ALL IN THE MIND

By the same auhor

The Blair Years

Alastair Campbell

ALL IN THE MIND

THE OVERLOOK PRESS
New York

First published in the United States in 2009 by

The Overlook Press, Peter Mayer Publishers, Inc.
141 Wooster Street
New York, NY 10012
www.overlookpress.com

Cataloging-in-Publication Data is available from the Library of Congress

Printed in the United States of America
FIRST EDITION
1 3 5 7 9 8 6 4 2
ISBN 978-1-59020-224-1

To
two parents, one partner, three children
and
one (single-handed) GP and two psychiatrists. They know who
they ae. I know what they did, and am grateful.

FRIDAY

1

Professor Martin Sturrock was feeling stressed enough already, even before the phone call from Simon telling him Aunt Jessica had died. Now, as he sat in his office waiting for his first patient of the day to arrive, he felt a rising sense of panic mixing in with the usual Friday tiredness. He tried to quantify the panic. Was it manageable, or did it herald a plunge? Would it fade as the day passed, or was he facing a weekend of angst and insomnia? He thought it was manageable. Just about.

Friday was usually Professor Sturrock's best day of the week because it was the day he saw David Temple, his favourite patient. But he could not recall a Friday that had started as badly as this one. He had woken up feeling low, a mood not helped when he glimpsed through a gap in the bedroom curtains a grey sky carrying a hint of rain.

Breakfast had been another silent stand-off with his wife Stella, who seemed to find something to be angry or sullen about most mornings, and today chose the fact he had opened a fresh carton of milk ahead of two cartons which had been in the fridge for three days already.

'I don't understand why you can't look at the date on the side,' she'd said on realising his error. 'You're supposed to be the one who likes everything ordered.'

'Sorry,' he replied mechanically, stuffing the carton back into the fridge.

On a good day, if his mood was up and the sun was shining through the kitchen windows, the pouring of fresh milk on to organic cereal could carry with it a sense of hope, vitality and energy for the day to come, whatever challenges it might hold. On a bad day, milk had all the emotional qualities of slurry, especially when his wife was making an issue of it.

He'd had a slight knot in his stomach ever since he woke up, and food was not going down well. The cereal lacked its normal taste and texture, and his coffee tasted burnt and bitter. But with the number of patients he was seeing today, he knew he had to eat. He thought about slicing a couple of bananas into the mix, as they were easily eaten and digested, and a good energy hit. He glanced over to the fruit bowl, sitting on the counter a yard or so from where Stella was rearranging the contents of a cupboard, noisily, for reasons known only to her.

There were plenty of apples, both green and red. There were at least four oranges, maybe more hidden below those he could see. There were a few plums which looked as if they were beginning to go off, and a small bunch of grapes which already had. There were only two bananas, lying on top of the apples, joined together, with the attached ends hanging over the edge of the bowl. But he felt the risk was too great. He might peel them, slice them, start to eat them, and only then would Stella turn from her cupboard rearranging and say, 'I was planning to have those for breakfast myself.' So he carried on chewing, telling himself he could buy a couple of bananas from the fruit and veg stall at Brook Green tube station, and eat them when he reached the hospital.

It was while Sturrock was taking his cereal bowl to the sink that the phone rang.

He thought about just allowing it to ring away in the hallway, leaving for the tube and letting Stella decide whether to answer it or not, but the milk-carton incident had left him feeling defensive. He went to pick it up.

Simon and he rarely spoke these days, so the second he heard his cousin say, 'Hello, Martin, it's Simon,' he knew what had happened.

'Hello, Martin, it's Simon. I'm afraid I have some bad news.'

'Oh dear,' said Sturrock, the formulaic tones of death already taking over the conversation.

'Yes, I'm afraid so. My mother passed away in the night.'

Aunt Jessica was the youngest of three and, Martin's father having died five years before, the last of that generation of Sturrock siblings to go.

'I'm so sorry, Simon.'

It's never easy to get the words right with deaths in the family, he thought.

It was different if it was a friend telling you about the death of someone you didn't know. 'I've been at a funeral,' a colleague might say. 'My uncle died.' 'I'm sorry to hear that,' you'd reply, and it would be no more or less than your colleague expected. They'd want you to sympathise but wouldn't expect you to go over the top about someone you'd never even met. With blood relatives, the death codes were not so simple.

He had been close to his cousin as a child. Though he grew up in Hertfordshire and Simon in Somerset, they had spent all their holidays together, and he had enjoyed many happy weekends staying at his aunt and uncle's cosy farmhouse with its blue-and-white crockery and worn pine furniture. His father was an engineer, whose work often took him abroad, and his mother thought that a bit of male company in the holidays would be good for him, rather than knocking around the house with her and his sister Jan. Fifteen months apart in age, he and Simon had played together, fought together, complained about their parents to each other, swapped ill-formed and confused fantasies about girls. But though there was kinship there, there was no lasting adult friendship. By the time he was in his mid teens, he had stopped seeing so much of Simon. The allure of trips to Somerset had vanished. Instead, he formed closer bonds with his own school friends, refusing invitations to accompany his aunt and uncle on holiday. And so, slowly, he and his cousin had drifted apart. Where once they would see each other several times a year, as young adults building their own lives, that dwindled to Christmas and Easter and now, as they neared pensionable age, it was usually weddings that brought them together, or funerals, the last of which had been Simon's father's.

Sturrock could tell that Simon had already made the call to several others. It was as though he had a script, and he was ticking off the main points.

- Passed away *peacefully*. Something of a *release* in the end.
- *Good innings*. Sturrock thought it odd that even people who knew nothing about cricket, and possibly had never watched let alone played the game, used this phrase to describe the life of anyone who had lived beyond eighty.
- Details of the *funeral* still to be decided.
- Then a couple of details from the last few days, in Aunt Jessica's case how they knew things weren't good when she refused blackcurrant crumble on Monday evening, even though it was her favourite pudding, and also the story of a row with one of the nurses at the care home who insisted on her sitting downstairs with the other residents to watch afternoon TV when she actually just wanted to stay in bed.

'She was feisty to the end then,' said Sturrock.

'Yes,' said Simon. 'Feisty to the end.'

It was strange to reflect how, in his youth, he really had thought of Aunt Jessica as 'feisty'. He'd loved her energy, the way she would bustle around the farmhouse, making everyone feel wanted and involved in everything that was going on. He'd loved her cooking and her relaxed approach to mealtimes, bedtimes, and her appreciation of his sometimes unconventional opinions and ambitions. He'd considered it one of the great mysteries of nature that his grandparents had produced two children as different as his father and Aunt Jessica. But then there'd come a moment when he wasn't sure they were so different after all.

'I'm glad it was fairly painless when she went, Simon,' he said. 'And if there is anything we can do, just call.' He was conscious of how trite that sounded, then taken aback by the response it provoked.

'There is something, actually,' said Simon. 'I was hoping you might do the eulogy.'

'Me?'

He tried to use his tone of voice to convey opposition to the proposal on several levels. He didn't want to. He didn't think he was appropriate. There were plenty of people who were better qualified. He hadn't seen much of his aunt for the past forty years. He didn't much like speaking at funerals. He didn't see why he, a mere nephew, should have to do it, when she had three sons of her own.

But Simon was not good at reading tones of voice. He interpreted the response as one of surprise, but delight and honour to be asked.

'She was very fond of you, and very proud of what you do, and you would be so much better at it than anyone else. I could do it but I'm worried I'll break down.'

'What about the other boys?' Sturrock asked, boys now with a combined age of 121.

'Well, Archie and she fell out quite badly over Dad's will, you remember, and Paul might have a few too many drinks to settle his nerves.'

'Are you sure I'm the right person?'

'Definitely. I'll give you all the facts and dates you need and if you could weave in a few nice stories, that would be great. Needn't be too long. Ten, fifteen minutes?'

Sturrock was losing the will to fight back. He thought it incredibly selfish of Simon to land him with a task like this. But then, perhaps *he* was the selfish one. Simon had no way of knowing that his cousin was tipping into one of his glooms. Indeed, Simon, in common with his dead mother, would have been very surprised to learn that cousin Martin experienced such glooms. That in itself was evidence of how distant they were, and yet here he was having to do the eulogy at Simon's mother's funeral.

'As soon as we've sorted the arrangements, I'll let you know,' Simon continued. 'There is a chance we might be able to get a slot at the crematorium on Tuesday. It's a bit quick, but the formalities are done and most people who would want to be there know she's gone.'

'OK,' Sturrock said, while secretly cursing to himself. If it was as early as Tuesday, he would have next to no time to rearrange all the appointments he had for that day, let alone deal with the inevitable knock-on consequences.

Though he didn't feel it this morning, Professor Sturrock was widely viewed as one of the best psychiatrists in the business. For a fair few London GPs, he was first choice for the mental health cases they felt they couldn't handle by medication alone. They would happily refer their patients to the Prince Regent Hospital off Oxford Street and its renowned psychiatric unit run by Professor Sturrock. He liked NHS work. He tended to get some of the toughest cases, and they always provided inspiration for his research work. But he also liked to provide real, quality care, and this took time. It meant he could see only a fraction of the patients doctors wanted him to see, especially as he insisted on one-hour consultations for his outpatients. This had got him into trouble with management from time to time, concerned as they were with 'throughputs' and 'patient experience'. But given his record and reputation, he was able to operate as something of a law unto himself. 'Patient experience' was important to him too, but in a very different way.

Stella's reaction, as she picked up on his angst about having to mess around his patients, had further worsened his mood as he gathered his papers and packed them into his brown leather briefcase.

'It's your aunt we're talking about, Martin,' she said as he headed for the front door. 'A little bit of humanity wouldn't go amiss.' He nodded, and left.

On the tube, he'd felt more than usually suffocated and starved of space, but now he was in his consulting room, he could breathe again. It was his sanctuary, the place where, when he was alone, he could think. Through the frosted-glass door he could see the shadow of Phyllis, his secretary-cum-receptionist, getting ready for the day ahead, just as she had done every weekday morning for the twenty-plus years she had worked for him. He buzzed through to her, to warn her she might have to rearrange things for Tuesday.

'Sorry to hear about your aunt,' she said.

She was a large, rather stern-looking woman, not terribly prone to laughter, who liked everything to run precisely as planned. It was exactly what bosses look for in a secretary, but at times it irritated him, particularly when she was unsympathetic to patients who missed their appointments. She seemed to have very little understanding of the courage it took for some of his patients to get themselves to the hospital. But he knew he was lucky to have someone who always appeared able to take changed arrangements in her stride. When she'd had three weeks off for an operation, he'd realised just how much he relied on her. The place virtually fell apart. But though he and Phyllis were such an important part of each other's lives, they were not particularly close. He gave her a small birthday present in March, and a larger Christmas present each year, but they never socialised.

His consulting room was on the sixth floor of the new Le Gassick wing, named after the businessman and philanthropist, Stuart Le Gassick, who helped to fund it. It was built five years ago, just before his father died. He had a nice view over low rooftops to the square nearby with its well-kept private garden in the middle, though an enormous new complex of business premises and luxury flats was in the process of being built in between. He feared that once it was completed, he would lose the little glimpse of grass and bushes he could enjoy when he stood at the far corner of the room. The furnishings were a mix of classic public sector functionality and several items – including his mahogany desk, his swivel desk chair, and the two brown leather armchairs he used for patient consultations – that he had brought with him from his old room in a part of the hospital that had since been converted to a lecture theatre.

He had just ten minutes before he was due to see his first patient of the day, Emily Parks. Just ten minutes to think about the four consultations planned for the morning, and in the afternoon the budget meetings and the appointment with Hafsatu Sesay, a young woman from Sierra Leone who had been the victim of a particularly brutal sex-trafficking scam. She was a patient whom Sturrock found particularly challenging. Ten minutes wasn't long enough. He cursed last night's dinner for a visiting American professor, who was over studying some of the work he had done on the use of dreams in the analysis of addiction and depression. The dinner hadn't finished until 11.20, so it was nearly midnight by the time he got home and he was too tired to do his usual day-before review and planning.

Each of the morning's patients was challenging in their own very different ways. Emily Parks was a burns victim who had lost half her face in a house fire three years ago and who was so permanently conscious of her disfigurement that she was scared to go out in daylight. At 10.15 he had David Temple, a serious depressive whom he worried might one day cause harm, to himself or others, and then at 11.15, Arta Mehmeti, a refugee from Kosovo who had been raped in her south London home while the rapist's accomplice held her young daughter hostage in the kitchen. In her dreams, Arta was stalked nightly by the rapist, making a normal sex life with her husband impossible. To wrap up his morning, at 12.15 he was seeing a new private patient who wanted to come and discuss his sex addiction. He was always keen to have private patients. The income helped him fund his various research projects, his current one being a study of the psychiatric impact of resettlement on asylum seekers, particularly from the Balkans and African war zones. But he didn't like sex-addiction cases. They made him feel uncomfortable.

Sturrock wondered whether David would turn up. He had missed several consultations in the past, unable even to get out of bed. If David didn't show today that would at least give him time to check his emails and see whether Arta had sent through her 'homework'. At the end of most appointments he would set his patients some task for the week ahead, and many of them, Arta included, would email it to him the night before they were due to see him. However, he worried that if he was deprived of the chance to talk to David, his mood might sink even further.

Sturrock marked his depressive patients on a scale of one to ten. Most of the people he treated were between five and eight. He had never had a ten. He put David at seven, which was bad. He put himself at six, but didn't let anyone know, which ran counter to the guidelines for psychiatrists who feel they may have their own psychological issues.

He knew the guidelines better than most, having updated them personally four years ago, but he could see no point, for himself or the department, in drawing attention to his own shifting moods. Instead, he tried to manage them himself. And seeing David helped.

Though in times of depression, David had self-esteem perhaps lower than Sturrock had ever witnessed, he had in his lucid moments an ability to articulate his depression that the psychiatrist found moving, humbling. He thought of one of David's descriptions now as he heard Phyllis greet Emily Parks in the waiting room outside. 'It's like a storm coming,' he'd said about the feeling before a plunge. 'There's a moment when the sky darkens, you know what's coming, and you're powerless to do anything about it.'

2

As Professor Sturrock was consulting his schedule, David Temple was already just a short walk away, sitting in a scruffy little café used mainly by builders working on the new shops and flats going up by the hospital. He sat drinking a mug of tea, pleased with himself that he had got this far. He had more than an hour to steel himself to take the final steps to the hospital and up the stairs to the sixth floor of the Le Gassick wing, where the kindly psychiatrist and his rather forbidding receptionist would be waiting. He had been in this position before, come all this way, sat in this same café, with its Formica tables and classroom chairs, and then decided he couldn't face it, and gone back home. Some days, it was just that he couldn't summon the will to talk about the way he was feeling. More often, he would ask himself what right he had to take up the time of someone like Professor Sturrock. Even now, looking around the cafe, he saw people who probably had far worse problems than his. Was it a problem demanding of a doctor that he couldn't get out of bed in the morning? It made him feel small, unworthy of the space he took up.

Yet despite everything these sessions stirred in him, he had come to depend on Professor Sturrock, almost to look forward to the weekly meetings where they went through his dreams and other homework tasks, and he tried to describe the shifts in his mood. They helped. And today he needed help. He was still shaken by his conversation with Amanda at work yesterday. With every conscious effort he made to shake it clear from his memory, its grip on his mind tightened. He watched a waitress wipe away a stain on the table as she brought him over another mug of tea. Why couldn't he wipe his mind clean so easily?

He had got this far, he told himself, so just do what the Professor said – a step at a time; live in the moment; look for the good things not just the bad. It had helped get him out of bed when he woke up with a seven-out-of-ten dead feeling. It had helped him out of the house, onto the tube, including a change of line, off at Marble Arch, then on the little stroll to the café. From where he sat, he could see the window of Professor Sturrock's room. So he was close. Live in the moment, he whispered to himself, then the next one, then the one after that.

David Temple was thirty-three but looked closer to fifty. He had been bald since his early twenties and his forehead was already quite heavily lined. He had realised, since seeing Professor Sturrock, that he had probably been suffering from depression all his life, but he had only been diagnosed as needing treatment three years ago when he'd tried, with no real risk of success, to kill himself through an overdose of his mother's sleeping pills. 'Can't even kill myself properly,' he said to the nurse in accident and emergency. It was a year later, when he became a so-called 'risk to others' that he was sent to have sessions with Professor Sturrock.

It had happened in a park near his home one evening. He had been feeling very low that day and everything at home was driving him deeper and deeper down. He lived with his mother in a rented two-storey flat in the shadow of Pentonville prison, having found life on his own worse than life with her, even though often she was the thing that sparked what Professor Sturrock called his 'plunges'. She knew the rhythm of his moods almost as well as he did, having lived with them for so long, but long and painful experience had made her no better at dealing with them. Her answer to everything was either to suggest he go and have a little chat with Father Nicholas, the priest at their local church to whom she turned whenever *she* had a problem, or that he have something 'nice' to eat or drink. Each exhortation, each suggestion of a new foodstuff would make him feel he was slipping down another notch. He knew the feeling too well, a gnawing emptiness expanding beyond his own body space. The empty feeling would start as a knot, somewhere close to his stomach. It would then grow outwards, sometimes in circles, sometimes in irregular shapes, but before long his entire insides felt as though they contained absolutely nothing. No flesh or blood or bones, no breath, no pain even, no feeling beyond a dull ache that he could only describe as emptiness. How was it possible, he wondered, to feel totally, absolutely empty, and yet to feel even emptier the moment his mother suggested another meal she might serve up to make him 'feel a bit better'?

'Perhaps not now, maybe later, I could do you a nice little Welsh rarebit.'

In his mother's world, food was always 'nice' and 'little', unless it was a roast, a bowl of pasta or a fry-up, in which case it would be 'nice' and 'big'. When he was fine, he was OK with her fussing around and feeding him. When he was down, it became unbearable.

Normally, his depressions were worst in the mornings, and got slightly better as the day wore on. But on the day of the incident, he'd felt the knot in his stomach tightening, and the void growing, and he was worried he was getting close to saying or doing something that would hurt his mother. He decided he had to get out, maybe go for a walk in the little park three streets away. But he knew she would be upset if he just walked out without saying anything, so he sat for a while, trying to summon up the energy to announce his departure. He ran the words around his mind. 'Just popping out for a breath of fresh air.' Or should it be 'Just going out for a walk'? 'Just going out for a little walk'? He wondered whether to try to add in an offer of service. 'Just popping out for a little walk, Mum – need anything from the shops?'

But even as he was rehearsing the best approach, he could see no way that she wouldn't engage, forcing him to feel the pressure to speak again, and he just didn't have the will for it. If he really dug deep now, he might get one sentence out, probably the short version saying he was popping out for a walk. But she was familiar with his rhythms, and she would be worried and the worries would come out in questions that would require a response. Questions like 'Where?' or 'Why?' or 'When will you be back?' He didn't know the answers to any of them.

'Where?' Probably the park. Possibly the canal. Or he might just go out and wander, street by street, until he felt a little better, or tired enough to sleep.

As to 'why?' he wouldn't be able to tell her the truth, which was that he was on the downward curve and when that happened, everything she said pushed him further towards the floor.

He loved his mother. She was in many ways his only true friend. He liked to think that the reason it was she who plunged him downwards when the rhythm kicked in was because she was the only person there, that if he was in different company, the words and motions of others would have the same dire effect. But he couldn't be sure. When the downward rhythm began, he avoided anywhere but home, any company but his own or his mother's. So how could he know? Perhaps she was the cause of the spiral and he grew more and more desperate because he wanted her to be the cure to its repetitive agonies.

He must have eaten up fifteen minutes running the various options around his mind. His inner voice told him unequivocally that he was not going to be able to articulate the simple concept that he intended to go out for a stroll. But he felt he owed it to his mother to try. She was not a bad person. She was a good person, and she had a lot to put up with, never knowing whether he was going to be up or down. Mostly she knew he was going to be down but she never stopped trying to jolly him along. He tried to say, 'Just popping out for some air,' but as the 'p' at the start of 'popping' formed on his lips, he pulled back.

'Did you say something, love?' she'd asked.

'No,' he'd said. He was fine with 'No', 'OK', 'Fine' and 'Yeah'. Beyond that, words were locked away until the rhythm turned upward, and he never knew when that would be.

Go on, he said to himself, one last try, really try, it won't hurt, it won't harm, just say it. But no. It was impossible because she wouldn't be able to let go, she'd be straight in there asking, 'Where, love, why, love, what time you going to be back, love, do you fancy a nice little chicken salad when you come home?' And then he'd be back to square one, but one notch lower, one ring wider in the emptiness bowl, swamping the odd shapes of emptiness that first surrounded the knot in the centre of the stomach. So now he was just playing a waiting game, pretending to read the newspaper he had placed on his lap, but just longing for his mum to leave the room, preferably to head upstairs, so he could slip out.

After what seemed like hours she said the words he wanted to hear.

'Just going up for a wee, love. You OK?'

'Fine,' he said.

As he heard her reach the landing he fetched his coat, picked up his key from the table by the front door, and fled.

The noises of cars passing or children laughing and shouting were less grating than the voice of his mother trying to persuade him to eat food he didn't want. The kids' noises were just noise, they had nothing to do with him. The cars came and went. There was a consolation in the dark. If nobody could see him, nobody could speak to him. Dark also heralded the time when he would be ready to sleep. Sleep at least removed several hours of the day, and meant he would be a few hours closer to the next upward curve of the rhythm, sometimes with dreams along the way that made him feel warmer and less anxious than he did in his waking hours.

He was rarely violent, but as he arrived in the park, he stumbled over a discarded petrol can, which unleashed in him such rage that he kicked the can, kicked it again, then stamped on it four times before picking it up, whirling it hammer-thrower-style round and round above his head, then letting it go flying into the night.

He had neither seen nor heard the two cyclists pedalling side by side along the bus lane which bordered the park. As the petrol can bounced towards the road, it clipped the front wheel of the bike closest to the verge. The cyclist jerked his handlebars to the right, so violently that the wheel touched the left foot of the second cyclist, who in turn pulled away, tried to click his feet out from the cleats on his pedals, but failed to maintain his balance and fell into the road, his friend falling on top of him a few nanoseconds later. The second cyclist was not wearing a helmet and his head hit the tarmac hard as he fell.

David looked around to see if anyone had witnessed what the Clerkenwell magistrate would subsequently call 'this mindless act'. A part of his mind was telling him to turn and run. Instead he walked over to the two men, started to help them up, and once he had done so, confessed he had thrown the can which had been responsible for their fall. 'I'm really very sorry. Here, let me help you.'

The helmeted cyclist appeared not to be hurt at all, though he was rubbing his hip and moving his neck and shoulder to check for strains. The second man had a large graze across the side of his head through which blood was beginning to seep. There was real hurt and anger in his voice as he railed at David. 'What on earth were you thinking of? You could have killed us. Imagine if a car or a bus had been overtaking us as we fell into the road. Bang, dead.'

'I'm sorry,' said David. 'I really am.'

'Is that it? Is that all you can say?'

'The problem is that I'm quite ill.'

It was the first time he had ever said it in those terms and they knew immediately what he meant.

'Care-in-the-community job, are we?' said the helmeted man in a tone that was surprisingly friendly. Even his angry, bleeding companion seemed to soften just a little. They were clearly disarmed by David's confession, his apology, and now this statement about his mental health.

'Hadn't you better call an ambulance for your friend?' asked David. 'Or the police?'

His lawyer would later cite this as a set of circumstances amounting to a 'cry for help', which would lead to David escaping with a small fine provided he agreed to undergo psychiatric treatment. And so Professor Sturrock entered his life. He didn't feel substantially better. But he felt a little better, some of the time, and he was sure this was in large part down to the Professor. It made him even more determined to make his appointment today.

David spooned the tea bag from his fourth mug of tea, squeezed out the last drops and placed it carefully on the saucer. He had another half-hour before he was due up there on the sixth floor. 'You can do it,' he whispered to himself. Professor Sturrock had such faith in him – he owed it to him. As he stirred the sugar into his tea, he remembered the scribbled note the Professor had put on his homework just before Christmas last year – '*Low self-esteem is not the same as humility. You may think that you are less important than others, but what I think you are is humble. And humility is a fine quality.*' He was pretty sure he was going to turn up now.

3

Matthew Noble QC had taken Friday morning off work in preparation for the ordeal of his first ever encounter with a psychiatrist, but the time was dragging. As he sat in the kitchen nursing his cup of coffee, his wife Celia insisted on reading out the latest piece of research on sex addiction she had found on the Internet. He thought the whole thing ridiculous, but Celia had been adamant he should get help, and he didn't feel he was in a position to argue. She had caught him out cheating on her, twice in fairly rapid succession. He knew he had left her feeling hurt and humiliated on both occasions, but she was clear that, despite everything, she didn't want to lose her marriage. They had recently celebrated their silver wedding, and whatever it was that had led him into his infidelities, he still felt something for her. She knew everything there was to know about him: what he liked to eat, what clothes he liked to wear, his little routines. The idea of living without her horrified him. Partly, he acknowledged, it was a question of self-image. There was something a bit sad and loserish about colleagues he knew whose marriages had ended because they had run off with younger women. But also he knew he depended on his wife. Who would book the holidays for a start? Who would run the house? And they still sometimes laughed together, not always at each other. So he was grateful that Celia was making such an effort to keep things from falling apart. He found it quite touching that once the initial shock at his infidelity had subsided, she changed her attitude, deciding to think of him as victim not sinner. He found it irritating, however, to be labelled a sex addict.

The days after Celia's discovery of his second affair had been torture. They skirted round each other in the house, avoiding any kind of conversation. Then, one night, after they had been lying stiffly side by side for hours, both wide awake, Celia had gone into the study and switched on the computer. By the time dawn broke, she was convinced that the Internet had explained her husband's betrayal. And she said that the volume of material on sex addiction – more than six million items on Google – meant it was likely to be straightforward finding someone to help him. She refused to countenance even the faintest protest from Matthew. All the evidence pointed in the same direction. For example, though their sex life might not have transported them to heavenly pastures too frequently in recent years, her research showed they had sex more often than the most regularly quoted average for their age group, only marginally, it was true, but he could not claim theirs was a sexless marriage. Yet he had twice put in peril a relationship that they, their children, their friends and Matthew's colleagues at the Bar all rationally analysed as a strong one. And the most common definition of a sex addict appeared to be someone who felt compelled to seek out new sexual experiences regardless of the risk to personal, family or professional life. 'That would seem to be you in a nutshell,' she'd said over breakfast the next morning, as she took him through printouts from the Web. 'Look at the facts,' she'd said. Though he didn't particularly want to, he had to accept that when she first caught him red-handed, professing love down the phone to Madeleine, a divorced solicitor, his reaction had been to go off immediately in search of another even bigger fix with Angela. Celia had articles on how the addict spent a great deal of time and energy planning the next sexual encounter, often making the arrangements more and more complicated as a way of heightening the eventual thrill, which in turn would lead to the need for greater complexity in future to maintain the thrill level. When he thought about the layers of subterfuge in his relationship with Angela, and the lies he told Celia about conferences that never happened, in countries he had never been to, he could see she had a point.

He'd sat and listened as she itemised all the chemical changes that take place in people's minds and bodies during and after sex. 'Your sexual wiring is different to most people's, Matthew,' she'd said. 'For you, the chemical reactions are more intense so you need one sexual sensation to be followed by another once the effect of the first one has worn off.' Apparently, he was among the 3 to 7 per cent of the population suffering some form of sex addiction.

Amid the relief at her apparent forgiveness, Matthew felt humiliated that he was going to see a psychiatrist. He paced up and down the length of their kitchen as he waited for the taxi he'd booked to come at 10.45, in good time to get him from upmarket suburban Totteridge to central London. From the moment he'd woken up, he'd felt mildly nauseous. If people who knew him were asked to write down one word to sum him up, 'robust' would feature high up the list, as well as 'strong-willed, independent, pragmatic, solid'. Mad, insane, loopy, deranged, depressed – the words normally associated with the need to see a psychiatrist – would not figure. 'Sex addict' would be even less likely. Yet here he was, about to visit the Prince Regent Hospital for a session with one of the country's top shrinks.

As Celia had wittered on at him over the last few days, he had developed his own picture of a sex addict. A man who woke up to a giant erection every morning, which he would immediately masturbate into submission before being able to face the day. Someone who lived in a hovel surrounded by old porn magazines and crumpled tissues. Who viewed every even vaguely attractive woman as quarry to be leered at, followed and hunted down. Who, when free sex could not be found, would purchase it without regard to the sordidness of the venue or the disgustingness of the body his penis would enter. Who would spend hours on the Internet flicking from one porn image to another before finding a video clip that could hold his attention and interest long enough to inspire and then exhaust the next erection. The sex addict was a sad, lonely, depraved individual of low income and low social standing, with bad teeth and greasy hair that left an oily residue on the collar of his anorak. So how on earth had he, a highly educated, married father of two, a respected barrister, a long-time top-rate taxpayer, likely one day to be treasurer or even captain of the South Herts golf club, been engineered by his wife into accepting that he had joined the ranks of the waxy anoraks? He who had lost his virginity later than all his close friends; who could count on one hand the sexual partners he'd had before he married Celia; who had only ever watched porn in hotels if they allowed a few minutes of free viewing and wasn't overly bothered if they didn't; and who had never once felt tempted to pay for sex or trawl the Internet for sexual contact or pleasure? He just could not imagine what sort of person would buy sex.

He had often wondered, as he stood in the newsagent's deciding which golf magazine to buy, who were the millions who sustained such a massive market in top-shelf literature? But although he had occasionally taken a glimpse at the covers, and even more occasionally looked inside, he had never felt tempted to buy one. Yet there they were, in shops up and down the land, presumably being purchased regularly or else the shops wouldn't bother stocking them. And, as Celia had been discovering, the Internet had seen the market expand beyond the wildest pornographer's wildest dreams; in cyberspace, a vast army of men and women indulged in any and every sexual practice for the titillation of a vast global army of consumers. Just not Matthew.

His problem was that he was currently powerless within the relationship. He was the one who had strayed. He was the one begging for forgiveness, desperate to stay in the marital home, and so avoid the anger of his children and the laughter of his colleagues. Celia would never be in a stronger position and he felt his weakness every time she came out with yet another Web-based assertion to back her basic case that he had a problem which 'together' they could solve. This was why he had no way of wriggling out when, to his considerable but unspoken annoyance, Celia said she was worried he would not tell Professor Sturrock the full story if he saw him on his own, so she was coming too.

4

It was 9.20 before Sturrock was ready to see Emily Parks. He hated running late so early in the day. He viewed his meticulous punctuality as one of the few positive qualities he had inherited from his father. But this morning, events were against him. He had been held up by a call on his mobile from Ralph Hall, the government's Health Secretary and the only senior politician he had ever treated. Hall had sounded hung-over, and panicky. He asked if Sturrock might be able to come and see him that afternoon, even though their next appointment wasn't until Tuesday. For obvious reasons, Hall didn't like to visit the hospital.

'Today is difficult,' Sturrock had said. 'I have patients most of the day, and budget meetings later. It's tricky.'

Hall seemed desperate. 'I wouldn't call if it wasn't important, Martin. It's just that I'm not sure I'm going to hold it together.'

In his head, Sturrock ran over his schedule again. His only options were to skip one of the budget meetings, or reschedule his afternoon appointment with Hafsatu, which cut both ways. Part of him was longing to see her, part of him dreading it.

'Look, Ralph, it is not impossible one of my patients won't show. It happens a fair bit. I'll call you later whatever happens, but if a gap appears, I'll find a way to get to Westminster.'

He walked over to the windows to rearrange the blinds. Though the sky was grey, the rain was holding off and there was even a bit of sun struggling to get through the clouds. He liked light, and when the sun was out, he preferred to have the blinds up and the sun streaming in. But Emily's sensitivity about her appearance seemed to be exacerbated by light. On her last visit, she had clearly been troubled by the sun, shielding her face from it and wincing, as if in pain. He had interrupted their conversation to lower the blinds, but this had made her more than usually self-conscious and they hadn't made much progress after that. So today he left two of the blinds up, lowering the one that would place her chair in shade. Then he went to the door to call her in. He always called the patients in himself. It was one of those little touches he prided himself on.

'Hello, Emily, would you like to come in?' He waited at the door, stepped back to allow her in, then watched as she walked to the soft leather armchair in the far corner of the room in her usual timid, hunched way. She stared into her lap while Sturrock gathered up a brown folder from his desk, and went to sit in his chair, a few yards from her. He smiled, waited to see if she had anything to say, and when it was clear she hadn't, he said simply, in as friendly a manner as he could: 'So?'

Sometimes, that simple little question was sufficient to get the patient to open up with a general assessment of their current mood, what they had been feeling, and what had been happening in their lives. Once or twice, that had worked with Emily. Today, she smiled weakly, but said nothing.

He was feeling stuck with her, a feeling not helped by the lack of time for preparation. Yet they had made good progress when she was first referred to him. So phobic was she of being seen in public that his first four visits had been to her parents' house, where she had been staying after the fire, 'OTOs' as Phyllis called them: out-of-the-office consultations. Sturrock had introduced her to strategies for coping in the street and now, though she still found it difficult, at least she could make it to the hospital. She always asked for the first appointment of the morning. It meant there were fewer people around to see her, fewer people coming and going in the little waiting room. Her mother would drop her as close to the hospital entrance as she could, then wait in the underground car park listening, as she did all day, according to Emily, to Classic FM. Sturrock knew that Emily found the journey agony. She would arrive in a state of distress, only calming down once they began talking over how she felt. In order to soothe her, he'd developed the tactic of asking after her friend Sami. He'd noticed that the only time she really lost her inhibition was when she talked about Sami, the Muslim owner of the twenty-four-hour corner shop where, once darkness fell, she would do her shopping.

Shopping was a huge challenge for Emily. When she had been staying in Hendon with her parents, it hadn't been a problem because her mother had done it all. But when Emily decided to move out and try to live on her own again, in a flat just off the Caledonian Road, she'd been forced to shop for herself. Since the nearest grocery was Sami's, she'd ventured in and immediately been struck by the warmth with which he'd greeted her. She felt as though he was not even conscious of her appearance. When he talked to her, he looked straight into her eyes. After that she did all her shopping at Sami's and he made it clear to other customers that, no matter what she looked like, she was a valued and respected customer. He had even intervened when Emily ran into trouble outside his shop one evening. She wore a dark headscarf to hide her disfigurement and once or twice, she was mistaken for a Muslim woman. A group of kids hanging around outside the shop had started jeering at her, shouting things like, 'Go back to Somalia!' then, 'Show us your tits, Muslim tart!' Sami had rushed out to defend her and had even closed up his shop so he could walk her home.

Sturrock liked the sound of Sami and saw him as a useful ally. He had recently set Emily the homework test of ensuring five new people saw her face each day, so he had been particularly pleased to hear that Sami had suggested she might help out in the shop from time to time, in order to get used to people looking at her. Emily's immediate reaction had been to say thank you, but no. But Sturrock hoped that, given time and Sami's encouragement, she might change her mind.

He knew that Emily's personality made it particularly difficult for her to deal with negative reactions to her condition. She was so fundamentally decent a person that she simply couldn't understand why one human being would abuse another, purely because of their appearance. She'd talked about her schooldays and how, even though there was plenty of bitchiness among some of her friends, it had never occurred to her to pick on someone because they were fat, or thin, or black, or Asian, or Irish. She was always the one who, rather than joining in with the taunts, would tell her friends off for making disparaging remarks. When, at one consultation, he'd asked her to bring with her the following week something she was particularly proud of, she'd come bearing a school report, at the bottom of which her form teacher had written, *'Emily is a strong role model for other girls. On more than one occasion, I have had Emily to thank for helping me to deal with unpleasant behaviour. She has a strong sense of right and wrong and a very clear moral compass. You should be very proud of the person she is becoming.'* So proud were her parents that they'd had the report framed, and hung it on the wall in the hallway.

The challenge was to persuade Emily she was the same person, despite what had happened to her, and to get her back to seeing the world as a benign place.

Sturrock had had a lot of experience of burns victims. He had been the duty psychiatrist on the day of one of London's worst indus-trial blazes, in which thirteen people had died, and many more had been seriously injured. It was then that his interest in the lasting psychi-atric impact of trauma had been aroused sufficiently for him to decide to write a book on the subject, the first he wrote. So for a year or two he had specialised in that field, the fire victims and the emer-gency workers who had tried to rescue them providing a huge resource for his research and his care for them, hopefully, doing some good. It was this work that first caught the eye of senior people in govern-ment, who put him on the list of likely contenders when outside experts were required for policy review groups.

Emily's fire had been far less dramatic and was deemed to merit just two paragraphs in the local paper headlined 'WOMAN HURT IN BLAZE', in which she was wrongly named as Emily Parker, and her age given as twenty-two when in fact she was twenty-four. But although it wasn't front-page news, the fire had left terrible scars, both physical and psychological, and the more Sturrock saw of Emily, the less sure he was that, despite all his experience, he was going to be able to help her. Though Emily's parents had been stalwart in their support for her, shocking themselves at how quickly they had grown to accept her disfigurement, her boyfriend of three years, Patrick, had been far less understanding, perhaps planting the seed of Emily's belief that she had changed beyond recognition.

Nine months after the fire, as she was preparing for yet another skin-graft operation, Patrick had written her a letter. Sturrock had a copy of the letter in his brown folder.

'I will always love you,' it had said, 'but – and I know how cruel this will seem given all you have to face – I cannot cope with what is happening to us. I thought our life would be together, that we would raise a family. But we both know it cannot be. Yours is the pain and the suffering, I know that. For you, there is no escape. It will be with you for the rest of your life. For the rest of mine, I will curse myself that I am too weak to see it through, or even to give you this message face to face. But that is the reality. I do not have the strength to see you suffer like this. I do not have the strength to stay by you and help you to recover. I cannot bear your pain, nor my inability to deal with it.'

In the first months after the fire, Emily had been forced to wear pressure garments, including a mask. To look at, the mask was less alarming than the scarred face it hid, but she complained it was tight and sometimes sore, and it drew glances from virtually everyone she passed. Sturrock had pressed her on their reactions, and why they mattered to her. Most had reacted with studied neutrality, she'd said, and a number of people had even given an intimation of warmth, like a nod or a smile. But some looked away, unable to conceal shock or disgust. He urged her to try to enjoy the intimations of warmth, and appreciate the fact that this was the way most people reacted. But it only took one bad incident to set her back. The worst had occurred as she was being dropped off at the hospital one day. Three men in the cab of a filthy lorry trailing a cement mixer had spotted her getting out of her mother's car. She was in tears as she recounted the story to Sturrock just moments later. The young man in the middle of the cab saw her first, and pointed. Then the driver honked his horn, so loudly it startled her. She looked up to see the three men now gesticulating and laughing. Her meekness vanished, and before she knew it, she was striding over to the lorry and ordering the driver to open the window. He did so, and the laughter calmed.

'Do you have children?' she asked. 'Do you have brothers and sisters? Do you have a heart?'

She said the man in the middle sniggered, but she could see her point had hit home with the driver, who was silent.

'When you go home tonight,' she said, 'ask your children to google "burns victims". Look at the pictures. Then imagine it's them, not me.' And with that, she turned and went into the hospital.

'How did you feel?' Sturrock asked. It was one of his favourite questions.

'I felt strong. I felt I was making a point I had to make. But then as I came up the stairs, I could feel myself collapsing inside. Why should I have to put up with that? What have I done in my life to deserve what has happened to me?' She was sobbing so heavily that Sturrock felt he had to get up from his chair and go to console her. In her diary of emotions which she submitted the following week, she said she sobbed in similar fashion on and off for three days.

Emily's mask was now a thing of the past, so it was the reality of the scarred face beneath it that she sought to hide from passers-by. She was a little out of breath as the consultation began because she preferred the breathlessness and the intense pain in her left thigh from climbing six flights of stairs to the feeling of being trapped in the corner of a crowded lift, with people pretending not to look at her, but sneaking glances in one of the tinted mirrored walls.

Sturrock felt that he'd made little headway with Emily in recent months. In fact, the only real progress was that she now removed her scarf when she sat down in the leather armchair. Once someone was used to her appearance, as he was, or Sami the shopkeeper, or Phyllis, Emily could cope more easily. But he was desperate for her to overcome her fear of strangers and that just wasn't happening. In general, she hated being seen, and devoted much of her energy to preventing it. That meant staying in during daylight hours, even though she knew that wasn't helping address what her GP called 'the underlying issue'. To her, there was no underlying issue. The issue was there for all to see, her face a hotchpotch of the skin she was born with, scar tissue and grafts from other parts of her body.

'So,' Sturrock said, realising that his first 'So?' had not worked, 'how has your week been?'

'OK.'

'Really?'

'No, not really.' She smiled.

'How did you get on with your homework?' he asked.

He had given her a book to read at the end of their last consultation, an anthology of stories of survival from around the world which the publishers had sent to him because he had treated one of the cases featured. He read widely and was always looking to find ways of sharing what he read with patients and colleagues. He had hoped Emily might get some kind of solace from learning about people who had suffered even worse injuries than hers, but who had gone on to rebuild their lives, one of them becoming a celebrated poet, another running a small bank in Illinois. Part of his assessment of trauma victims was that they needed to know there were others like them.

'I'm afraid I didn't really get into it. I will try, I promise.'

'Only if you want to,' he said. 'There's no pressure. I thought it might help to read of others who have gone through something similar.'

'Sorry.'

'Not a problem. What about the raisins?'

He had asked her to study a box of raisins as part of a cognitive therapy designed to change the way people think about the world around them and, hopefully, their own lives.

'Sorry. I will, I promise.'

There was a pause. Then Emily broke the silence.

'I spent a lot of time looking in the mirror.'

'And what did you see?'

'I covered the bad side of my face with a towel, and stared, just stared at the good side.'

'And saw . . . ?'

'Pretty. Saw that I was pretty. Clear blue eye. Nice high-set cheekbone. Nice ear. I remembered how Patrick used to nibble it when we made love. Then I stared into the good eye for as long as I could and tried to remember what it was like when all of me was like that. I tried to smile but half a smile looks odd. You need the whole face for a smile to work. So I tried to imagine the mirror changing shape so that instead of half a face looking out at me, the good side was reflected and the face became whole again.'

'And how did it feel to imagine your face whole?'

'I don't know because then I dropped the towel and the ugliness came back.'

'And how did that feel?'

'Disgusting. And I thought if *I* feel disgusted by what I see, why shouldn't others?'

She had been in her second year as a primary-school teacher when she was burnt. He had no doubt she was good with the children, and though she said some were cheeky from time to time, they adored her. She loved the work. The day before the fire, she said, she felt she would teach for the rest of her life. Today, she couldn't see herself ever being inside a classroom again. The children would not be able to look at her. As for having children of her own, even if it was physically possible, which seemed to be doubtful, she didn't believe it would happen.

'Children can be very understanding,' said Sturrock. 'They might surprise you. They might just see you as the same person they knew before.'

'But I'm not.'

'I think you are. All that's changed is how you look, and that changes how you feel.'

'But what I feel dictates what I am,' she said. 'I don't feel like I used to feel because I am not who I was.'

'I think you are *who* you were. You're not *what* you were in that you look different, but what has happened to you is part of who you are.'

'I was happy,' she said, 'and now I'm not. I was pretty, and now I'm not. I was confident, I was whole, and now I'm not. I wasn't scared, and now I am. I wasn't angry, and now I am.'

'And that anger is part of who you are.'

'What good does it do me?'

'What harm does it do you if it helps you come to terms with what's happened?'

'I don't know that I can ever come to terms with what's happened.'

'You might, Emily, we just don't know. You thought you were going to die, didn't you? Yet here you are. Not long ago, I had to come to your parents' home to see you because you wouldn't go out in daylight, but here you are. And you're living on your own now. This may not seem much to you, but it's progress, I promise you.'

Sturrock was never afraid of silence. He often used it to let a point sink in. He used it too to let the patient take that point wherever they wanted to in their minds, and then say whatever they wanted to say once their mind had played with it. He assumed Emily was reflecting on what he had just said, and would come back at him in a softer, mellower way. He was wrong.

'What are you thinking?' he asked.

'I'm wondering how different you would look if you had all these scars. And I'm wondering if you'd still feel you were the same person.'

'The you I see is the only you I know, and it is a full you, a real you,' he said. She nodded but in an unyielding manner that said to him he was failing. He felt the failure deeply, felt it was his fault, something he was doing wrong. How could he convince her she was making progress if he didn't even believe it himself, or believe that he knew how to help her?

'But there is a difference with me,' she said. 'I have seen a different me. The one that was pretty and whole. The one whose only scar was a tiny little mark below my ear, hidden away by my hair and so small it was hardly noticeable anyway. You can imagine the other me, can't you? But could you really imagine yourself looking like this? Do you really think you would still be saying I'm the same me?'

There was a short silence.

'I don't know,' he said. 'You're right. I don't know.'

He felt even more stuck with her now. The only good thing had been to see her showing a bit of fight and spirit. But he knew he was clutching at straws. They wrapped up early. As she pulled her headscarf tightly around her face, she said, 'Thank you,' as she always did, and left.

Sturrock went back to his desk, and sat motionless for several minutes. He felt almost numb. He couldn't recall the last time he had experienced a collapse of confidence like that during a consultation. Not since his student days. Usually, no matter how low the patient might be, he was able to come up with an idea, a strategy, something to help. But today he had been weak, drained of inspiration. As he tried to think what else he could have done, he reflected that Emily had lost her health, her looks, her confidence, her job, her sense of belonging and her boyfriend. It was hardly surprising she failed to buy into his assertion that she was the same Emily as before.

He had a spare ten minutes. He edged his hand towards the mouse of his computer. As happened far too often when he was low, he thought of Hafsatu, and felt an overwhelming urge to see her. A few months ago, she'd told him how her captors had posted videos of her on the Internet. She had described them in detail. How they had forced her to have sex with three white men, filmed her, shouted at her to look like she was enjoying it, then sold them to a company that specialised in interracial sex websites. Ever since then, he'd been looking for the videos. Even though it meant sifting through thousands of pornographic images, even though he felt sick with himself for doing so, he couldn't stop himself: he needed to see them. But just as he was about to open a new site he had not known about till now, Phyllis came in with messages.

With her usual efficiency, she went through her list. The organisers of last night's dinner called to thank him for going. Could he phone his research director about a couple of fund-raising leads they had? Next Wednesday's budget meeting was being moved. And his wife had called.

The message that his wife had called was one that Phyllis conveyed often. She always did so in a totally deadpan manner, as if it was entirely usual for a wife to make so many calls to her husband at work. Sturrock wondered if she even noticed the way his face fell a little each time she said the words. He suspected not. For a secretary to a psychiatrist, she showed a remarkable lack of interest in human nature.

He and Stella had been married for so long, and spoken by phone so often, that Stella liked to say she always knew when it was her husband calling. Statistically, that was a fair bet. She phoned him at least four times a day, sometimes half a dozen, and very occasionally the number of calls to poor Phyllis would reach double figures. He almost always called back. There was a time, just after the texting craze began to catch on among the older generation, when she got into the habit of sending messages to his mobile saying 'please call'. But it led to so many consultations being interrupted by the pinging sound of a message coming in that he'd had to turn off the phone and ask Stella to go through Phyllis like everyone else. Needless to say she was aggrieved that yet again, in her mind, he was putting his care for his patients ahead of his care for her.

He still had a bit of time before David was due to arrive – if he decided to come. He picked up the phone, and dialled home.

Stella answered after one ring, which meant she had been sitting there waiting, phone in hand. There was no hello from either of them. There rarely was.

'It's me,' he said. 'Phyllis said you called.'

'It's Jack's birthday on Sunday. Have you remembered?'

'Oh yes, of course it is. Twenty-eight, isn't he?'

'Will you get a card on the way home? We can talk about a present tonight.'

'Fine, yes, OK,' he said.

Sturrock suspected Stella's next call would be about what present to buy for Jack. He tried to say goodbye but she went into a long explanation of the comings and goings – or rather non-comings and goings – of a delivery man who was supposed to be bringing the new lawnmower she had ordered. He let her roll out every inconsequential detail, quelling with difficulty the urge to shout out that he had just spent an hour with a woman almost burnt to death, he was about to spend an hour with a chronic depressive, then see a woman who had been raped with a knife at her throat, and did she ever think that she went a bit over the top in complaining about her lot?

'I'd better go,' he said. 'I have a patient coming. I'll get the card.' And he hung up.

5

Phyllis was close to sarcasm when she buzzed through to say that David had arrived.

'He's here, lo and behold,' she whispered, and Sturrock hoped she wasn't pitching her voice just loud enough for David to hear.

'Good,' he replied. 'Excellent.' The relief was as much for himself as it was for David's well-being or Phyllis's schedule.

He walked over to his door. Through the frosted glass he could just make out the form of David, slumped in one of the chairs outside his consulting room. He smiled on seeing the familiar blue coat, hands plunged into side pockets. It was his first smile of the day. He smiled again to himself, thinking that it was a depressive who was making him happy.

On the surface, there was little in David's background to explain why Sturrock had so taken to him. David came from a broken home from which the father had fled when his son was just five, leaving his Irish mother, Nora, to cope alone with financial hardship and, as David grew older, her son's evident psychological problems. He, on the other hand, came from a well-off, middle-class background which, if unloving, had been comfortable and stable. Sturrock was a husband and a father. David had difficulty forming any sort of relationship. Sturrock was a highly educated, well-paid, respected professional. David earned seven pence above the minimum wage in a packaging warehouse in Dalston, which took a quota of 'disabled' people as part of its social responsibility programme.

Secretly, though, Sturrock knew that as well as treating David, he used him to deal with his own depression. In his behaviour and his words, David articulated a lot that he himself was forced to suppress.

So whenever David didn't show up, Sturrock knew why. Often he too felt like not turning up, but he was the doctor, and he had to. Only twice in his career had he missed a consultation because he felt psychologically unable to face it. He'd told Phyllis he had a migraine and she'd told his two patients he had food poisoning. It was the closest he'd got to asking for help. He'd sat with the phone in his lap, and begun to call his former colleague, Michael Wells, who had recently retired and was living in Bath. He got as far as the 01225, then stared at the keypad for a while, and pressed the red button. He could just about bear to admit to a general feeling of being beleaguered. He could not bear to admit all the reasons though.

It was one of the great ironies of his life that he urged his patients, and friends in his own circle, to be open about their own feelings and experiences, yet remained so closed about his own. Several times in the past, he had been asked to examine fellow psychiatrists who had either developed a particular condition that worried them or, more likely, who just felt life and the pressures of work getting on top of them. They were all encouraged to ask for help if they felt they needed it. Perhaps that was why the suicide rates among psychiatrists had fallen substantially since the days when Sturrock started his career. But he never felt able to follow their example. There were depressives who scored four or five who were under regular care and yet he, sometimes self-analysed as a six, had always resisted doing what he knew he should. It was partly the fear of damaging his own reputation inside the profession, or within the politics of the hospital. There was also a little arrogance in there, the belief he could analyse himself better than others could.

In truth, it was often David who provided the analysis. Sturrock was constantly amazed by the way he managed to describe with such vividness the knots, the chasms, the spaces, the voids and the vacuums that tormented him.

There had been several moments when he had wanted to tell

David that he experienced something very similar, but that he had learned how to hide it from others. He wanted to say it not in any 'I feel your pain' kind of way, but so that David might take some pride in his feelings and his ability to articulate them. David had never felt special about anything. He had been a failure at school and in work, and a failure in relationships. Yet he had a very special way of describing his depressions once he had left them, or they had left him, and Sturrock experienced a profound empathy.

Once, about six months ago, they'd had a longer than usual session, during which David had attempted to describe the mental tortures he inflicted upon himself as he tried to lift his head from his pillow, then his body from the bed, then go through the seemingly endless processes of cleaning and clothing that have to be done before a 'normal' person can begin to live a 'normal' day.

He'd talked about what it was like to experience a plunge, a sustained period of unrelenting agony, which then ended as quickly as it had begun. 'I felt like I had lived through a storm,' he said, 'and not a blade of grass had moved.'

Sturrock was so struck by the beauty of the words, and how they spoke to his own condition, that he wrote them down. When David left, he stood by the window, staring at those words, reading them again and again. Then he let his head fall against the glass, and started sobbing. He was feeling close to physical collapse, about to fall to the floor, when Phyllis came in to tell him he was running late for his next patient. She saw he was distressed, saw also the zeal with which he sought to recover himself, and neither of them ever mentioned it again. He hoped she assumed he had been given some bad news by his wife who had been particularly persistent in her calls.

When David had been referred to him, the diagnosis had been that his condition was chemical and he had been prescribed a variety of drugs. Sturrock hadn't been so convinced and had lowered the doses, cutting out some of the drugs completely. In one of their first sessions he'd talked to David about the demons and angels inside everyone, and how on some days demons could get the upper hand, making a person think bad thoughts, feel bad feelings and occasion-ally do bad things.

'But why do my demons always have the upper hand?' David had asked him. 'And what are they?'

'I don't know if you don't know,' replied Sturrock. 'That's what we're here to try to find out.'

Deep down, though, he was pretty sure that David's demons lurked somewhere in his relationship with his father. When they talked about Leonard Temple, David's recollections were minimal and fluid, details large and small changing with each account. Sturrock believed David felt somehow responsible for his father's departure and his mother's subsequent misery, though on the one occasion he talked to Mrs Temple, he discovered that after the shock of her husband's leaving subsided, she began to prefer life without Mr Temple to life with him, which had included persistent verbal and occasional physical abuse. David could remember none of it.

Today Sturrock wanted to focus on David's 'best–worst' list, a new piece of homework he had introduced a few weeks ago. The idea was that David should record, at the end of every day, the best thing and the worst thing that had happened to him. It didn't have to be an event as such. It could be a thought or a memory. Nor did he have to do it literally at the end of the day. Any time he felt like noting down these moments and thoughts, he should do so. The basic purpose was to try to show David that even on bad days, good things could happen, and he should recognise them, and try to build them into a pattern.

'How are you getting on with the best–worst exercise?' Sturrock asked, once David had settled himself into the leather armchair. 'Do you find it useful?'

David looked a little suspicious of the question. He didn't answer immediately, but after a few seconds he answered firmly, 'Yes, I do.'

'Because?'

'Because if I am kind of OK, not on a downward curve, just OK, average, it makes me look around for the good things, and maybe appreciate them. Something like that.'

Sturrock smiled. He felt pleased. At least one of his patients was benefiting from the homework exercises he was setting. 'Good. Well, let's keep it up as part of the weekly rhythm, shall we? Every day, let's try to record it, one of each at least, more on the good side if you want to, and then every week send it in for me to have a look at before we meet. That OK?'

'Yeah,' said David. Then he paused, and the suspicious, hesitant look returned. 'It's hard when the "worsts" are really bad, though. Like yesterday.'

Sturrock glanced down at the piece of paper resting on top of the file, angry with himself that he hadn't had time to look at it properly before David arrived. He had clearly missed something. He decided to play for time, and give himself the chance for another look.

'Let's read through what you've written, shall we? And you can talk me through it.'

He picked up the printout and read:

Friday. Best – warm sunshine when I was walking to the tube from the hospital. Really nice chat with Amanda at work. Worst – got bollocked again for not responding to tannoy message at work. Argument with Mum when I told her.

Saturday. Best – thinking a lot about Amanda. Worst – really empty at start of day because of last night. Mum hyper. Rhythm kicking in, slipping down. Key trigger Mum turning on radio and responding to something on a phone-in, then asking my views.

Sunday. Best – walk by canal. Forgot myself. Worst – couldn't sleep.

Monday. Best – felt confident. Had planned to ask Amanda to go for a drink after work. Worst – decided against, and felt a bit low.

Tuesday. Best – slept OK. Felt OK. Worst – bit of a fall as walked home from work.

Wednesday. Best – good conversation with Amanda. Worst – some guy giving me a really funny look, sort of contempt but worse than that because it said 'you don't count'. Rhythm down.

Thursday. Best – woke up thinking today was going to be a great day. Worst – really bad conversation with Amanda.

Sturrock wanted to probe first on the trigger points that had set off a clear downward curve from last Friday into Saturday. Did the curve down begin when he was told off at work, when his mum reacted in a way he didn't like, during the night, in his dreams, or when he woke up the next day? David thought it was probably a combination of all of them. But if he had to pick out a particular moment, it would be when his mother reacted as she did.

Alongside David's best–worst printout, Sturrock also had a copy of David's account of his dreams for the week. He asked most of his patients to keep a 'dream register'. He urged them to get into the habit, as soon as they woke up, of recording as much as they could remember. It was an article of faith for Sturrock that dreams were a nightly conversation between the conscious and the subconscious. There was, in his opinion, no detail too small to be of interest. But, for David, there were too many mornings in which he woke up in what he called his full-on catatonic state, and even committing thoughts and memories to print was beyond him. He also claimed he had never been much of a dreamer. Sturrock had heard this from dozens of patients down the years, but he knew that, once they acquired the discipline of noting down their dreams, first they realised how much they dreamed, and then they became more adept at remembering them. There came a point with most patients required to keep a register where they suddenly realised that even as they were dreaming, part of their conscious mind was trying to store away details to record as soon as they woke up. One patient complained that it led to her becoming a virtual insomniac. She was so keen to commit her dreams to memory that as soon as one began, she woke up and reached for her pen.

The only dream David had noted from Friday, the night of his plunge, was of him and his mother in a cafe. He couldn't decide what to order and his mother was getting more and more agitated, not on her own account, but for the waitress who was standing there waiting to write down what he wanted. David thought the waitress seemed content to wait for as long as it took, and he went back to the beginning of the menu and began to read slowly through the list of starters. His mother shifted about on her chair, the waitress remained impassive and David was resolutely indifferent to both. He ended up ordering a glass of water and salt in a pepper cellar, which the waitress took at face value, but which agitated his mother even more. She wanted him to have some vegetables too.

'What do you make of that?' Sturrock asked.

'Dunno,' said David. 'Just Mum and her food again, isn't it?'

Sturrock noted that the woman called Amanda figured several times, and was clearly responsible for a second downward curve. David had never mentioned her before, yet it was clear they saw a good deal of each other.

'Who's Amanda?' he asked. 'This is the first I've heard of her.'

David looked pained. 'We're all allowed secrets,' he said.

Sturrock nodded. 'We are indeed. But she's not secret any more, is she? She is on your best–worst list, prominently.'

David looked over at the window. He seemed unsure how to respond. Sturrock asked him whether she worked in the same department at the packaging warehouse, where David was a porter. His job was low-paid, not particularly challenging, but it suited the rhythms of his depressions. When he felt OK, he could join in as part of a team, and it was clear that at times he even quite enjoyed himself. When he was down, the routine work allowed him to avoid being drawn into other people's lives or conversations.

'She started out as a porter,' said David, 'but she's so much better than me that she got promoted fast.'

Apparently Amanda was now in overall charge of one of the most important packing stations, which handled women's fashionwear. At first David hadn't thought she was any different from all the other employees who spent their time chatting about telly and fashion and football, tracking who was going out with who, and complaining about how stupid the bosses were. She would tease him about his scruffy clothes, or ask if he had his eye on any of the girls at work. But then one day she'd asked him if he suffered from depression.

'I don't know why,' said David, 'but I kind of trusted her. The other packers and porters just think I'm weird, and mostly avoid talking to me. But Amanda has always been friendly. It turns out her dad was bipolar, so she knows all about depression. She even went to my line manager to ask him about me, whether I was bipolar and stuff.'

'How did you feel about that?' asked Sturrock.

'About what?'

'About her asking your boss personal questions about you.'

'I felt quite touched that she bothered to,' said David.

After she had told him of her father's illness, David said, Amanda had stuck up for him if anyone gave him a hard time.

'A couple of weeks ago, there was a forklift-truck driver waiting for a container of packages that I was supposed to have put in his next batch for moving. I wasn't feeling great and I was late getting round to where this guy was waiting and when I got there he starts mouthing off at me, really going for me, and Amanda is standing there watching, and she lets it go, but then this guy calls me a "nutter" and she just goes for him, marches right up to him and says, "You just leave him alone or else you've got me and the rest to answer to."'

'The rest?'

'I don't know what she meant by that. Most of the time the rest of them just ignore me, but she's a bit of a leader at work, and it shut the guy up big time. I just chucked the packages in and off he went.'

'She sounds quite a character,' said Sturrock, smiling.

'Like I say, a leader. She's special.'

Sturrock noticed that David's face changed when he talked about Amanda. The lines around his mouth relaxed a little, and he no longer narrowed his eyes. He began to open up, and his account became a melange of his words and hers as he explained how he tried to thank her for what she did.

'I didn't say anything for a few days, but then I dug in a bit, and I got up the courage to go up to her in the tea break to say thanks, thanks, Amanda, for what you did the other day. And she's like smiling, and probably wondering why it took me so long, but she says, "No worries," and how she hates bullies and she could tell I was having a bad day, and I say, "Yeah, most of my days are bad days, but that day was worse than most, so thanks."

'And then she goes into a big thing about her dad and how I remind her of him, how one minute he could be warm and loving, the next he'd go all withdrawn, sometimes unable to speak or even hear what she was saying to him. She said he could go for days on end, locked away in his room, and her mum would pretend everything was fine, how he was just tired and needed a rest, and she and her sisters had to be quiet and good, but she says even when she was little she knew it was bad, and then she said how horrible it was sometimes, having a dad there who wasn't really there at all, just this big bad cloud hanging over the place.'

'Did that make you think of your own father?'

'No, it made me think of my mum, and how she must feel about me. No wonder Amanda wants nothing to do with me.'

Sturrock glanced down at David's homework and his 'worst' entry for Thursday: *really bad conversation with Amanda.* He was angry with himself. How had he managed to miss picking up on that?

'How do you know she wants nothing more to do with you?'

David's narrow-eyed, troubled look returned. He was staring down at his hands, and running them over his knees again and again.

'No point.'

'No point what?'

'No point talking about it.'

'Are you sure?'

'Hmm . . .'

Sturrock realised he was going to have to come at it from another angle.

'So from what you've told me, she stands up for you, and she understands you, and she sympathises with you, so you like her, yes?'

'What I liked was having someone to talk to who had this incredible feel for the mood I was in. It was uncanny really, how she would always know when I was up for a chat, and when I just wanted to be left alone. One day I said to her, "Do you know that apart from my mum and my shrink, you're the only person I really talk to?"'

'How did she react to that?'

'Good. Big smile. Said she was glad. And I wanted to say something nice to her. And I had the words coming up through my mind – "You're really nice." I can feel them coming up into my head and they're almost at my lips but then I'm getting different messages from my inner voice. First, it's telling me to say it, tell her she's really nice and see if she's still smiling, and then it comes in again and it says, "No, play safe, sit tight, it'll come out wrong."'

'So what did you do?'

'I listened to the second voice. So I'm standing there and it's just silence, till eventually she gives me a little smile and she says, "Any time you want to talk, you just say."'

Sturrock asked him how that made him feel.

'Good. I thought that was just so nice, so incredibly nice. And when I'm walking home that night, I'm thinking there's something happening here. She can have her pick of all the blokes at work, but I'm the one she seems to really like.'

'Do men find her attractive?'

'Oh yeah. She's not what you call a classic beauty, but she's got such a strong character and a strong face and a great body, and she's got these really toned shoulders and big breasts that the guys are always ogling because she wears tight lacy bras and the uniform for the women is these pretty thin polyester blouses, so yeah, most of the blokes fancy her rotten. She's got long curly red hair and she's always fiddling with the curls, and I was convinced she fiddled with her hair more when she was talking to me. I was sure of it. Sure of it.' He stopped, and Sturrock could sense that, as he told the story, David's mind was already moving to the moment of rejection.

David had only ever had one serious girlfriend, Catherine, twelve years ago. He had told Sturrock about her in his very first piece of homework, when he had to write out his whole life story as he saw it, all the good things and the bad things that had happened to him. Sex for the first time with Catherine went down on the bad side.

'I guess I saw Amanda as the one really, the one I could finally make some kind of relationship with, and her saying what she said made me feel even more like that. It seemed such a lovely thing to say: "Any time you want to talk, you just say." It showed how well she got me, because sometimes I can't talk because I'm on a downward curve, but sometimes I really do want someone to talk to. But I didn't know how I would let her know that I was in talking mood. "I want to talk" sounds too stark. "Amanda, you know you said just say any time I wanted to talk, well, how about now?" I'm thinking that sounds a bit clumsy. I thought maybe I would just start chatting to her, like we'd been doing, and then let it develop. I had this idea that I'd take her out for a meal, ask her to suggest somewhere. I thought about it all weekend. I just couldn't stop thinking about it – while I was helping Mum sort out the washing, while we were eating, while I was cleaning my face, brushing my teeth. I got to bed and I'm lying there just thinking about her and it makes me . . . you know. And it's not just sex either. It's like in my head, I'm making these plans, thinking one day I'll be leaving home and living with Amanda instead.' He stopped, and shook his head.

'So Monday comes,' said Sturrock.

'Yeah, and I was sure I was going to ask her out, but when it came to it, I bottled out. I needed more time to think how to do it. But then, yesterday, we were chatting and I got the feeling she was playing with her hair even more than usual. She does this thing where she twiddles her finger in her hair then pulls it away from her head, lets go and the hair falls back in a little curl, then she starts all over again. I love it when she does that.

'She was smiling a lot, and then she tells me this silly story about a package that went missing yesterday, and later turned up in the finance director's office, and she lets out this really lovely laugh. So it felt like the moment to make the move and I couldn't believe how fast my heart was pumping. For a second or two I was worried I was going to faint. But I held it together, I looked her right in the eye and I went for it.'

David's face fell again.

'What did you say?' Sturrock prompted.

'I said, "You know you said 'any time you want to talk, you just say'?" and she goes, "Yeah," and I go, "Well, I can't tell you what that meant to me, Amanda. It was one of the best moments of my life," and she goes like, "Wow, that good?" and I say, "Yeah, yeah it was, and there's something else I want to say, Amanda, which is that I think you're a really good person, I mean like the nicest person I think I've ever met, and you've made me feel happy by the way you talk to me and the way you are with me."'

'How was she reacting?'

'You know, I was concentrating so hard on what I was saying I can't say I noticed. It was like, I'd rehearsed these words hour after hour in the mirror at home and I was just desperate to say what I planned to say and get my words right, so maybe I wasn't paying attention to how she was reacting. And it must have been weird for her, I guess, because normally she would drive the conversation, it would be thirty words her and ten words me, but this time was the other way round, I'm doing the talking and she just throws in the odd word.

'So I'm steaming on now, just full-on going for it, like I've practised and I go, "What I've been thinking in the last few days, maybe, I dunno, I hope maybe you've been thinking something of the same thing, is that, maybe, we could carry on our talking away from work, maybe go out together somewhere, just the two of us, away from here, carry on talking like we do here, and if it feels OK, maybe be more like boyfriend and girlfriend, not just working together."'

He stopped again, stared down at the hands on his lap, then looked up at Sturrock.

'And then?' Sturrock asked gently.

'And then, well, she had this look on her face, and part of me is trying to tell myself it's just shock that I've come out with this stuff, but deep down I know it's disgust. All of a sudden her eyes look mean, and her lip is curling up a bit. But I'm hoping maybe it's just shock, so I ask her what she thinks and she says she doesn't know what to think and how she has never really thought of us in that way, and I go, "Well, can't you try?" and she says she doesn't think so, so I go, "Why not?" and she says because it just isn't like that, and it wouldn't work. So I say, "Why not?" again and she says, "David, honestly, it wouldn't work, let's just not go there," and I say, "But I want to know why," and maybe I should have turned and walked away right then but I keep at her and eventually she says there is no point talking about it and I say, "Why?" again and of course she tells me the truth.'

'Which is?'

'She says I've read too much into things. She's nice to me because she feels sorry for me. She feels sorry for me because her dad was ill like I get ill and she knows how hard it can be and she thought if she could help me a bit like she was never able to help her dad, that'd be great. But going out together? Boyfriend and girlfriend? "No, David," she says. "I really don't think so."'

Seeing his favourite patient collapse back in his chair, Sturrock felt the full force of Amanda's rejection himself. For a few moments he didn't know what to say. In the end, he resorted to his favourite question.

'So how did that make you feel?'

'Shit. Like shit. Like I will never get anything right. Like why did I even think she might be interested? And you know how sometimes the downward rhythm creeps up slowly, takes you bit by bit?'

Sturrock nodded.

'Well, this time it came all at once, an instant hit. Straight in the guts. Bang. Empty. Sick. The big void. Do you know what I'm saying?'

'I do, David. I'm sorry.'

'I remember thinking that at least I'd have something to talk to you about. That's about the only thing to be said for it, I guess.'

'Well, I'm glad you did. Thank you.'

Sturrock looked at his watch. There wasn't much time left. He had Arta Mehmeti next who was always on time, and he did not want to keep her waiting. But he worried about David heading into a weekend with the feeling of rejection so strong in his mind.

'Do you wish you hadn't asked her out?'

'Yeah.'

'You shouldn't. You should be proud you felt the courage to ask her.'

David looked unimpressed.

'And just remember that however bad you felt, it will pass. You know that from so much of your experience, that these feelings can pass. OK?'

'I guess.'

'Look forward to when the storm is over, David, and not a blade of grass has moved.' He paused, and smiled. 'You said that.'

David didn't smile back.

Sturrock noticed a book on his shelf – one that he had been intending to give David in the next week or so. Perhaps now was the moment. He took it down.

'Have a look at this, David,' he said, 'and try to do the exercise in chapter three. I think it might help.'

David looked dubious, and Sturrock couldn't deny that he, too, felt on shaky ground.

6

While Professor Sturrock and David were talking, his next two patients were making their way through dense London traffic, Arta Mehmeti on the 148 bus from Elephant and Castle, Matthew and Celia Noble in a taxi from Totteridge. Though coming from opposite ends of London, their routes briefly converged around Marble Arch where the Nobles' taxi cut in front of Arta's bus, forcing it to brake hard. Arta stumbled, dropping the notebook she was holding on to the floor.

For the whole journey, Arta had been fretting about her homework. She was normally punctilious about getting it to Professor Sturrock the afternoon before her appointment, but the last few days had been busy, mainly because her husband Lirim was having to work so hard. He was expanding his small car-wash business and didn't have so much time to help out with their two children, Alban and Besa. Last week Professor Sturrock had asked her to be more detailed when she recorded her dreams, and also to keep a separate record of what she would like to dream about if she had the ability to control her night-time thoughts. This request for more homework, and his demand for detail, had further upset her daily routine. She found it hard to write down her dreams at the best of times. She always slept badly and woke up feeling tired. And there was always too little time to get the family up and running, Lirim off to work, Alban off to school. This week, instead of writing more about her dreams as requested, she found she had written even less.

Arta was a Kosovar Albanian who had come to Britain with her family when President Milosevic was engaged in his policy of ethnic cleansing, purging Kosovo of all but the Serbs. The journey had been long and at times they had thought they wouldn't all make it alive. The process of settling had been even harder than she had expected, but Lirim's little car-wash business was now bringing in a steady income, and she had a part-time job in a launderette. They had a perfectly good flat and Alban had settled well in school, where the teachers and most of the other children made him feel welcome.

The attack had taken place on a Tuesday morning when she opened the door to two men, who forced her back into the narrow hallway. As they came through, they put on balaclavas, making it impossible for Arta to give anything but the vaguest of descriptions of them, beyond their thick south London accents, and the rapist's dulled blue eyes, when the police interviewed her later. The bigger of the two men dragged her three-year-old daughter Besa into the kitchen while his partner pushed Arta into the sitting room. He forced a gag into her mouth, silencing the scream she had let out as Besa was taken from her. 'Shut it, or the little girl gets hurt,' he said. 'My friend has a knife and if I shout to him to "cut"' – he lowered his voice to a whisper to say the word 'cut' – 'he will cut her. Do you under-stand?' Though she nodded, he kept the gag in her mouth throughout, occasionally making her retch. 'And if you annoy me, my friend will come through to watch, and bring your little girl with him. OK, you got that?' She nodded again. He had a knife in his hand. He put it to the side of her neck, said, 'Just do as you're told,' then tossed the knife to the floor while he started to undo his trousers.

She had heard so much about rape during the onslaught of the Milosevic forces. Twenty thousand was the figure most commonly used of Kosovar Albanian women raped by Serb soldiers. Enough to fill the national stadium in Priština. There remained such a feeling of shame attached to rape that the actual figure was almost certainly far higher. Arta had friends who had been gang-raped by Serbs, including one who had been killed afterwards. Stories of suicide were common. Less so the stories of women who became pregnant through rape and kept their sons and daughters. Rape, particularly in the Balkan region, appeared to be a fact of war. But Arta and Lirim had fled the war with their newborn son, Alban. He now spoke with a London accent and wanted an Arsenal shirt for his birthday, and of course Besa, born in England, had no memory of Kosovo at all. They lived in civilised London in a nice flat provided by the local authority which one day they hoped to buy. She had Sky TV and a discount card for the local superstore. She had English friends and Kosovan friends and her son was getting fantastic reports in school, and her daughter about to go to the nursery.

She had been cleaning the kitchen floor, listening to the pop-music station favoured by Alban, and thinking about taking Besa out for a walk to the car wash, where she would deliver a packed lunch for Lirim and his four staff as a little surprise. As she was forced on to the sofa, she felt physically and psychologically powerless. She believed the man when he said his friend would harm her daughter who even now she could hear crying out for her. She felt she had to submit, that the quicker he entered her, the quicker he would be done, and the sooner she could call for help. She tried desperately to think of other things to block out the smell of the man, the noise of his grunting, the feel of his penis first jabbing against her thigh, then inside where till then only her husband had been. She now knew why it was called making love. She and Lirim made love. This was hatred, not of her as an individual, but of women, or of humanity, possibly a deep self-hatred inside the man who was doing this to her. She was gorging on the gag, trying not to let him see her tears, wondering whether once he was done, he would swap roles with his friend, wondering what her husband would say and do, whether he would feel as powerless and helpless as she did. She wanted to shout out Lirim's name and say she loved him, but was scared her attacker would see it as an act of defiance. As he raised the volume of his grunting and pumped his semen into her, she tried to summon up the faces of her children, of her mother and father. 'Sorry,' she whispered beneath the gag. 'Sorry.'

He was done, his final grunt followed by a snarl as he put his face right against hers and pretended to spit. He slid out of her, wiped himself with his shirt tail, did up his trousers, stood over her, made to hit her but pulled back, then laughed and left the room. She lay there, tears now flowing, then heard the door to the flat close quietly as her daughter came running towards her.

She was referred to Professor Sturrock by one of the GPs helping with his research programme on asylum seekers and refugees. She was plagued by nightmares in which the rapist and his accomplice reappeared, and she and Lirim had not had sex since the attack.

For all the talk of rape during the Kosovo war, Arta had never given any real thought to the consequences of it before. Rape was something best dealt with by being content that one never had to deal with it.

Once, in a cafe in Priština, her mother had pointed out a young woman with a son who was known to have been fathered by a Serb soldier who had raped her inside a mosque. Arta had been interested enough to watch the interaction between mother and son, and had a sensation somewhere close to pleasure on seeing how the boy so clearly enjoyed his mother's touch and company. The young woman looked little more than a teenager yet was clearly comfortable with the mechanics of motherhood, the juggling of the various objects her son was playing with, the challenge of keeping him from her hot drink even when he grabbed for her, the skilful use of a smile or small talk to defuse any embarrassment if he ran into a waitress. Yet, the young girl had surely hoped to raise a family through the love of a husband, not a soldier's hatred for her and her race. Would she ever now be able to find a man willing to love not just her, but her mixed-race son created by the sperm of a grunting brute cheered on by his friends and fellow conquerors? It looked to Arta as though the girl was able to separate love for her son from hatred for his father. But could a woman really love a child half made by hate and evil in the same way as she would a son fathered in love?

That was as far as she ever got in her reflections on rape. She had a new life now. England was her home, and Priština a place she visited once a year, each time feeling less of a desire to go back to settle, as she used to imagine she would.

Once she was a rape victim herself, she thought of little else but the consequences of it. She was tormented by questions. Had Besa suffered lasting damage as a result of what happened, or would she be able to forget, provided the reminders were taken away? What was her husband really feeling beneath the attempts to sympathise and support her? Did he feel at fault in not having been there to protect her? Was there a part of him that felt she should have been able to fight off her attacker, cry for help, take greater risks than she had to alert neighbours and passers-by on the walkway outside their front door? Would he ever be able to make love to her again without thinking that someone else had been there and hurt the only woman he had ever truly loved? Would she? And finally, the question that took her to Professor Sturrock's brown leather armchair on the sixth floor of the Le Gassick wing at the Prince Regent Hospital: would she ever be able to sleep again, without the rapist intruding night after night into her dreams?

As she sat on the bus, desperately trying to recollect details from the dreams of the last week, she calculated that the rapist had entered her subconscious on every night but one. He had raped her twice, once on Sunday, in a muddy field in pouring rain, with Arta feeling she was sinking into the ground, and she wanted the sun to come out and bake the mud into a coffin shape and take her to her death; and the second time on Tuesday, when he raped her in the hallway, watched by his accomplice, Besa and Lirim. Yet she was just as scared by his presence in the dreams where he didn't rape her, where he just looked and smirked and insulted her.

Professor Sturrock had told her his task was to help her to accept what had happened, to help her to believe her life could be good again, persuade her that, with time, the memory and the pain could fade. But no matter how many times he told her there was no shame attached to what had happened, she felt it.

They talked about the kind of dreams she'd had before the rape. She struggled to recall any in detail. In so far as she had a recurring dream, it was of their journey to England, where they were carrying all their possessions in canvas bags, climbing a long, stony hill, reaching the summit only to find that it wasn't the summit at all but a short plateau before the hill stretched upwards again, ahead of them a single file of humanity fleeing fear and persecution, their certain knowledge of the reality of both sufficient to keep their feet shuffling forward. Alban was thirsty but she had no milk or water to give him.

'Did you ever reach England?' Professor Sturrock asked.

'Not in the dreams,' she said. 'Only in real life.'

'So life can be better than our dreams,' he suggested.

Arta knew that her homework this week was not as good as either of them would want it to be. She preferred to type it up and email it to him, but today was still scribbling in her large handwriting as the bus ground its way into the centre of town. She was always nervous on the bus, especially the first part of the journey from the Elephant, worried that some of her friends might see her. They knew what had happened to her, and had been as supportive as they could be, but there was a limit to what friends could do. In any event, she didn't like to talk to them about it, especially now that a little time had passed, and she didn't want anyone but Lirim and her GP to know that she had weekly sessions with a psychiatrist. Should she bump into anyone she knew, they would ask her where she was going, just to be polite, and she would feel she had to say something truthful. She thought that 'into town' would be OK, but then they might ask 'what to do?' and she'd feel obliged to say she was going for a medical appointment, taking the conversation down routes she didn't want to go.

Last week, Professor Sturrock had said to her that it was possible the nightmares were recurring because, even though women knew that rape existed as a phenomenon, particularly where she came from, there was no part of her basic belief system that could incorporate such a terrible thing even in theory, let alone in practice as a victim. So the rapist's constant appearance in her dreams was a reminder not just of how awful and traumatic the attack had been, but also that she was a good, decent person with good, decent values. The basic vision she had of herself was as a devoted wife and mother. The rapist must not be allowed to take that from her. He credited her too with being a great survivor, who had come through dreadful experiences in making her way to Britain, and she had to draw on those qualities as a survivor in how she responded to what had happened to her. But he had also said that so long as she allowed her life to be dominated by bad memories, the chances of a good life slimmed down. He had said it kindly, but it felt harsh at the time.

He had asked her to plot any changes in the rapist's appearance and behaviour in her dreams. The bus had slowed to a halt and was waiting for traffic lights to turn from red to green. Arta closed her eyes, and tried hard to think. When he raped her in Sunday's dream, he had a knife and he was wearing the balaclava. When he raped her on Tuesday, he was wearing the balaclava, but he had no knife. She thought it possible that he hadn't grunted so much either. It also helped that she could see her daughter and husband who, though immobile and seemingly unable to help, had love in their eyes, almost as if they saw only her, not what was happening to her. She opened her eyes and wrote it all down, until the bus braked and she dropped her notebook.

The taxi had arrived early for Matthew and Celia Noble. It was one of their regular drivers, Alan, who turned up, which meant they couldn't really talk to each other much about what lay ahead. They just gave him a postcode, which he tapped into his satnav console.

'It's got the Prince Regent Hospital coming up,' he said.

'Yes,' said Celia. 'We're going to a shop just round the corner.' She slid her hand over to touch Matthew, who was staring out of the window, wondering if he would ever have sex with Angela again.

He looked back on the two affairs as unfortunate accidents really. He had reached a point in his professional life where he was established, knew what he was doing, did it reasonably well and had more or less given up thinking he would ever be anything more than a good, solid, middle-aged, jobbing barrister who could make a tidy living without ever becoming the star QC he had once thought he might be. Their two children had left home, one to university, one to 'travelling', and though he missed them, a little, he didn't get much sense that they missed him or Celia, so he felt freed from many of the emotional stresses they once put upon him.

He had quite fancied Madeleine, the first of his two adventures, but no more than he did plenty of other women who flitted in and out of his radar. She was nothing special in the physical stakes: a few years younger than his wife, a bit slimmer, but her face was nowhere near as striking, nor her mind as sharp. She didn't even make him laugh very much.

There was nothing that he could remotely term magical in the sexual encounters they enjoyed. 'Enjoyed' was as high as he would put it. He was only a few weeks into the affair when he wanted out of it. He wondered if he hadn't deliberately gone for someone not too attractive, so that he wouldn't be drawn in too deeply, and would be able to end it without too much pain on either side of the ledger. The problem was that, even before he got to that stage, Celia found out, in circumstances that were cruelly unlucky.

Celia worked three days a week as the assistant catering manager at the offices of a rival law firm. Though she had a second-class degree in fine art, she had been a full-time wife and mother for most of their marriage and it was only when the first of their children left home that she asked Matthew to help her find something to do to get her out of the house a bit more. She had no relevant experience in catering other than running a small household, but Matthew was a close friend of the head of the divorce specialists, Durrants, who agreed to take her on. Once she got the hang of it, she loved it.

Her discovery of the affair with Madeleine resulted from the simple fact that the combined volume of a flushing toilet, a running tap and a ringing mobile phone is louder than the turning of the key in a front door, the closing of said door, and the movement of feet on carpet. Celia had left for work at 8.10, forgoing a goodbye kiss because Matthew was in the downstairs loo, reading *The Times*. Overall, he had preferred the newspaper when it was a broadsheet, he was thinking, even though a tabloid was a lot easier to read when sitting on the toilet. 'Goodbye, darling, see you tonight,' she had shouted, and as he heard the front door close, he took his mobile phone from his trouser pocket, and sent Madeleine a short text message. '*Safe to call xxx.*'

Madeleine tended to respond to texts with an immediate call, one of the signs that had suggested to Matthew that she might be becoming more intense about their affair than he had ever intended. With that thought very much in mind, and with it an accompanying sense of disappointment, and slight dread at the day ahead, he flushed the toilet, then walked the four steps to the sink to wash his hands. It was now 8.11. As the toilet gurgled away, and as he washed his hands under the cold tap, his phone rang.

Unbeknown to Matthew, at the moment he was pressing the answer button on his phone to silence the final ring, Celia was turning her key in the front-door lock, having come back for a letter she had forgotten to post. Worse, she was passing the door as he uttered the words, 'Listen, Maddie, here's a plan. I have a case first thing, but it won't even see out the morning, so what do you say we meet for an early lunch, at the little Italian we went to last Tuesday, one course, quick as you like, then back to the flat, and I promise you, by the time we're finished, you will be in no doubt how much I love you.' Then she opened it.

Matthew was so shocked he dropped his phone. When he picked it up, he told Madeleine that he was cancelling lunch. 'Something's come up,' he said. Half an hour later, he ended the affair by text. *'Celia heard us talking. I've promised her it's over. Sorry.'*

He felt that, if he could last the first twenty-four hours without being thrown out, he would be able to make it through. He could live with being ejected from the marital bed for a while, and with the kids away, he had plenty of spare rooms to choose from, but he positively did not want to be kicked out of the house. Matthew was not far off the truth when he said to Celia that there was nothing much to the affair, that it was classic midlife crisis stuff, he had been flattered into it, now wished it had never happened, and how it made him want to be with Celia for the rest of his life, which all being well could be another three decades or so.

The second affair lasted longer than the first, its intensity was stronger, the sex more joyous and there was even a brief moment when he really believed that he would happily end his marriage for a future with Angela. She was the junior brief for the defence in a case where Matthew was prosecuting two young Turks charged with beating up a minicab driver. The second he set eyes on her, across the corridor as he walked towards the courtroom, he was possessed by a desire to know her. She was tall, with long brown hair and green eyes and a smile that mixed mischief with warmth. The case lasted four days and throughout he couldn't have cared less how he was viewed by the judge or the jury. He was performing for her alone. He was not known for being sociable at the Bar, but he engineered several meetings between the prosecution and defence teams so that he could get closer to her. By the time the case ended, with a guilty verdict, which had given him more pleasure than any verdict he had ever secured, because she *must* have been impressed by the way he secured it, he felt he had met her often enough to ask her out for lunch. The moment she said yes, he knew they were going to have a totally inappropriate, highly unprofessional relationship.

In the weeks that followed, he felt he was truly in love for the first time in his life. He awoke each morning, happy to be alive. They spoke in any spare moment. They met as often as their schedules would reasonably allow. He shocked himself with the risks they took. He would collect her from her office, knowing he might be seen by her colleagues. They ate out together, went to cinemas and theatres together, even spent weekends away together in country hotels on the pretext that he was speaking at legal conferences.

As what he believed to be his love for Angela grew stronger, he began to think about leaving Celia. He worked out how and where he was going to tell her – in the car, as they arrived home on one of those rare nights when he collected her from Durrants after work. He would just tell her straight out: he had met someone else, this time it did mean something, and he was really sorry, but he was going to move in with Angela, they hoped to marry, and therefore he would be looking for a divorce. Then one afternoon, as he and Angela lay in bed post-sex, he told her what he was thinking about. She was appalled. Of course she loved him, she said. She was having the time of her life. He was great fun to be with, and a terrific guide professionally. Of course she wanted to carry on, but she was almost twenty years younger than he was. She never for one moment imagined they would spend their lives together.

From that moment, the affair began to die. He felt hurt by her reaction. 'Us? Married?' She had almost laughed and for the first time, he saw a harshness in the smile. For months, she had made him feel so young and alive but her inability even to imagine that they might have a future together made him suddenly feel old. Silly. Old. Man.

Perhaps, somewhere in his subconscious, he wanted Celia to discover that a young and beautiful woman had fallen for him, albeit not sufficiently to wreck their marriage. In any case, this time it was a silly lie that led to his being found out.

He and Angela had gone to a nice hotel in Ireland for a weekend. He had told Celia he was going to play golf with friends in Scotland. A golfing weekend in Ireland was just as plausible as a golfing weekend in Scotland. So why did he say Scotland when his credit-card bills would show Ireland? Why did he take his passport to 'Scotland' when normally he used his driving licence as ID for internal UK flights? Why did he take the little stash of euros she kept in the top drawer of the bedside table? And why didn't he take his golf clubs?

Unfortunately, Celia had seen the offending American Express bill: *12 February, Aer Lingus, 230 euros. 16 February, Galway Bay Hotel, 348 euros.* She had checked out the website of the Galway Bay Hotel: it didn't even have a golf course.

To make matters worse, she decided to use his clerk, Julian, to shame him. Angela had sent him a text just as he arrived home from work one evening. *'How about coming round to see me now?'* He couldn't resist. He'd told Celia the text was from Julian, asking where he was, reminding him he was supposed to be at a late-night meeting about a case next week. He went into a great fandango about how stupid he had been, went to get his coat and briefcase, and convinced himself he had been utterly convincing.

'What time do you think you'll be back?' she'd asked.

'God knows, love. Don't wait up. Complicated case. Five defend-ants all with their own briefs, turning against each other.'

When he got home at eleven, Celia had met him in the hallway. She gave him a little kiss, which surprised him, and asked if he wanted a drink. 'I'd love a tea,' he said. 'Awful meeting. Cut-throat defence looming.'

'Who was there?' Celia had asked as she led the way towards the kitchen. The 'J' of the word Julian was beginning to form halfway between his teeth and the roof of his mouth as he walked into the room. The 'u' was forming at the front of his mouth, just behind the top lip, as he caught sight of his clerk sitting at the table, his hands curled around a large whisky tumbler filled with sparkling water. It was too late to get the word back into his mouth. By the time the third syllable arrived on his tongue, all strength and confidence in the voice had gone. He felt momentarily faint. He kept looking at Julian so as to avoid looking at Celia. Julian appeared confused, and a little scared. He didn't know what was going on, having been called out of the blue by Celia and asked to come and see Matthew for an urgent meeting, but he didn't like it.

'I think you have been a pawn in a little private difficulty between a man and a wife, Julian,' Matthew said. 'I'm sorry you've been drawn into this. It's my fault. You should go home now, and I'd be grateful if you didn't mention what happened to anyone.' Julian left.

To Matthew's surprise, Celia continued to make him tea. She stood watching the kettle boil, and said nothing. She didn't look at him. She was waiting for a confession, and he knew he had to provide one.

'I don't know what to say,' he said. She said nothing, just stared at the kettle, and waited to see whether he could bear the silence. He couldn't.

'Sorry for lying,' he went on. 'But I thought the truth would be worse.' He longed for her to say 'tell me the truth then', or even 'go on', anything that would spark a dialogue. But she was still staring at the kettle and he knew he was on his own.

'She's called Angela,' he said, and she nodded to the kettle, as though the name of someone she had never met, nor ever would want to, somehow helped it all to make some kind of sense. 'She's thirty,' he said.

'Young enough to be your daughter,' she said, quietly, as she dropped a tea bag into a cup.

'I know,' he said. 'I'm sorry. Pathetic really.'

'Is it about sex?' she asked. 'Is that what this is all about?'

'Probably,' he said. In truth, he didn't know whether it really was all about sex, but he felt it was what Celia wanted to hear, and it was at least believable, allowed itself to be rationalised as true.

'Do you love her?'

'I thought I did, for a while. But no, not really, not the way I love you.' Again, he didn't know for sure whether any or all parts of that statement were true, and it was quite a while since he had told Celia he loved her, but it felt about right. He felt he was getting the tone of these exchanges right, much better than when he was confronted about Maddie.

'So it's all about sex really, isn't it?' she said. It appeared to be her big point.

'I suppose so.'

'Is it really that bad? Between us, I mean?'

'No, of course not.'

'So what's the problem?' It was his turn to be silent.

Now, as the taxi drove through an amber light at Marble Arch, accidentally cutting up a bus and getting a blast of its horn, Matthew felt increasingly sick. Celia was holding his hand, and smiling. He looked into her eyes, and smiled back, hoping she couldn't tell just how much he was hating every single second of this.

7

As Arta settled down in the brown leather armchair opposite Professor Sturrock, she pulled out the notes she had scribbled about her dreams.

'I'm sorry I not email,' she said, handing them over. 'Lirim is very busy in his work and I have little time.'

Sturrock was taken aback to see the homework. Because nothing had been emailed, somehow he hadn't expected it, and he had spent the few minutes before he called in Arta reflecting on whether to go for a high-risk strategy that might begin the process of breaking her free from the imprisonment of her rapist. Now that she had given him her dreams, he would have to read through them, which would take a few minutes, and then ask her about them, which would take a few minutes more, and possibly lead to further avenues of discussion. The dreams exercise was part of a cognitive-behavioural therapy he had worked on in an earlier research programme on dreams and post-traumatic stress, which had formed the basis for one of his books. The idea was to help train the mind to know when it was dreaming and, when recurring bad dreams cropped up, to develop the ability to force events to go in the direction the dreamer wanted them to. It was called lucid dreaming treatment, but, so far, Arta had not responded well.

The upside of her handing over her dreams register was that a short discussion would give him more time to work out whether she was in the right frame of mind for the high-risk strategy. If she was closed up and unyielding, he would continue to probe gently the nature of her dreams about the man who had, to use her own words from their first meeting, 'destroyed' her life. If, on the other hand, she appeared to be open to a different form of dialogue, he was going to try his new approach. He would rely on instinct.

He quickly noted that the rapist appeared to have been less violent in the past week than he had in previous weeks. He noted too that, although her attacker continued to wear his balaclava, when he raped her on Tuesday night, he wasn't holding his knife. It also struck him that she had once again, with regard to Sunday night's rape, equated what happened to her with death.

In their discussion, he focused more on the first observation, the fact that the rapist seemed to be raping less and simply observing and abusing verbally. He asked if she thought this was significant, and whether in the dreams it made her feel any differently.

'I don't know,' she said. 'Maybe a little, I don't know.'

He felt himself being pushed towards his high-risk strategy.

The danger was that she would feel he was minimising her suffering, and it might lead to something of a rupture in the relationship he had slowly developed with her. She had definitely become more open, willing to accept that only she could really change the way she looked at the world. But he knew from some of his research on asylum seekers and their efforts to integrate that there were cross-cultural clashes that he needed to be more sensitive to. It was particularly hard for her, a Balkan Muslim, to talk to him, a Western man, about some of the issues they discussed.

He always tried hard to imagine how his patients felt. Often, it was easy. With David Temple, for example, and his unknowing ability to capture feelings in a way that sometimes captured Sturrock's own moods better than he could. But with Arta, it was more of a challenge. It was clear that before the rape, she was someone who, despite, or perhaps because of, the suffering she endured as she fled Kosovo, was warm, optimistic, generous and very happy with what life gave her. He would certainly assume that her general disposition was sunnier than his. The rape, though, had left her with overwhelming feelings of hurt and fear. The fact that it had taken place in the country to which she fled, rather than the one she was fleeing, where so many women had been raped, added to her bewilderment.

There was a feminist view in psychiatry, not widely held but occasionally put to him by his young colleague Judith Carrington, that only a woman psychiatrist could properly treat women patients. Sturrock rejected that entirely. He felt he was just as capable of treating women as men, and giving equal quality care to both. If a patient were to say to him, 'You've no idea what it is like to be a woman,' he would argue back that he could understand what it was the woman was feeling, and why. There were sufficient solid principles in his approach to psychiatry to make him feel confident in making that case. But when someone said, as Arta had the last time they met, 'You have no idea what it is like to be raped,' he had to accept that was true.

He had tried, many times, to imagine. What would it be like, for example, to be sodomised by another man against his will? When he tried to picture this, he always saw himself fighting off his attacker. When he made himself imagine that he failed and was instead being held down by others, it was still difficult to summon up the feelings of pain, hurt and humiliation that a woman must feel. In his imagination, though he knew a man could be raped face to face if held down, he was always raped from behind, his face against the ground; whereas a woman would more likely be forced to feel a man's breath over her face, forced to see his eyes, forced to feel his penis in a part of her body she had only ever shared with a husband or boyfriend. It was the invasion of body space that seemed the greatest difference. A heterosexual man was likely to be raped in a part of his body he shared with nobody. And so Sturrock believed – though never having counselled a victim of male rape he had no idea if this was true or not – that male rape was less likely to destroy the victim's long-term interest in a sex life with a female partner. Arta's problem, as well as the dreams, was that she now couldn't face sex with her husband. Though Lirim was clearly trying hard to be loving and understanding about what had happened to her, there was no doubt it was leading to tension in the marriage. Sturrock knew too, from previous patients, that rape of a woman could change her partner's self-image which in turn could badly affect not just his sex drive, but his self-esteem.

Arta was looking at him, waiting for him to say something. He was trying to gauge how much she meant it when she said she had been feeling 'just a little' different in her dreams. He desperately wanted to see her make progress. He was going to try to speed things along.

He sat up straight, and sighed deeply, trying to indicate that this was an important moment for them. Arta picked up on the signal, and shifted a little in her chair, then she too sat up, put her left arm on the arm of the chair, and put her right hand on top of her arm.

'I'm going to ask you to try to do something very difficult, Arta. Do you think you could do that, something difficult?'

'I have done difficult things before. It depends what it is.'

'That's very true. You have done difficult things before. Brave things. Things that when you set out to do them, you weren't sure you would be able to see them through.'

She nodded. The warmth in her eye had faded a little, though he might have been reading too much into that, and anyway he was now set on his course. He was letting his instinct drive him forward.

'The difficult thing is this. I want you to try to forgive the man who raped you, and the man who frightened Besa.'

She said nothing. She looked at the floor, her right hand clenching her left arm so tightly he could see the nails digging in. He wanted to wait until she said something but the silence was too strong.

'Do you think you could do that? Find forgiveness?'

She showed no reaction, apart from lifting her eyes towards him. He sensed she was computing what he had said, trying to decide whether to be angry and upset, or intrigued.

'It doesn't mean you accept what they did was right, or justified. It doesn't mean you forgive the act. It just means you forgive the people.'

'Why?' she asked.

'Why should you, do you mean?'

She nodded.

'Because only if you forgive them will you set yourself free from them. I think. I could be wrong, but I think it's possible. You will never forget, but you can forgive, and then you may be free.'

She was saying little, but at least she wasn't rejecting him out of hand. She was a bright woman, and he sensed she was really thinking now about what he had said. He was content to wait. They endured a longer silence without too much tension. It was Arta who broke it.

'I can't,' she said.

'Can't, or won't?'

'If I saw them here now, I would wish them dead. They have destroyed my life, and they have destroyed my family's life. Even if I could forgive them for what they've done to *my* life – which I can't – I couldn't forgive them for what this has done to my family.'

'But they're not in your life now. You are the one who controls your life. Your family are still with you, and they love you, even more than before. The men are gone. The family are with you.'

He paused.

'I would like you to think over the next few days about whether it might be possible, not now maybe, but sometime, that you can forgive them. Your anger is totally understandable. But anger can either motivate, or it can entrap, and at the moment, you are trapped by it. Forgiveness might let you escape the trap.'

She shook her head.

'You don't know what it is like,' she said. 'How many times I try to tell you what happened. I tell you how I felt, how I feel now, how I feel when he comes at me night after night, always different ways, different places, and I wake up scared of the dark. I am scared of the light, scared of my own husband lying next to me, I spend all day tired and scared and thinking I am letting my family down and sometimes I wish he had taken that knife and cut my throat so I didn't have to feel like this one day longer, and still you don't know what it's like.'

'I accept that. I don't know what it's like. But it happened, and now we have to try to rebuild. Forgiveness may be the first very difficult step you have to make.'

It was when she stood up that he realised his gamble had failed disastrously.

'You said, "Can't, or won't?" Like that was a choice I had. I have no choice. I can't. I can't forgive them, and if you really think your place is to ask me to forgive them, you have more concern for them than you do for me.'

Her words really hurt him. He felt like he was being punched in the stomach. As when Emily left his consulting room earlier, he felt a sense of failure, this time far more profound. Three patients in one morning, and none had left any happier. Arta walked out in such a state of anger and shock that she didn't even say goodbye.

Phyllis came in, troubled that another one-hour consultation had ended early.

'Fuck it,' he said, banging his fist on his desk. 'Fuck it.' It was the first time he had ever sworn in front of Phyllis. 'I should have waited another week, maybe two,' he said. 'I should have given her more to read. I should have spoken to some of the Kosovo people. She needed more time. I went at it too quickly. I totally screwed it up.'

'Am I getting her in next week?' Phyllis asked matter-of-factly, and he looked at her, failing to hide his irritation that she seemed more concerned about her appointments system than the success or failure of the consultation.

'You can try,' he said. 'I doubt she'll be coming.'

'OK,' said Phyllis. 'By the way, Hafsatu Sesay called.'

'Oh.' He looked at her more intently now.

'She said she's very sorry but she has a meeting with her police handler which can't be moved and she can't make it this afternoon. I've fitted her in on Monday.'

'OK,' he said, feeling a mix of disappointment and relief.

'Do you want to see Ralph Hall instead? He called again to see if you've got a gap.'

'Good idea, yes. Can you fix that?'

'I will. Oh, and Mrs Sturrock called. Said it was quite urgent.'

Sturrock went over to the window and stared out. He wondered where Hafsatu was amid the mass of humankind that filled London's streets. He wondered whether her police handler was a man or a woman. He hoped it was a woman. He wondered if she was in danger, if the sex-trafficking gang she gave evidence against had tracked her down, and she was being moved again, perhaps this time further out of London. That might be the best thing all round, if she was given a new life and a new identity somewhere else. He would miss her. But it would definitely be for the best. And if she stayed in London, he knew he couldn't go on treating her. It wasn't fair to either of them. She inspired in him feelings he felt he couldn't control, a desire so strong he felt his stomach turning to mush, and his mind dissolving, so he was deprived of the ability to think straight. It meant he was not giving her the treatment she needed and was entitled to. He made a mental note to write to Judith Carrington later, and ask if she would take on Hafsatu as a patient. He would tell her Hafsatu had had so many bad experiences with men that he felt she would better respond to a woman. But could he really give her up? He knew that what she stirred in him was wrong, but it was real, and he wasn't sure he could let go of it, lose the chance to see her and fantasise about her and let those fantasies fill some of the gaps in his life.

The building site below was teeming with people and trucks and lorries. He could not believe how quickly the previous buildings had gone, and the foundations for the new ones had been laid. He wondered how many of the people he could see were less happy than he was. He looked down to the pavement cafe on the far side of the road. Three workers from the building site were sitting outside on white plastic chairs, still in hard hats, drinking tea. They were laughing, one of them almost uncontrollably. A nice-looking waitress came out with a trayful of food and within seconds was joining in whatever joke it was that Sturrock couldn't hear. One hundred per cent of the people down there are happier than I am, he said to himself. He looked over to the big office blocks now dominating the skyline down towards the river. Inside those buildings, he thought, the figure might be lower than 100 per cent. But not by much.

He walked over to his desk, sat down and called home. Stella wondered if he could pop into Waterstone's. There was a book Jack had mentioned he was interested in getting, she said, a collection of aerial pictures of the great European cities. It might make a nice birthday present.

'Yes,' he said, 'I can do that. I've got one more patient before lunch. I'll go out then. Or I could do it this afternoon. I have a patient to see in Westminster.'

He rang off, and as he did so, he realised neither of them, in the two conversations they'd had on the phone that morning, had mentioned Aunt Jessica. He made a mental note to call Simon to check on the arrangements for the funeral. As he reflected on the effort it would take him to research, write and deliver the eulogy, he sat back, let his head fall over the top of his chair and stared blankly at the ceiling.

8

It was when Matthew caught sight of an elderly woman in a wheel-chair being lifted from the back of an ambulance that the full horror of his predicament hit home. This was a hospital, full of sick people being cared for by doctors and nurses; and to the medics and the management, he was one more sick person, even though he did not consider himself to be ill at all.

As he and Celia walked into the teeming foyer, he could tell that, like him, she was hoping they would be able to find directions to the psychiatry department without actually having to ask for them. Until now she had been brimming with confidence. But since they'd arrived, in a real hospital with real sick people and real doctors, he sensed Celia had started to feel a little of what he had been feeling. It was all so dreadfully embarrassing. Fortunately, at the information desk was a board with a map of the building and an index below it, so they could work out where to go without having to utter the word 'psychiatry' to anyone.

He felt very self-conscious pressing the button for the sixth floor in the lift and hoped that the young man in a white coat might think he was going for renal surgery rather than psychiatric care, since the two departments shared the same floor. He accepted it was odd that he would rather have it thought he was about to lose a kidney than admit to requiring treatment for sex addiction, but he had always believed psychiatry was a branch of medicine dedicated to helping life's losers, not good decent people like himself. It was never pleasant when your long-held, comfortable assertions and prejudices were challenged by experiences as bad as this. He tried to recall the last time he felt quite so humiliated. He had been caned twice at school and it was probably the second caning that took him closest to the awful sick feeling he was trying to conceal as the lift doors opened on to the sixth floor and a blue arrow pointed them left to the Le Gassick wing, and 'psychological medicine'. It was a good job he had never told Celia about the reason for the caning. Had he done so, she would certainly have been using it in recent days to bolster her current theory about his sex addiction. His 'crime' had been to make a highly aggressive pass at a fifteen-year-old girl from a visiting school. A few fifteen- and sixteen-year-olds from St Hilda's School for Girls had been brought in to help his boys-only school put on a perform-ance of *Henry the Fifth*. Matthew had a fairly small part as Lord Scroop, one of the conspirators against the king. During a longish period when he was not required onstage he misread signals from the girl playing Queen Isabel. He forced himself upon the girl in full view of his drama teacher, Mr Burrows, creating a disturbance which could be heard by the audience in the main hall, just as Henry was about to deliver the battlecry. The girl made a complaint, refused to take any further part in the performance, and the combination of his amorous advance and the fact that Queen Isabel, who was important in the final act, had to be played by Mr Burrows as the play reached its climax, left the headmaster convinced he had to punish Matthew in the conventional manner.

The caning was humiliating at the time, but signing in for a session with a top psychiatrist for a discussion about sex addiction, with his wife present, was even worse, though at least there were few people around to notice him and he was pleased that the receptionist did not look at him in anything other than a perfectly friendly and entirely normal way. She was getting on a bit and so was presumably used to dealing with all manner of deviants and inadequates. He couldn't help noting, however, that, on a single-page printout marked 'Schedule, Friday', she had scribbled, alongside his name, the letters SA, which he assumed to refer to his alleged ailment. A lifetime's commitment to his personal and professional development, now reduced to two letters. S for sex, A for addict. A fresh wave of nausea surged through him, though his attention was then diverted to what he could only describe as a kerkuffle as a door opened loudly and an Eastern European-looking woman in a flowery dress stormed out, slamming the door behind her, then rushed past them and ran down the stairs.

He saw Professor Sturrock's nameplate on the door she had just slammed, and wondered what on earth he was letting himself in for.

'Take a seat,' said the receptionist. 'I'll tell Professor Sturrock you've arrived.'

The short wait was excruciating. But then the psychiatrist appeared at his door, apparently unruffled by the storming out of his patient, though he seemed surprised that his new patient's wife had accompanied him. It required him to make a slight rearrangement to the chairs in his consulting room.

'Welcome,' he said, once Matthew and Celia had sat down. He was a little older than Matthew had been expecting him to be, a bit shorter too. He was wearing a short-sleeved light blue shirt and a grey tie. He didn't have spectacles. Matthew had imagined he would have glasses. He had a long thin face and deep lines running down from the side of his nose. When his face was in repose, the lines gave him a slight resemblance to a walrus, Matthew thought.

'I wasn't expecting both of you,' said Professor Sturrock, 'but I'm sure it's very good that you have come together.'

'We see this very much as Matthew's problem, but one which we can face together,' said Celia.

'Excellent,' said Professor Sturrock. 'Of course, it may be that at some point I will need to talk to your husband on his own, but let's see how we go.'

He turned to Matthew and smiled.

'Mr Noble, I wonder if it might be best if you say in your own words why you're here.'

Matthew nodded, paused, sighed very loudly, looked at Celia, sighed again, shook his head a little, looked up at the ceiling, licked his lips, looked at Celia again, then at Professor Sturrock, then at Celia again, who whispered the single word 'sex'.

'Sex, I suppose,' said Matthew. 'I have a very happy marriage in many ways, far better than many of my friends and colleagues, I think, but I've had a couple of relationships with other women which have made me, made Celia and me, I guess, think that perhaps I have a problem in that area.'

'The problem being?' asked Professor Sturrock.

'Sex addiction,' said Celia.

'I see.'

'Well, Celia has been doing a lot of research into this and thinks perhaps that I'm possibly a sex addict.' Even as the SA words left his mouth, he was struck by what a waste of everyone's time this was. He was a busy lawyer with a lot of work to do. Here in front of him was a busy psychiatrist with a busy department to run, in a large city full of people with serious mental illnesses, and instead of the poor man's time going on helping the real unfortunates of the world, he was having to listen to a heap of nonsense about Matthew's sex addiction.

'What do you think?' Professor Sturrock asked. 'Do *you* think you're a sex addict?'

'Well, it's interesting, isn't it?' Matthew said. 'I mean, I had one affair, and the minute it was over, I had another, and all the time I have this OK marriage at home. So it is quite odd really, and I can see where Celia's coming from.'

Professor Sturrock asked to be taken through the exact sequence of events as the affairs unfolded, and Matthew did his best to indicate to Celia that he would prefer her not to interrupt quite so often.

Then Professor Sturrock asked him in rapid succession about his sexual history, masturbation, pornography, the frequency of marital sex, the frequency of urges to stray. Matthew tried to be as honest as he could without the whole thing becoming too embarrassing, and he was encouraged by the gentle nodding of Professor Sturrock's head as he made notes of his answers.

'Finally,' Professor Sturrock said, 'have you ever paid for sex?'

'No, never,' Matthew said, taken aback by the suggestion.

Professor Sturrock turned to Celia.

'Mrs Noble, I think I should probably talk to your husband alone for a while, but tell me, what is your assessment? I would really value that.'

Matthew sat back as Celia let out a stream of facts and figures, citing as incontrovertible proof the findings of a website run by Sex Addicts Anonymous.

'Thank you,' said Professor Sturrock, 'that's fascinating.'

When she had left and gone to wait for Matthew in the waiting room, Professor Sturrock sat in the chair she had just vacated, looked at him, and smiled, a very warm man-to-man smile that made Matthew feel more at ease than he had done at any time since he caught sight of Julian the clerk sitting at the kitchen table after his last and indeed final orgasm chez Angela.

'What do you really think?' Professor Sturrock asked.

Matthew took a deep breath. Sturrock seemed trustworthy enough.

'I think you know what I think. I'm here because I was unfaithful to my wife. Neither of us wants to split up, but Celia needs to have a reason why I strayed and it has to be a reason in me, not in her, or in us. That's what I think.'

Professor Sturrock smiled, and nodded. 'I don't think you're a sex addict either. You have what seems to me a pretty average interest in, and experience of, sex and you also have a higher than usual interest in saving your marriage. I would be happy to help you.'

Help involved entering into something of a conspiracy: Matthew would come to see Professor Sturrock, no more than half a dozen times, but could tell Celia that the course of treatment was likely to last longer. Before they left today, Professor Sturrock would have a private word with Celia, explaining to her that this complaint was quite common, quite straightforward to treat, but that it was best done by a series of one-to-one sessions.

Matthew was delighted. The cost of six mock sessions with Sturrock was negligible if it meant he could placate Celia without actually having to become a real sex addict.

Professor Sturrock suggested they went through a few motions. He advised that Matthew start to intimate to Celia that he would be getting into a major exercise regime. 'She needs to think you're taking on board what she says, and changing. Get her involved in helping you with a big fitness drive, maybe take up cycling. It will do you good and it will make your wife feel more secure, that you are channelling your energies in a direction she knows about and approves of.' Matthew liked Professor Sturrock's style.

As they went out to rejoin Celia, Professor Sturrock told her, 'I'm really grateful you came along today, but it will work best if I see him alone from now on in. You've done the hard work. Now leave the easy bit to me.'

'What a lovely man,' she said as the lift took them down to the ground floor.

'Yes, very,' said Matthew. 'Older than I thought he would be.'

'Wise,' she said. 'Wise, I would say.'

'Oh yes, very sharp.'

'What did you talk about on your own?' she asked.

'Nothing too much,' he said. 'Same as when you were there really. Bit more detail, I suppose. He did say he thought I needed to get myself a really serious exercise regime beyond golf.'

'Oh, good idea. Do you want me to sign you up for the gym? They have really good personal trainers.'

'No, I think I'm going to get myself a bike. He seemed to think a bike was the right thing for me.'

'A bike?' she said, and he read in the question mark the intimation that he was too fat for a bike. 'What a great idea,' she added, picking up on his reaction.

As the lift slowed to a halt and the doors opened, Celia went over to kiss him on the cheek. It was the first time she had kissed him in a while. He took her hand and squeezed it. He felt a little embarrassed, almost like he was touching her for the first time, but once it was done he felt better about the way things were going. He kissed her on the lips.

'Thank you for coming today,' he said. 'I had my doubts but I'm glad you came.' He reflected for a moment on whether he meant it, but before coming to a conclusion, he moved on to an assessment of which bike shop was nearest to their house. He had decided not to use the Internet, which was very much Celia's domain.

'You know something, I think with that nice psychiatrist's help we'll crack this,' she said.

'Yes, I think we will,' said Matthew, who was now longing to get to chambers, where he had a case conference planned for 2.30.

9

Sturrock watched as Mr and Mrs Noble made their way towards the lift, then he went back into his consulting room, and gently closed the door behind him. Every limb in his body was weary. It felt like something worse than Friday tiredness. His brain was barely functioning.

He liked to make notes on his patients as soon as practicable after they left his room, to supplement those he made while they were with him, but today he was finding it difficult to remember who he had seen when. He needed his schedule to remind him. It was only four hours since Emily came in, but he struggled to remember the detail of their conversation. He scribbled down, '*Zero steps forward, three steps back. Not really engaging. Rejecting empathy strategy. Seems to be retreating more and more into herself.*' Of Arta, he was even more gloomy. '*Tried forgiveness. Total rejection. Anger entrapping not motivating. Fear rupture.*' Of David, he made a few scribbles on his dream register and best–worst list, then added on a separate sheet of paper, '*First mention of Amanda. Seemed hopeful of proper relationship. Rejected badly. Bound to be stirring feelings of past rejection. Worrisome for next few days. Maybe call Sunday.*' About Matthew, he had little to say. '*Wife says sex addict. Not. Go for sport and support.*'

The only positive thing to come out of the morning was that David had confided in him, although his pleasure at this was marred by concerns that David's rejection by Amanda would trigger one of his really deep depressions, the kind which reduced him to near speechlessness. Mostly, though, Sturrock simply felt he was looking back over a morning of failure. The appointment he felt worst about was Arta's, because he knew he had made a mistake. He hated making mistakes. Was it because he was too tired? Or had he been too keen to try something different and dramatic because he wanted to see whether he could relate it to his asylum-seeker research project? If so, that was bad, he said to himself. Was he doing it for her, or for himself? Right now, he genuinely didn't know the answer. He was feeling shattered and the effort of trying to think it through was making him feel even more so. This was happening too often, that he beat himself up when things didn't go exactly as he had planned for them to go. His only consolation was that his words had provoked a strong reaction in her. But where that reaction would lead was what worried him.

He called his cousin Simon to see if there was yet a confirmed date for the funeral, but the number was engaged. Please God, let it not be on Tuesday, he thought. And then felt instantly guilty. He pulled a piece of paper towards him and picked up a pencil. '*I will always remember my aunt for her . . . what?*' he wrote. He sat there, pencil poised for a moment, but no words suggested themselves. It was as if all his memories of Aunt Jessica had vanished from his mind.

He sat back in his chair and tried to recall how she had looked when she was the happy-go-lucky holiday hostess who used to make such a fuss of him. No image came.

It was a row about religion, with his father at the heart of it, that led to his falling-out with Aunt Jessica. He forgot when it was exactly. Maybe forty-five years ago. It was the last day of what became his last holiday at her Somerset home. His father and his sister Jan had come to collect him and the two families were having Sunday lunch together before the Sturrocks set off back to Hertfordshire. It had all been perfectly jovial with his uncle getting out his best wine and Aunt Jessica chatting happily to Jan when his father started preaching to Aunt Jessica about the benefits of a church-school education, and criticising her and her husband for not sending Simon to such an institution.

'But, Dad,' Martin had shouted across the table, 'you don't *know* God exists any more than I know for sure that He doesn't. You believe simply because you were brought up to believe, the same as Muslims believe in the Prophet Muhammad because that's what they're brought up to believe. How do you know you're right and they're wrong? You don't. You just think that, because you think it, it must be right.'

Until his mid teens Sturrock had gone along with the education his father believed in, positively enjoying the religious as well as the social side to the weekly Sunday-school sessions that followed church. At one stage, he'd even gone so far as to ask his RE teacher how you became a vicar. But when he went into the senior school, he started to emerge as something of a star in all the science subjects, and medicine or possibly his father's chosen profession, engineering, seemed more obvious careers. It was also around that time that the rather indistinct but negative feelings he had about his father began to form into something vaguely approaching rebellion, and religion came into his sights as something to rebel against. Compared with some of the tales he heard from patients, for whom a mother and father were considered the trigger for violent and destructive acts of rebellion, up to and including murder, Sturrock's protests were small-scale. He undid his school tie as soon as he left the house. He smoked one or two cigarettes, but so hated the taste and the smell that there was never any chance of him engaging in anything stronger. He had a similar experience with alcohol. At a friend's sixteenth birthday party he drank four pints of cider, relishing with each gulp the idea that he was doing something of which his father would thoroughly disapprove. But when he found himself being sick in his friend's back garden, he decided that drink, like cigarettes, was probably not for him.

By far his greatest act of rebellion was his announcement at Aunt Jessica's Sunday-lunch table that he doubted there was a God. It was the beginning of what would become his hardened atheism. Looking back, he realised that, as much as rejecting God, he was rejecting his father, and his father's interpretation of what God meant in their lives. But it led to such a scene that he'd felt he had to hold firm, not retreat from what he'd said, so that doubts about God's existence became a conviction that God did not exist. As he grew older, he came to doubt his own atheism. Stella's faith was strong and they talked a lot about religion. But even though she often implored him to come to church with her, he always refused. He felt he had expressed his disbelief so forcefully in the past, he couldn't now air any doubts he might have.

His father was not used to being spoken to as his son spoke to him that day in Aunt Jessica's kitchen, and responded by launching into a full-scale defence of Christianity. He could see his aunt start to look concerned. This was the kind of conversation he could enjoy having with her, but they had both noticed the telltale red flush rising on his father's neck, which signalled that he was about to lose his temper.

'Now, now, let's just finish lunch and leave this for another day,' she'd said.

'Yes, George,' said his uncle. 'Let me pour you another drink.'

'No,' he'd said, 'let's carry on. Let's for once say what we think.'

'Martin, I really don't think it's sensible to say what you think right now,' his aunt had said, smiling ingratiatingly at her brother. 'You're too emotional and het up.'

'That's exactly why I should say what I think.'

He had heard Aunt Jessica say some very cutting things both about her brother and about the Church, but here she was simply trying to shut him up, and take her brother's side.

She tried a different tack.

'Jan, what do you think?' she said, clearly hoping Martin's younger sister might cool things down.

'Well, even at Sunday school we've had a session called "Does God really Exist?",' said Jan diplomatically, 'so perhaps it's OK to ask the question.'

'Of course He does,' said his father. 'Everyone knows God exists.'

'Everyone?' he'd said, raising an eyebrow in a way guaranteed to infuriate his father. 'The Muslims don't believe in your God. The atheists don't believe in any God. If everyone knows it, why are there so many empty churches on a Sunday?'

'That's to do with television and cars and people having other things to do now,' said Aunt Jessica.

'Is it? Well, here's another one – why is there so much starvation? Why are there wars? Why are some people rich and other people poor?'

'But God is a guide for our world. He doesn't run the world.'

'I thought He created it. If He created it, maybe He should run it, and run it better?'

He knew he had incurred his father's deep displeasure, but he felt he was crossing the Rubicon, and he might as well go the whole way now. He put a sliver of roast beef in his mouth and chewed slowly for a few moments, thinking about how to express the view that, if God was as He was described in church and Sunday school, there should be more love in their family, and less fear.

'God as an instrument of love I can believe in, God as an instrument of fear I cannot.' That was a good way to put it. Then he would add, 'In our house there is a God of fear, not a God of love.' It was a big call to make, and he could feel his heart pounding as he sought to bring the words from his mind to his lips. He breathed deeply a couple of times, conscious that nobody else was speaking, so the only sound was of his breath, and the occasional clink of knife and fork on china. He ran the words once more round his mind, then again, then breathed deeply again. It was his father, though, who broke the silence. He looked directly at Aunt Jessica and said, 'Thank you, Jess. I don't think I will have pudding. I'm afraid the discussion has put me right off my food. I think Jan should help you with the washing-up, and Martin, you can go to your room until we're ready to leave.'

His father stood up, pushed his chair under the table, tossed his napkin onto the side plate, turned and left the room. He thought for a moment about sharing with Jan and Aunt Jessica the thought he had stored at the front of his mind. But the moment had passed, and the target had gone.

He went upstairs and, once his rage had calmed a little, he decided to write a letter to his father. He took an age to decide whether to start with 'Father', 'Dear Father', or 'Dear Dad'.

'*Father,*' he began, '*Jan and I try really hard to be good children. We work hard at school. We do well in exams. We get good reports. We take part in school plays. We both play musical instruments. We help Mum around the house. Neither of us has ever had to be sent home early, or given a detention. What more do we have to do before we have a father who looks like he wants us to be his children? As for today's discussion, am I not allowed to have my own thoughts? And if I have doubts about something as important to our lives as God's existence, with whom am I meant to raise them if not you? What is a father for, if not to listen to a son's concerns?'*

There was a knock on the door. It was Aunt Jessica.

'Are you all right?'

'Not really, no.'

'You shouldn't upset your father like that.'

'Why don't you go to him and say, "You really shouldn't upset your son like that"? And why did you take his side when I know you agree with me?'

She was standing at the desk, where he was sitting writing his letter. He made no effort to shield it from her view.

'Don't send it, Martin. Nothing good will come of it.' And with that, she patted him on the shoulder, and walked out of the room.

As his father drove them home in silence that evening, he felt a sense of real betrayal. Just a day earlier, he would have named Aunt Jessica as the adult he felt closest to, the one he could really confide in. That closeness had vanished.

Sturrock put down his pencil and sighed. He felt exhausted. And he was frankly irritated that several of his patients, all living, all in need of his help, all people he saw regularly, were to be majorly inconvenienced because of the funeral of someone he had seen three times in five years.

He looked at the clock, and reckoned he could steal a short nap before heading to Westminster to see Ralph Hall. Phyllis had put a sandwich on his desk, but he didn't feel like eating it. He adjusted his chair so it was reclining and shut his eyes. Immediately, an indistinct image of his father started to form in the middle distance of the darkness that his closed eyes had delivered. That was definitely his hair, before he went grey, and that was the jawline. The image faded as quickly as it came. George Sturrock had been dead five years, but most days Sturrock would see him, somewhere. He had very few photos of him around the house, and those he did have were put out by Stella not him, but he had a series of images that intruded on his mind, often, as now, when he was tired. In most of the images, his father was in his forties. He never smiled. He never spoke. Nor did he stay long. Other thoughts and images would crowd in and chase the image away. It was strange, he thought, that even though his father came to him as a relatively young man, it was always thoughts of his final days that these unexpected visits inspired.

George Sturrock had been well into his eighties when he died, but even a couple of weeks before his death, he seemed to be strong and healthy. Sturrock had never thought of his parents as a very close or loving couple. Their life revolved around certain constantly observed routines in their eating habits, sleeping patterns, leisure pursuits and holidays. But in his final days, George Sturrock began to show a humanity to his wife sadly lacking during the half-century they had known each other. He had liked to describe himself as a God-fearing man, and perhaps it was a fear of God, and what awaited him if indeed God's judgement was to fall upon him, that led him to try to change his ways so late in life and he began to treat his wife with an almost embarrassing solicitude. It had been hard to watch his father fawning over his mother like that – it seemed so hypocritical. He didn't have to put up with it for long. Once the seeming switch in his father's personality clicked in, the decline towards death was rapid. He ate little. He resisted visits from the doctor. Sturrock and his sister Jan visited him on a kind of rota basis, and with each visit he saw decline matched by a rise in serenity and acceptance of what was coming. When finally his father passed away, quietly in his sleep, he had been at his bedside. He was unprepared for the grief. He began to cry, and after several minutes wondered if he would ever stop. Jan appeared moved, then surprised, then a little worried, then embarrassed. They had talked so many times about how cold and distant their father had been. They had talked openly about whether to try to persuade their mother to leave him. Jan had once put it this way: 'Mum, why did you have us when it is so obvious that one of you didn't really want us?'

His father had never been violent, though he could look it, and at primary school, a teacher was once concerned enough about a drawing Martin had done of 'My Daddy' to bring it to the head's attention, so dark and violent were the images surrounding the matchstick man at the centre of the page.

He was not even particularly strict. It was worse than that. He seemed indifferent.

'Why does he show such little interest in who we are and what we do?' he had once asked his mother.

She looked saddened. 'He's not a bad man, your father,' she said, which was not the most loving or fulsome of endorsements. 'He's of a very different era. His father was even harsher, and colder. Dad went to boarding school when he was four. He once went three years without seeing either of his parents, because when he came out of school for the holidays, they were then living in India and thought it was best not to have him travel out on his own, so he lived with his aunt. Imagine how that felt, that his parents didn't want to see him when they could.'

'So why does he want us to feel the same, even when we live with him?'

He had wondered if his mother raised what he had said with his father. Certainly, for a week or two, George Sturrock seemed a little bit warmer, asked once or twice about homework, and even tried to engage him in conversation about a film he had expressed an interest in seeing. But he then had to leave for South America for a couple of weeks, where he was involved in a major bridge-building project for the Brazilian government, and when he came back, the coldness came back with him.

Just as husbands and wives get into ruts, so do parents and children. He had seen it many times in the key relationships of his patients. They would know they had to change, but they didn't know how. He had longed for his father to change, but it was clear that would never happen. So he and his sister tried to change instead, but every change they made just seemed to make things worse.

He tried to talk to his father about it the night before he died. It was obvious he was fading, and Sturrock was moved by the calm with which his father was approaching death. George talked about his wife with much greater affection than he had ever showed to her when he was healthy. Sturrock sat and listened, feeling for the first time that his father was talking to him as if he was truly his son. 'Why?' he wanted to ask him. 'Why did you find it so hard to touch, or be there to listen to me when I was confused? Why did you never hold me when I was scared? Why did you never tell me I did well when I passed exams, or made things, or said things that most children are not capable of thinking? Please, tell me.' But the scars of six decades of resistance had built up. Even as his father was seeming more human and vulnerable, Sturrock couldn't bring himself to get the words out. So he sat by his bedside as his father drifted in and out of sleep, and just asked the questions silently to himself, as his mother fussed around, she too seeming calm and serene as the moment of death neared. And when finally his father passed away, he was sad at the loss, as any son would be, but his real sadness was the lack of love they had had for each other in life. That was what he was really grieving, and had grieved ever since. He felt his father had left him a bitter legacy – that of being a distant parent. He tried to comfort himself with the thought that he was of a different generation to his children, and that the cultural and social differences meant that it simply wasn't possible for a parent of one generation truly to relate to a child of another. But then he saw others who seemed to be able to do it, and he was left with the thought that his father had been a bad parent and he had followed in his footsteps.

Sturrock opened his eyes. The thoughts of his father had filled him with blackness. He realised his mind was working too much to allow even a short doze, so he gathered his file on Ralph Hall, said goodbye to Phyllis and left.

It was difficult to induce himself to go into Waterstone's for Jack's present. The shop was crowded and it seemed unlikely he'd find a book of aerial photography with ease. In the event, there was a stack of them near the staircase on the second floor. He had a flick through it. It was interesting enough, particularly the pictures of Berlin and

Barcelona, but not the sort of thing he would want himself, not for a birthday. He liked pictures of people, portraits which captured a moment or a feeling in their lives. This book suggested buildings, not people, were what mattered. But Jack had very different interests to his own, so perhaps it would please him.

Though he never said so, and emphatically denied it if asked, Sturrock was disappointed that neither Suzanne, Michelle nor Jack had followed him down the medicine route. He suspected his own father had felt the same about him and engineering. They never really discussed it. Sturrock's children did not get a science A level between them, so from their late teens, it was clear they were not going to follow his chosen path. But by then, he already felt the distance between himself and them, particularly Jack. Having had two girls, he longed for a son, and it was perhaps that longing, and with it the expectations of a classic romanticised father–son relationship, that led to his disappointment being even greater when, other than fleetingly, that relationship did not materialise. And of course the biggest disappointment of all was that the children appeared to drain all the joy and energy out of his wife. Where once life had seemed to please and excite her, motherhood and the running of a home made her tired, a bit miserable, and jealous of what she imagined his life to be.

He went to the till to pay for the book. There was a woman in front of him who was rummaging around in her handbag trying to find a credit card. The shop assistant looked cross. Sturrock stood for a moment, closed his eyes and wished away his tiredness. But he was jolted back to reality by the angry shop assistant demanding payment for the book. He paid, stumbled outside and hailed a cab.

On the short cab ride to Westminster, he looked through his notes on Ralph Hall. Yet another really difficult case and the last thing he needed on a day like this. But there was no getting out of it now. He imagined Hall sitting nervously in his House of Commons office, waiting for him to arrive, gearing himself up for their secretive meeting. It had been such a huge effort for Hall to admit he needed help in the first place, he couldn't let him down.

He had first met Hall when the politician was a Minister of State heading a policy review on care in the community, and Sturrock was an adviser to the review team. After that they met a few times socially, first with others, then just the two of them over dinner at the House, when Ralph admitted that he had occasional panic attacks, particularly when feeling under pressure. Sturrock gave him one or two interesting thoughts and insights about possible associations with feeling trapped, and also the link to anger. He suggested they keep in touch on the subject.

A couple of weeks after their dinner, he watched Ralph doing a difficult TV interview, and noticed that the minister's hands were shaking slightly as he spoke. He called him the next day, said he had noticed and Ralph suggested they meet again. They had dinner at a little French restaurant not far from Buckingham Palace.

'I feel I can trust you, Martin, so I am going to tell you something I have told nobody else.'

'Yes, if it relates to a health issue, Ralph, I assure you that you can trust me to be one hundred per cent discreet.'

The minister took a deep breath, then rushed out the words, 'I think I may have a drink problem.'

Sturrock could see the effort that had gone into his saying it. At the time he had thought that, with the confession having been made, the battle was half won. Now he wasn't so sure. Ralph was more scared of his problem being made public than he was of what drink was doing to him. It explained the lengths he went to in order to conceal his drinking habits from everyone around him, even his wife. Sturrock knew from bitter experience with other alcoholics that, until someone was prepared to face their problem openly, it was unlikely ever to go away.

As the cab drew up outside the Houses of Parliament, he tried desperately to drag his mind away from its dark thoughts and into professional mode. 'Get a grip, Sturrock,' he said to himself. 'Hall's relying on you. But if you go to pieces, there'll be no one there to pick them up.'

10

Ralph was finding it hard not to blame Sandie. If only she didn't keep disappearing off on business trips, he thought, it would be easier for him to stay sober.

As he prepared to head to the Commons for his hastily arranged consultation with Professor Sturrock, he cleared his desk in his enormous fourth-floor office at the Department of Health, took a final shot of Scotch from the hip flask in the second drawer of his desk, and walked over to the bathroom to brush his teeth. Sandie was currently in Jordan, after a tip-off from a colleague about the possibility of acquiring a sizeable collection of paintings by one of Jordan's most renowned artists. It had been a last-minute thing. She'd heard about the possible sale at a breakfast meeting in Chelsea on Monday morning and caught the first available plane out after going home to Pimlico to pack. When she called Ralph from the taxi taking her to Heathrow airport, he felt torn, between his desire to support her, and his feeling of abandonment. He hated arriving home at night to an empty house.

Yet it had been he who had encouraged her to turn a lifelong interest in Middle Eastern art into a little business, importing and exporting paintings and artefacts. The children were grown up, she had got the MP's wife role off pat, there was nothing to stop her, he'd said. But the business had been more successful than he'd expected and she was often away. Whereas, before, her presence would help to keep his drinking in check, now things were getting out of control.

He was just removing the cap from the tube of toothpaste when the phone rang.

'Damn it,' he said, walking back to the desk and picking up the phone.

'Yes?'

'It's Mrs Hall, Secretary of State. It's not a very good line.'

'OK, put her through,' he said, while simultaneously saying to himself, 'must brush teeth, must brush teeth, must brush teeth.'

'Hello, darling.' Sandie sounded very chirpy, and very far away. She had been due home that night, but the deal was taking longer to conclude than she'd thought.

'So when will you be back?' he asked, trying but failing to hide his disappointment, and wondering as he tried whether it was disappointment, or just irritation.

'I'm checking the flights now, but all being well by lunchtime tomorrow.'

'OK,' he said. 'Just make sure you get the train straight up to Newcastle in time for the dinner with the Chamber of Commerce people. It's important that the constituency still sees that I've got you by my side from time to time.'

'All right, my love. See you tomorrow. Everything OK?'

'Yes, fine. Better go now. I've got a meeting.'

He went over to the Commons on foot, and arrived in the central lobby to find that Professor Sturrock hadn't yet got there. The delay was excruciating for Ralph. It meant that there was a possibility one of his colleagues, or even worse a journalist, would come up to him, and be there as Professor Sturrock arrived, and either recognise him, or ask who he was. Since he wanted nobody in his office to know about these meetings, he had to escort Professor Sturrock to his Commons office himself rather than send a secretary to collect him, but it was high risk. He found himself rehearsing answers to any curious questions: 'Professor Sturrock has kindly agreed to advise our mental health strategy review,' or, 'I'm just introducing Professor Sturrock to the chairman of the health select committee.'

He was absolutely paranoid about anyone knowing he was seeing a psychiatrist, even more so since his promotion from Minister of State to Health Secretary, his first Cabinet position. He was under little doubt that he would have to resign if his problem became public. Times had changed. MPs could happily regale each other with tales of George Brown's antics as Foreign Secretary under Harold Wilson, and Ralph, in his after-dinner speeches, often used a colourful version of Brown's drunken threat to invade Israel. But one of the reasons MPs found the stories so amusing was because they involved behaviour that, in today's more censorious, media-sensitive age, a senior politician might not be able to survive. They might wish it wasn't so, but it was, and that was that. Ralph knew that at least three backbench MPs had been ruled out of the last junior ranks reshuffle because the chief whip reported that they spent too long in the bars.

It had taken Ralph a while to decide upon the best place to see Professor Sturrock. He'd pulled out of the first appointment, which had been scheduled to take place in his office at the department, because he was worried about some of his more observant staff members putting two and two together and, for once, making four. He now insisted on all his meetings with Professor Sturrock being either at his home first thing, provided Sandie was away, or at his Commons office, normally unattended unless he was over there for voting.

Professor Sturrock finally arrived, looking slightly harassed. He had been held up by queues at the security checks. Ralph gave him a hurried handshake and rushed him along, through the door by the message board next to a huge statue of Winston Churchill, then up dozens of stairs to his office.

It was only when they were both settled in Ralph's office, Ralph on the green sofa, Professor Sturrock on the fake leather swivel chair, that Ralph realised that, although he had been desperate to see the psychiatrist all day, he didn't really know what he wanted to say to him.

Professor Sturrock was looking at him with his usual gentle, patient expression.

'So, Ralph, what's been going on?'

Ralph felt a sudden caving in of his stomach, a desperate desire to confide.

'Sandie's away.'

'Ah . . . And?'

'And I've been drinking too much.'

'More than usual?'

'A lot more.'

At their first meeting five months ago, Professor Sturrock had asked detailed questions about his consumption. Ralph had been modestly relieved when Professor Sturrock said that, though he was drinking more than was good for him, he was drinking a lot less than some of his really bad cases. Still, Ralph had had to admit he couldn't remember the last day he had gone without a drink. The closest he had got was the previous Sunday, when he'd had four glasses of wine. Most days he would have a couple of drinks on his own in the office, hopefully with nobody else knowing. If he had a lunch engagement, he would drink if others were, maybe a few glasses of wine. He would always have wine with his dinner, and if possible squeeze in a few spirits beforehand, and always a few more at home before he went to bed. But he knew his consumption had been rising in recent months, which is why he had begun to worry.

He had sensed Professor Sturrock's concern when he confessed that not long after he woke up, he would think about when he might be able to have a drink, either publicly without people thinking it odd, or privately without being discovered. He had a secret stash of spirits in his office. He used toothpaste and breath fresheners to conceal the odour when, as happened fairly frequently, he had a drink between meetings. He drank from bottles as well as glasses. At official or social dinners, he would drink wine as would others, but also try to pull a waiter to one side and order whisky and water in a long glass, with a fair bit of ice, so that it looked like a soft drink.

'Is that why you wanted to see me today?' asked Professor Sturrock. 'Because Sandie is away?'

'Maybe.'

'Is there anything else?'

'There is one thing,' Ralph said. 'Most mornings now, especially if Sandie's away, I'm forcing myself to vomit soon after I wake up.'

'I see.'

'I thought I should tell you.'

'Yes. Thank you.'

Ralph was looking closely to see how the psychiatrist reacted to a piece of information that had been worrying him a lot. He had held back from telling him, but as he was throwing up this morning he had decided that having trusted Professor Sturrock so far, he should trust him the whole way, and with every detail. Professor Sturrock just made a note, in the same calm and unperturbed manner he made a note of most things, nodded, and then asked, 'Every morning?'

'Pretty much, these days.'

'And as you're throwing up, what are you thinking about?'

'Hoping I'll feel better when it's done. Thinking about the day ahead, what meetings, what gaps in the day, what problems to deal with as soon as I get in. Even when I'm chucking up, I'm thinking about that.'

'And how are you feeling about *yourself* when you're chucking up?'

'Pretty crap, I suppose. Not great, is it? Hands on the toilet bowl, knees on the floor, head down, fingers down the throat, waiting for the stuff to churn up. Not great for the self-esteem.'

'And as you do it, which of these thoughts is closer to your mind: "I'll never drink again" or "I wonder when I can get my first drink of the day"?'

It was the moment Ralph realised he had been right to be worried, and right to see Professor Sturrock today.

'The second of those, I'm afraid. Every time.'

'And which of these thoughts is closer at that time: "I would like a drink right now" or "I will wait a few hours"?'

'Both,' he said. 'I don't do the hair-of-the-dog thing, as you know. I hardly ever drink before midday, but I have various moments of struggle before I get there.'

'Including when you're being sick?'

'Sometimes, yes.' He whispered it. He knew it was a serious admission to make.

'And why are you so afraid today?'

'Because I probably drink more when Sandie's not there to keep an eye on me.'

'Do you resent her being away?'

'A bit.'

'Yet her art business was your idea?'

'I know,' he said. 'Life is full of unintended consequences, isn't it?'

'Do you feel jealous at all?' asked Professor Sturrock.

'Not jealous, no. But I thought it might be a way of filling the gap left by the children. Instead, I can see it has maybe filled some of the emotional space she saves for me. She's always been such a support, right from the start, but it's changed.'

Sandie had known about his political ambitions from the moment they met at university. He'd once confided in her that he felt destined to be Prime Minister and though it had sounded boastful and arrogant, it did not sound totally absurd, as are so many of the claims made by students for their own future. She supported him too when he stood for a hopeless seat in the Midlands, driving him around from village to village, town to town. On the night he became a Member of Parliament for one of the new Newcastle seats, she told him she was really proud of him, happy in the knowledge that he would be doing what he wanted to do, and happy to take a back seat, and hold home and family life together. He was soon seen as something of a rising star, though it took longer than he would have liked, and longer than some of his peers, before he was made a minister. It also irked him somewhat that though he was still seen as relatively young in political terms, the Prime Minister was even younger.

'Shall we take a look at your drinking diary?' asked Professor Sturrock.

'I suppose, if we have to.'

The only homework Professor Sturrock asked Ralph to do was to keep a diary, in which he was supposed to record not just what he drank, but when and where, as well as what was happening around him, and what feelings he had about himself and others at the time. Given how busy Ralph was, it was a lot to ask for, and when he had set the task, Professor Sturrock said he understood it might not always be possible to do it in detail. Also, Ralph was so terrified of his problem being uncovered that he had been very hesitant at first, fearing that he would write it all down, then lose the document somewhere when under the influence, only to see it surface in a Sunday newspaper, fuelling an enormous media frenzy which would see the Prime Minister express initial support, then throw him overboard as the frenzy failed to calm.

Ralph took out the little soft-backed notebook on which he had written 'DD' on the cover. He had taken to writing with his left hand so that if he accidentally left it lying around the office, he could feign ignorance as to what it was. He had a code for different drinks – w for whisky, w2 for a double, w3 for one of the really large ones he sometimes had at home before going to bed, ww for white wine, wr for red. He used Roman numerals to record the time of day at which he was drinking. If he was drinking alone, he put a little letter 'i' inside a circle alongside the nature and quantity of the drink consumed. If he was at an official event, he would mark it with the letters 'oe'. If he was at a social event, he recorded that with 'se'. Recording his feelings was harder. There he relied on a number of key words, on which he would elaborate when he saw the Professor. He was quite pleased with all his little codes and his terrible handwriting. He was confident that even if Professor Sturrock were to stumble across the diary, he would not be able to decipher all its contents.

'So which was your worst day?' asked Professor Sturrock.

'Wednesday, by a mile,' said Ralph, flicking to an entry that ran to three full pages littered with increasingly erratic scribbles.

Professor Sturrock moved to join him on the sofa so that he could get a proper look at what Ralph had written. He pointed to a line where Ralph had written, *'Is dd mkn m d mr so v mr2pt? Rbsh. Sf/srv. Stop.'*

'What's that?'

Ralph translated. '"Is the fact of doing a daily diary making me drink more so I have more to put in it? Rubbish. Self-serving argument. Must stop thinking that." Or maybe it's "must stop drinking"? That's one of the limitations of my codes. Sometimes I can't remember what I meant.'

Professor Sturrock asked him to talk him through the day.

VII (7 a.m.) saw him starting with a morning vomit for the second day running. It was the full horrible works, four heaves, each one burning the throat more painfully, each one like a punch to the stomach until all its contents were gone. But it was only once he had been sick that he felt his real head was back on his shoulders. He had a note alongside his record of being sick, to the effect that the vomiting was so violent he had suggested to himself he should try not to drink anything that day.

'How long did that last?'

'Till 11.50.'

He had a single w to record a small shot of whisky slugged from his top-drawer hip flask as he dealt with correspondence before a noon meeting with the Chief Medical Officer. Alongside, he had noted that he could probably have waited till lunchtime, but he didn't like the CMO and he felt a quick hit might help him get to the other side of the meeting more quickly.

'Did it?' asked Professor Sturrock.

'Not sure.'

'And the next drink?'

'I had lunch at La Barca with the chairman of one of the big employers in my constituency. He was in town for an industry awards ceremony that evening, so in a good mood.' He pointed to the entry – 'ww4, w2'.

During the afternoon, spent in his department, he recorded three single ws. Alongside the second, he noted feeling that he would end the day absolutely smashed. Alongside the third he had written 'mst pc' (must pace myself). He had also recorded cancelling an early-evening office team meeting, telling his secretary he needed time to start writing a speech he had to make in his constituency on Saturday.

'Was that true?'

'No. I just wanted to sit on the sofa and see if I could go half an hour with the hip flask in front of me, but not drink from it. It was tough, but I did it. Then I went for a pee and washed my face, then came back and had a very small swig.'

'Because you thought you deserved it for going through the half-hour?'

'I suppose so. It felt good, having forced myself to wait. The warm glow you get, it was warmer because of the wait. Then I had to go to a farewell party for one of the senior civil servants. I asked if I could make the speech early. I stuck to two wines before speaking, just about got through it even though I barely knew the guy, then really started to pick up the pace. Ww4, wr2. Back to the office, return a few calls, sign a few letters, brush my teeth, wash my face, then out for dinner.'

He had a monthly dinner with a group of his parliamentary colleagues, those he had been friendly with on entering the House, and even though some were now ministers, and others still on the backbenches, he and the other ministers had kept up the routine, pulling out only if really unavoidable.

'Ww5, w2. One or two of the backbenchers were drinking heavily so I was probably thinking nobody was really noticing how much I was packing away.'

'My God, Ralph, this is one bad day,' said Professor Sturrock.

'I told you it was bad. It gets worse.'

He told Professor Sturrock how his driver had dropped him off at home, a couple of streets behind the Tate Gallery, shortly before eleven, and how the moment the car had sped off, he felt liberated to let his drunkenness flow.

'I just thought to myself, "Fuck it, you're pissed out of your brains, and now there's nobody to hide it from." I just wanted to be a normal badly behaved drunk.'

He'd had a dozen yards to walk from the road to his house, the last few feet of which required him to climb seven steep steps to his front door. He stood for a while, ministerial red box in hand, head slumped into his chest. He spat on the ground, though some of the spittle hit his coat on the way down. He made a strange snarling sound, then looked from right to left, caught sight of a builders' skip two houses away, snarled at the skip, spat again, then staggered towards the door. He rummaged around his pockets, found the door keys, plonked his red box down on the top step, spent thirty seconds or so trying to open the door, enjoyed the failure to do so, put the Yale key in the Chubb lock and laughed at his inability to make a connection. When eventually he opened the door, he returned to the step, picked up the red box and slowly made his way back to the door, slamming it behind him. The house was dark, empty of all human life but his. He threw the red box on the floor. 'You can fuck off for starters.' He laughed, then kicked the red box. He switched on a light. He went into the lounge, switched on the light there too, turned on the TV, snarled at the correspondent pontificating about Iran on *Newsnight*, then stood channel-hopping for a while, settling on an old black-and-white film that was showing on the Turner Movies channel. He snarled at the actors. 'You can fuck off too. You're probably dead now anyway. Look at you, you're not even in colour,' and he laughed at his insult. He went over to the cupboard in the corner, opened it, took out a bottle of Johnnie Walker Black Label and went to sit, still wearing his suit and coat, in the chair closest to the TV. He knew the actress wasn't Jayne Mansfield, but she was of that era, and he called her Jayne, apologised for being rude earlier, said he hoped she wasn't dead, made a mental note to ask Sandie when she was back whether Jayne Mansfield was dead because it was the kind of thing Sandie would know without looking it up. She would even know what she died of, if she *was* dead, and what she was up to and where she was living, if she was alive.

He put the bottle on the floor beside him and pressed the remote control so that the time would come up on screen. It was 11.48 p.m. He set himself a test. Not a drop till midnight. Go on, Ralph, you know you can do it. Just twelve minutes, it's not long, and get through twelve minutes and you'll deserve it. A w3 coming up, sir, no ice, no fucking glass, mate. A nice w3 straight from the bottle. You cannot beat it, sir. 'The wife is away, the mouse will play,' he said, then laughed again.

He reckoned he could waste at least five of the twelve minutes just channel-hopping. 'Cheerio, Jayne. Live well.' He skipped over the news channels, where a bunch of journalists were talking to each other about tomorrow's papers. He gave twenty seconds or so to each of the pop-music channels, whizzed through sport, and settled on one of the TV shopping channels where a young black woman was urging him to call the number on the screen to make a bid for an enormous punchbowl. He could not work out how the price kept changing, and how the young black woman seemed to know, but he imagined it had something to do with supply and demand, and assumed the names appearing on a rolling ticker tape at the bottom of the screen were affecting the price. £5.99 seemed quite reasonable if you liked the look of the punchbowl. He thought it was hideous. He wondered what sort of people were up at this time of night watching a nice-looking young black woman trying to sell punchbowls, and then he started laughing again. 'You, you daft cunt. You're fucking watching it, and you're the Secretary of State for Health in Her Majesty's government. What excuse do all the other sad fuckers have?'

He had three minutes to go. He pulled out his drink diary from his inside pocket. He had recorded nothing since the farewell party, so he tried to remember how much he had drunk at dinner, and scribbled it down. He started laughing again. 'I'm on for a record here,' he said. 'I'm on for a fucking record.' He looked down at the bottle of Johnnie Walker. 'You and me, Johnnie, we are heading for the record books. Nice Professor Sturrock is going to be so pleased that I've filled this all in, and we're going in the record books, Johnnie.'

At one minute to midnight, he gave up the wait. 'What difference does one minute make, one tiny little minute made up of sixty silly little seconds?' The black woman was going off shift at midnight and saying goodbye to her viewers, so he said goodbye to her, picked up the bottle, unscrewed the top, then held it under his nose and breathed in deeply. W8 later he went to bed, still wearing his suit, though he had at least removed his coat and shoes at the bedroom door.

'Oh dear,' said Professor Sturrock as he registered the w8.

'I'm guessing at 8. There was about a quarter-bottle left and I just downed the lot.'

'How did you feel?'

'I didn't feel anything,' he said. 'I just wanted to finish the bottle, and I did. And then I went to bed.'

'Can you remember going upstairs?'

'Not really.'

'Can you remember what you were thinking?'

'I was just trying to get up there. I think I brushed my teeth. When I woke up one of the photos on Sandie's dresser was broken. I don't know if it broke because I was bouncing around, or whether I smashed it. I just don't remember.'

'What was it of?'

'Our wedding day,' he said, knowing as he said it Professor Sturrock, probably rightly, would assume he had smashed it in a drunken rage because Sandie wasn't there, just as he had kicked his red box around downstairs, causing it to fly open and his papers to scatter around the hallway, because he felt his career was not going where he wanted it to.

'I honestly don't remember,' he said. 'I don't remember smashing the photo, and I don't remember smashing up the box. They were there in the morning, in bits. I don't remember.'

He couldn't decide whether the look on Professor Sturrock's face was disapproval, or sympathy.

'So what do you think?' he asked the psychiatrist.

'I think it's serious, Ralph, and getting worse. You know that. It's why you called me first thing this morning, and why you kept calling Phyllis.'

'What do we do?'

Professor Sturrock looked out of the window, clearly needing time to think.

'Is there no way you could go to the Prime Minister, tell him you have a problem, and ask if it is possible to take leave of absence for a while? In the meantime I could fix you up with a proper course of treatment, possibly at a residential treatment centre which will put you in touch with Alcoholics Anonymous.'

Ralph looked down towards the floor, shaking his head.

'It's a bit hard to be anonymous when I'd be all over the front pages for weeks on end if I did that,' he said.

'There is that, I suppose.'

Ralph said there was not a single person in politics that he trusted sufficiently to tell he had a problem, not even his closest friend and ally, Daniel Melchett.

'I took a big gamble on you, Martin. You know that, don't you? I'm trusting you because you're a psychiatrist. But politics is a very different world. I'm truthful with you. I couldn't be truthful with anyone else about this.'

11

When Sturrock emerged from the Houses of Parliament, he switched his mobile phone back on, and within seconds it pinged with a text from Phyllis. 'Please call Mrs Sturrock.' He sighed, scrolled down to their number in his directory, then pressed the green button to call her.

'Martin, is that you?' his wife shouted when she answered.

'Sorry about the noise,' he said. 'I'm in Whitehall.'

'Are you going for the book?'

'I've got the book. All done.'

'How much was it?'

'Can't remember – £19.99 or something.'

'Oh.'

'Did Simon call?'

'Oh yes, sorry. He did.'

'And?'

'Noon, Tuesday.'

'Damn. Where is it?'

'Yeovil crematorium.'

'Yeovil! Shit.' He had been hoping Simon might decide to have it nearer to his own home in Berkshire.

'He said they had a cancellation,' said Mrs Sturrock.

'What, someone decided not to die?'

'No, there was another one planned, but they couldn't release the body.'

'Well, it's bloody inconvenient. That's the whole day gone, might even need an overnight stay for Christ's sake.'

'Martin. Someone has died. Your relative.'

He recalled her earlier chastisement in the kitchen about his seeming lack of caring about Aunt Jessica. He knew she was right, but he didn't like to be told by her what he should feel. Perhaps if she tried a bit harder to imagine how he felt most of the time, he would allow her more say over his emotions.

'I know someone has died, and I know she was my relative, and I am very sorry. But I am dealing with the living and I have one or two people due to see me on Tuesday who need me rather more than Aunt Jessica does.'

There was a pause, and the silence was filled by the sounds of traffic, including an ambulance heading down Whitehall, siren wailing.

'What a din!' said Stella, somehow making him feel as though he were personally responsible for the sounds of busy central-London life intruding into the kitchen of their suburban Chiswick home.

'By the way, Simon asked if your mother would be going to the funeral. I said I didn't know.'

That brought him up short once more. He had not even thought of his mother, and whether she would want to attend her sister-in-law's funeral. He hoped not. It would be hugely inconvenient to have to ferry Sheila Sturrock from her care home in Hertfordshire, all the way down to Yeovil, then back again, and doubtless it would fall on him to sort it out. He suspected that she would want to go. She had been very fond of Aunt Jessica – perhaps the only other woman she knew who had really understood what it was like to live with George Sturrock.

'I'll ask her when I go over at the weekend,' he said.

'What time are you home?'

'Oh, I shouldn't be too late. I've got a couple of budget meetings back at the hospital, then I'll tidy up. I'll probably be back around half seven.'

'What sandwich did Phyllis get you today?'

It was the kind of question that demented him. What did it matter what he had in his sandwich? It was of no interest to anyone but himself and Phyllis who had gone out to buy it, and the Pret A Manger staff who supplied it. As it so happened, the uneaten sandwich had been a BLT. But if he said it was cheese and tomato, it would make no difference to Stella's life whatsoever, so why was she asking? It would make no difference to his. It was a detail of no importance to anyone.

He recalled David Temple's view that his mother was obsessed with other people's food because it was a way of interfering in other people's business. For his wife, there was the added dimension of making him know that she was sitting there at home feeling that she was reduced to asking about sandwiches because that was the only kind of conversation he allowed her to have with him.

'BLT,' he said.

'Nice?' she asked.

'Yes, fine.'

He had almost reached Trafalgar Square, but felt a sudden need to sit down. He thought about walking down to the Embankment to sit on one of the benches by the river, but even thinking about it drained him of a little more energy. Instead, he sat on a metallic chair outside a cafe. It was grey overhead and he could feel tiny spots of rain on his face. He felt overwhelmed by lethargy, as if it would be too much effort even to put his mobile back in his pocket. Ralph Hall had been the final dispiriting consultation of an utterly dispiriting day. He had never finished a week feeling quite as bad as this.

There was no doubt Ralph's drink problem was worsening, but Sturrock felt completely unable to see a way forward. Another patient consultation, another sensation of being blocked. He was surprised Ralph's colleagues had not noticed the beginnings of physical change. There were some unpleasant-looking red lines on his nose. His face was puffier, yet his body weight was, if anything, down. His trousers looked a little too big for him. Perhaps Ralph's fellow MPs *had* noticed, and Ralph didn't realise.

Had this been a standard patient, one without a public profile and position, Sturrock would have gone for shock tactics, confronted patient and family with the reality, got him into a drying-out clinic, and then monitored him through the standard Alcoholics Anonymous twelve-step programme. But that wasn't possible with Ralph. Instead, he'd have to try to manage the situation, stay vaguely on top of this until the summer recess, and hope that somehow the circumstances would emerge that allowed him to get Ralph onto a proper addiction programme, starting with total abstinence and withdrawal. Perhaps he could stretch out the treatment a bit by going into the marriage and career issues more deeply, to establish whether they were the problems Hall was trying to block out. He also intended to do the full emotional background, from childhood on, to see whether the reasons for his drinking stretched further back. But it was really a patch-and-mend situation. He felt a little weighed down by the enormity of the secret. A newspaper billboard across from the cafe advertised the news that a junior defence minister had once owned shares in an arms company. A nothing story compared with the Health Secretary being secretly treated for alcoholism, he thought.

He decided that, the next time they met, he would urge Ralph to confide fully in his wife. The way Ralph talked about her, Sandie came over as a pretty solid citizen, a woman who would stand by her husband. It made him think of Stella, the conversation they had just had, the life they lived together, and it made him sink even deeper into the tiredness he was feeling. He felt a little guilty too, for even as he'd told Stella about the budget meetings, he'd known he was lying. He had no intention of going back to the hospital.

The staff inside the cafe appeared to have realised he was simply resting for a few moments, for nobody came to serve him as they prepared to close up. He called Phyllis.

'I'm not going to make it back in time for the budget meetings,' he said. 'Could you go, give my apologies, and just take a note for me?'

'OK,' she said. 'What reason shall I give?'

'I got held up on a very tricky OTO.'

The rain was getting a little heavier as he stood up and began to walk towards Soho. He stopped at a cashpoint just beyond the National Portrait Gallery, and took out £140, his body as close as he could get it to the keypad, so he could shield his transaction from the Italian couple in the queue behind him. He was very rarely in this part of town at this time of day, and he could scarcely believe how busy it was. There was a steady flow of people pouring in and out of Leicester Square tube station, locals, tourists, people clearly rushing to work, meeting friends, going to the cinema, going to get something to eat before the theatre, whatever, but what he knew was that every single one of them was going somewhere to do something or see somebody, and all of them had a story behind them that stretched way back to the day they were born, then back again to those who went before them, and the bustle they created was making him feel a little queasy. He stopped to catch his breath, resting his hand against a bollard.

A young woman was emerging from the Underground now, and he watched her for a while, putting up a tiny pink umbrella, crossing the road, clutching her handbag tight against her waist, her ponytail swinging from side to side as she ran the last steps to avoid a black cab coming towards her, then skipped up onto the pavement. She must have been twenty-five, maybe twenty-eight. He would probably never see her again. Yet her life was just as important as his, he told himself. Her family history was every bit as rich. Like everyone, she would have issues to deal with, problems that kept her awake at night. He would never know what they were. Perhaps 'never' overstated it, but the odds on him ever knowing must be in the billions-to-one area. She looked grounded. She had a thin smile on her face that said to him she was fairly comfortable in her own skin. But he couldn't be sure of that. She could have just been released from prison and be on her way to meet her old mates for a night on the town. She could be a schizophrenic dependent on regular medication. She could be a teacher, doctor, student, painter, actress, call girl, anything at all. She stopped by a newspaper kiosk outside a packed coffee house, and was greeted by a young man who kissed her, twice on the lips, once on the forehead, then took her hand and they headed towards the Square. Sturrock smiled, pleased that she appeared to be loved. Though what did he know?

He felt a little re-energised at having been able to focus on one individual amid this mass of humanity that appeared to grow and grow, becoming noisier and more boisterous as he continued up towards Soho, hoping that he would be able to have the same woman as last time.

Sturrock had first paid for sex forty-two years ago, aged nineteen, when he was in his first year studying medicine at university. It was a fellow medic who told him that the anonymous-looking grey building at the end of Hopton Street was a place where sex could be bought, with a discount for students. And so, one Tuesday afternoon, he went in, paid up front, told the prostitute he had never had sex before and could she show him what to do. It was a lie that he'd never had sex before. In fact, he had lost his virginity two years earlier with Rosalie Curtis, and his visit to Hopton Street was probably an attempt to put behind him the awful memory of that first sexual experience.

Rosalie was the daughter of a family friend and near neighbour. He had known her since primary school and had always thought her a little stuck-up. Yet one autumn evening they met, as she was walking home from a choir rehearsal, and he was walking home from a school trip to a local museum. The clocks had just gone back, and as they walked together, kicking leaves and laughing, talking about mutual friends and acquaintances, and sharing thoughts about what hopes they had for the future, something clicked in a way that neither had expected. When they reached Rosalie's house, they paused for a moment, then carried on walking. They must have walked for more than an hour. As darkness fell, they reached a little park where, side by side on a bench, they kissed and tore at each other's clothes until, at the time he was normally sitting down for his dinner, he had her knickers in his right hand, while she had his penis in hers.

His knowledge of sex was at that time limited to what he had learned in biology lessons, what he had seen in films, what he had read in magazines, and what he had picked up listening to his more street-wise friends. He had hoped his father might explain a thing or two to him, and when he was fourteen had asked him straight out, his stomach churning as he did so, whether he would tell him about sex.

'Don't trouble your mind with all that, son,' his father had said. George Sturrock must have mentioned something to his wife, because a few days later, his mother gave him a booklet to read which had pictures of organs, and explained where body hair came from, and what a condom was. It was all very interesting, but didn't exactly answer all the questions his body and mind had been asking of him.

So now here he was, in the cold autumn air, and stuck-up Rosalie from Lavender Park Avenue was yanking her hand up and down his penis, he was clutching her knickers, and all he really knew was that he had to get his penis to where the knickers had been and hope for the best. It was too cold, and possibly even a bit damp, to get down on the ground, but he had never seen a film in which the love scene took place on an oddly shaped park bench with intricate metalwork at either end. He stuffed Rosalie's knickers into his pocket, and while her right hand continued to play with his penis, his moved down to pubic hair which felt very different to his, crinkly rather than soft. He worried she might resist as he started to push his hand hard between her legs, but she was making little purring noises that made him think he was doing fine. He levered himself up, pushed her skirt up and tried to roll his chest onto hers, trailing his legs behind him.

'Ow,' she said, as her back dug into the bench, and her arm brushed the metalwork.

'Oh, sorry. Are you OK?'

She wriggled her back into a more comfortable position, pulled his head towards her and as they kissed, he manoeuvred his body into what he assumed to be the right place. He wasn't sure where his penis was in relation to where he wanted it to be, but when her hand curled round it once more, and she pulled him towards her, it felt right. Then as her hand joined the other on his neck and she started making more purring noises, now with little squeals punctuating them, he was pretty sure that he was losing his virginity. He didn't know, technically, whether loss of virginity related to penetration only, or whether it required a climax. Either way, one appeared to be completed and the other was not far away. It was then that his problems started. He climaxed, trying not to make too much noise for fear of passers-by seeing them, and as he finished, Rosalie began to punch his back, then his chest, shouting 'off, off, off', and he was deeply confused. He had had his first orgasm inside a woman, who until a moment ago appeared to be a consenting partner in this but now, immediately post-orgasm, was trying to banish him. He felt this would be one of those moments that would stay with him for some time, even qualify as one of the final thoughts flashing through his mind on his deathbed. He pulled away from her, at which point she stood up, brushed herself down and ran away, leaving him alone with his rapidly softening penis, her knickers in his pocket, and a worry about what he had done wrong, and how he was going to explain being late home for dinner. He dumped the knickers in a builders' skip two streets from home.

One evening, as his father was gardening, he decided to tell him about what had happened – not in full detail, but sufficient to explain that he didn't really know what he should have done differently. But as he walked towards him, his father looked up, and though he smiled, it was not a smile that welcomed him in. He stood for a while, looking for a more positive signal.

'What is it?'

'Oh, nothing, just wondered what you were doing.'

'Spot of gardening. Tell your mother I'll be in in a minute.'

And he wondered whether 'in in a minute' was some sexual code known only to people who have graduated in the basics of sex. Perhaps he should have told Rosalie that he was going to be 'in in a minute'. He didn't like the thought that he would have no further relationship with the girl who took his virginity. He wondered how many women his father slept with before he met his mother, and indeed how many since. It was a question he never asked, not even when he was trying to make up for lost time, talking to his father on his deathbed many years later.

He was confident that when he got to university, he would not want for sexual partners. But it didn't really happen. And that was what had led him to Hopton Street, which became a regular haunt until, in his third year, he met Stella, fell in love and, for the first time in his life, learned what it was to enjoy sex. For years, it never crossed his mind to visit a prostitute. But recently he'd become an increasingly frequent customer.

The worst thing about going to a whorehouse was the moment

of entry. Once he was in a private room, with the girl who had been allocated to him, he felt safe. But walking through the main door off the street was a moment of high risk, and high pressure. It was usually pretty obvious what kind of establishment he was entering. And who knows how many of the people walking past might have met him – as colleagues, students, patients or friends? The anxiety would linger, even once he had crossed the threshold, for though he could no longer be seen, how was he to know he hadn't been seen already? Then there was always a bit of hanging around in an inevitably decrepit reception area, where he felt the soles of his shoes sticking to the carpet, as he waited to be told where to go.

He had only been once before to this particular place, with its 'Girls, Girls, Girls' red lights flashing above the doorway, and though it was pricey, they were quick and efficient. He saw one other customer, who looked and sounded like a tourist.

He wondered whether, if he was seen by someone he knew, he could say he was seeing a prostitute as a patient. On the surface, it was implausible that he would do OTOs at a brothel, but perhaps their customers more than anyone would understand why prostitutes had serious psychological issues. Like Hafsatu. Of all his patients, she was the one who most challenged his own self-worth and sense of his personal morality. But it didn't stop these visits, nor his fantasies about arriving in a brothel and finding Hafsatu was there waiting for him. How could he listen to Arta talk about being raped, and Hafsatu describe her experience as a prostitute as 'being raped for a living', and then come to a place like this and do what he did? But he could, and he did.

He asked if the same girl he saw the last time was available, but the woman at the desk couldn't remember him, so obviously couldn't remember the girl. He tried to describe her, but after a while gave up. 'It sounds like Carina,' she said. 'She's not on till later. You can have Angharad. Room 4. Go in and get undressed and she'll give you a nice rub-down. She won't be long.'

It was less a room than a booth, with a large massage table in the centre. There was a TV screen on each wall, playing a fast-moving compilation of pornographic images. He undressed, hanging his coat and jacket on the two hangers behind the door, then the rest of his clothes over a small red chair in the corner, next to a sink. He kept on his underpants and slowly climbed onto the table.

Angharad – he assumed all these glamorous-sounding names were invented – came in, said 'hello, my love' in a cheery Welsh accent, turned down the lights with the dimmer, walked over and playfully smacked him on the backside. 'Come on, fella,' she said, 'we can get rid of those.' So he removed his pants, and her voice, and signal of intent, began to arouse him in a way that none of the films playing on the four screens had done.

She massaged his back and shoulders quickly, then worked on his thighs, letting the side of her hand brush his ballbag every time she worked up to the top of his leg. Once she knew he had an erection, she asked him to turn onto his back, and worked around his stomach and the top of his thighs.

'OK, time we put a bit of protection on there,' she said, her accent appearing to grow stronger the more he heard her. She went over to the cupboard by the sink and took out a condom. She rolled it on, asked him to get off the table, rolled down the tracksuit bottoms she was wearing, leaned over the table and said, 'Now you take Angharad from behind, love.'

She had a huge barbed-wire tattoo across her lower back, and a scar on her left thigh. As he entered her, he closed his eyes, not out of pleasure, or because of shame, but because he wanted to block out the gaudy, multicoloured tattoo and the pasty white skin it decorated, and imagine that the body he was now inside was Hafsatu's.

Hafsatu was black, and muscular, and it was her skin he wanted to be touching, her voice he wanted to be hearing exhorting him to go faster and harder. He rocked his head back, and as he held onto Angharad's hips, and moved his body backwards and forwards, he forced an image of Hafsatu on to the darkness behind his eyelids, and inside his head he was telling her how nice it felt to be with her, here, just the two of them, no danger of anyone else coming in and finding them doing what both of them had wanted to do for so long, and for a few brief moments, he was almost there, the fantasy real, it was her body that he could feel against his, it was her moving back towards him as he moved forwards to her, and she was saying she loved him, and she loved the way he made love to her, and as she said it, he felt love and sex were as one, as once they had been with Stella, but now it was Hafsatu who infused sex with love, and love with sex, and gave him these few fabulous moments at the end of a dreadful, dreadful day, but even as his fantasy mind was trying to summon up and hold on to that joy, as he came, his rational mind cut in forcefully, reminded him where he was, what he was doing, and he opened his eyes, saw the tattoo on the pasty white skin, and felt an intense longing to be out of there.

Walking out into the street afterwards, he felt a familiar, but this time more profound, sense of self-disgust. It was the same every time. The urgency to get there, the excitement when he arrived, and then the shame once it was all over. But this was worse than shame. This forced him to confront a question he couldn't easily answer. What right did he have to be treating people, interfering with what went on in their minds, when his own mind was so sordid?

The shame sat with him all the way home. Usually, he liked to look around the carriage on the tube, study his fellow passengers, take a glance at what they were reading. Today, he had eyes only for his own reflection in the window across from his seat. He looked old, tired, unclean.

When he got home, he told Stella he had a dreadful headache and went to lie down. He spent two hours staring at the wall and then fell into a troubled sleep in which Hafsatu, his father, his wife, Aunt Jessica and David Temple were all vying for attention and he didn't know what to say to any of them. When he awoke, startled by a dream in which he was giving a consultation to a regular patient about whose condition he could remember absolutely nothing, the house was pitch dark and he could hear Stella breathing alongside him as she slept. He lay for a while in the dark, then got up and went for a shower. It was 4 a.m.

SATURDAY

12

Lirim's dream took him back to Kosovo. He was fishing on the banks of the River Sitnica, at a spot he had loved since he was a boy. It was a beautiful, sunny day and Arta surprised him by arriving with a lunch of sandwiches, cakes, fruit and wine. They started to eat and drink, but soon they were touching each other, taking off their clothes. As they knelt face to face, slowly kissing, Lirim thought he would like to stay like this for a long time. But his desire grew stronger and he knew he wanted more than to kiss her, so he took Arta by the shoulders and gently pushed her to the ground, rolling himself on top of her in the same movement. And then, suddenly, a farmer came towards them shouting, 'Hey, stop, this is private land.' Lirim woke up.

For a few moments, he was still in Kosovo, and happy to be so, though scared of the farmer he imagined to be shouting at him. Then he blinked his eyes open and realised amid the near darkness that he was at home, in London, in bed with Arta. He had no idea what time it was, somewhere between midnight, when they had fallen asleep, and 7 a.m., when his alarm would ring to get him up for work. Arta seemed at peace, the rapist absent from her mind, the turmoil of yesterday's confrontation with Professor Sturrock seemingly gone.

As Lirim's dream faded, and with it the hope of making love, he lay still, trying to make sense of what had happened with her psychiatrist yesterday, and the violent reaction he had provoked.

He hadn't expected to see his wife till the evening. He had a particularly busy day at the car wash because they were preparing for their first Sunday opening. He'd told Arta he wouldn't be home till gone seven, but there she was, at two in the afternoon, crossing the street towards the car wash. He could tell as soon as he spotted her, pushing Besa in the buggy, negotiating her way through the queue of cars waiting to be cleaned, that she was upset about something. He hoped she wasn't bringing him problems. He was on the phone in the little cubbyhole that served as an office, renewing the ad he had placed in *Southwark News* for two more staff. His current team were all Kosovans, as was the builder who rented the space to him. Now that he had decided to turn the business into a seven-day operation, he needed extra manpower. He paid his boys, as he called them, just above the minimum wage, and they were allowed to keep their own tips. Lirim had got his first customers through a heavy leafleting drop in the area, which he'd done himself. After that, he'd built up a good pool of regular clients, and word of mouth was doing the rest.

Lirim smiled as he watched his daughter enjoying the noise and the splashing of the power hoses being trained on the car at the front of the queue. He held up a finger to say he would be one minute and tried to finish his call as quickly as he could. His staff noticed Arta, and shouted hello. They knew what had happened to her, but it was a while back now, and their greetings were nothing more than happy hellos from people pleased to see the boss's wife.

As Lirim came off the phone, he could see that she was agitated.

'I tried not to come,' she said. 'I tried to stay home and calm down but I can't. I had to come and tell you.'

'What is it?'

'The psychiatrist. He really hurt me.'

'What? How?'

'He says I have to forgive the men who did it. I said I can't do that, and he said it's not that I can't, but I won't, like it was my fault that I feel like this, my fault I have all the dreams, my fault that I can't let you touch me. It upset me so much, I just had to get out of there and get away from him.'

When she had started talking, Lirim had had the improbable thought that the psychiatrist had physically attacked his wife, and so felt relieved when she explained herself in more detail. But his relief was short-lived. It had been some time since Arta's appointment with the psychiatrist and yet she was still extremely angry. What if she didn't get over this? What if she stopped wanting to see Professor Sturrock? Lirim had been so glad when their doctor had managed to get her those first appointments at the Prince Regent Hospital. Until then he had felt completely alone with the problem, as if he was the only person who could help Arta. Everything he had heard about Professor Sturrock made him feel he was a good thing, and important to Arta's recovery. But this morning's appointment, and his demand for forgiveness of the rapist, had put all that at risk.

Until the rape, life in England had been good for Arta and Lirim. They were amazed how quickly they recovered from the ordeal of the journey, and they had impressed themselves and each other with how they had become virtually fluent in English, though Alban would still occasionally gently mock their accent. Their son's school reports were beyond reproach. He was a good football player. His parents were proud of him to the point where Lirim knew that sometimes Alban found it embarrassing, the extent of praise they lavished upon him.

So that was how it was – a nice, tidy home, a business being established, the children doing well – when Arta was raped. They continued to live in the nice, tidy flat in one of the huge blocks near Elephant and Castle tube station. The business, a short walk down Walworth Road, continued to expand. And the children continued to do well. But life had changed for all of them. Much as she tried, Arta could not get through a minute, let alone an hour, without thinking about what happened. Lirim had suggested they move house, but she felt she had to stay and conquer the feelings she was having, added to which the children had had to suffer enough with what had happened to her, and she didn't want to unsettle them further.

Once he had got over the initial shock, which made him want to roam around the streets looking for a man in a balaclava, and kick him to death, Lirim had done everything he could to support Arta, sitting with her as she spoke to the police, stroking her hair and her hand, just being there. She told him she had worried he would be angry with her. He was angry only with the people who had hurt her, and desperate for them to be punished.

He had been told by the victim support officer that sometimes women who were raped by strangers would find it very difficult to resume a sex life with their husband or partner, and it was important he tried to understand that, just be supportive, be patient, help what could be a slow recovery. At first he'd found it easy to be patient. It was his natural instinct to do what was best for Arta. But recently he'd found it more difficult. He was pouring himself into his work, but he was surprised by how many of his waking moments were dominated by two men he had never met, the rapist and the psychiatrist. He had put a lot of hope and trust in Professor Sturrock, but now it looked as if he might be back on his own with the problem.

Arta was crying and Lirim noticed his staff looking over at them. He led her into the little cubbyhole office.

'Why does he say that? Why does he say "Can't or won't?" like I have the choice?' she asked.

'He must have his reasons. He is the doctor. He is the one who knows how the mind works. You have to ask him.'

'But I don't want to go back. I can't go back.'

'You said before he is a good man, and kind. He hasn't changed, has he? All that's changed is he asked you a question you didn't like. Don't turn your back on him yet.'

Arta had given him a weak smile, and then trudged off to collect Alban from school. All that evening, he could sense her anger simmering. But although he was worried, in some ways, he actually found it reassuring to see his wife angry about something other than the attack itself. It felt as if she was coming back as a full human being. And he surprised himself by thinking the psychiatrist might have a point.

He got out of bed and started dressing for work. He was about to leave the room when Arta started screaming in her sleep. He rushed over and shook her awake.

'Arta, Arta, Arta, wake up, wake up, it's OK, it's OK, you're here, it's fine.' As she opened her eyes, she looked petrified, then realised she was safe, and flung her arms around his neck, breathing deeply as the fear began to fade.

13

Lorraine Parks woke, as she did every morning, to the sound of Classic FM on her clock radio.

She had never been a classical music fan, until the fire. She'd always listened to Radio 2 in the car, middle-of-the-road CDs at home, and the last time she'd been to a concert it was to see the Eagles at the old Wembley with a friend who'd won two tickets in a radio competition. But the nurses had Classic FM playing in the background at the burns unit where she had spent hundreds of hours beside Emily's bed, many of them watching her daughter sleep. The music became an important part of her life as she tried to come to terms with what had happened.

Most of the time, unless she made a point of listening to the announcer's voice, she had no idea whose music she was listening to. But it was rare that she didn't find it soothing. Sometimes she found it deeply moving, either stirring in her enormous hope that Emily would one day rediscover her beauty and zest for life, or mirroring the hopelessness she felt at what Emily's life had become. Whichever set of emotions was stirred, she was lost in wonder at the ability of a sound to provoke them. It could have been Mozart, or Bach, or Beethoven, or Wagner, she had no idea. She didn't know their first names, let alone what they had composed, but at least now she knew why their names and their music had endured. They had created works of art which, centuries later, performed by people not even alive when they wrote their music, could help a mother who was struggling more than she dared to admit with the despair of her daughter. Within a few weeks, despite initial opposition from her husband, the radios in the kitchen and the bathroom and the family car were all tuned to Classic FM. She saw it as a little piece of good to emerge from something terrible.

Lorraine had managed to get through more than twenty years of motherhood without ever receiving the call that every parent dreads. She and her husband were having dinner. They were irritated when the phone rang, but they answered, as they always did, in case it was one of their parents who were getting on and had a few health problems.

It was the hospital, with a few words of introduction, and then: 'I'm afraid your daughter has been involved in an accident.'

Lorraine couldn't get the moment out of her head. She played it, over and over.

'I'm afraid your daughter has been involved in an accident.'

And everything stops, and you fear the next sentence, that she's dead, but there's a little pause and so you fill it, by asking the question, 'Is she . . .' But you can't bring yourself to utter the word, and the voice fills the gap, says, 'No.' But now your husband has picked up on the worry, sees the colour draining from your lips and your face and the life flowing from your eyes, and he is saying, 'What's wrong, what's wrong, what is it, is it your mum?' because your mother is elderly and has been having tests on her heart, and you're trying to hear the voice on the phone which is saying there has been an accident, Emily is alive, but she is badly burnt and this is the address you need to go to. And you tell your husband, and then there's a couple looking in each other's eyes, and they may think they know everything about each other but they have never seen this look of fear and panic, the fear of loss. How have they let this happen? they think. Why weren't they there to protect her? And they're asking each other questions they can't possibly know the answers to, like 'What happened?' and 'Was she on her own?' and 'How long will they keep her in for?' and then rushing to put on shoes and coats and find car keys, leaving pets unfed and TVs unturned off and dinners uneaten on the table because they've had the call that every parent dreads and they know this is a moment where their life departs its comfort zone and takes them to pain and a challenge they're not sure they can meet.

Lorraine could sense that her husband, Ken, was determined to be strong when they were taken in to see Emily. He knew that Lorraine would be crumbling inside, and he felt he mustn't crumble himself. They had half an hour – twenty minutes driving there, five infuriating minutes trying to find somewhere to park, then five minutes getting from the car to the hospital – to become accustomed to the idea that Emily had been burnt. They both had very different pictures in mind. Lorraine couldn't recall if the woman who phoned said fire or not. She just heard 'accident' and 'burnt' and, in her mind, she saw blisters and scaldings on Emily's hands. Perhaps a pan of boiling water had fallen from the gas rings and caught her on the way to the floor. She hoped she was wearing shoes. She was always warning her not to cook barefoot. Ken had visions of her being dragged from a fire, choking and spluttering, and imagined his daughter suffering from the effects of smoke inhalation.

Neither was remotely prepared for what they saw. Both were crushed, instantly. Lorraine didn't know whether she could touch her own daughter. Ken burst into tears, and was close to gagging. If the call had said she was dead, and this was a visit to the morgue to identify the body, they would have been no less devastated.

Yet little by little, in the following months, they coped far better than they ever imagined they would, and they had come to accept Emily's disfigurement in a way that she couldn't. Their real distress was caused by her evident suffering in trying to come to terms with what had happened to her. Yesterday, as she came out of her appointment with Professor Sturrock, the good side of her face was flushed and her hands were shaking visibly.

Lorraine had been sitting in the hospital's basement car park listening to Debussy's 'Berceuse héroïque'. She turned down the volume.

'What's wrong, love?' she asked. Emily shook her head. Lorraine started the car, drove out of the car park, turned left onto the main road and began the journey home.

'How was it?' she asked once they were well away from the hospital. She was never sure if she would get an answer after these sessions with the psychiatrist, but she always asked.

'Not great,' said Emily.

'Why?'

'I think he was a bit cross that I didn't read the book he gave me.'

'Why didn't you read it, Em? He is trying to help.'

'I know. I'll read it at the weekend.'

'Was that it?'

'No. Don't be angry, Mum, but I was a bit harsh with him. He was trying to tell me I was the same person as before, but I said there was no way he could know how I felt, and he looked a bit hurt by that.'

'You shouldn't talk to him like that, love. Who knows what he's been through in his life? He could have had all sorts of tragedies for all we know. And, even if he's had a trouble-free life himself, he's bound to have had a lot of experience dealing with people who haven't.'

'I know,' said Emily. 'I know he has a point. I know he is trying to help. And at least he always gives me something to think about.'

Her mother looked over to her. She could only see the right side of her daughter's face. She looked lovely. She always did when they were driving, and the burnt side of her face was hidden to Lorraine. The music ended and they broke for an ad break, which always irritated her. There was such a horrible clash between the beauty of the music and the awful jingles they played for the adverts.

One such jingle came on now, as she lay in bed thinking about Emily. 'Rediscover the real you, with Olay Definity Self-Repair Serum – ignites skin's natural ability to self-repair for diminished discolorations, dullness, brown spots and wrinkles.'

Lorraine tutted loudly and turned off the radio in disgust. If only life were so simple.

14

Celia was already up and about when Matthew opened his eyes on Saturday morning. She had half opened the curtains and through the window he could see it was a bright, crisp autumnal day. The wind had chased away yesterday's rain and a sliver of sunlight fell on the bed – a bed which last night, for the first time since the visit of his clerk Julian, had seen Matthew and Celia doing what husbands and wives are meant to do from time to time. It wasn't as if they hadn't been getting on prior to the visit to see Professor Sturrock. After the initial fury Celia's mood had improved steadily as, first, he'd agreed with her analysis of his problem and, second, promised to get help. Yet he had still not felt confident enough to indicate any sexual desire or intent. She had been almost impossibly nice, but he assumed that anger at his betrayal was never far below the surface and he should pander to her enjoyment of being in control, and let things evolve on her terms, at her pace, and not push his luck. Also, despite his official diagnosis as a sex addict now being recorded somewhere in Professor Sturrock's files, he had rather liked the enforced deep freeze and its accompanying celibacy. It had reminded him of the time, pre-marriage, when his body was his own, with no calls upon it to perform when he was feeling weary or out of sorts with his partner. But when, last night, he had sensed Celia inching across the mattress, then felt her thigh against his and her arm circling his shoulders, he knew it would be churlish to be anything other than surprised and pleased. She rolled him onto his back, which was where he stayed as, here too, she was clearly enjoying being in control. Perhaps it was this surprise, and the pleasure of knowing his marriage was resuming something approaching normal service, that led him to climax way too soon. As she continued to bounce up and down on him, hoping to reach orgasm herself, his mind began to wander. It travelled via next week's case, his golf swing and Angela's neck, finally arriving, as Celia collapsed on top of him, moderately satisfied, at thoughts of what kind of house Professor Sturrock lived in, and whether he played golf. He didn't look like a golfer, but then, Matthew didn't look like a cyclist.

After breakfast, he walked to Mitchell's Bikes, not the nearest bike shop to his house, but according to Celia the best in the neighbour-hood. It was run by a former PE teacher who had decided teaching wasn't for him and, with financial backing from his father, had decided to become a sports businessman. Frederick, known to his regulars as Freddie, was hoping eventually to run a London-wide chain of gyms but for now he had to content himself with selling bikes to the cyclists of Totteridge and its surrounds.

Matthew didn't have a clue what kind of bike to get, so even before meeting Freddie or knowing he existed, he'd decided he would happily be led in his decision-making. The sun was so strong it was almost hot as he set off, dressed in the tracksuit Celia had bought him for Christmas last year, prior to another failed Get Fit kick. As he walked, he decided what he would say to the people at Mitchell's – that he had not ridden a bike since his teens, that he wanted to get into it in a serious way and didn't really mind the cost.

He went inside, where a young assistant was helping an elderly woman choose a helmet. Scores of bikes were racked up against two of the walls. The rest of the store offered a bewildering array of shoes, cycling tops, gloves, hats, glasses, computerised speedometers. There was a cupboard with about eighty different watches locked away. Even water bottles had their own little section. There were two huge fridges filled with energy drinks and a shelf next to them offering a choice of energy bars and food gels. He had no idea that there was so much paraphernalia attached to bikes. And this was just downstairs. He noticed a clear divide between customers in the main bike section, and those amid the paraphernalia. The bike buyers tended to be mums with kids or people like himself, older sorts who had bought into the fitness craze. Then in the paraphernalia sections were men in their twenties and thirties, many already kitted out for cycling, fit and lean, and chatting away about the new products that were on the market. He wondered if he was the first customer to be here because a psychiatrist had suggested he get fit, and to show his wife he was serious about it.

It was pretty clear who the boss was: the tall stocky man wearing a white T-shirt with 'Mitchell's' emblazoned front and back, and who had a quiet authority as he walked around making sure his staff were taking care of the various queries customers had.

'Excuse me,' Matthew said, 'I've not cycled since I was a student. I really want to try to get into it. Do you think you could advise me?'

Seventy minutes later, Freddie Mitchell had a new favourite customer, and Matthew Noble had a new carbon-frame racing bike and assorted paraphernalia that in total cost him well into four figures.

Walking home, pushing the bike, he could not recall the last time he felt so excited. Back at the house, he went straight upstairs to change. The padded shorts, and leotard-style braces, were tight. When he'd complained to Freddie that they showed off his gut far too graphically, he'd told him it was a good incentive to do the kind of distances that saw the gut come down. The great thing about bikes, Freddie said, was a lack of snobbery among those who rode them. From slim men on the best racing bikes burning up the road, to fat old ladies grinding their way home, the cycling community was a broad church, and nobody would think any the worse of you because of a gut, even one as large as Matthew's. Matthew wasn't so sure. Even breathing in hard, he looked like an overweight wrestler. But he had a strong frame and his legs were not in bad shape. He slipped on the multi-coloured mild-weather zip-up top, which Freddie had told him was totally windproof, and studied himself in the mirror. He looked faintly ridiculous. But then he recalled feeling exactly the same the first time he looked at himself in the mirror wearing a QC's wig. Come on, he said to himself, it's not how you look, it's how you feel, and what you do to look and feel better. And then he thought about Angela and how, when he was seeing her on something close to a daily basis, he had been so carried away by it all that he became in his mind's eye a very different figure to the one he saw when he looked in the mirror. Angela had a classic young English woman's body, firm shoulders and breasts, a slim waist, long legs. He had a classic middle-aged lawyer's body, and yet somehow it had worked between them.

He realised he was allowing Angela to occupy too much of his mind. He needed to think bike again. What a wonderful outcome it would be if he genuinely got into cycling, became fit and lost weight, and managed to make Celia happy as she witnessed an unhealthy addiction being replaced by one she could live with.

He put on his trainers, and wondered whether he should have bought proper cycling shoes with cleats to click into the pedals. On Freddie's advice, he had decided against getting them at this stage. Freddie had said it was best to get used to the bike first, get to know the roads. Cleats became one of Matthew's ambitions for the future, like fidelity.

He ran downstairs, relieved that Celia smiled rather than laughed when she saw him. He showed her the bike, and explained how the computer on the handlebars worked, demonstrated the gears. She walked with him to the front door, where he put on his shiny silver helmet and his wraparound cycling glasses, which Freddie had explained were as much to keep dirt, flying objects and insects out of his eyes as to block out the sun. He was excited at the prospect of cycling so fast that he could catch insects in his eyes.

'Here goes then,' he said, manoeuvering himself on to the bike. 'I'll just go up and down the road for a bit to get used to the gears.' Celia waved him off. He must have looked impossibly large as he perched on the tiny saddle and he could sense Celia shared his worry that he would fall off. But the moment he turned into the road, he felt he was beginning a great new adventure. He didn't have a clue where he was going, or how far, and it took him a while to figure out the gears. But within minutes, he was loving it. The sun was on his back, cold air was blowing into his face. He felt free. He felt young. Hills were hard, but he soon learned to go into the lowest possible gear and just 'twiddle' – it had been Freddie's phrase – his way back to the flat. Cars were scary, but if he stayed a couple of feet out from the kerb, the cars might not like it but they pulled out to give him room. He found himself being overtaken several times by other cyclists, but he consoled himself with the thought that they were half his age with ten times his experience, and vowed that one day he would overtake more than overtook him.

Only once, on a particularly steep climb through a nearby village, did he get out of breath, but he just turned round and freewheeled back down the hill, taking an easier, longer route home. He put the bike in the garage and went upstairs to have a shower. He'd worked up a mild sweat, his legs were tired, and his arms ached a little from all the vibrations on the road, but once he'd washed and got dressed, he felt a glow every bit as warm as the one which followed sex with Madeleine. With time, he was sure it would match the post-Angela glow too.

15

It was mid morning before Sturrock finally managed to set off for the village of Coldicote to see his mother. Despite the fact that it must have been evident he was so tired he could hardly get out of bed, Stella had sent him to the supermarket first thing to buy some bits and pieces for Jack's birthday lunch the next day. He really resented the way she set him little tasks on Saturday morning. It was her way of indicating that she didn't think he made a sufficient contribution to domestic life. She knew he was usually exhausted on Saturdays, but nevertheless she always made her point, getting him to clean the car, trim the hedge, mow the lawn. He felt worn down by it. 'Can't she see,' he said to himself as he turned onto the North Circular from the Chiswick Roundabout, 'that far from bringing me closer to the family, it drives me away?' He occasionally thought about saying so, but he could never face it.

He visited his mother in her care home once a week, partly out of duty, and a genuine fondness for her, but also as a way of getting out of the house for a good chunk of the weekend. Stella and his mother had never really got on, so Stella rarely came with him, unless it was a special occasion. On his mother's last birthday, they'd taken her a present and a cake which Stella had bought at Marks & Spencer, but then taken out of the packaging and put in an old baking tin.

On a good day, it would take him just over an hour to get to the Grosvenor Vale Home for the Elderly, seven or eight miles from his childhood home in Hitchin. Every week, he said to himself he would go and take a look at their old house, but he never did.

He would often stop for a coffee on the way, and another on the way back, and with the hour he spent with his mother while he was there, he could eat up a very substantial part of the day. This morning, however, he decided to drive straight to the home. He was eager to get the visit over with, nervous about telling his mother about Aunt Jessica, and how she would react.

As he picked up speed on the A1, he wondered if the sight of his mother, and the inevitable talk of death and memories of the past, might turn his worsening mood into something more serious, sending him off into a plunge. Yet even as he wondered, he reflected how, usually, if he predicted that a specific event would cause a plunge, the plunge never came. Or if it did, it came later, when he was not expecting it.

He hoped his mother would be in her room when he got there, not downstairs where the old people sat for part of the day in a semi-circle, chairs pointed towards some inane daytime TV programme. He couldn't bear to see her just staring at the TV, occasionally looking round when she heard some of the other residents laughing at what the presenter was saying, she a woman whose intellect he had always admired, and who had taught him so much. The chances were she would be downstairs though, as it would be close to midday by the time he arrived, and they liked to get them down for lunch if they were mobile.

He parked behind a builder's van, walked in to the smell of old age, cleaning fluids and institutional cooking, signed himself in and took the lift to the third floor. Even though he suspected she would be in the ground-floor main lounge, not in her room, he was letting his hopes take him where they led him. As he walked down the corridor to her room, he bumped into her being wheeled towards the lift.

'Oh, look who's here, Sheila,' said one of the nurses. 'It's your little lad Martin.' His mother's head was lolling forward and sideways, but she managed to straighten a little and there was at least the hint of a smile when she saw him.

'That's nice, isn't it, Sheila?' said the nurse, who spoke very loudly and very slowly, as if, thought Sturrock, she was speaking to a deaf child. He didn't much like the home, or the staff, but he could hardly criticise. They looked after his mother every day of the week, which was more than he did. Shortly after his father died, he had suggested to Stella they build a granny-flat extension in Chiswick, but Stella rightly said she would end up looking after Sheila because he would be busy looking after his patients, and it wasn't fair to expect *her* to look after *his* mother.

'I'll tell you what, Sheila,' the nurse went on. 'It's about forty minutes to lunch so why don't we wheel you back to your room? That way, you and Martin can have a nice chat, and then he can bring you down for lunch with your friends.'

'Allow me,' said Sturrock, taking the handles of the wheelchair.

Back in her room, he wasn't sure whether to lift her out of her wheelchair into the worn velveteen armchair in which she spent most of her waking time. It seemed a lot of effort.

'Shall I put you back in your chair?' he asked, hoping she would say no. She didn't answer. 'Perhaps best to leave you where you are, then, rather than lift you out now only to have to lift you back again when you go downstairs for lunch.'

When he told her, quite matter-of-factly, that Aunt Jessica had died, she remained impassive, so it was difficult to know what she felt. That had always been the problem with his mother, he thought. She didn't like to betray her feelings. Perhaps it had been a reaction to living with his father, who tended to seize on any display of emotion as a sign of weakness. Whatever the reason, it had always annoyed him. He'd wanted to have a mother who laughed and cried, rather than one who met all events, be they happy or sad, with the same measured attitude. 'I'm going to become a psychiatrist, Mum.' 'If you think it's the right thing to do, that's fine.' 'I've just been appointed a government adviser.' 'Well, I'm sure you've worked hard for it.' 'I fell out with Aunt Jessica because she sided with Dad when we had an argument, and I knew she actually agreed with me.' 'Oh, Martin, there really is no point falling out over that!' She had been a fiercely intelligent woman and he knew she felt things deeply, she just never let him in.

'Simon said it was a release in the end,' he said. 'She had been getting very confused, and he said she was suddenly very weak.'

His mother nodded, and gave him a little smile.

'You're still here though,' he said, picking up on what the smile and the watery eyes were trying to tell him.

'Still here,' she said. 'Just.'

'You'll be here a while yet,' he said.

There was a fairly long lull before he said, 'The funeral is on Tuesday, in Somerset. I don't suppose you can go, what do you think?'

He was conscious of loading the question in a manner designed to illicit the reaction he was hoping for, namely that she would say she was not strong enough to travel, as it would complicate his day even more if he had to take her.

'I should go,' she said. 'I think it would mean a lot to your father.'

Even accepting his disappointment at the answer, Sturrock felt dubious that his mother's attendance at the funeral would have meant anything much to his father, who had shown little regard for Aunt Jessica when she was alive. His mother was doing what everyone did when confronted with death, saying what she thought she ought to say. It was the same sentiment that had led to the glowing tributes made to his father on his death. Martin had read them all, including the obituary in *The Times*. He hardly recognised the man they described. They set out places he had lived, jobs he had done, professional achievements, but said nothing about what kind of person he was. The only reference to his family was in the final sentence of the little piece in *The Times*: '*He is survived by his widow Sheila, and a son and daughter.*' That was it. George Sturrock's contribution to a new style of bridge in Morocco, which had a whole paragraph, was deemed more important than his life as a husband and a father. Yet as people came up to him at the funeral, touched his arm and said how sorry they were, and he nodded in silent appreciation of their sentiments, they were doing so because they assumed he was feeling the deep loss of someone he loved and who loved him in return. In truth, he was feeling the deep loss of a love there had never really been. When ordering the headstone, his mother asked that they put 'engineer, husband, father'. At one point, Jan suggested putting 'loving' before husband and father, but he and his mother felt it wouldn't flow. 'Engineer, loving husband and father' sounded awkward. And you couldn't say 'loving' before 'engineer'. So 'loving' was dropped, and he had felt pleased at that. George Sturrock was indeed an engineer, a husband and father. They were facts. He was not loving, at least not till the end, when, in Sturrock's mind, he had demonstrated affection merely in the hope he would get a late pass to Paradise rather than Hell and damnation.

His mother looked tired now, and her head was beginning to fall to her chest. He knew it wouldn't be long before her funeral too. He loved her much more than he had ever loved his father. Yet he doubted he would shed as many tears as he had then.

The thought of his father's grave aroused in him a fresh wave of anxiety about the eulogy he was supposed to deliver on Tuesday. He had spent his professional career helping people to see the best in themselves and yet he had difficulty seeing the best in Aunt Jessica. For years, he had loved her, perhaps as the emotional mother he never had. One lunchtime argument had changed that for ever. Ever since, she had seemed to him a weak woman – someone who pretended to have independence of spirit but was in fact as awed as the rest of them by his father's bullying authority.

Downstairs, he could hear the bell ringing, announcing that lunch was ready. He wheeled his mother towards the lift, longing to be back in the car, alone.

16

Ralph Hall was feeling very pleased with himself as the train pulled into Newcastle station, and he stepped on to the platform, virtually sober. Throughout the three-hour journey, he had managed to limit himself to a couple of the tiny bottles of white wine from the complimentary drinks trolley which, taken as an accompaniment to a late breakfast of scrambled eggs and smoked salmon, seemed to have gone unnoticed by his fellow passengers. For the first hour of the journey, he ploughed through a boxful of paperwork. Once the effects of his hangover had worn off, he whizzed through it, congratulating himself on the speed with which he was able to dispatch work. Over the years, he had developed a fairly acute sense of what was important and what was not simply from glancing at the paperwork. Like people, some papers looked more important than others. He sometimes felt bad when he dismissed a complicated position paper in a matter of seconds. He would skim-read it before rushing to the final paragraph in bold at the end, which would ask him to make a decision, yes or no, agree or disagree, and he would tick or circle and move on. His box also contained letters whose authors had agonised over every word, thinking deeply, consulting widely, and then sending them off with enormous hope in their hearts that he would agree with their proposal or argument, or accept their invitation to speak at the event they were planning. Yet such letters often came to the minister with a squiggled one-line interpretation and recommendation at the top, penned by a private secretary, and Ralph would tick yes or no and that was that. He was rushing more than usual today because he also had his homework from Professor Sturrock which he was determined to get done before the weekend was out.

Professor Sturrock had asked him to write two separate lists, one on the left-hand side of the page, the other on the right. On the left-hand side, he had to write sentences beginning 'I want'. On the right, sentences beginning 'I need'. They did not have to be obvious pairs. Indeed, he could write five successive wants for every need if he so chose, though the Professor said it was probably best to aim for a similar number of each. He told him not to rule out anything that came into his mind. 'I want world peace' was no more or less important, to the psychiatrist, than 'I need a bar of chocolate'.

The carriage was less than half full, and Ralph had managed to get a table to himself, so once his box was done, and his scrambled eggs played with and pushed to one side, he settled down to it.

He took out his A4 pad and drew a reasonably straight line down the middle of the page. He wrote a small w on the left of the page, a small n on the right. Professor Sturrock had told him he must put down his thoughts as they came, but Ralph was not happy with the first want that came into his head – 'I want to be Prime Minister.' He looked out of the window. A farmer was leaning against a tractor, drawing on a cigarette. The farmer was gone. Will I ever see that farmer again? he asked himself. Probably not. As the green fields sped by, he wondered how many of them belonged to the farmer he had seen. Or perhaps he was a mere labourer, paid a lowly wage to tend the land and do the farmer's bidding.

Ralph forced his gaze back to the A4 pad. He realised he was deliberately turning his mind away from the task in hand as a way of avoiding dealing with the simple fact that, when he began to analyse his needs and wants, 'I want to be Prime Minister' was the first thing that came to mind. He wondered about starting again, so that he would not have to deal with Professor Sturrock making too much of such a clear and unequivocal statement, but then the Professor's words came back into his mind: 'It's important to be honest, and to be open to whatever comes in. If you're not honest and open, we'll be wasting our time.'

He looked around him for one last check that nobody could see what he was writing, and committed the thought to paper. 'I want to be Prime Minister.' Nothing wrong with that, he thought. Plenty of people in Parliament thought he might be up to it. Every now and then, his name popped up in media speculation, albeit usually towards the end of a fairly long list. His son told him the bookies had him at 33–1, but that was before the new man came in, and he would have lengthened by now.

If that was the first want to come into his head, the first need was a toss-up between two thoughts that filtered into his head at roughly the same time. There was no chequered flag inside the mind to tell him for sure which came first, no video replay of his mental processes to give him absolute definitive proof. So he had to work it out for himself. It was a close call between 'I need to keep busy' and 'I need to drink'. OK, he thought, I cannot be one hundred per cent sure which came in first, but I can at least reflect on which carries more weight, or holds the greater truth. 'I need to keep busy.' That was true. He had always been a busy character. At university, he was involved not just in student politics, but sport and amateur dramatics. His ministerial life was a busy one, long hours with myriad different issues and situations to deal with. Was it a want or a need? 'I want to keep busy.' Was that true? Yes, it probably was. 'I need to keep busy.' Probably, yes. He wrote them both down, on either side of the page.

The question now was whether 'I need to drink' came on top of 'I need to keep busy' or whether he could honestly put it second. He scribbled on a separate piece of paper, 'I need to be busy every day,' and alongside it, 'I need to drink every day.' There was, sadly, he realised, no contest. The second of those statements was the truer. He wrote 'I need to drink' at the top of his need list. 'I want to be Prime Minister' sat oddly opposite 'I need to drink' but both were true.

Even as the thoughts were coming and going, he had Martin Sturrock inside his mind. He was not simply thinking the thoughts but analysing what the Professor might make of them and what he might do with them. What the Professor would love to see, he was sure, was 'I want to stop drinking' and 'I need to stop drinking'. He could do need on that one, but could he do want? Did he really *want* to stop drinking? Not really. He wrote down 'I need to stop drinking' below 'I need to be busy'. Two out of his first three needs related to drink. He wrote another: 'I need to face up to my problems.' Professor Sturrock would like that one.

He was short on the want side, so he slid his mind and his pen to the left half of the page. 'I want to live for a very long time' popped into his head, so he wrote it down. His mind took him back to the need to stop drinking. If he wanted to live for a long time, he definitely needed to stop drinking. He wondered about drawing a dotted line between the two so he could remember the thought when he saw the Professor, but it was such an obvious connection, it didn't seem worth it.

His first want spoke to ambition, his second to the longevity of his own life. What about others?

'I want a good marriage,' he wrote. Was that true? Was that up there with his political career and his desire to live to an old age? Yes, it was. But was it a good marriage he needed, or was it Sandie? 'I need Sandie,' he wrote, but it looked a little pathetic. He started to cross it out and replace Sandie with 'a good marriage', but that felt a bit harsh, even though she had annoyed him by being away longer than she had intended, so he made it 'I need Sandie / strong marriage'.

'I want the children to be happy and fulfilled.'

Did he need that too? Well, yes, but not in the same way as he wanted it. Instead, he wrote, 'I need to know the children feel they are part of a family.' That didn't look right, or feel right. He crossed it out. He would come back to the children.

'I need holidays.'

'I want holidays.' Trivial. Cross it out.

But was it so trivial? No, put it back. 'I need to get proper rest.' 'I want more holidays.'

'I want a drink.' He crossed it out. He had a drink, so what was the point of that one? But he did want a drink. The drink was sitting

there and he wanted to lift it to his lips and there was nothing wrong
with that because it was afternoon now and it was hardly the end of
the world if he had a tiny bottle of railway-trolley white wine. It
would only count as WW1 or maybe 2 in his drink diary. He lifted the
glass to his lips and sipped the white wine. Did it change the way he
felt? He didn't think so. Did it make him want to empty the whole
glass down his throat and then order another one when the pretty
Polish girl with the trolley came by again? Not really. So what was
the big deal? The big deal was that in many moments of most days,
he wanted a drink and he felt he needed a drink. He had to acknowledge that. He couldn't run away from it. He wrote, 'I want a drink,
too often.' 'I need a drink, too often.' He wrote, 'I want to stop
drinking', but it wasn't true, so he crossed it out. He wondered if
Professor Sturrock could live with 'I would like to stop drinking', but
he had been pretty clear. This was a want/need list, and it was the
definitive nature of the statements he was required to make that
would help the Professor do something with the information.

Two more linked thoughts came into his mind, and he wrote
them down. 'I want to increase my majority.' 'I need to spend more
time in the constituency.' Then two more, which at first he thought
were linked, but then realised perhaps they weren't. 'I want Sandie
to be happy.' 'I need Sandie to be at home more.'

'I need more sleep.'

'I need more exercise.'

'I want to be more appreciated than I am.'

'I need to be more appreciated than I am.'

Now he was motoring, and needs and wants were coming in at
all angles.

'I want to be happier than I am.'

'I want a new private secretary.'

'I need a new private secretary.'

The children filtered back in.

'I want the children to stay in touch more.'

'I want to be a grandfather.' Was that true? Kind of. But totally,
a real want? Not really. He crossed it out.

'I need new challenges.' Like what? Don't know, but I do. Keep it.

'I need more big moments, less grind and routine.' Definitely.

'I want to make more of a difference to the Health Service.' Really? Yes.

'I want to be able to relax more.'

'I need to relax more.'

But his career came to the fore once more.

'I need to widen my circle of support.'

'I need to improve my operation.'

He looked out of the window again, and sat back. He felt tired. He had been poking around in his own innards and it had taken more out of him than he anticipated. At least he had broken the back of the job. He would have another think about it tomorrow. He hoped Professor Sturrock would be pleased with him. As he surveyed his list, it was perfectly clear what he needed to do if he was to have a chance of his wants happening. And that was to stop drinking. He downed the last of the Sauvignon, and told himself he would have no more until mid-afternoon at the earliest, but when the Polish girl with the trolley came back from her journey through standard class, he helped himself to the last little bottle. He had done a lot of work, he had almost finished his homework for Professor Sturrock, so he thought he deserved it.

17

The voice on the warehouse tannoy was muffled, as ever, but David heard it clearly enough, and felt it, like a blow delivered straight to the guts.

'David Temple to Packing Station 15. David Temple to Packing Station 15.'

He had been at work for an hour. When he arrived, he had a few packages to take to sport and leisure, a batch of letters for the postroom, but was then able to hide away behind a pile of cardboard boxes hoping no one would notice him. The tannoy message was the call he'd been dreading, because Packing Station 15 was Amanda's. He had no choice but to face her.

The morning had begun badly. If Friday had started with a seven-out-of-ten dead feeling, today it was closer to nine out of ten. It had been a struggle to force himself out of bed, then get his mind in some kind of working order, finish his breakfast without exploding at his mum, then get to work. He knew he was in for a bollocking, having failed to turn up yesterday afternoon after his appointment at the hospital, but he just had to face it. They were fairly used to him missing Fridays, but if he missed Saturday too, he might get another warning letter.

Amanda and Professor Sturrock were dominating his every waking thought. As he brushed his teeth, he wondered if he had been wrong to tell the Professor about her. At the time of telling him, he'd felt a little better, but this morning he was less sure.

Maybe it was his own fault for taking so long to tell him, but he didn't feel Professor Sturrock had given him much by way of advice on how to cope with Amanda's rejection. Normally, the doctor was great at coming up with strategies for facing down the problems that David took to him, even if David wasn't always capable of implementing them. But yesterday, all he'd done was give him a book by some American professor of psychiatry, and ask him to read it. David had started looking at the book on the tube home, but could see no relevance to his current needs.

It was all about training your mind to think as you wanted it to, so that negative thoughts could be parked and positive thoughts brought to the fore. Professor Sturrock had told him that once you got through the American style and the over-the-top claims the author made for himself, there were some really interesting thoughts in there, particularly about death, and the importance of death to the process of life. He wanted David to focus on the death chapter for his homework, and do the little exercise on the final page.

The American professor said that, as we go through life, we should not fear death but know that one day it will come, and be ready for it. He also said we should think about how we want to be seen by others when we die and allow that to influence how we live when we're alive. He said it was good to imagine our own funeral, think about who we would like to come, what hymns and readings we wanted, who we thought should deliver the eulogy and what we hoped they would say. Beneath the text was a little drawing of a headstone. It was a simple design, rounded at the top, with the words 'Here lies . . .' written across it and then a gap for a name, and a tribute. A note beneath it read, '*Exercise 19. Fill in above as if it's your gravestone. Do not worry about space. Write as much as you like but try to imagine the words that best describe how you'd like to be remembered.*' And then, with a further irritating reminder that the author was American: '*And please, guys, no false modesty.*'

The book had annoyed David, because he couldn't understand why Professor Sturrock had chosen this particular moment to give it to him. Usually he felt he could see the reasoning behind the doctor's homework tasks. But not this time. He wondered whether Professor Sturrock had actually been responding to their session of a week ago, when he'd talked about feeling dead inside, and had not really been listening when David talked about Amanda. How on earth was an exercise about his own death the appropriate response to an experience of rejection as bad as the one he suffered on Thursday?

All of Friday evening David had felt weighed down by rare feelings of anger towards the doctor, but now, hiding away in his corner, he tried to find a way out of the blackness he was feeling. Perhaps Professor Sturrock had just been having a bad day, he thought. It was possible. After all, he was only human, the same as everyone else. He told himself to try to imagine what a Sturrock on a good day, an on-form day, would have suggested. He was pretty sure the Professor would think that David saw in Amanda someone who could look after him as his mother tried to, but without all the irritation and with a sexual element added to the relationship. He would also think that Amanda's rejection reinforced the feelings he had deep inside him as a result of the rejection by his father. He was always tracing things back to his father running off. Why hadn't he said so this time then?

As to how David should react when he saw Amanda again, he suspected Professor Sturrock would advise him to be pleasant, try to be as they were before he had felt the little spark between them, and rebuild the friendship if he could. He wondered if the Professor had ever been rejected.

Rebuild the friendship. That's what he wanted to do, but it seemed impossibly difficult. That was why he wanted to hide away in his dusty little corner. But he knew he couldn't stay there all day, and now he'd got the call to go to Packing Station 15, he would have to decide for himself, without Professor Sturrock's direct advice.

Amanda worked from a waist-high metal desk where she could sit if doing paperwork, or stand, as now, if she was organising shipments of goods to leave the building. She looked up as David approached, pushing a large trolley with an empty canvas bag. He worried that the bag wouldn't be big enough to take the dozen or so packages she had ready for him. It might mean two visits. A week ago, that would have been a cause of some excitement. Today, it made him feel even more anxious.

'Hi, David, how are things?' She too was trying to behave as though nothing had happened, but it was clear she was tense.

'OK,' he said.

'How was the shrink yesterday?' A few days ago, he would have seen this as nothing more than a friendly enquiry, an indication of how close they had become. Today, it felt like an insult. 'Shrink' showed a lack of respect, to him and to Professor Sturrock. He just nodded.

'We talked about you,' he said.

'My God. I don't know whether to be flattered or worried.' Again, he didn't like the tone. There was the tiniest hint of mockery in 'My God', and the use of the word 'worried', he felt, was designed to convey the idea that she was sane and he was not.

'You shouldn't be either of those things,' he said. 'Just that I always tell him the good and bad in my week, so you came up.'

'Oh.' There was a pause. 'Good or bad?' she asked.

'Both. In that order, I suppose.' She flicked her head back in a way that he read as indicating that she wanted the conversation to end. But he was determined to try and make up with her.

'Why did you do that?'

'Do what?'

'Flick back your head like you just did.'

'I didn't know I had.'

'Yes, you went like that,' and he flicked back his head, much further than she had, but he also added in a little curl of the upper lip.

She laughed. 'I didn't do that. I was just like, I don't know, you said what you said and I just . . . Don't worry about it. It meant nothing.'

'What meant nothing? What you did . . .'

'Yes.'

'Or you and me, what we were?'

Amanda frowned. 'David, there was no you and me,' she said.

'Oh, I see. What's that supposed to mean?'

He could tell she was beginning to lose her patience, but he couldn't let it go. He knew that, if they didn't resolve things now, there was a danger he would walk out of the warehouse and never come back. That would be that. No job. And, more importantly, no more Amanda. Even after being rejected, he wasn't sure he could face that.

Amanda spoke very slowly, as if she were talking to an idiot. 'David, it is not meant to mean anything beyond what it says. You say "you and me" like we were an item, a couple, boyfriend and girl-friend. It was never like that, and I'm really sorry if you think I did anything to make you think it was. OK?'

'So not even a friendship?'

'Look, David, I've got lots of friends, right. You're different. You're a workmate. I felt sorry for you.'

He looked intently at her lips as she spoke. He had so hoped to kiss them. But now he saw them not as objects of beauty and desire but purveyors of the bad feelings she had for him. Words were leaping from them, each one hurting, every syllable hurting, reminding him of how foolish he had been to think she might have liked him.

She realised she was making things worse not better.

'Come on, David. We've both got work to do. You take those packages. I've got another order to get ready.'

As he packed the boxes into the canvas bag, he made a mental note to record this as his worst moment of the day, the moment he realised she had complete contempt for him, the same as all the rest. And he would tell Professor Sturrock it was fucking obvious what he would write on his headstone: 'Here lies David Temple, a loser – in life, in love, in everything.'

18

Emily sat down in her favourite chair and studied the box of raisins in her hand. Her anger at Professor Sturrock had been intense through yesterday afternoon, and lingered all evening, but she had woken up regretting that she'd been so confrontational. She felt bad about herself, bad that she had possibly made him feel he was to blame for her sense of utter hopelessness that anything was ever going to get better.

She thought it might somehow help to make amends if she finally did the exercise he'd set as her homework a couple of weeks before.

'When you next go to Sami's corner shop,' he'd told her, 'I want you to buy a little box of Sun-Maid raisins. Take the box home, and really spend some time looking at it, feeling it, thinking about it. Then I want you to look even more closely at the raisins inside. I don't want you to eat them until you've really, really looked at them. And I want you to record what you think.'

It seemed an odd exercise, and she felt nervous as she turned the little box over in her hand. Her worry was that if she got nothing out of it, then she would lose even more faith in Professor Sturrock's ability to help. And yet she so wanted to trust him, as she had done in the beginning. She remembered how reassuring she'd found his manner, when he first visited her at her parents' house in Hendon. She was so impressed, moved even, that he'd understood how scared she was about venturing into town, and agreed to travel all the way out from central London to see her. She'd liked his crinkly forehead and his kind hazel eyes, and the long thick lines on his face that gave him a look of wisdom. He didn't make false promises, or try to minimise what had happened to her. He didn't make any effort to say it was going to be easy. On the contrary, he emphasised how awful it was to have suffered as she did, and how that suffering would only ease, never fully go away, but he wanted her to try to help him ease it for her. She'd appreciated the way he looked her full in the face, rather than focusing his eyes on her undamaged side. After a few home visits, she finally felt able to travel to the hospital in her mother's car. The Friday sessions went well at first, and she felt safe and confident in his care. But over the following months, she'd begun to doubt him. Every week she would make the excruciating journey into town and most weeks she came home feeling just as bad.

Moving into her new flat hadn't helped. Professor Sturrock had seen it as a big step forward towards a new life, but, for Emily, it was just a reminder of everything she had lost. The flat was on the first floor of a modern apartment block just off the Caledonian Road. She'd chosen it partly because the building had a fire escape, but it felt impersonal and cold, unlike the characterful place she'd lived in before, on the top floor of a tall Victorian terraced house in Hackney with a great view over London. But the Hackney house had turned out to be a fire trap. The investigation into the cause of the fire had proved inconclusive, but Emily was convinced that it had been started by the man in the flat below, who was a heavy smoker. He'd fallen asleep in front of the TV. His wife had been woken by the smell of smoke and they'd both got out before the fire spread. Emily was asleep in her bedroom at the back of the house, oblivious to the shouts of people down in the street below, or the stones they were throwing at the window. As she was a relatively new tenant, none of the other occupants had her telephone number. By the time she was finally woken by the sound of fire-engine sirens, the staircase was ablaze.

She threw on a dressing gown and shoes, then went out to the top of the stairs. The stairwell was filled with smoke and below her she could hear the crackling of flames. She felt paralysed. There was no way she could climb or jump down from the window of her flat. The only way out was through the fire. She took a chunk of dressing gown, held it in front of her mouth, closed her eyes and raced as fast as she could down the stairs and out of the open front door. Halfway down she was conscious of her hair and her clothes being on fire. She kept running. The worst damage was done when a huge lump of burning plastic, part of the low-budget new roof recently put in by the landlord, landed on the side of her face and shoulder. As she reached the street, the small crowd gathered outside began to scream and it was clear they were screaming at the sight of her, flames running down her side. She fell to the ground, rolled around on the floor as people rushed to try to help her. She was coughing and choking and could vaguely hear someone shouting, 'Lungs, lungs.'

An ambulance was there in minutes. She knew from the panic in the paramedic's eyes that her life had changed forever. Though she was sedated, the pain was worse than anything she had ever known or imagined. She touched the side of her head where her hair had been burnt to a crinkly stubble. She looked at her lower arm. It resembled the remains of a half-eaten pizza. Although she tried to concentrate on the fact that she was alive, she was safe, her mind kept flashing towards the future, a future in which she would never look the same.

In the following months she lost her teaching job, her boyfriend and with him, she feared, her hopes of raising a family; she lost her home, her sight in one eye, and, at times, her will to live. She had first-, second- and third-degree burns. At least she had heard of those. The specialist had to explain to her what fourth- and fifth-degree burns were, when he told her she had suffered them, and it meant that some of the muscle in her arm was irretrievably lost.

When finally she was released from hospital, she felt none of the joy that people going home are supposed to feel. Unable to face going back to Hackney, she went to live with her parents until she worked out what to do with her future. They tried their best to give her the love and emotional support she needed. But it wasn't easy. Whatever she felt about herself – whether it be anger, fear, or self-pity – they felt part or all of those emotions for themselves and on her behalf. She lived with the physical pain and disfigurement. They shared the mental load, but they also added to it. That was why eventually she decided she wanted to live on her own again. She knew the pressure she was adding to their lives by staying, even if she was adding to her own pressures by leaving. Her moods were like a dead weight around the house.

She knew her parents were good people, but they were not up to the task of helping her through this. She had decided to put her faith in Professor Sturrock as the man to do that. Which is why recent weeks had been so frustrating, but also why she was so cross with herself for being rude to him yesterday, and determined to complete all the homework tasks today.

Emily placed the box of raisins face up on her knee. It was one of six she'd bought at Sami's shop a few days ago. The exercise required just one box, but they were so small she worried Sami would think it odd to buy one, so she put half a dozen into her basket, along with the other groceries.

The box was about one and a half inches long, an inch wide and half an inch deep. It was predominantly red. In the top half was a picture of a red-hatted, brown-haired, red-lipped young woman carrying a huge bowl of grapes. Behind her and encircling her was a picture of the sun. Sun-Maid. It was the kind of picture celebrated as Art in totalitarian states where the virtues of working people were extolled as a matter of cultural policy. The woman looked a little like Emily before the fire. Perhaps that was why Professor Sturrock had asked her to do this. Then she looked more closely. The woman wasn't so like her after all. Beneath the picture were three lines of writing. First, in big yellow letters, SUN-MAID. Then, on the second line, smaller, in white, NATURAL CALIFORNIA. Then, bigger than the California writing but smaller than SUN-MAID, the single word, also in white, RAISINS. The back of the box was identical. On the top and bottom of the box, NATURAL CALIFORNIA was dropped. There, it said simply SUN-MAID and, on the line below, RAISINS. The sides of the box had the same message, though the shape of the box meant the two words could run together on the same line. On one side, beneath SUN-MAID RAISINS, was the message 'For nutrition information, write to Sun-Maid growers of California, Department R, 13525 S. Bethel Avenue, Kingsburg, CA 93631, USA'. So this tiny box came from America. She wondered where the raisins themselves came from, when they were picked, how many different processes they had been through, how far they had travelled.

The box was well made. Though small, it felt solid. The flaps into top and bottom were firmly inserted. She rolled it around in her hand for a while. If there was such a thing as a cardboard box nice to the touch, this was it. She was hoping this was the kind of reaction Professor Sturrock would be looking for. His whole thrust with her seemed to be encouragement to see good in things she had previously never noticed.

She flicked open the top with her thumb. There was no internal packaging, no plastic or cellophane, which pleased her. Just the raisins, tightly packed. The raisins at the top were all dark brown, though two looked closer to black. They all had a very wrinkled look, but on some there were gaps between the folds, while on others one wrinkle ran into another, so the wrinkles took up more space than the gaps between them. One in particular reminded her of her skin where the burning had been particularly intense and the scarring severe. She took one of the raisins out and rolled it between her thumb and forefinger. Not only did the raisin as a whole change shape, but the wrinkles took on a different form too. She placed the reshaped raisin in the palm of her hand. It looked like an angry old man with a mop of hair and a big bushy beard. She shook her hand so that it rolled to a different position. Now it looked like a dead fly. She shook her hand again. It looked like a log lying in the hearth of a fireplace.

She poured the contents of the box onto her lap, and then counted the raisins one by one, laying them in a line on her right leg as she counted. There were thirty-four. She looked at them for a long time, as Professor Sturrock had asked her to. They weren't exactly pretty but they were interesting. Each one looked slightly different to the next. Every time she moved one, even by a couple of millimetres, it took on a different look.

She picked up the smallest one and put it into her mouth. There was no real taste until she bit into it and then a juice started to form which softened the texture and meant eating it became more pleasing as she continued to bite it into ever tinier pieces. There was a short aftertaste which made her want to eat another. Just as they had looked different, so they felt different on the tongue and tasted different. She saved the biggest for last. She let it rest on her tongue for a few seconds, and reshaped it with her teeth without biting into it. Depending on where in her mouth she put it, it had a very different feel. When she bit through it with her top middle teeth, the juice was sweet and if she moved her tongue she could take the sweetness to different parts of her mouth. She ate the residue in a kind of shredding motion and forced the juice to the back of her throat before swallowing.

She flicked the box closed again and started to jot down what she had thought, as Professor Sturrock had instructed. Her main point was that every single raisin was different. She concluded by writing, 'If every raisin can be different, so can every living thing.' Was she simply saying that because she thought it was what Professor Sturrock wanted to hear? Perhaps, but somehow, looking at the raisins had made the idea feel more real.

She stood up and went into the kitchen to make herself a cup of tea. She could sense a shift in her mood, a lightness that came from having done something she thought would gain Professor Sturrock's approval. At the same session, he had suggested she go for a walk in daylight. She'd dismissed the suggestion when he made it, but the raisins exercise had left her feeling more settled and more emboldened. She looked out of the window. It was one of those rare autumn days of bright sun. Perhaps she should go out now. If she went out in the light, there would be no hiding place, she knew that, but maybe she could deal with whoever and whatever was out there. She recalled how scared she used to be when, as a child, she jumped into the water at the Finchley Lido, where her father taught her to swim, and then how much she loved it when the initial shock had subsided and her body grew used to the cold water. She felt that fear now, but perhaps, like the cold water, it wouldn't be so bad after she made that initial leap.

She wrapped her headscarf tight around her face, put on her jacket and set off.

19

An accident on the A1 South reduced the motorway to one lane each way, and it took Sturrock almost two hours before he was back in the Chiswick area. Even with the delay, though, he couldn't face going back home straight away, so stopped at a little coffee shop near Gunnersbury station. He was killing time.

There were eleven tables in the café. Three were empty. Seven were taken by families or groups of friends. He was the only one there who was alone. He ordered a coffee and a tuna sandwich, and went to sit down. At the table next to him, a couple with a young child in a pram were talking about whether to go to the swings, or whether to go home. The man wanted to go to the swings. The woman thought it was too cold. At the table behind him were two married couples dressed for a long walk. The men were looking at a map, and plotting their route. Their wives were talking about who was doing what and who was going where at Christmas. One of them had a dispute with her sister as to which of them would have their mother. So far as he could tell, both the sisters actively wanted the mother to be with them, which was nice, he supposed. He wondered where the mother wanted to be. Dead, possibly. That was when he knew he was on the verge of a plunge, possibly even well into it. Such a tiny trigger for his thoughts to turn to death.

As the Eastern European waitress brought over his coffee, he felt close to being overwhelmed by the sense of solitude that had been growing all day. He had been with his mother, but had wanted to get away from her. He was heading home to his wife, but didn't want to get there. He was dreading the visit from his son tomorrow, because he was sure it would go wrong, no matter how hard he tried. All around him was the noise of families and friends enjoying their weekend, but not his family, not his friends. By the time his sandwich arrived, he was lost in thoughts about Stella, and whether there was any hope for their marriage.

When he met her, almost forty years ago, Stella had been a bright, exuberant young medical student, hoping one day to follow in her father's footsteps and become a general practitioner. They first encountered each other one Tuesday morning coming out of a lecture. He wasn't looking where he was going, bumped into her, and amid all the mumbling and stumbling that followed, they agreed to go for a cup of tea. Both were finding it more difficult to be away from home than they had admitted to anyone else. They became friends quickly, lovers more slowly, and married in their final year of studies. But marriage was followed swiftly by one child, then another, both girls. Stella was thinking about getting back into medicine when she became pregnant again, and their only son was born. By the time Jack had reached primary-school age, she feared medicine had passed her by. She resented it, and at times resented the seemingly effortless rise her husband was making through the ranks of the medical establishment. Even before he graduated, he was being talked about as the best of his generation. It came as something of a shock to his fellow medical students when he opted to specialise in psychiatry, but he felt his strengths lent themselves well to a branch of medicine he thought to be wrongly regarded as the Cinderella service. He was right. He soon became head of the Department of Psychological Medicine in a leading teaching hospital, the youngest doctor ever to do so. For six years, he ran it brilliantly, before deciding he wanted to concentrate on consulting and research.

Sturrock liked to think he was a skilful and profound observer of human nature. But when it came to his own wife, he had failed to see the effect his success and her sense of imprisonment and disempowerment was having. By the time it all poured out, during a dreadful holiday in North Devon when Jack was five, it had felt almost too late to repair the marriage.

They were staying in a rented cottage. The children had gone to bed and Stella had had a little too much to drink. She laid into him with a venom that he had never imagined her to possess. He had been completely taken aback, as if he were witnessing a completely different person telling him about a life he knew nothing about. In the sour silent days which followed before they could pack up and head home, he realised that Stella had been trying to send him signals about her unhappiness before, but he had always been preoccupied with something else. That was the problem. There was rarely a moment when he wasn't preoccupied with something else or, more accurately, someone else's psychological problems. He had thought Stella understood, that she shared his commitment to the well-being of others, but he had been wrong. Her anger genuinely shocked him.

'All these poor unfortunates coming in to see you,' she'd shouted, 'and you sit and you listen and you tell them what to think and what to do, and they think you're God, so *you* think you're God. You think you know all that goes on within their hearts and minds, but you know nothing about what's going on in mine, because you don't even think about it. I'm just the one who will look after your kids while you're caring for everyone else's. The one who will feed and water you. The one who will occasionally let you screw me because you spend so much of your time talking about sex to your patients you remember you're supposed to want to have sex with your wife.'

Sturrock felt one of his skills as a consulting psychiatrist was an ability to defuse anger, and an ability to respond to anything his patients said. But this was Martin the failing husband and father, not Sturrock the brilliant doctor, and he was clueless as to how to respond. Stella was breathing very heavily, almost hyperventilating, fiddling with the silver cross she always wore on a chain round her neck. She had turned her chair around so that she was now looking across the garden, not at her stunned, confused husband, but still attacking him. 'I'd love to come and hear you talking to your patients. I bet it's hilarious, you with your great wisdom about feelings and families, when your own feelings are locked away, and your own family sometimes wonder if you even exist. Do you sit and listen patiently, nodding sympathetically at all their moans and groans? Well, maybe you should listen a bit to me, and maybe you should listen to the kids and ask them, "Is it true you said to Mummy that I'm never here and I'm always tired when I am here?" Yes, Martin, that's your own son Jack speaking and you have no idea. But every little bit of every patient's life, you listen and you think and you tell them what they can learn from it and how all they need is love. Is that what you tell them? Is it? Well, it's what we need too, Martin, and we don't get it, and it's time you knew it.'

'I'm sorry,' he said. 'I had no idea you felt like this.'

She snorted at him, the snort signalling more clearly than any words her view that it was entirely his fault that she felt as she did, as was the fact that he didn't know about it until now.

He remained silent. He felt that, with her anger so intense, anything he said would provoke it further. He hoped there would be a calm after the storm, and her rage would cool.

He was close to saying something he said often to his patients, namely, 'We cannot change other people, the only person we can change is ourself.' He was even rehearsing in his mind how to say it without it sounding like a criticism, but he concluded that, given her current frame of mind, she would take it badly however he said it.

He recalled the last time he had offered this particular piece of advice to a patient – a depressive named Bernard who was convinced his wife deliberately set out to depress him. Bernard's response had been to ask him to visit his house. 'See for yourself what she's like,' he'd said. 'It's not me that needs to change, it's her.' Sturrock had felt that a home visit wasn't appropriate for the doctor–patient relationship as it stood at that time. Perhaps he was wrong and Bernard was right. Perhaps he should have gone to his house.

'What are you thinking about?' Stella asked, only slightly less accusingly.

He didn't dare tell her he was thinking about one of his patients.

'I'm thinking I should have seen this coming,' he said. 'And I'm thinking I normally know what to say, but right now I don't.'

Almost a quarter-century on, he now realised what a turning point that was, and felt ashamed at his failure to practise what he preached. It hadn't crossed his mind it was he who needed to change. Despite all the hurt, he was sure that, eventually, Stella would see the importance of his work and the sacrifices it entailed.

His tuna sandwich lay on the plate in front of him, untouched. His coffee was almost cold. The two couples he had listened to at the table behind him got up to go, full of purpose as they set off on their walk. He noticed one of the men take the hand of his wife as they left the cafe, and tried to remember the last time he and Stella had held hands. They were in a dreadful, dreadful rut, and neither appeared able to do anything to shake themselves out of it. He tried to imagine what he would say if Martin Sturrock the husband and Stella Sturrock the wife came to see Professor Sturrock the psychiatrist.

What was the problem? The problem was that when they started out together, they were equals, both clever and idealistic, with powerful if unformed ambitions for themselves and, once they fell in love, for each other. He'd told her he finally realised why they called it 'falling' in love. It was like a dive into somewhere warm and safe, but also edgy and exciting. He'd said he could see to the ends of the world now and wanted to go there with her. She'd pushed the end of his nose and giggled. Now all that felt like a scene in a black-and-white film telling the story of life in Britain hundreds of years ago. The arrival of their children totally changed the nature of their lives, and the relationship between them. She, despite being the one who had most wanted to start a family, seemed to resent the grind and the loneliness attached to motherhood. He could see she was stressed, but not that she was unhappy. He was stressed too, but he was fulfilled in his professional life, and underestimated how much that grated with her. He would come home, play with the children if they were not already in bed, try to share some of his day with Stella, and expect her to share hers with him, and he just didn't notice that she was becoming more distant.

He began to withdraw into his work. He recalled one morning, when he was running a bit late, and Jack was playing up, building for a major tantrum. Stella looked exasperated. He'd gone into the playroom to remonstrate with Jack but then pulled back, saying to himself that if he engaged, he would be there for several minutes, and he was late already. So he just turned and left, hoping Stella wouldn't notice, which of course she did. Outside on the front doorstep he'd stopped and listened to the cacophony inside – Stella calling him back, Jack screaming. Then he'd started to walk, and didn't give it another moment's thought for the rest of the day beyond the insight, which came into his mind right then, as he walked, that he was walking away from his family. It felt like a point of departure.

After that, her resentment grew. His resentment at her resentment grew. The rut developed. A fault line formed. They rubbed along, kind of, especially when anyone else was around. Their friends and neighbours would not have thought for one moment that they were anything other than a happy, loving couple. But they were neither happy nor loving.

Their sex life had gone from poor to virtually non-existent. He had been shocked by how readily both seemed to accept it. How many times had he urged his patients to work at their sexual relationship with their partner, to try to be more tender, to try to find the points of connection that had drawn them to that person in the first place, to understand that it was easier to love someone who was acting in a loving way towards you? He'd lost count of the number of people whose problems he'd traced back to issues in their marriage, and whom he'd helped to a better place. Yet in his own life, he had been hopeless, absolutely hopeless. And what was his response to the collapse of his sex life? Not to try to be more loving and tender, but to go out and buy sexual gratification elsewhere, which in turn, as he knew it would, bred guilt and angst, which in turn fuelled the depressive streak in him that had always been there, but which he had just about managed to keep under some kind of control. And now there was Hafsatu. A wonderful, mesmerising, torturing symbol of the guilt invading his professional life, poisoning everything.

He hated feeling like this. Hated being like this. Hated the fact that he ought to take a lead in resolving the problems in his marriage, but he couldn't. He ought to forgive Stella for the way she had changed, forgive her rages and her tantrums and her attempts to make him feel dreadful about himself, but he couldn't. And the worst thing of all was that as he surveyed the wreckage of their marriage, he heard so many echoes of another marriage, that of his parents, and he saw in his own weaknesses so many of the things he used to criticise, silently, angrily, in his father.

And what would Stella say, if she was sitting there on the sixth floor of the hospital, alongside Martin the husband talking to Professor Sturrock the great solver of mental problems? She would sit with her arms folded across her chest and say that she might have been at fault at times, but it is so painful when your husband doesn't seem to understand what you feel and why you feel it, and wants you to share his concerns for these other people that he is looking after when he can't even look after you. He could hear her saying it: 'Do you have any idea what it's like to feel you are trying to hold a family together but your husband and partner is more interested in other people? I wouldn't mind if he looked after us as well as them. But he looks after them instead of us. And it hurts. It really, really hurts. And what hurts most of all is that he doesn't even notice that it's hurting.'

Sturrock laid his head down on the café table and tried to stop the voices in his head. Conscious of the waitress standing close to him, he sat up, but he could still hear Stella. He buried his head in his hands, told himself to stop listening, stop hearing, stop letting Stella's voice and her anger take over his mind. But he was stuck there, Sturrock the Professor, hearing an everyday story of marital breakdown and its attendant psychological agonies. Professor Sturrock knew what to say. But Martin Sturrock wouldn't be able to deliver. What was the point of Martin Sturrock keeping a dream register or a best–worst list? He would never change. He just couldn't do the forgiveness.

His sandwich untouched, he left a ten-pound note on the table, and walked slowly back to the car. There was no doubt now, this was serious, the kind of plunge where he couldn't function, couldn't communicate. But he had so much to do. The funeral on Tuesday. The fund-raising for his research. All his patients – he had so many cases on the go, and some of them really tough. If this was a plunge as serious as he feared, it threatened to be catastrophic. He couldn't let that happen. He had to find a way of stopping himself going further down. As he sat in the car, he tried to calm himself, using a technique he often recommended to his patients – the 'running commentary'. It involved the articulation of a feeling, verbally not just internally, exactly as it was being felt. The only rule was that every sentence had to begin with the words 'I am'.

'I am feeling empty,' he said to himself as he turned the ignition and started the journey home.

'I am wondering why it is that I am feeling empty.'

'I am thinking that it is because my marriage is so poor.'

'I am feeling bad that I want the weekend to pass.'

'I am feeling bad that I have deliberately tried to stay out of the house to avoid contact with Stella.'

'I am thinking I have no choice, because we seem unable to speak to each other.'

'I am feeling guilty that I did not want my mother to come to Aunt Jessica's funeral.'

'I am wishing it was Wednesday, then the funeral would be over.'

'I am hoping that I will be able to see all the patients I need to next week.'

'I am worried about Arta. I am hoping she will come back.'

'I am worried about Emily.'

'I am wondering if David is OK.'

'I am sad that all my father's family are now gone.'

'I am wishing I could hear my father's voice speaking to me when I am troubled like this.'

'I am wishing I heard it when he was alive.'

'I am thinking that I should not be worrying about things I cannot change.'

'I am wishing I did not have to do the eulogy on Tuesday.'

'I am wishing Aunt Jessica had stood up for me.'

The traffic was heavy, but for once he didn't mind. He was lingering at traffic lights. He was stopping to let cars out of side roads. He was changing gear slowly, very deliberately, trying to make each moment last a little longer. It was like living in slow motion, another symptom of the plunge.

He was hoping that a little more passage of time might lift him, and make him feel better prepared for going home and seeing Stella. But every time he felt he was able to focus on her, and try to be positive, even for a few moments, another person, another thought, another image would crowd her out and make him more pessimistic about his ability to lift things. Aunt Jessica crowded in. Emily Parks crowded in. Arta crowded in even more. He thought of Arta's recurring dream about trying to leave Kosovo, and the obvious message it carried that no matter how hard the journey, there appeared to be no ending.

Sturrock didn't write down his own dreams. He had done so only when he was running a research project on dreams and depression. But he had a recurring dream of his own, not dissimilar to Arta's, though without the background of ethnic and military conflict. He was at an airport, late for a plane, running up a gently rising travelator which gave the appearance of moving, but though everyone else on it appeared to be moving forward, he was making no progress at all. The people around him were not even moving their legs, yet they were moving forward. They were in small groups, mainly families smiling and sharing the excitement they felt at heading away to new destinations, or they were groups of friends all enjoying each other's company. Sturrock appeared to be the only one alone. He was running hard, yet staying in the same spot. The harder he ran, the more happy, smiling people glided past him. They headed to the next stage of their journey, while he never moved beyond the gaudy poster advertising a West End musical which had closed long ago. When he looked more closely at the poster, his father was among the cast, looking morose and unyielding amid a stage full of smiles.

It was a fairly basic anxiety dream. Had it been a patient's dream, he might have said it revealed a loner, something of a perfectionist, forever striving but never truly content. He would have further concluded that he saw his father as a distant and aloof figure unable to help him in any struggle he had. But he knew all that anyway.

When he finally got home, Stella was busy in the kitchen.

'Dinner won't be for a while,' she said, perfectly nicely.

'I'm fine,' he said. 'I was hungry when I left Mum's, so I picked up a sandwich.'

'OK.'

'I was there longer than I planned to be. I've got a bit of work to do now.'

'How was she?'

'OK. Same really.'

'Not coming on Tuesday.'

'No, she is.'

'Oh.'

'I'm going to see if Jan will take her.'

He went to his study, muttering to himself.

'I am thinking I should have been able to engage in a better conversation than that.'

'I am relieved I am on my own again.'

'I am hoping this gloom will lift.'

'I am seeing and feeling nothing to suggest it will.'

20

'Can't or won't? Can't or won't?' Professor Sturrock's question had been echoing around Arta's head all day. Last night, as happened most nights, she'd dreamed of the rapist, but this time her psychiatrist had been there too.

He was wearing casual clothes, which surprised her, as usually he wore a jacket and trousers, or a navy-blue suit. They were meeting not in a consulting room but on a train, in a crowded, rickety carriage that was taking them through what seemed like an industrial waste-land, dark lifeless buildings on a snow-covered plain. The seats on the train were brightly coloured, a lurid mix of pinks, purples and yellows, colours so shrill they made her want to look away, stare out of the window. She was embarrassed to be talking to a psychiatrist in front of others. 'What did it feel like, Arta, when the man entered you? Try to describe for me both the physical sensation but also what was happening inside your head.' She wanted to say that she had tried to force her mind to think thoughts so powerful and loving that she felt nothing but she hadn't managed to. She wanted to say she had felt a failure as a parent because she couldn't protect Besa, a failure as a wife because she had allowed a strange man into the flat. The thoughts were clear inside her mind, and close to coming out. But the other passengers were listening, even though some pretended not to, and when she opened her mouth she found she couldn't speak. Professor Sturrock normally spoke softly but tonight he was talking in a clear, precise voice, and loud enough for anyone in the carriage to hear. She looked out of the window and when she turned back to Professor Sturrock, there was a little crowd of people behind him, all staring at her. Among them was a man with a cruel smile. The rapist. This time, she had given him dark hair, brown eyes, a scar across his top lip, a brown leather jacket and yellow T-shirt. He was unshaven. He wore a badge on his leather jacket, based on the three-fingered salute of the Serbs. He had raped her, and he was smiling.

'I can't say,' she said. 'I can't say with all these people here.'

'Can't or won't?' Professor Sturrock said. 'Can't or won't?' the passengers behind him joined in. Then the 'can't' was dropped and they began to chant and stamp their feet. 'Won't, won't, won't, won't, won't . . .'

Arta had been shaken awake by Lirim. 'Arta, Arta, Arta, wake up, wake up, it's OK, it's OK, you're here, it's fine.' The hurt and fear she felt in her dreams started to mix in with the feelings of relief and warmth as she realised where she was – in her own bed, not on a train with the psychiatrist, the rapist and a baying mob.

'It's OK,' Lirim said, sensing the calm coming over her. 'It's OK. What happened? Him again?'

'Yes, but not attacking me, laughing at me. The doctor was there, saying, "Can't or won't?" Why does he say that? Like I have the choice.'

Lirim was in a hurry to get to work. She had her arms around his neck. He eased her grip a little, then held her close to him and kissed her on the forehead. 'Sorry, I've got to go. We'll talk more tonight. We will get there in the end, Arta.'

As he reached the bedroom door, he looked back at her. 'Don't forget to text me if there are any goals in Alban's match,' he said. And, with that, he was gone.

As soon as the door closed, Arta picked up her notebook from the bedside table and tried to record her dream. It struck her that, of all the faces on the train, Professor Sturrock's was the only one with a kindly expression in his eyes. For a moment her anger towards him softened, but then the humiliation of yesterday's appointment, which had clearly provoked the dream, came flooding back. Professor Sturrock always encouraged her to write exactly what she felt in her dreams. She wrote: '*I was angry with you in real life, because you asked me to forgive those men, and I was hurt in my dream that you did not defend me when the other passengers were shouting at me.'*

Once the children were up, Alban buzzing with excitement about his match, she was able to silence the taunts in her head, and concentrate on getting them ready for the day.

Alban's only unhappiness was that his father was unlikely to be able to watch him play. Unlike Arta, Lirim loved football. Yet it was she who would be going to Herne Hill to support him. Lirim had popped in to see Alban in bed the night before, to tell him he would try to get along if he could, but he was pretty clear the chances were slim. Arta had listened outside the door. 'This is a big weekend for us at work and I need to make sure everything goes according to plan,' Lirim had said. 'But I'll be thinking of you.' When she went in to give Alban a goodnight kiss, she could tell he had been sniffing back tears.

Arta knew next to nothing about football, but she knew this match was important to her son. The day he was told he had been picked for the school team he was so excited he could barely get the words out when he got home. It was a London Schools Cup game too, and she gleaned from the conversation between Lirim and Alban that this made it even more exciting. It meant playing on a proper, full-sized pitch at the Herne Hill Velodrome, with a team bus to take them there and their own changing room. Arta walked with him to school to wave him off, then she and Besa took the 196 bus and arrived at the ground as the teams were warming up.

Alban's school was playing a team from another school in Elephant and Castle, so Arta recognised quite a few of the faces. She felt out of place among the other parents. Mostly it was the dads who had come, and she was the only woman with a pushchair. Alban was trying hard not to look nervous, but she knew him too well. She worried that some of the players on the other team were much bigger than him. She worried too that the pitch was so huge, that he would need to conserve his energy if he was to last the course. She was surprised at how many spectators there were, at least fifty, maybe even a hundred, mainly parents and other family, but also, she heard one of the other parents say, scouts from Charlton, Millwall and Queen's Park Rangers. She found it astonishing that professional football clubs would send people to watch ten-year-olds.

She knew what the objective of the game was – to put the ball in the opponents' net – but she had little understanding of how that was made to happen, or what made one team better than the other. For large parts of the match, Alban didn't touch the ball, but she heard his team coach shouting 'well done' to him a couple of times, so she assumed he was doing fine. But then something terrible happened, which challenged fundamentally her own understanding of her son.

She was watching Alban run alongside another boy, trying to get the ball from him, when suddenly Alban deliberately tripped the boy, and gave his leg a sharp kick as he fell. She put her hands to her mouth as she watched the victim of Alban's aggression fall to the ground clutching his shin and screaming. The referee ran towards him but was beaten to it by three or four of the other team's players who were shoving and pushing Alban, now defended by his own teammates. Several parents were edging from the cycle track on to the pitch, shouting angrily. Arta could tell from the look on one woman's face that she was the mother of the boy who lay on the floor. She was of a type very familiar to Arta from her life on the estate. White working class. Overweight. Unhealthy puffy face. Pink tracksuit. Holding a cigarette. Alongside her, another parent was shouting, 'Kill the little sod.' Others were calling for Alban to be sent off. 'Red card, red card. It's got to be a red card.'

Arta just stood watching, half an eye on Besa who was playing behind one of the goals with a little friend she had found. Alban had the look of a cornered animal. She just wanted the game to resume and all the shouting to stop. She wished Lirim was there. He would know how to handle this better.

Alban was given a yellow card, to the evident annoyance of many of the parents, who were now shrieking abuse at the referee. As Alban walked away, the boy he had fouled stood up. Even though she was on the other side of the pitch, Arta could hear him shout at Alban, 'Why don't you fuck off home, you asylum-seeking little wanker?'

A minority of the spectators cheered. Arta noticed that the pink-tracksuited woman was not among them. She threw her cigarette angrily to the ground, and stamped on it. Although the referee had clearly heard what the boy said, he ignored it and blew his whistle for the free kick to be taken. Alban turned and looked at the boy, walked straight over to him, and punched him twice in the face, left fist, right fist, and the boy fell to the floor once more. Parents from both teams ran onto the field and for a moment it looked as if they too were going to start fighting. Alban's coach managed to protect him from the worst of the abuse as he escorted him from the pitch, not needing to wait for the red card. He brought him over to Arta, whose hands were shaking. To her, Alban was the kindest, softest, gentlest son. Out on the football field he had behaved like a monster. He had a look of fury in his eyes.

'What happened? What happened to you?' she said, fighting back tears.

'He'd been having a go at me the whole game. Asylum seeker this, asylum seeker that, go home, foreigner –'

'You should have ignored it and played on.'

'Would Dad have ignored it?'

The game had resumed. The coach said to Arta it might be an idea to take Alban home to avoid any further flare-up at the end.

She could feel his agony as he sat staring out of the bus window.

'Sorry,' he said.

'It's not me you should be saying sorry to, but the boy you hurt.'

'No way,' he said.

'Let's see what Dad says.'

'Do we have to tell him?'

'Don't be ridiculous, Alban. Of course we do.'

They told Lirim when he got home from the car wash. Arta was surprised by how lenient he was. Usually he came down hard on any bad behaviour from Alban, but this time she felt he was just going through the motions, pretending to be cross, giving his son a friendly cuff around the ear. He seemed more interested in knowing whether he would be suspended from future matches than what it said about Alban's character. Perhaps he was tired, she thought, or overexcited about the new Sunday opening. She suspected, though, that part of him was secretly proud of Alban for standing up for himself.

As she washed the dishes after dinner, she heard Alban asking Lirim whether he could stay up to watch *Match of the Day*.

'Of course you can,' said Lirim. 'Glad to see today hasn't put you off football.'

Arta was furious with both of them. It was bad enough to be violent, as Alban had been, but she found Lirim's virtual condoning of the violence even worse. It disgusted her. As she heard the two of them chatting away about the match they were watching next door, she tossed aside the dishcloth, went into her bedroom and gathered up a pillow and a blanket. Then she went into the children's room and lay down on the floor next to the bed in which Besa was sleeping soundly.

Ten minutes later, Lirim came in.

'Arta, what are you doing?' he whispered.

'What does it look like? Sleeping here. Alban can share the bed with you since you're both so pleased with yourselves.'

It pained her to see Lirim looking so crestfallen, but she felt too angry to change her mind, and too proud to back down.

'What on earth is the matter?' he said.

'I don't want to talk about it. Just let me sleep.'

'But you'll be uncomfortable.'

'I'll move on to Alban's bed. Now go please. I'm tired. We'll talk about it in the morning.'

Lirim gave her a final, beseeching look and then tiptoed out of the room, closing the door quietly behind him. For hours Arta lay in the dark, listening to her daughter's soft breathing and fearing the arrival of sleep which would take her back to her nightmares.

SUNDAY

21

The light on David Temple's digital alarm clock showed it was 3.12 a.m. He'd been lying awake for over three hours, and he knew the void inside was growing. He watched the little electronic dot between the 3 and the 12, which flickered silently on and off to record every passing second, and with each flicker, he felt his mind filling with a familiar painful emptiness. How can emptiness be painful? If there is nothing there, where does the hurt come from? How can a void be full of emptiness? And if it is already full, how come it feels that with every new second it is getting fuller? And why ask these questions, he said to himself, when I know I don't know the answers, and at times like this, I know I never will?

Then the void started to fill, as his mind was taken over by what he called his water torture. Every flicker on the clock was a tiny drop of water trickling through a slightly open sluice gate into his mind. One drop was next to nothing. But a minute delivered sixty drops, an hour 3,600, and if he stayed awake all night, that would be going on for 30,000 drops of water, an unstoppable force, drowning his mind. He didn't want to drown. He wanted to sleep.

He craved the oblivion that sleep delivered, and the possibility that, on waking, he'd find himself on an upturn from the downward curve of the rhythm. He couldn't recall an upturn following a bad night's sleep, but perhaps he was thinking so negatively about everything that no positive memories were being allowed in.

All evening he'd tried to dredge up positive thoughts without success. He and his mother had eaten dinner in silence, he picking at the enormous plate of minced beef, carrots and mashed potato she'd dished up for him. He'd watched her mouth, chewing and chewing. Open, shut, chew, chew, chew, chew, open, shut, chew. On and on . . . It seemed like it might never stop. Afterwards she'd watched TV for a while and he had watched her watching, a book on his lap. He had no intention of reading the book. It was his device to stop her from talking to him. Occasionally he looked down and turned the page but somehow the book always fell back open on page 166.

He knew it was wrong to feel the way he did about his mother. His rational mind said she had done more for him than anyone could expect, but his inner voice kept saying harsh things. His rational mind knew it should be his father he blamed for the way he was, but he couldn't help thinking his mother must have done something to drive his dad away.

But look at her. She was kind, she was thoughtful, she would never harm anyone. So it must have been me, he thought. I was the change in their life that he couldn't handle. That must have been the reason he left.

Over the years, he'd considered tracking down his father, and trying to punish him. But where would he start? His dad had left almost thirty years ago. He could be anywhere in the world. He could be dead. The thought of hunting him down never stayed long.

His mother had made them both a cup of tea just before eleven. She took hers to bed, her last words, as on so many nights before, 'Don't stay up too long.' He'd sat for an hour in the living room with the lights off, and then dragged himself to bed. He wondered why he'd bothered. What difference did it make to be awake and alone with his thoughts here in bed, in the dark, or awake and alone with his thoughts downstairs in the dark?

He thought about getting up, had a conversation in his head about whether to stay where he was, or to walk around the room. Staying was easier. He wondered what Professor Sturrock would advise. He would probably tell him he needed to sleep, but if he really couldn't, then perhaps he should get up for a while, and look over recent dreams, or review what he had done of his homework so far, something that would allow him to think in a more structured way of the issues that were clearly keeping him awake. He would almost certainly advise against looking endlessly at a little flashing dot between the hour and the minute on a digital bedside clock.

David wished he was in the comfortable armchair in Professor Sturrock's consulting room right now, talking about his dreams, listening to the doctor's gentle voice telling him that eventually he would be able to sleep again, eventually the emptiness would go and everything would be all right.

When he first started visiting Professor Sturrock, he hadn't seen the point of all the dreams analysis. Sturrock had told him how we dream all the time, and our conscious and subconscious minds help each other sift out what matters and what doesn't. He'd said that, if you worked hard at it, you could start to see patterns in your dreams and try to make sense of them. It had amused David to call the psychiatrist's bluff. In addition to what he actually dreamed, he would sometimes invent detail too, just to see whether Professor Sturrock would invest the invented detail with any significance. Once, David had told him about a dream he'd had where he was locked in a gas chamber with his mother. Many of the details were true – the chamber, the pipes, the colourless gas that starting hissing into the room. But he'd invented a drawing of a church on one of the walls, close to where the gas pipes entered the chamber. He'd said that out of the church was filing a crowd of people lined up behind a bride and groom. Apart from the church, his account of the dream was pretty faithful. As the pipes began pumping gas into the room, his mother had screamed for help. David told Professor Sturrock how, in the dream, he'd felt strangely calm. He was upset for his mother who was shouting, 'God, what did I do? Take me but do not take my son,' but he did not believe they were in danger. And he remembered thinking that, even if they were in danger, it wouldn't matter.

Sure enough, the Professor had skipped over the gas chamber element of the dream, dwelt a little on the contrast between his mother's panic and David's calm – a familiar theme – but then lingered at length on the drawing of the church and even more so on the bride and groom coming out of it. Could David make out who they were?

Were they happy? Did one seem happier than the other? David said he couldn't remember. It was just a sketch on the wall. He knew that Professor Sturrock wanted this to be a subconscious sighting of David's parents so that he could ask how David had felt on seeing his father in the picture. He pressed and pressed, until David confessed to making up the picture of the church and the wedding. He thought Professor Sturrock would be angry with him. Far from it. Apparently, even inventions, especially when they might concern his parents, gave Professor Sturrock something to work with.

From then on, David had taken the whole thing more seriously, writing copious notes for Professor Sturrock each week. Sometimes he would fill pages. But tonight he felt so dead inside he couldn't imagine having the energy even to pick up a pen. In any event, he couldn't sleep, so he would have nothing to record.

He wondered what Professor Sturrock was dreaming about tonight. Did he analyse his dreams? Did he wake up and immediately obsess over a minor element of his reverie – why the walls kept changing colour from red to blue to green to yellow, why the man at the back was carrying a cross, why the radio announcer was speaking Portuguese? These elements had all been in David's dreams recently, and Professor Sturrock had spent a few minutes on each. What details of his own dreams would the psychiatrist analyse, if he did? Or did he get someone else to analyse his dreams? Who did psychiatrists see when they were feeling shaky up top?

David worried that, once again, he was allowing his mind to fill with questions he couldn't answer. Maybe Professor Sturrock didn't worry about his own dreams. Perhaps he was a heavy sleeper and when he woke, he was immediately busy, rushing to get up, to prepare himself for a day trying to analyse others. It couldn't be much of a life, David thought, having to sort out everyone's prob-lems. What did he think when David left the room each week? God, what a loser?

He wondered what kind of house Professor Sturrock lived in. It was probably big. Were psychiatrists well paid? No idea. Did he sleep in a big bedroom with paintings on the wall and little statuettes that he and Mrs Sturrock picked up on their summer holidays? Maybe Mrs Sturrock was dead. He was a widower. Or he was divorced and now on the second Mrs Sturrock, and he had a complicated family set-up, kids from his first marriage, kids from hers, kids they shared between them. What would it be like to have a father who took you on holiday?

How can I be sure he has kids? David thought to himself. I bet he does, but how many? Two? Three? No, five. I bet he's a good father. Were they grown up now? Must be. How old is he? Sixty? Bit younger, bit older, round there I would reckon, so his kids, what will they be? Thirties, maybe forties, twenties if he started late. I bet he's a grandad too. I bet he has a picture of his grandchildren in his wallet and when he has no patients around, he gets it out and puts it on his desk, and it cheers him up to think he's taking them to the park at the weekend.

David wondered if he would ever have grandchildren. He doubted it. You needed children first and to have children you needed a woman, and you had to have sex with the woman and she had to get pregnant. Amanda's sudden return to his thoughts was like a punch to the chest, and he rolled over, pulling a pillow against his head. How could he have imagined Amanda would have gone out with him, let alone had sex with him? No chance. Why couldn't he have seen that before he made such a fool of himself? Maybe he should have stayed with the fantasy, not listened when his inner voice was telling him to try to make it real. But fantasies don't make love, they don't make children. They're sterile, ultimately they're dead.

He wondered what Professor Sturrock made of his story about Amanda. Had he spent any time, even a minute, even a few seconds, thinking about it over the weekend?

He was suddenly confronted, and frightened, by the thought that one day, maybe soon, Professor Sturrock would retire. Perhaps he was nearer sixty-five than sixty. Maybe he won't retire, he thought. Maybe he'll stay on for a few of his really tough cases and I'll be one of them. I can tell he likes me. I don't believe he puts as much thought into everyone else's problems as he puts into mine. Look at all the homework I do for him, and he has always read it, digested it, printed out my emails and put little circles around points he wants to discuss at greater length. Sometimes I can tell he's gone back over some of the homework from months earlier, checking for the rhythms and the patterns. I bet he doesn't do that for everyone. How could he? He wouldn't have the time, for heaven's sake. So what do I do if he goes? What if I get transferred to someone else and have to go through all the same old same old, the weeks and weeks of talking we did before I felt he was on my planet, somewhere inside my head? And what happens if I don't like the new one? What do you do if you just can't bear to be in the same room? Do you walk? Do you ask for a different one? But what will they say? You've just had a new one, you can't have another one so soon after. Even if Sturrock does keep me on after retirement, it can't last forever, can it? He could grow old and senile. What havoc a gaga shrink could wreak. But maybe by then it would be like with Mum, I will know the Professor so well that I'll be able to predict his reactions, and maybe get guidance that way, even without actually seeing him.

Yes, he reckoned Professor Sturrock had five kids. Lucky bastards, to have a father like that who would talk to them and guide them through life.

He still couldn't sleep. He thought about getting up to read the American book again. There must be method in the Professor's madness. He wondered about calling him. Professor Sturrock had given him his mobile number for emergencies. But then he thought about the big bedroom with Mr and Mrs Sturrock fast asleep in it. No, he couldn't call. He'd have to get through this by himself. He rolled over again to check the time. It was 4.15. He was sure the dot between the 4 and the 15 was flashing more slowly than the last time he looked.

22

When Sturrock finally woke on Sunday morning, he knew he faced a struggle to get out of bed. He'd slept through Stella's alarm clock, which she had set for 8 a.m. to give her plenty of time to prepare for the birthday lunch for Jack. It was now ten o'clock, and from downstairs he could hear the vacuum cleaner, and with it the message from Stella that she was up and about, and he was lying in bed doing nothing. Sleep had failed to alleviate his tiredness, or his irritability.

An odd dream from the night just gone came back to him. He'd been pruning a rose bush and a panther had sprung out at him. David's influence again. David often dreamed of cats who turned violent, and had spoken recently about a dream in which a ginger cat had suddenly transformed itself into a panther. More often than he liked to admit, Professor Sturrock found details from his patients' dreams entering his own. In the past few weeks it had been as if David's dream-life had invaded his. He told himself that this was because he saw David on a Friday and he tended to dream more at weekends, when he slept a little longer. But he knew there were other reasons. Even within the dream, he was having to acknowledge that this was David's influence and he was trying to fight off not merely the animal, but the influence.

He lay there for a few moments, trying to persuade himself the inertia would pass, and he would soon be leaping out of bed and facing the day with confidence. But even as he tried, he knew he would fail. There was no doubt. The events of yesterday had taken him into a plunge, and sleep had taken him lower. His mind was filling with more of the same negative thoughts he had endured all day yesterday, and the thoughts kept his head pinned to the pillow. His marriage; his son and his worries about whether he would be able to engage with him when he came to celebrate his birthday; his mother's health and his selfishness about it; the patients he had to see next week, and all the problems they would bring; Tuesday's funeral and the wretched eulogy he still hadn't even started to write. He felt incapable of facing up to any of these challenges, and there was no one he could ask for help. He felt totally alone.

He found himself thinking of the time David Temple's mother called him, in a terrible state, because David was so bad, so low, she was desperate. It was about ten months ago, and it had led to his one meeting with her, and his one visit to David's home.

David had had an appointment that day but despite his mother's efforts he had refused to leave the house, and she was sufficiently worried about his state of mind to call the hospital. She spoke to Phyllis, said that David was worse than she had ever seen him, and she was worried what would happen if he went another week without seeing the doctor. Fortunately Phyllis had the sense, despite her annoyance at the missed appointment, to put Mrs Temple through so she could speak to Professor Sturrock directly.

Mrs Temple was hugely apologetic both about David's failure to keep the appointment, and for taking his time on the phone. She thanked him at length for all the help he gave to her son. 'You're like a lifeline to him sometimes,' she said. Although she couldn't say hand on heart that David's condition had permanently improved in the months of treatment under Professor Sturrock, she had noted that he sometimes came back from his hospital visits with a little more energy. He also enjoyed most of the tasks Professor Sturrock set him, though he didn't like her to read what he wrote. And it was clear to her that David had a respect for Professor Sturrock that she had never seen him have for any other man. He could be scathing about his work colleagues. He had refused to engage with the man from the community crisis team sent by Professor Sturrock after a previous failure to keep an appointment. 'I have never heard him say a bad word about you, Professor. You are unique in that.'

Sturrock asked her what David was doing. She said he was sitting in a chair by the kitchen table. He had been sitting there all day. He had failed to go to work and when his line manager called to find out where he was, David wouldn't take the phone. He was just staring at his knees. His eyes barely blinked. His limbs didn't move. He was so still she wondered if he was even breathing.

'It must be very worrying for you, Mrs Temple. It sounds like he's at the bottom of one of his curves, doesn't it?'

'Well, yes, but usually when he's there, there are flashes of anger, or looks of hurt or hatred at me, or something. There is nothing, Professor. I am looking at my own son, my own flesh and blood, and he looks more dead than alive.'

'Have you asked him why he doesn't want to see me?'

'Yes, he just stares and moves his shoulders a tiny, tiny bit, not even a shrug, but I know I'm meant to see a shrug.'

'Yes, that is quite normal. It means he wants to engage and answer, but he feels he can't. I know it's not easy to live with, but I promise you this is quite normal for someone like David. It happens to quite a lot of people.'

'I just don't know what to do though,' she said, and beneath the words he could sense her struggle to hold back tears.

'I assume he's not with you at the moment.'

'No. I think he would be cross if he knew I was calling you.'

'You've done the right thing in calling. If you're worried, I'm worried. I'm worried about you too. You sound under great strain.'

She let out a rather embarrassed laugh, which unlocked a tension that had been growing all day and she began to sob. She kept the phone to her ear the whole time, and the sobbing went on, so long and so hard it sounded like the insides of her chest were caving in.

'It's OK to cry,' he said. 'You just cry for as long as you like, and then I've got an idea.'

'I can't believe I'm crying down a phone, on to the shoulder of someone I've never met,' she said. 'I'm sorry.'

'Don't worry. Sometimes these illnesses can be every bit as bad for the family as for the sufferer, so I do understand.'

Once she had recovered herself, he told her his idea – that she take the phone to David, and tell him Professor Sturrock was on the line, then put the phone to his ear. He said he would ask David if he would like him to come to see him at home tonight when he was finished at the hospital.

As he expected, though Mrs Temple held the phone close to his ear as instructed, David did not respond at all when he offered to visit him.

'OK, David, well, you think about that and if you want me to come, just ask your mum to call me.'

When Mrs Temple came back on the line, he tried to reassure her.

'It doesn't seem to me that he's a danger to himself. He hasn't said anything for now, but he will think about it, and he may want to speak later. If he does, and he wants me to come, call me. Or if you want me to come, just say. I will be here till quite late.'

'Will you tell your secretary I might call?' she asked.

Sturrock laughed gently. He knew Phyllis could be fierce with patients and their families sometimes. 'Why don't you take my mobile number and I'll keep it on? Just call if you think I should come.'

Two hours later, she did. She said David had just been sitting staring at her while she watched TV. She'd asked him every now and then if he was all right, and he'd just carried on staring, but then after a while he'd said something which sounded like, 'Do you think he would come?'

She'd got up from her chair to turn off the TV, gone over to where he was sitting, knelt down with her hands on his knees, and seen a tiny hint of life in his eyes.

'I said, "Would you like him to, love?" and he kind of nodded. It's like he's really, really trying to tell me something, like a massive effort going on and he's in agony, but I'm sure he nodded, I'm sure of it.' She paused. 'So do you think you can come?'

Sturrock arrived just after 9 p.m. He was surprised by David's home. He always developed an impression in his mind of his patients' homes, and he had imagined David in a block of flats, graffiti on the communal staircase, a green door, one of ten, along a dank third-floor corridor. His mind's eye had him in a very small and cramped bedroom leading off from the top of a mini staircase, opposite a bathroom with a leaking tap and a shower curtain that failed to hold in the water. But the house was not as he had imagined at all. David actually lived on the top two floors of a well-maintained, fairly modern red-brick house in a development near Pentonville prison. There was a thick blue carpet on the shared staircase up to the Temples' door and signs of his mother's Catholic faith everywhere. Jesus on a cross was the first thing he noticed going through the door, high on the wall to the left. A classic Jesus and Mary portrait hung over the fireplace in the kitchen where David was sitting. Little frames holding cards with lines from the Bible were dotted around the room.

He had also got Nora Temple wrong. When she had come up in his discussions with David, Sturrock saw a woman of medium height, very well built, with solid legs, a thick head of brown hair and a bossy manner. In reality, she was tiny, no more than five feet tall, with thin wrists and arms and a bony face beneath perfectly symmetrical jet-black hair. She looked at the end of her tether.

'Thank you for coming, Professor. And sorry about earlier.'

'Not at all,' he said. 'I know how hard it can be for the families of people who suffer like David.'

He picked up a chair and went to sit close to David.

'Well then,' he said, with a smile. 'This isn't so good, is it?' David shook his head very slightly from side to side.

'What have you been thinking about sitting here all day? Can you tell me?'

David exhaled a very long sigh, let his head fall backwards so that he was staring at the ceiling, and shook his head, more forcefully.

'You can't tell me, or you don't really know what you've been thinking about?'

David's head fell forward. 'Dead,' he said. 'Been feeling dead.'

'And what does that feel like, feeling dead?'

Sturrock knew the answer, having felt dead himself several times, though only once so dead that he had been in a state like David's, but it was important to get David to open up.

'What does dead feel like, David?'

'Bad,' said David, with just the tiniest hint of a laugh. Sturrock smiled back. It was like an in-joke. 'Feels bad. Like nothing there. Nothing. Just dead. Can breathe, can hear, can see, can smell, but can't feel. Nothing. Can't feel anything. Nothing. Just dead.'

'Like before, or worse?'

'Dunno. Can't remember before when it's like this. It's like this is all there is, all there has ever been, all there's gonna be.'

'But you have been here before, David. Many times. These feelings do pass.'

David nodded, but then his head slumped forward. He was exhausted. The effort of speech had sucked all the energy from him, and he was going to have to dig again before he could say any more.

'Is he OK?' asked Mrs Temple.

'Yes, he's OK. For someone in the state he is in, what he did in speaking just then was equivalent to running up stairs with a ton of bricks on his back. Big effort. Now he'll be tired. But it'll be OK.'

Mrs Temple made some tea and put out three slices of a lemon cake she had made, which went untouched.

By ten to ten, David was ready to talk some more.

'It's like there is a part of my mind that knows what I have to do, and the other part is stopping me. The first part is saying be nice, be good, get involved, because that's what will make you happy, and it'll make Mum happy. But the other part is saying you can't do it, you shouldn't do it, don't do anything because it's all bad anyway, and it won't work, and you'll make things worse, so just sit down and shut up, you useless little fucker.'

Mrs Temple put her hands up to her mouth as he swore, something he rarely did, and crossed herself.

'It's OK, Mrs Temple,' said Sturrock. 'It is important he expresses himself as he feels it.' He turned back to David.

'Did anyone ever tell you to sit down and shut up, David? Did anyone ever call you a useless little fucker?'

David was staring at his knees again, and shaking his head.

'Is that no, nobody did? Or you can't speak again?'

David shook his head, slowly. 'It's not about him, it's about me.'

'Not about who, David? Who is him?'

'You know.'

'So why do you think it is all about you?'

'Because it is. Because I can't seem to get anything right.'

Sturrock looked into his briefcase and rummaged around, eventually finding a rubber band. He took David's hand in his, and slipped the rubber band over his wrist. David looked down at it, suspicious.

'That's your positive-thinking band,' said Sturrock. 'Every time you have a negative thought about yourself, I want you to flick the band against your wrist. I want you to try to force yourself to have a positive thought. If you're thinking of something you feel you cannot do, flick the rubber band. But then try to think of something you can do.

'There is a lot you can do, David. Just try to think a little bit positively. Can you do that for me, do you think?'

David nodded, then he slumped again, and as he stared at his knees, Sturrock took Mrs Temple through to the sitting room and asked her about David's father.

'He did hit me a few times, but I don't think he ever hurt David. He wasn't a good man, but I don't think he did any of that.'

He asked how David had been when he realised his father had gone and wasn't coming back.

'It's hard for me to remember. I was so shocked at first, but then I was glad, and I had this vision of a wonderful life bringing up David on my own, not having to worry about his dad and what his moods might bring home with him. And sometimes it's been great, you know. And lots of times, it's been like today.'

As Sturrock lay in bed, Mrs Temple's words – 'lots of times, it's been like today' – ran round and round his head. He tried to tell himself he had so much more going for him in life than David, or many of the other patients he treated. He tried to list the good things in his life, but they were quickly drowned out as the same old concerns came crowding in.

Then he could hear Stella walking up the stairs.

'Are you up, Martin?' she shouted from the floor below.

'Nearly,' he said.

'Jack will be here soon.'

'OK.'

He looked through the drawers of his bedside table, found a rubber band, and slipped it over his wrist.

23

Ralph Hall woke up on Sunday morning in a strange bed. His first thought, as his eyes blinked open, was that he felt even more ill than yesterday morning. He felt tired too. Tired and ill. No, ill and tired, in that order. He needed to be sick, but he wasn't sure he had the strength to get out of the strange bed and drag himself to the toilet, wherever that may be. He needed to find out where he was before he could face the day. This was not his own house, the little three-bedroomed semi he had bought when he first went for the seat to satisfy his local party that he intended to 'live locally'. It wasn't a hotel either. It was too lived-in for that. So he assumed he must have been taken here by a friend last night, when he knew he'd had way too much to drink. But which one?

He'd spent the day running around the constituency. He did eleven visits in all, and managed a drink at five of them. Then he had a double Scotch at home while he changed into black tie for the dinner at the local Chamber of Commerce. He needed it to calm down. Sandie had phoned to say her flight had been delayed so there wasn't time for her to get up to Newcastle for the dinner. She'd see him at home in London tomorrow. He was furious. It was the only thing he'd asked her to do in weeks and she'd let him down.

He'd been called on to say a few words at the dinner. Conscious of having had too much to drink already, he spoke briefly, telling one joke and making a couple of points about the state of the economy before hurrying off the platform. He couldn't remember what the two points were. He remembered the joke – or vaguely funny story at least – which was about the time he was mistaken on a train for one of the characters in *Emmerdale Farm*. It usually got a laugh, but he couldn't remember if it got a laugh last night. He could remember that he had been sitting next to David Marchant from the Bank of Scotland who was complaining about a proposal in the new Enterprise Bill. He could remember the MC saying the formal proceedings were now over but the bar was open till 1 a.m. and he could remember shouting 'Amen to that' and then heading off to get a whisky. He'd had three or four large single malts and also, accidentally on purpose, a couple of other people's drinks from the bar. One was a pretty tired-looking champagne. The other tasted like gin and tonic. He could remember thinking that it wouldn't matter so much if he was drunk tonight because he was among his own people, away from the London limelight, most of the killjoys had left and everyone else was drunk or close to it.

Then he remembered the woman in the long lime-green dress, with swimmer's shoulders and a sexy laugh. Did she really take his hand and say she was going to take him to paradise, or did he dream that? He sat up and saw his jacket on the floor.

'Oh no. Oh God, please tell me no, please tell me I didn't. Please tell me this is not the bed of the woman in the green dress. Did I? Oh Christ, I think I did.' He now had a pumping heart to add to the sore head and parched throat. He sat up, threw back the sheets and jumped out of bed. He thought if he moved fast enough, and panicked enough, he would wake up and find it was that awful panic you get in the last few seconds of dreams so scary they wake you up. He thought he might wake up and find he was actually at home in his own bed and this was just a nice dream with a bad ending. But as he looked around the room for clues as to where he was, he saw the red chesterfield sofa in the window and draped across it the lime-green dress. On the floor beside it was a black lace basque. He suddenly remembered helping the lady in the lime-green dress to take it off, and then she became the lady in the black silk basque and he helped her to take that off too, which was the cause of a lot of laughter and a lot of fiddling with little hooks that increased the laughter. Where was she?

'Hello?' he shouted.

No reply.

'Hello?'

He worked out that the frosted-glass door in the corner must lead to the bathroom. The after-effects of last night's alcohol and the electric panic he was now feeling combined to make him vomit as soon as he reached the toilet. As he waited for the next heave, staring at the red, brown and yellow mess that swam around in the bowl, he found space within the heaving to ask himself how his life had come to this. He had been a rising star. Though some said he lacked charisma – clearly not the lady in the lime-green dress – nobody ever questioned his judgement or competence. He had a good marriage and a good family. He still thought he might one day be Prime Minister. And yet here he was, stark naked, his belly hanging down, his knees cold on the linoleum floor as he chundered into a toilet bowl and tried to remember who it was he screwed last night. If a line-up of eight moderately attractive women in their mid-thirties was brought in now, like some kind of identity parade, he would struggle to pick her out. Whereas her perfume . . . he remembered that. The thought of it brought on the next heave.

As his vomiting cleared away some of the debris from his body, his mind started to throw up details of his encounter. She had bumped into him in the foyer as he arrived, late. She'd said hello and showed him where to go. Later, after he'd made his little speech, she'd come to see him at his table. She said she was getting more interested in politics, she was sick of all the cynicism and she would like to join the party and help in the next election campaign. He mumbled something about how they needed all the help they could get and gave her the number of his constituency office. As he wrote the number on the back of a menu, he was conscious of people looking at him, asking themselves who this attractive woman was he was giving his number to. But he was more conscious of how close she was standing to him and how nice her perfume was. She stayed close as she said how he had always inspired her.

He was then surrounded by some of the black-tie great and good who wanted their little bit of attention from the minister, and though she stood there for a while, she eventually returned to her table. He was pleased when he spotted her in the bar later. He went to talk to her, found she was the marketing manager of a travel agency, separated, looking for a new challenge in life. Again, they were disturbed by men in dark suits and bow ties. But as he was fetching his coat from the cloakroom, he met her again. She stopped him, slid her hand into his, and asked if she could give him a lift home.

He had been driven around all day by a local party supporter who had irritated Ralph by asking him if he was all right more and more frequently as the afternoon wore on and Ralph became increasingly tipsy. It was 1 a.m. and the driver was still waiting outside. Ralph called him, apologised for being so late and said he was going to stay a little longer but a friend would take him home. Ten minutes later, having said goodbye to the organisers, he was being shepherded to the door by the lady in the lime-green dress. On their way out, they were stopped by a young couple who asked if they could have their picture taken with the minister. He felt rather puffed up as their friend snapped away, and his shapely companion hung back a couple of feet from his side.

He asked her to stop at an all-night off-licence where he bought a bottle of champagne and a carton of orange juice. He opened neither. The moment they were inside her house, he was helping her undress. At one point, as he was on top of her, trying to enter her, he somehow rolled over and fell off the bed, then made a joke about needing a sexual satnav.

'You are close to your destination but no longer on your planned route,' he said, as he climbed back on to the bed, and they laughed even more than when he was trying to undo all the hooks on her basque. They had sex once then he crashed out.

He had finished being sick. Picking out the newest-looking toothbrush from the cup by the sink, he gave his teeth a vigorous brush. He needed to shave but there were no razors in sight. Putting on his black suit and frilly white shirt, he caught a glimpse of himself in the mirror and winced. He stuffed his bow tie into his pocket and then looked around the house. Three bedrooms. A study without books. Downstairs a big kitchen and a small lounge. A dining room with a table but no chairs. And no people. He drank from the tap at the sink. He picked up the carton of orange juice. He walked to the front door and opened it. It was sunny but cold outside. It was when he saw a photographer and reporter on the doorstep that he realised the extent of the calamity he had brought upon himself.

'Mr Hall, what were you doing here at 65 Westmoreland Terrace with Davina Owens?'

So that was her name . . . It was a question both difficult and easy to answer. He narrowed his eyes against the glare of the sun and recognised the photographer busy snapping him as the man who had taken the photograph of him with the young couple the night before. He realised the whole thing had been a set-up. What was more, there was a camera crew filming from across the road.

'Don't worry,' said the reporter, 'they're with us.' How that was meant to stop him worrying was not entirely clear. He didn't have a clue where Westmoreland Terrace was. He was not even sure what town he was in. He began to walk towards what looked like a main road with road signs in green and blue, which meant taxis might come by. He was followed by the reporter, the camera in the van, and the photographer walking backwards and still snapping. His best picture was of Ralph hurling the orange-juice carton at the reporter. 'Not clever,' whispered the snapper. 'Really not very clever, Ralphie.'

The reporter was now in full flow. 'Can you confirm you are Ralph Hall, the Secretary of State for Health? Can you confirm you have just left the house behind us where last night you had sex with Davina Owens? Will you confirm, as Ms Owens has told us this very morning, that you met her at a Chamber of Commerce dinner, that you told her your driver had gone, and asked if she would give you a lift?'

'That is not true,' shouted Ralph.

'Well, tell us what is then.'

'I am saying nothing till I have spoken to my office.'

'Oh, don't worry. Number Ten should have told them by now. We've asked them for a comment.'

Ralph pulled his mobile out of his pocket. Seven missed calls. Oh shit. Why did he have it on mute?

'Go on, Ralph, answer,' said the snapper. 'Put the phone to your ear. Need a shot of you getting the call from the boss to ask what the hell you've been up to.'

'Fuck off.'

But he was discovering there was no point saying anything. The reporter pretended to be filing a story on his mobile.

'Health Secretary Ralph Hall launched into a foul-mouthed tirade as he was confronted over his sordid sex romps with gorgeous single mum Davina Owens yesterday . . . Owens told how the wannabe PM forced himself upon her after she invited him for a cup of coffee to discuss joining the party . . . But the drunken minister, a married father of two, insisted on plying her with champagne and having his evil way with her . . . Last night devastated Davina said, "I feel used. I wanted to talk about politics and he was just after one thing. He abused his authority and now I will have to pick up the pieces. He is not fit to be in Parliament if you ask me."'

As the photographer leered and the reporter laughed at his own wit, Ralph knew he was finished. He knew that it didn't matter if the details were false, because the basic story was true. He got drunk. He got laid. He couldn't deny it. 'Davina' could say what she liked, and if they didn't like how she said it, they could make her say more.

'She says you only wanted one thing,' said the reporter. 'How do you react to that?'

'Nothing to say.'

'She said you slagged off your Cabinet colleagues, including the PM. What do you say to that?'

'Rubbish.'

'So you deny slagging off your colleagues but you don't deny shagging Davina Owens. Can you confirm that?'

He was sweating heavily, and could feel his guts churning and raging. He was desperate to go to the toilet and throw up. Finally he saw a yellow light coming his way and ran towards it, chased by the photographer.

He got into the cab. 'Anywhere,' he said. 'Anywhere away from those bastards.'

'How's it going now, Mr Hall?' said the cabby. 'You havin' a bit of a bad time with them then?'

He got to his house. Another photographer and reporter waiting for him. He knew his career was over. He wished his life was. He felt it might as well be. When he was inside, he shut the door, leaned against it, slid to the floor and started crying. He didn't know what to do, who to call, who to reach out to.

24

There were at least two points of connection between Emily Parks and the small, tidy woman kneeling in prayer at the end of the pew. One was the obvious: they had both walked into the same church. The other, though neither knew it, was Professor Sturrock. The small, tidy woman was Mrs Temple, who was praying for the Professor, praying that he continue to find the strength to help David, who had accompanied her to church this morning, and was now waiting outside for her.

Emily was attending Mass for the first time since she'd left school. Though she'd gone to a Catholic girls' school, she remembered their visits to church more for the laughter and the larking around on the way there. God and Jesus were like names in a book, or lyrics in a song, and she did love to sing along. But she'd listened to the Mass every week without it ever meaning as much as it seemed to mean to other girls. She was not from a very religious family. Her parents were irregular churchgoers, though since the fire, her father had taken to going more often, especially during the week when nobody else was there, to pray for Emily. She'd hated the idea of him doing this – wasting his breath on a God who perhaps didn't even exist. But now, as she watched a queue of worshippers shuffling forward to take communion, she felt she understood her father better. She felt calm, at peace within herself.

It was a feeling that had begun on her walk the previous day, the first time she'd gone for a walk in daylight. She'd set out without a destination in mind and somehow found herself able to go as far as the Holloway Road, even though the pavements were packed with

Saturday shoppers and football fans heading towards the Emirates Stadium, where Arsenal had a home match. At first, it had been terrifying, for she knew she was heading towards an area even more crowded than the Caledonian Road. When she went out in daylight to the hospital, she had no choice, and she had the cocoon of her mother's car, and with it her mother's smothering concern. Here, each step was a choice, and as she made another step forward, she felt a tiny grain of confidence building within her. She pulled her headscarf tighter around her face and avoided looking at anyone. She just focused on one step at a time, and got caught up in the crowd, all now moving towards the same destination. She turned with the masses into Drayton Park, and walked past lines of police vans, programme sellers and fast-food outlets. Then, as she passed the stadium, she found hundreds of people now moving towards her, as they too headed to the ground. She knew she ought to feel scared, but she didn't.

She came to Gillespie Park, the council-run ecology centre where once she had taken her class for a whole day's nature study, and as she left the crowds, and opened the wooden gate into the park, she found herself smiling as she breathed in the cleaner air and enjoyed the sudden quiet. She walked past the smaller of the two ponds, down the little trail towards the bigger pond, and sat down on the long bench that overlooked it. She blew out her breath and saw the beginnings of a fog in the air. A young couple walked by, so lost in each other that they didn't notice her, and she smiled at that too. To her right, an elderly man was painting the scene, equally oblivious to her.

She sat for a while, watching two ducks glide slowly across the pond. One was leading the other, very slowly, so they left barely a ripple in the water behind them. She made a note to tell Professor Sturrock that she sat for a good half-minute and watched the ducks glide by. He was forever telling her to find new experiences and record them in her 'Pain Diary'. 'Pain Diary' was Emily's term for it, not Professor Sturrock's. He had simply asked her to divide each page into two columns and record her feelings, good on the right and bad on the left. She called it her Pain Diary because page after page was filled with bad feelings, while the right-hand column was largely empty. But, little by little, as she sat by the pond, she started to find things she could write in the diary to go alongside the bad. The ducks. The calm she had felt on entering the park. The feeling of the cold air on her face. The low autumn sun on the water. Even the occasional muffled roar that emerged from the stadium had a vibrancy that pleased her. She wished she had brought her notebook with her, so she could record all this while it was there in front of her.

This morning, she'd gone for the same walk. The streets were deserted compared with yesterday, yet still she was being seen by dozens of people. She was able to walk a little more quickly. Close to the entrance of the park, a man was walking two dogs, one a Dalmatian, the other a terrier of some sort that was constantly jumping up and down against the Dalmatian's side. She wasn't sure what possessed her, but she lifted her hand to her neck and loosened her scarf, pushed it back so that it rested at the top of her head, and flapped fairly loosely around her neck. As the man got nearer, she told herself to say 'Good morning' in a neutral, friendly way. It was the kind of thing that, before the fire, she always used to say to strangers out walking their dogs. She couldn't stand all that reserve that went with living in a busy part of the metropolis. It was why she used to love her visits to her grandparents in their little village in Warwickshire where on a Sunday morning all you could hear were the church bells and the echo of 'good morning' as people greeted each other as they went about their business. But that was then and this was now and she knew it was a big moment for her. She was about to say it, but he beat her to it.

'Morning,' he said. 'Bit cold, but stayed fine.'

There was no doubt about it: her face was clearly exposed to view. He must have seen it, but his expression had not changed.

'Morning,' Emily replied. 'Yes, isn't it a beautiful day?' And he was gone.

She walked into the park, and as the second pond came into view, glinting in the morning sun, she started to run down the muddy trail towards it. As she caught sight of the ducks, she felt a sensation as close to happiness as she had felt since before her disfigurement. She had brought some stale bread with her and she broke it into little pieces and tossed them onto the water. Immediately, seven ducks came towards her. She couldn't be sure if the two from yesterday were there. They're like raisins, she thought. No two ducks are the same. Once the bread was all gone, she sat on the long bench. She stayed there for an hour. For twenty minutes she studied the trees, watching one leaf and counting how many times it moved in a different direction. Seven. For half an hour, she looked at one small area of the pond. She watched the light patterns change, tried to follow one ripple and see where it led, waited for one of the ducks to come through that part of the pond, then followed the duck for a while, loving the little line it left behind it, then loving the way the line disappeared.

On the way home, she'd passed the church. The doors were open, and a hymn was being sung by a large congregation inside. She had only a vague purpose in entering. She thought it would be nice to hear the singing, and it would be a good place to have lots of new people see her face. But once she was inside, she found herself whispering her thanks.

She couldn't really explain how she had got here. It had happened so quickly. It was as though all the different parts of a psychological jigsaw had been hanging in space above her, sometimes moving to fit another shape, but then breaking apart again and flying elsewhere. Some were her own pieces. Some were her family's, their desires and fears for her. Sami the shopkeeper, with his kindness and offer of a job, was a big piece of the jigsaw. So was Professor Sturrock and the things he had said to her, which at the time she hadn't really taken in, or even listened to: his ideas on what makes a person, what is good and what is bad, what a lesson about the past really means, dreams, forgiveness, grief for what we lose when alive, living in the present tense. All these different ideas flying around in the space above her head and then somehow coming together in a way that made her want to see and be seen. The raisins and the ducks and the light on the water. How could it be that a fire had destroyed her and a raisin had helped to rebuild her? But it had. A humble raisin had taught her a lesson that no RE or social sciences teacher had ever been able to.

Last night, before going to sleep, she'd read a few chapters of the book Professor Sturrock had given her, about people who had survived trauma and disaster. She found herself flicking through to find the stories that involved fire. They included examples of suffering far greater than hers. A soldier with third-degree burns to most of his body and who was now running a soup kitchen for down-and-outs in Detroit. A firefighter who defied the orders of a superior in entering a collapsing warehouse to look for one last remaining person, and who broke his neck and back, and was burnt all over his face and body, when the roof caved in. There was a picture of him before the accident, resplendent in a new fire uniform, a huge smile creasing his face, and another of him now, in a wheelchair, wearing a neckbrace, an old fire brigades union baseball cap covering the damage to his scalp, his face scarred almost as much as Emily's. But the smile was the same, and the caption said simply: 'Kenny Macleod, firefighter, Glasgow, Scotland – "I lived to tell the tale."' And a nine-year-old girl who was the sole survivor of a blaze in Northern Ireland which killed her parents, two sisters and two brothers. The little girl was quoted as saying, 'When I heard the others were dead, I wanted to join them, but I had such a lot to do, what with the operations and the grafts. I live with my aunt and uncle now and they've been a real help. I miss everyone a lot but my uncle said so long as I'm here, a little bit of them is here, and I like thinking about that.'

Emily felt bad that she was grading the disfigurement of the people she read about, but she couldn't help herself. She put the American soldier at five stars, the Scottish fireman and the little girl from Northern Ireland at four, maybe three and a half. She put herself at three slash two and a half. She wondered if that was why Professor Sturrock had given her the book, to lead her to the insight that there were people worse off than she was. But she liked to think there was more to him than that. She doubted that he graded suffering. He struck her as someone who would look at every case on its own merits, and do his best for each. She then graded them for inspiration value. This time it was the little Ulster girl who gained five stars, while the fireman and the soldier got three. Perhaps it was the fact that they were doing a job they would expect to take them into dangerous situations, so perhaps had more forewarning, whereas she was just a little girl sleeping in the wrong place at the wrong time. She had lost loved ones, not merely her health.

She thought about how many stars she would give herself for inspiring others. It was an important moment, and a very solitary one. Even if she really tried to put a positive gloss on how she had handled herself, she could only go to one. Without the gloss, she wondered if she wasn't closer to zero. Perhaps that was why he gave her the book to read. Perhaps this was the conclusion she was meant to reach, that how she inspired or sought to inspire others would decide how well she recovered from the mental scarring. Yet far from inspiring her family, she knew she saddened them. She had walked away from them, preferring her own company to their constant efforts to make her feel better. As for inspiring anyone else, she had been avoiding people. The thought of baring her scars to a charity's cameras was one she had never had.

She was analysing not just her own reactions, but how they might fit into the psychiatrist's expectations of the process. She was determined to make her next session with him more productive and less confrontational than the last. She had noticed before how much their discussions on the Friday played around in her mind over the weekend. It must be strange for the Professor, she thought, to have all your patients out there at the weekend, ruminating, reflecting, some getting better, some getting worse, but all linked in to him, putting hopes in him. And it wasn't just the patients who did this, it was people like her mum who liked to think that he was some kind of miracle worker who would succeed where they had failed.

She reached for her Pain Diary, which she kept on the floor beside her bed.

'I cannot describe the feeling as I sat by the pond,' she wrote. 'I felt a serenity today that I cannot explain. It was a feeling of being alone, but I was fine about being alone. I felt vulnerable, but that was OK, because we *are all vulnerable. Out in the park today, I felt that there was a greater power than all of us, and it was guiding me to a better place. It was telling me to appreciate beauty wherever or whatever it may be. It was telling me that I came close to losing my life, but I still have life, and I should make of it what I can.'*

She wrote a final sentence. *'I feel like I have been walking through a forest where the trees are so tall and so tightly packed together that there is no light to guide me. Then I have seen a clearing and followed the trail that it's exposed. The trail was a long hilly climb through the last part of the forest. And then I find myself standing at the top of a mountain range and below me hills are rolling down to a beautiful lake, water shimmering in sunlight, and I am standing in awe of what I see.'*

In the church, the choir had started to sing again. Emily joined in.

25

David leaned against an unkempt family mausoleum in the graveyard outside the church and listened to the faint sound of the choir and organ. His mother had looked a bit hurt when he said he couldn't go in with her, but he'd given the excuse that Professor Sturrock wanted him to look at gravestones. She was sceptical but when he showed her the book, and the little drawing of a headstone, she accepted it. After God, Professor Sturrock was, for her, the voice of authority.

There were all sorts of gravestones and monuments in front of him, which he hoped would inspire him to do a good piece of home-work, and maybe even lift his mood a little. He liked the simple ones best. He found the enormous square plinths with their heavenward-pointing angels over the top. He was no keener on the heart-shaped headstones which were clearly becoming fashionable. He liked a plain slab of marble, with a simple cross, and a simple message.

He started to walk around the cemetery, stopping occasionally to read an inscription. Most were purely factual. Name, dates, brief description. Some stressed work: *Malcolm Rowan, banker,* for example. David wondered whether it was Mr Rowan (1929–2003) who chose that one-word description of his life, or his family. If his family, why did they not want to be recognised as part of his life and death? Or perhaps he lived alone all his adult life, and being a banker was all he or anyone else could think to say about him. Four stones down lay Iris Silver (1911–1999). *Much loved by 7 children, 29 grandchildren and Bertie.* He assumed Bertie was a pet, probably a dog. Again, who decided that Bertie should be included as part of the family on her gravestone? And why was there mention of the children and grandchildren but no mention of the man or men who fathered the seven children? Bertie couldn't have been the father, surely, tagged on at the end like that? David assumed Mrs Silver had a single husband who predeceased her. If so, why no place, on such a large headstone, for a little mention that Iris was joining Mr Silver in heaven?

The graves of children were the most moving, and often the best kept. Martha Rudd (1989–2001). *You lit up our lives every second you graced our world*. It wouldn't be true of course. There would have been times, during her twelve years, when little Martha must have annoyed Mr and Mrs Rudd. But they wouldn't remember those. The tragedy of a child dying young would leave them memories only of the joy and beauty they now missed so much. It was a nice thing to have on a headstone, he thought. He reflected that even Mrs Temple would be hard pressed to say of her own son that 'he lit up our lives'.

Who would 'our' be? There was only his mum really, and truth be told he often darkened her life with his terrible moods and his incessant staring at a fixed point in the near or middle distance, which is why she relied so heavily on God and Father Nicholas. When he felt his equilibrium was kind of OK, he made her life hard enough, but when, as now, he was low, he knew he made it even harder. He loved her for the way she just kept going, trying to make him happy and comfortable, even when she probably thought it was a lost cause, but it wasn't enough to lift his mood.

If he were to drop down dead right now, he thought, there wouldn't be many at his funeral. A few people from work, a few more from up and down the street, provided they could get time off, and no doubt Mum would round up some from church. Would his dad come? He doubted it. How would he know David had died? And how would he cope with the guilt he was bound to feel, surely, at leaving him so young, and wondering whether he had something to do with his early death? Or perhaps he wouldn't feel any guilt. Perhaps he'd forgotten David long ago. Perhaps he had a new family who knew nothing of his old one.

He took out his notebook and tried to write an inscription for himself. Really, it just boiled down to his mum, and his being a troubled soul.

'Here lies David Temple, a troubled soul, loved by his mother.' Was that it? Was that how he wanted to be remembered?

He tried again. 'Here lies David Temple, a troubled man who did his best to look after his mum, and look after himself.'

It didn't read right. 'Did his best' sounded so weak.

He walked a little further to study more graves. He preferred the messages that gave a sense of the person's character rather than what they were or did. 'He blessed us with his love' was a nice one. 'One of life's givers' was OK. 'You were a friend to all who knew you' a bit yucky, and probably untrue.

David found a little grass bank opposite a section devoted to over-seas servicemen and women, mainly Poles, who died in the Second World War. He sat down and turned to a blank page in his notebook. Then he drew his own gravestone. He based it on the rusty-coloured stone about eight yards away. It was taller than most, with a small cross at the top, then a name, Pawel Dabrowski (1922–1942), followed by a brief message in Polish.

David drew a clutch of flowers at the base. Then he faltered. Did he have any quality that was worthy of note? He thought again of the line Professor Sturrock had put on his homework once. '*You may think that you are less important than others, but what I think you are is humble. And humility is a fine quality.*'

Humility. It was one of Professor Sturrock's favourite themes. He believed that humility was the key to self-respect and mutual respect. At first when Professor Sturrock had called him 'humble', David had read it as meaning he was lowly and insignificant. But gradually he'd come to realise there was a more favourable interpretation, and though he would never go so far as to say it had made him feel special, he felt he understood what Professor Sturrock meant. He remembered an occasion when Professor Sturrock told him there was a humility in the way he gave expression to his feelings that he rarely saw in people far better off and far better educated than he was, and it was something he should be proud of.

He remembered too the time when he was complaining to Professor Sturrock about how some of the people at work treated him.

'You don't behave like that, David,' Professor Sturrock had said, 'because you have a sense of humility. If you can understand humility, then you have the key to life.'

Looking at the gravestones, David thought that maybe he was beginning to understand why Professor Sturrock had set the exercise. He took his pencil and filled in his gravestone.

Here lies David Temple
A humble and loving son.
Through his mother, and through struggle in life,
he learned that humility is the key to humanity.

He was pleased with it.

Several weeks ago, Professor Sturrock had asked him to write something about humility. Now he felt ready to do so. He turned to a fresh page and started to write, hoping the service inside the church would not be ending any time soon.

26

It transpired that even the little Ralph Hall knew about Davina Owens was false. She was not in marketing: she was a former model. It was not her house she had taken him to, but one that had been rented for the night. She worked part-time for a freelance press agency which specialised in undercover scams. They had been put on to Ralph by the *Sun* who sometimes used freelances in these kind of operations in case things went wrong and they could have a little bit of deniability.

Who had put the *Sun* on to Ralph, he could only imagine, but he clearly had an enemy out there. Not for the first time he kicked himself for indiscreet phone calls made from the car when he knew his London driver was a man who nurtured a grievance. But he couldn't believe his driver had the initiative to set up something like that. No, it was someone with more clout. Someone after his job perhaps.

Once Ralph had summoned the energy to pick himself up off the doormat of his house, he had a shower, shaved and dressed, and then went to phone Sandie. Then he changed his mind and called Number Ten instead. He told the PM's private secretary the facts – that he had got very drunk last night, he had been targeted by a woman and he had slept with her. The *Sun* had interviewed the woman and he feared the worst. He asked whether the PM had been told anything. 'Yes,' the private secretary had said, curtly. He asked how he had reacted. 'He just wants to know the facts before he can decide anything.'

'But he didn't say it was curtains per se?' asked Ralph, conscious of how pathetic and pleading he sounded.

'No, he didn't. As I told you, he's waiting for the facts.'

Ralph said he was heading back to London, he would be saying nothing to the paper, and he would keep in touch.

'Yes,' said the Number Ten official. 'Let's keep in touch.'

He bottled out of the conversation with Sandie and decided to text her from the train instead. If he asked her to collect him from the station in the car, he thought, he could get her away from the reporters who would be sure to gather on his Pimlico doorstep as soon as he got back, and also use the short drive to tell her what had happened.

There was another photographer waiting at Newcastle station. 'Damn,' said Ralph, realising he should probably have got the cab driver to take him all the way to London. It meant they knew what train he was on so there would be more than Sandie to the welcoming party. Once the train had pulled out of the station, he texted Sandie to say his driver was ill and he couldn't get an ordinary cab because of the nature of some government papers he was carrying. It was lame, he knew, but the best he could think of given his hangover and his general state of mind. 'I'm jetlagged,' she texted back. 'Can't you get another driver?' 'Please xxx,' he replied. 'OK,' came the response, her reluctance clear.

The train was due in just after half past two. He spent most of the journey staring out of the window and trying to avoid conversation with the couple at his table. The man had nudged his wife and motioned towards Ralph as he sat down. She had looked a little perplexed, then her husband whispered, 'Ralph Hall, the politician,' and she said, 'Oh yes,' and smiled.

'Just telling the wife,' said the man. 'Recognised you.'

'Like it's a fucking quiz game,' Ralph thought of saying, but instead he just smiled.

'You must get used to it. Sorry,' said the man.

'It's fine,' said Ralph. 'If you can't stand the heat and all that.'

He thought ahead to tomorrow, and the conversation his travelling companions would have when they learned they had sat on a train with a man whose sexual shenanigans would be all over the news, and possibly lead to his demise as a minister.

He studied the woman's thin lips and imagined her leaning on a garden fence telling the neighbours, 'You'd never guess for a second he was in trouble. Like butter wouldn't melt in his mouth.' Now she was looking at him, smiling.

When the food and drink trolley came round, Ralph bought a small bottle of white wine, a cheese sandwich and three bottles of water, which he drank so fast the woman opposite appeared mesmerised. As the trolley went into the next carriage, he pretended to be going to the toilet, but actually followed it in order to get three miniatures of whisky. Then he did go to the toilet, to drink them.

Another reporter and photographer greeted him as he stepped off the train on to the platform at King's Cross. The couple from his table were just behind him. 'What a life,' said the husband to his wife. 'Having the press turn up wherever you go.'

'Do you have anything to say, Mr Hall, about the claims made by Ms Owens?' asked the reporter.

'I don't,' he said. He was aware of how ghastly he must have looked leaving Davina Owens's place, so he agreed to stop and pose for a photo in the vain hope the paper would use this one rather than the shots of him emerging bleary-eyed and half dressed from what the paper would call the 'love nest', not to mention the shot of him throwing orange juice at a reporter. He also hoped that if they got a picture now, and got the message he wasn't talking, they might leave him to walk to meet Sandie alone. He had no such luck.

He didn't know how to begin to tell Sandie what a mess he was in. All these years, she had supported him and now he was about to put her to the kind of test no politician could wish for his wife. He knew how humiliating it would be, for both of them. But at least it would be more humiliating for him, and he was hopeful that she would see the whole sorry episode as a twisted way of getting his problem out in the open, and stand by him. Clearly, he would have to say something when the story broke, and he thought that Sandie would want to as well. He imagined her in one of her smart dark suits walking calmly down the steps from the front door at home, standing absolutely still until the media had settled and were listening politely, then telling them it would take much more than one drunken night and a newspaper set-up to destroy their marriage and their family. Then she'd hire someone to run the business for her and take six months off to help him fight the demon drink. Telling her about last night would be tough, but though he was almost sick with nerves, he retained confidence in her and confidence that, together, they'd get through this.

The reporter and the photographer followed him all the way to the car park, the photographer walking backwards and so drawing unwelcome attention to Ralph holding his suit carrier and his red box. Sandie was parked just round the corner from where a little queue of tourists were having their photo taken by the Harry Potter wall, Platform 9¾. Ralph was desperate for her to stay in the car and not get out to meet him. He hurried to the car, opened the boot, threw in his bags and jumped in. The photographer was crouching over the bonnet getting shots of both of them, Sandie looking confused, Ralph looking flustered. As he tried to shut the car door, he found the reporter's body in the way.

'Mrs Hall, has your husband told you about Davina? What do you have to say?'

Ralph banged the door hard against the reporter's hip, three times, and eventually he was able to force him away and slam the door shut.

'Go, go, go, Sandie. Go. Fast.'

But she was going nowhere.

'Who is Davina? Who are these people? What is going on?'

The reporter was tapping on her window, asking if she realised she had a rival. The photographer had a fantastic shot of Sandie looking thunderstruck as Ralph put his head in his hands.

'Please, Sandie. Please drive. I'll tell you what's happening when we're away from these animals.'

Reluctantly she started the car and sped off. After a quarter of a mile, she turned off York Way, and parked up opposite a little hotel.

'Right,' she said. 'What's happening?'

'I don't know where to start.'

'Start with Davina.'

'Can I start earlier?'

'OK. Start earlier, and end with Davina.'

'I haven't wanted to worry you but I've been seeing a psychiatrist for a while. About my drinking. I met him through a policy review and when I realised I had a problem I asked for his help.'

'And he suggested Davina as a cure?'

'Please, Sandie, don't make this even harder. He suggested I try to stop drinking. But I can't. I have been drinking quantities like you wouldn't even imagine.'

'You seem to think I'm blind, Ralph. I have seen a few signs.'

'It's worse than you think. Far worse. Anyway, it's been going on for a while and getting worse and worse and last night I'm afraid I got absolutely smashed, and I seem to have been targeted by this woman and it turns out she was doing it for a newspaper. So the top and bottom is I'll be all over the *Sun* tomorrow, and it will be absolutely humiliating and I will probably get the sack.'

Sandie had both hands on the steering wheel. She sighed and her head fell forward, almost hitting her hands. Then she sat up and looked at him. He was trying to read her eyes. There seemed to be more understanding than hurt or panic.

'You know, I've been expecting something like this, Ralph. You've been slipping away from me.'

'Sandie, I promise you it's not what you think.'

'Do you really know what I think? Do you ever take the time to consider what I might think?'

'Of course I do.'

'No, Ralph, you don't, because you never take any initiative unless it's to do with you, your work, your career. Things just happen to you, as if it's not your creation – like this woman who "targeted" you. I suppose that's your way of saying you had sex with her.'

'Look, Sandie, I can barely remember meeting her.'

'Did you have sex with her?'

'I think so.'

'You think so? That sounds like a yes to me.'

'I honestly can't remember, Sandie, but she will certainly say I did and much else besides.'

'And what do you expect me to do in this situation?'

This was a question Ralph had not anticipated. He had expected Sandie to intuit what was expected, without him having to tell her, and regardless of how hurt and angry she might be. He remained silent, trying to make himself look as penitent as possible.

'I suppose you want me to pose with you in front of the world's press and talk about all the terrible pressures poor politicians are under, don't you?' she said. 'Well, I'm sorry, Ralph, but I'm not going to be humiliated. I've given my life to your job, and now I want to do something for me.'

Ralph felt as if he was going to be sick.

'Sandie, please don't do this to me. I am going to lose my career in a matter of hours. Don't take away my marriage too.'

'You should have thought of that when Davina seemed to be targeting you.'

'One chance. Just one chance. It might not be as bad as I think.'

'Ralph, I don't care how bad it looks in the papers. I care how bad it *is*. And it is bad.'

'What if I give up the job, and I get proper help, and we try to make a new start of it?'

'I just can't see it happening,' she said. 'I can't see it.'

Ralph could feel tears welling up behind his eyes. He hoped that if he cried, she might think again.

'Please, Ralph, don't cry,' she said, looking as if she might break down herself. For a moment she hesitated, then she got out of the car and started removing his bags from the boot.

'I don't think I can take you home with all that's coming our way,' she said. 'I suggest you find a hotel. That one over the road might do. I will put together some stuff for you and your driver can collect it when he's feeling better. We can talk about lawyers in a few days' time when the dust has settled. I will talk to the children and if they want to speak to you, they will. Now, in the name of God, go.'

He was stunned. He had imagined every possible reaction, but not this, not straight away, as soon as she heard. He stepped out of the car, retrieved his bags from the pavement and watched as Sandie drove off at speed. The road was empty apart from a bus making its way towards him. For a few moments he thought about jumping in front of it, but decided it was not going fast enough to guarantee killing him, so he watched it go by then waved down a cab and asked to be driven to the Health Department in Whitehall.

The call from Number Ten came five minutes after he got there. The switchboard operator, polite and friendly, said, 'Good afternoon, Secretary of State, I have the Prime Minister for you.' He then had to wait almost a minute as she linked up the various officials who would listen in to the call.

He knew from the tone of the Prime Minister's very first syllable – 'now' – that his instinct had been right. He was about to be sacked.

'Now, Ralph. I've made a couple of calls about this situation, and I'm afraid it's not good. I think people might just about understand the sex thing, though it's not exactly what they want from their ministers. But they will rightly worry about the judgement attached to getting into this situation in the first place. So having thought about this carefully, I've decided I am going to have to ask for your position.'

Ralph tried to protest, but the Prime Minister wouldn't let him. The b in 'but' had barely left his lips when he was shut down.

'You are more than welcome to pop over to Number Ten but I'm afraid there is no discussion about this. I've decided. It is tough, I know, but sometimes leaders have to do tough things.' As he spoke, Ralph could picture the Number Ten officials scribbling that down as they listened, ready to brief the media on how tough and decisive and moral the young twenty-first-century Prime Minister had been.

'Ralph, this does not mean that one day you cannot come back, and I will say some very nice things about you in the exchange of letters. What I advise you to do is try to save your marriage, work hard in the constituency and, though it pains me to say this, I think you need to see someone about your drinking. We've had a number of reports to the effect that you have been the worse for wear in public places, and I think you need to sort that out.'

Ralph was shocked that the PM knew about the drinking. He even wondered whether his reference to 'seeing someone' was made because he knew he already was.

He had uttered not one single word in the entire call, just half a 'but', and he had very little to say now.

'Very well, Prime Minister. I have made a mistake and I understand why you want to deal with this before the media creates a great frenzy out of it. Just one thing. Could I ask who will be replacing me?'

'Daniel Melchett, so don't worry. The department is in good hands. Now you take care and let's keep in touch.'

The line went dead and Ralph sat holding the phone in his lap, not quite daring to believe that what he'd just heard was true. He looked around his vast office. By morning, Daniel Melchett would be here, master of all that Ralph surveyed. For one, horrible moment he remembered how friendly Melchett's driver was with his own. Surely Melchett, his closest friend in politics, wouldn't be capable of such treachery? He started to dial his number. But what would he say? 'Congratulations on getting my job'? It would not be an easy conversation. He decided not to call.

As it was Sunday, he didn't even have any staff to help him clear his desk or make a cup of tea. He opened the top drawer, took out the hip flask, and emptied it in seven enormous swigs. Then he picked up the phone to call Martin Sturrock. He wasn't entirely sure what the psychiatrist could do to help him, but he felt an overwhelming need to see him. Unfortunately, Sturrock's phone went to voicemail. He left a plaintive message. 'Martin, it's me, Ralph. Please, please, please call as soon as you can. I am desperate.'

Number Ten had wasted no time in announcing his 'resignation for personal reasons' and the media were gathering outside. He persuaded a weekend security man to drive him out of the back. The security man said he could not leave his post for long, but would get him away from the immediate area.

'Is this OK?' he asked as they reached the south side of Westminster Bridge, by County Hall.

'Yes, it's fine, thank you,' said Ralph.

'Take care of yourself, Secretary of State,' said the security man.

Ralph stood on the pavement and muttered the words 'Secretary of State' to himself. One minute he was. Now he wasn't. He was no more or less important than the tourists heading for a trip on the London Eye. He watched two nurses laughing as they walked towards St Thomas's Hospital, and reflected that they were still part of the NHS, and he was not.

It was getting dark, and the lights from the cars and buses and buildings gave him a headache, not helped by the cold and oppressive air. But he thought the Houses of Parliament looked more glorious than ever, lit up against a gloomy sky.

He stood and stared at the building, remembering the first time he arrived there as an elected member, and how Sandie had taken his hand as the cab took them through the members' entrance, and said he could go as high and as far as he wanted and she would always be there beside him. Then there was his maiden speech and the nice write-up in the *Northern Echo*. He could see the lights on in the room where he attended his first select committee. He recalled his first speech as a frontbencher and the nerves he felt, even in a chamber nearer empty than full. And he thought of some of the great characters he knew, and the friends he thought he had made. Yet he looked now at this beautiful building as though it had just materialised from an alien planet. It had nothing to do with him any more. He was finished.

He had no idea where to go, so walked south down Westminster Bridge Road. Through the windows of the Crown and Cushion pub he could see a TV screen and pictures of himself at the last general election, kissing Sandie as his increased majority was announced. He stood at the window and watched the tickertape box at the bottom of the screen where the words were changing every few seconds as the story was being told.

'Minister Hall sacked over sex scandal.' Then: 'PM regrets "tough decision".' . . . 'Wife stays silent.' . . . 'Tabloid about to expose drunken sex romp.' . . . 'Melchett takes over as PM acts fast.'

There were about fifteen people in the pub. Only one appeared to be watching the breathless reporter standing outside Downing Street.

Ralph walked on, then through a side street into a local estate where he sat on a bench overlooking a tiny children's playground, and tried to think. There was no one he could turn to. His dad was old and frail – the news might give him a heart attack. And besides, he felt far too ashamed to call his father. As for his children, there was no way he could face them in this state. The thought of spending a night in some anonymous hotel, worried that the staff might tip off the press, and even more worried that he might empty the minibar, filled him with dread. He had to get help.

He tried Professor Sturrock again. Still voicemail.

27

'I'll be having that,' said Stella, whisking away her husband's mobile and putting it into a drawer. 'Today is a family day. No patients allowed.'

Sturrock felt too weak to protest. He'd been trying to send a text message to Phyllis about the patients whose appointments she would have to cancel as a result of Tuesday's funeral. Now he'd be worrying about it all day. He pulled quietly at the rubber band on his wrist and let it snap back against the skin. Think positive. He was finding it hard though. He'd taken an age to get dressed, then spent much of the morning sitting in the kitchen drinking tea and watching Stella bustle about. She seemed happy, excited about the prospect of some time with her son. She even hummed. He felt pleased she was happy, pleased for her, but also glad she was too preoccupied to notice how low he was.

When Jack arrived with his friend Charlie for lunch, he went to meet them at the door. He never quite knew how to greet his son, who was not the most expressive of characters, at least not with him. He had planned on hugging him and saying 'Happy birthday' as he arrived, but for some reason Charlie came in first, his son trailing behind, so the moment for a hug passed. Professor Sturrock made do with a friendly tap on the shoulder, and said, 'Happy birthday, Jack. Mum's through in the kitchen.'

Stella was putting the finishing touches to a chocolate cake, as well as getting lunch together, so she gave her son a quick peck on the cheek and then gestured to her husband to get the champagne, indicating with her eyebrows that he was to kick off the festivities.

Sturrock realised he hadn't got off on the right foot. The champagne bottle felt heavy in his hands and he wasn't confident about getting out the cork without the stuff spraying all over the place. Jack came to his rescue, giving Charlie a look which Sturrock read as saying, 'Feeble my dad, isn't he?'

'Michelle said she might make it after lunch,' Sturrock said, making a stab at conversation. His elder daughter Suzanne lived with her husband in Italy, so couldn't come, but Michelle was not far away in Notting Hill.

'Oh, I just got a text from her,' said Jack. 'She can't make it. Got a friend who's playing in a rugby match or something. Said to say hi.'

The news came as a blow, although neither his wife nor his son seemed to mind. He'd been looking forward to seeing Michelle. She was the only one of his children who could make him laugh, and he felt particularly close to her. But she was a fashion designer and her work often took her overseas so visits were rare.

'She's always so busy at weekends,' said Stella. 'If she's not working, she's catching up with her friends. It's nice to know she's got such a full life though.'

Sturrock took it more personally. Why was someone's rugby match more important than seeing her father? He felt slighted, even though he knew he probably shouldn't. Again he pulled at the rubber band on his wrist.

'Would you like your present?' he asked. But Stella had it worked out. 'No, no, Martin. We'll have lunch, then we'll have the cake and the present.'

They all stood in the kitchen sipping champagne and trying to make conversation. Jack was taciturn as usual. Sturrock wished one of his talkative daughters was there to keep things going. Suzanne, who had gone to art school in Rome, and settled there after marrying one of her teachers, was now making sculptures – not very good ones, in his opinion, but they always provoked discussion and she could be guaranteed to burble on about the latest happenings in the art world. But they saw her less and less.

Jack was trying to make it as a music producer. His friend Charlie was already quite well established and worked in something called 'final production', which Sturrock understood to be the final mixing and improving of sounds on CDs. He had worked on a recent album which got a lot of attention because there was no physical product as such. It was download only and had earned a fortune in related advertising. Charlie was always very well dressed, and groomed. He had immaculate short hair, wore jewellery that was fashionable without being gaudy and overly expensive, and he had quite a feminine way of walking and moving. Sturrock was sure he was gay, which of course had him wondering about his son. Jack had had girlfriends in the past, but his one serious relationship had ended when the girl got a job in the Midlands and he hadn't brought another home since.

He was sure he wouldn't mind if his son was gay. He'd had many homosexual patients over the years and his emphasis with them had always been that there should be no stigma attached to it. Some were absolutely tortured by their sexuality, their fear of discovery and what their family might think. Yet mostly, once they discussed the issue with their family, they found acceptance. That being said, only three weeks ago he'd had in his consulting room a young man traumatised after a homophobic attack which left him wanting to go back to a state of denial about who and what he was. He couldn't bear it if Jack suffered similar abuse. But no, thought Sturrock; whether or not Jack was gay was not the issue. Of course he hoped to be a grandfather but he knew his daughters would eventually provide on that front. The issue with Jack was that he didn't know about his son's sexuality, he didn't know how to ask, and it made him feel deeply inadequate as a parent that Jack never really confided in him. He was forced to acknowledge that whereas hundreds of people saw him as the first person they would want to talk to if they got into emotional or psychological trouble, Jack wasn't among them.

Stella's theory, most dramatically aired on their holiday in Devon all those years ago, but more subtly expressed on many occasions since, was that the children understood their dad wanting to put other people first in theory, but found it harder in practice. It was a philosophy that led to them feeling alienated from him. His theory was that his own father's habits were deeply ingrained in him and though he tried to do better as a parent, and did do better, he was starting from so far back that he didn't have a chance. When it came to patients, he had learned how to act with them. It was a skill that he had developed and improved over time. But with his family, he got into certain habits early on, and never really changed the skills set. So Stella was the one they looked to because she had been the one who was always there. He played at it. He contented himself with being a better, more attentive and loving father than his own father had been. But to a modern child growing up in modern Britain, that was not nearly enough. And now they were grown up and, to quote a phrase Jack was overfond of using, 'we kind of don't give a fuck'. Only he knew that they *did*, just as he didn't go through a single day without at some point giving a fuck about his father.

So they talked about whether the BBC should allow advertising on its main channels, and Charlie tried to explain the copyright issues that were making life hard for many record labels, and then they talked about how Catch Up TV had changed their viewing patterns. With a bit of small talk thrown in, those topics just about got them through lunch.

It was after lunch, when the cake had been eaten, the book of photographs admired and the coffee drunk, that things started to flag badly. Sturrock wanted desperately to go up to his bedroom, draw the curtains, lie down and shut out the world. He caught Jack giving his friend amused glances and was sure they were laughing at him. He was asking himself if he was being paranoid, but concluded he had reason to be. He wished they were gone.

By teatime, when Stella began bringing out the biscuits, they had all descended into silence. Jack was just suggesting watching a DVD together when the doorbell rang.

'That might be Michelle after all,' said Sturrock hopefully. 'Perhaps her match has finished.'

Stella went to answer the door, and her face as she walked back in revealed very clearly that it was not their daughter.

'I don't have a clue what's going on here, Martin, but Ralph Hall is at the front door. I explained that we were in the middle of a birthday celebration but he seemed to think you would want to see him.'

Sturrock saw on Jack's face the adult version of a look he recalled from when his son was growing up. It was a look that would appear whenever he was forced to take a work call at home, or when he had to miss attending a school sports event or a parents' evening because one of his patients 'needed him'.

'Excuse me,' he said. 'I'll try to be quick.'

Ralph stood on the doorstep, where Stella had left him. He looked dreadful. Tired, yet agitated, almost manic.

'I am so sorry to do this to you, Martin, I really am.'

'That's OK. Come in.'

He took Ralph into his study, and offered him a cup of tea.

'I know your job is to stop me,' Ralph said, looking shamefaced, 'but I really could do with something stronger.'

Sturrock hesitated for a moment, but he realised that there was little point trying to put Ralph on a detox programme at this precise moment. They could come to that later.

'How about a WI?' he asked, trying to convey in his smile both gentleness and concern.

'W2 would be better,' said Ralph. He smiled too, but the smile was too weak to detract from the wretchedness written all over his face. He seemed a lot older than he had on Friday. He looked grey and a little jaundiced and his hands were shaking.

'You don't look too good, Ralph,' Sturrock said as he retrieved a bottle of Macallan he kept in his filing cabinet. 'I ought to warn you, this whisky is at least three years older than it says on the bottle. We're not big drinkers.'

He sat down opposite Ralph and said, 'Now, Ralph . . .'

'My God, you sounded like the PM then.'

'I didn't mean to, I can assure you. Now what's happening?'

Ralph was barely coherent as he tried to rattle out what had happened in the last twenty-four hours. When he came to the end, he put his head in his hands.

'Martin, I'm finished. I'm dead. It's all over. This is worse than anything I have ever imagined and you have to help me.'

Sturrock looked at the broken man in front of him and felt his own anxiety ratcheting upwards. Ralph Hall was investing his last hope in him, without realising that he, too, was on his way down, incapable of holding a proper conversation with his family, let alone helping someone else through the biggest crisis in their life, all in the gaze of a cruel and prurient media. He searched his mind for the appropriate response. Fortunately, something clicked and years of experience helped the words come out, almost without him thinking about them.

'Well, Ralph, I can't say I'm well qualified to handle all the ramifications politically, but from my point of view the questions are these: What do you want to happen? Is there any chance of you getting back with your wife? That's really very important, because I don't like the idea of you on your own at the moment. And finally, how are you going to handle your drinking in the short term, when you'll be feeling under much more pressure and with a lot more focus on you?'

'I can't get through this without a drink, Martin, I'm telling you that for nothing.'

'What about my first question? What do you want to happen?'

'I want to survive,' Ralph said in a voice choked with emotion. He then began to emit a sound that Sturrock could only describe as wailing. He sounded like a baby. 'I want to survive. I want to survive.'

Stella popped her head round the door.

'Are you going to be able to watch this film with us, or shall we start without you?' she asked. Then she noticed Ralph Hall was crying, and left before her husband could answer.

Ralph sobbed for a few moments, apologised, pulled himself together a little and said, 'Martin, you have to understand – this is everything I am. Politics is my life and it is draining away. By the morning I'll be a laughing stock. I could have been Prime Minister but instead I will be a national joke. Because I got pissed. Again. Because I can't stop drinking and I can't stop drinking because . . . Because why, Martin? Why can't I?'

'Because it has a hold of you. It's called the demon drink because there is a demon in there somewhere and it loves to make you feed it with drink. It has a hold of you because there is something in you that you want to forget and not have to worry about. It may be something in your past. It may be your feeling that you're not fulfilling your ambitions. It may be a sense of inadequacy you don't want to acknowledge. It can be many things but it has got a hold and we have to break it.'

'How?'

'Ralph, it is not for me to tell you what to decide, but your health has to come first. In my opinion, your marriage is part of your health, and your career is the cause of your ill health. That is my professional analysis. I hope it helps you to think about what to do.'

'But I want to survive. I don't want to be humiliated.'

'I know. But the papers will give up on you after a while. You'll still be there, having to live with yourself, whatever it is that you're doing, in or out of politics. That is more important.'

'I want to survive.'

'Ralph, this is going to sound harsh. But you have lost your job and with it, so you think, your career. You have lost your wife, though I am not convinced that cannot be salvaged at a later date. You have lost everything because of your own actions, driven by drink. But you need to know if you carry on as you are, next on the losing line is your life. Do you understand that?'

Put so starkly, it pulled Ralph up short, and for a moment he put his glass down.

'Yes I do,' he said, before looking intently at the glass and then picking it back up.

'You think this has happened to you suddenly, but I think it has been building for years. That's how it works, and then once it has worked its way in, it can be hellish to get out. And even if you were able to stop drinking, the chances are the demon will still be in there, trying to get you to drink again, or do something else you shouldn't in order to feed it. You have to see it in those terms.'

'But how do you beat it? I can't even begin to think of how I would get through a day without drink right now.'

'I understand that. But you're going to have to. You have to see this as the low point. You're close to the gutter, Ralph. You've held it together after a fashion because you've had to observe the norms and do all the things expected of you. But that's all gone. You're out, and you'll never get back unless you clean up your act. So you have to clean up.'

Ralph looked at him, full of fear. 'I know, I know, I know. There's no point keeping on telling me. But how? Just tell me what I have to do.'

'Check yourself into a drying-out clinic tomorrow first thing. Get the shakes and the sweats and the elephants going up the wall, and then get on to a proper programme and take it a day at a time. It's the only way I know. I've not been able to push you towards it because I've been sympathetic to the extra pressures your career and your profile have put you under. I understand why Alcoholics Anonymous was not an option before, but it might be now. I'll give you some numbers to call. Find a hotel tonight and then ring them in the morning.'

'I can't see it. I can't imagine a waking hour without drink.'

'You will. Or if you don't, you're dead. Your call.'

Ralph's head slumped forward as he cupped both hands around his glass. 'It's not a great day to start.'

'It is the best possible day to start.'

'I can't, Martin. I know I can't. I have to get a few days the other side of this. And then take stock. But I can't not drink. Not tonight. Not now. I just can't.'

Ralph helped himself to the Scotch. Then came another little blow.

'I can't face staying in a hotel, Martin, with all the prying eyes and the people who'll tip off the press for a few quid.'

He looked beseechingly at Sturrock, who knew what was coming.

'I don't suppose I could stay here, could I? It'd be just one night . . .'

Not for the first time that day, Professor Sturrock felt what little energy he had seep out of him. He couldn't deal with this, not on Jack's birthday, with Stella on the warpath, all the preparation he needed to do for his consultations the next day, Aunt Jessica's eulogy. But there was no way he couldn't say yes.

Just as he was about to speak, Stella came in again. She had her coat on.

'Would you like to come and say goodbye to your son?' she said, deliberately not looking at Ralph.

'Is he going?'

'Yes. And I'm going with him.'

'What do you mean?'

'I can see you're busy, so I thought I'd go with Jack to his flat and have dinner there tonight.'

'I see.'

Sturrock didn't see, but he was conscious of needing to maintain his equilibrium in front of Ralph. He went out into the hall with Stella.

'There you go,' said Jack.

'By which I think he means "par for the course",' said Stella.

'I'm very sorry, Jack,' he said, ignoring Stella's barbed comment. 'See you soon, I hope.'

'Yes,' said Jack.

'You won't tell anyone Mr Hall is my patient, will you?'

Jack shrugged, a shrug that said, 'You just don't get it, do you?' and followed his mother and Charlie out of the house.

'Fuck, I really am sorry,' said Ralph.

'Don't worry,' he said. 'Today was always going to be a disaster on that front. If it hadn't been you, it would have been something else.'

Later, he showed Ralph to the spare bedroom, found a new toothbrush, toothpaste and razor, and suggested he tidy himself up and try to get a little rest.

He needed rest too. He felt so weighed down he could sleep standing up. Not only was the eulogy unwritten, he hadn't sorted out how he was going to get his mother from her home to the funeral in Somerset. He would call Jan in the morning. As he went to the bedroom, he wondered whether to go and read his emails, and prepare himself properly for the patients he was seeing tomorrow. He knew he should. But he felt too exhausted. He felt weak. He thought if he could get to bed early, he could wake up early and do today's work tomorrow before he headed to the hospital.

Stella phoned as he was climbing into bed. She said she was staying the night at Jack's.

'OK,' he said. 'Probably for the best, Ralph Hall's still here . . . Will you be back tomorrow morning?'

'We'll see,' she said. 'I need to think a little. Today was just . . .'

'I know,' he said.

Lying in bed, he was conscious of the rubber band tight around his wrist. He wanted to take it off, fling it into a corner, but he forced himself to keep it there. Then began the long wait for sleep to come. Despite everything, he missed having his wife's body alongside his. Often Stella's breathing would lull him to sleep, and tonight he needed that more than ever. He knew from experience that sometimes the desire to sleep, when he felt under pressure or was in the midst of a plunge, was matched by an inability to do so. He prayed to nobody and nothing in particular that tonight wouldn't be one of his nights without sleep. That added to the sense of beleaguerment.

He tried to tell his mind to be still, but it ignored him. He tried to tell it to think of one thing at a time, but it refused. Little fragments of thoughts and fears were flying in from many different angles, some causing him to wince a little. In an effort to calm things, he started to plan out tomorrow's cases, patient by patient, but the strategy failed when he got to Hafsatu Sesay's appointment and his mind immediately began tracing the curves of her body. He felt all the old shame welling up in him.

At around ten past three, he heard a noise downstairs. He got up and tiptoed down the stairs. The light was on in his study. He went in to find Ralph lying on the floor. He had clearly waited till Sturrock was in bed and then gone downstairs to resume his drinking. The Scotch bottle was empty. He had begun to demolish a bottle of gin, neat. He was now lying on his side, and had a cut on his head, presumably from hitting it himself on the corner of the little table by the fireplace as he fell. At first, Sturrock thought he might need a stitch in it, but he cleaned it up and put a plaster on it and felt that would be enough. Ralph was incapable of speech. Sturrock was incapable of carrying him up the stairs. He hauled him on to the sofa, took off his shoes and went to get a blanket. By the time he came back downstairs with it, Ralph was vomiting. Sturrock felt himself plunge another notch as he went to fetch a bucket. It was almost 4 a.m. and he was going to have to spend the next half-hour clearing up another man's sick from the carpet and sofa, and do it sufficiently well for his already furious wife not to notice what had happened if and when she came back to the house. By 4.30 he had mopped up the worst, settled Ralph and gone back to bed. He finally fell asleep just before five.

28

'Lirim,' Arta whispered. 'Lirim. Are you awake?' It was just after 4 a.m., and she knew he was asleep, but she was desperate to talk to him. She couldn't bear the fact that they hadn't really resolved their argument which had hung over them all weekend. Waking him was the only answer to her own inability to sleep.

'Lirim, are you listening to me?'

Without opening his eyes, her husband moved closer to her in the bed. She placed her hand firmly on his arm, and squeezed it hard.

'Lirim, I want to say I'm sorry. I shouldn't have got angry. I shouldn't have slept in the children's room last night. Can you hear me? I'm sorry.'

Lirim turned over and nuzzled into her neck. She put her arms round him.

'I hear you,' he said. Then he kissed her gently on her cheek.

It had been such a strange day, she didn't know what to feel about anything. Lirim had left for the car wash early without speaking to her. She'd been lying awake on the floor by Besa's bed, and heard him getting ready for work. She was longing for him to come in and pretend there was nothing wrong, but all she heard was his morning cough and the sound of the front door closing behind him. Breakfast was just as lonely, as she avoided Alban's reproachful gaze. Then the doorbell had rung.

She hated the ring, partly because it was a harsh, tinny sound, but more for the memories it brought back every time she heard it. Yet Lirim had offered to change it many times, and she always refused.

She shouted to Alban not to answer, and walked slowly down the hallway. As she looked through the security spyhole, she noticed the pink tracksuit first, and alongside it, the little boy Alban had fouled and punched yesterday. He looked smaller out of his football gear. He had a bruise at the side of his nose, a plaster across the top.

Suddenly, Arta felt scared. She turned back to Alban.

'It's them, the boy from the football and his mum.'

She took another look through the spyhole. The boy looked as she felt. Anxious, scared. The mother looked much softer than she had yesterday. She had her hand on the back of her son's head, and was patting him gently. He was staring at the floor.

Arta freed the security catch, and opened the door.

'Hello, I'm Maggie Phelps,' said her visitor. 'This is Dean.'

The tone was friendly, almost embarrassed. Dean was still looking at the floor.

'I hope you don't mind us just turning up.'

'How did you know where we lived?'

'We live over there,' said Maggie, pointing to the next block. 'It's how Dean knew who your boy was.'

'Oh.'

'Anyway, Dean's got something to say, haven't you, Dean?'

The boy nodded.

'Go on then, son.'

'Sorry,' he said.

Arta was taken aback. She stood in silence, not knowing how to respond.

'Sorry for what I said,' added Dean.

'Is your lad in?' asked Maggie.

'Yes,' said Arta guardedly, about to make some excuse about how they needed to go out. But then she stopped herself. This woman and her son had clearly made a big effort to come here. She should be polite to them.

'Come in, please,' she said.

Alban was standing at the kitchen door.

'Let's go through to the kitchen,' said Arta. 'I'll make some tea.'

Alban and Dean avoided looking at each other. But as Arta made the tea, Maggie said to Alban, 'Dean has something to say to you.'

Alban looked at the boy for the first time.

'Sorry,' said Dean. 'Sorry for calling you an asylum seeker and telling you to go home.'

Alban nodded. 'OK.'

'Is that all you have to say?' said Arta.

'I'm sorry too,' he said. 'Sorry I fouled you. Sorry I punched you.'

Arta and Maggie were both smiling. Dean nodded.

'And I'm sorry we lost the match,' said Alban. Maggie laughed, then Arta joined in.

The woman and her son had ended up staying for lunch. Arta had served up the dumplings and stuffed courgettes she was planning to make for dinner, which was a Kosovan speciality, and Lirim's favourite meal, then Dean and Alban had gone off to play Pro Evolution Soccer on the Xbox. When Lirim got back in the evening, tired and wet through, but beaming with pride about the success of his Sunday opening, she'd run to embrace him.

He told her how well the day had gone, how they had taken more cash than on any day since they opened. He told her about the two young students who had answered his ad and how pleased he was to get some part-time workers who were Brits and could mix in.

'These are the kind of English people we should have in our hearts and minds,' he said. 'Not the two who have been there too long already.' Then Arta and Alban told him about the extraordinary visit from Maggie and Dean, which he said was more proof that the English were basically good people, and they had so much going for them in their life in south London.

They hadn't discussed the events of the night before, or Professor Sturrock. Instead, they'd toasted the success of the car wash and gone to bed early. But Arta couldn't sleep. For once, it was less the fear of the rapist troubling her dreams, than her worries about how to face Professor Sturrock at her next appointment, and how to get close to her husband again.

'Lirim,' she said, stroking his hair, 'please help me. Tell me how I can escape from my nightmares.'

He was properly awake now, and he propped himself up on

his elbow to look at her, her face lit by the glow of the bedside clock.

'I can think when I'm washing the cars,' he said. 'The work requires little concentration, so I have been thinking about this all day.'

He said he thought the Professor was right. He may have made the call on her to forgive too early, but he was right in his general stance. 'What happened happened, and can never be undone,' he said. 'How we all feel about it will change with time.'

'But even if I forgive them for myself, I can never forgive what they forced Besa to endure!'

'But Besa is fine,' Lirim interrupted. 'She is a happy child. She is loved. She will forget, if she hasn't already.' He looked at her closely, clearly waiting to see if she pushed back once more. She was still.

'What your Professor Sturrock is suggesting is like a mental equivalent of a major operation. If you had a tumour, the doctors of the body would remove it, cut it out. With you, it is as though the rapist has left a tumour in your mind, but there is no form to it, no cells, nothing that would show up on an X-ray. It is a psychological residue of a physical attack and though the attack has stopped, you can't make the residue go away. The harder you try, the more you remember what happened, the more it grows. And every night, as I know too well from hearing your groans and your screaming, the rapist adds to the residue, and the invisible tumour grows.'

She listened, motionless and silent. Then she nodded a little.

'You thought all that as you washed a car?'

'Yes, I did. And I thought about your Professor Sturrock too. You said he was old, yes?'

She nodded again. 'Sixty, I think.'

'How many rape victims has he counselled? Maybe hundreds. So why did he do what he did, suddenly urge you to forgive, when he must have known there was a chance it would upset you?'

'I don't know.'

'Maybe because he wanted to upset you, because he wants you to see things in a new light, and start to shake the residue out of yourself. It is like the surgeon's knife going in, only it's not a knife, it is a thought.'

'So you can forgive a man who did these things to your wife?'

'There is not one hour in any day that I do not think of them. So I cannot forget. To forgive sounds much harder. But maybe it is easier.'

'Easier to forgive than to forget?'

'Maybe.' He pulled her closer and kissed her on her forehead.

'I would like to meet your Professor Sturrock,' he said.

'Why?'

'Because I am worried that you don't want to meet him again.'

'Mmm.'

'Is that a "you're right to worry" mmm, or a "I would like you to come with me" mmm?'

'Not sure.'

'We mustn't give up on him. You are his patient, but this affects all of us.'

She stared intently at his mouth as the words came out. She could tell he had really thought this through, as methodically as he thought through his business plan for the car wash, or their journey from Kosovo. He was speaking more slowly than usual. He was concentrating on every word. He relaxed a little as he sensed she was not reacting against what he was saying.

'It is odd for me,' he said. 'The two most important men in my life, and I have never met them. The rapist who hurt the only woman I have ever really loved. And the doctor who is trying to give her peace of mind. I see one as my enemy and one as my friend. But I do not want to meet my enemy, I only want to see my friend. If I could will the enemy away, kill him even, then fine, we would know he was not here. But I would be in jail, and he would be the one who put me there, just as he is the one who has put you where you are, in a prison inside your own mind. Our enemy wants you to stay there. Our friend wants you to be free. And he has freed women from rape before, I can sense that. I feel from everything you have told me he is a good man, and he is trying to help you as he has helped others.

But he knows if he asks you to forget, it is impossible. So he asks you to do something far harder, yet simpler too. Forgive. Don't try to understand. Don't torture your mind by wondering what kind of people they are, what kind of people their parents must have been, what kind of lives they lead. We will never understand them. But we can try to forgive them.'

She could feel the beginnings of a film covering her eyes, and a tear forming in the corner of her left eye. As it became whole it trickled across the top of her nose, down her right cheek, and disappeared into her neck. Lirim wiped it away with a corner of the sheet, and then kissed her on the neck, just where the tear had ended its flow.

'Think about it,' he said.

'I will.'

MONDAY

29

Matthew reckoned it would take him a maximum of one hour to cycle to chambers, which wasn't much longer than it took to drive. He had gone into the office last night with a clutch of suit carriers and bags containing shirts, ties, socks, shoes and underwear, as well as a change of cycling gear. He intended to ride to work every morning, lock the bike up, shower and change in the office bathroom, do a day's work, then change back into his cycling gear and ride home. His only concern was how to transport his files and papers back and forth. Celia, who had gone in with him to help think through the logistics, had the answer.

'You can take the small packages in a little backpack. Mitchell's will know which ones work for bikers.'

'Cyclists, love. Bikers drive motorbikes. Cyclists ride bikes.'

'Oh yes, of course. Anyway, backpack for small stuff. Big packages we put it in a cab, on the firm's account. Sensitive stuff, I drive it in for you. How's that?'

'Sounds fine,' he said. 'Thank you.'

As Matthew wheeled the bike to the roadside, Celia told him she intended to go online to look for a proper new cupboard for the office, and she was also going to work out a laundry system.

There was far more traffic than at the weekend and he found himself slowing more often than he liked. But he felt fairly comfortable with the mechanics of the bike now, and was starting to gauge distances better. He relished cycling past cars stuck in jams or traffic-light queues. 'You and me, babe,' he said, hitting the handlebars as he picked up speed coming off a roundabout into Muswell Hill Broadway. 'We're an item.'

He was surprised just how often he found he was talking to himself or talking to people in their cars or passers-by who couldn't hear him. When he reached Archway Road, he noticed a woman cyclist about seventy-five yards ahead. She was on a pretty ramshackle old bike but, nevertheless, it would be a marvellous moment if he could overtake her. She would become his first conquest. He looked at his speedometer. 23kph. 'Not very good on the flat, Matt,' he said to himself. 'Come on now, lower gear, higher cadence, then get the legs pumping and move back up to higher gear.' He was up to 25, then 28 and then, as he went downhill, he was on and then over 30. 'Twenty miles an hour, Mattie. If you were by the school in Sutherland Road you'd be breaking the speed limit. There she is now, not far, closer every stroke, she has no idea what is steaming up behind her. Go on, hit it harder, pedal harder, up down up down up down, faster, faster, nearly there, go on. You've got her, she's there, you can take her, you've got her, you've done it,' and he let out a huge cheer, turning back to see a sturdy, serious woman in her late forties or early fifties looking at him as if he were deranged. The advanced age of his competitor did nothing to diminish his elation. 'I have lost my virginity,' he shouted to the sky, 'and, darling, it was wonderful.' He laughed all the way to the next lights and then thought he'd better keep going in case she caught up with him and recognised him as Mr Noble the serious lawyer not Mattie the cycling legend. He felt that going through red lights was going to be one of the best parts of his new life.

When he arrived at the office, his secretary was already at her desk sifting through the weekend emails. She appeared stunned to see her boss walk through the door with a tight-fitting cycling top stretched over his considerable belly and padded shorts that showed off the size of his backside.

'Change of regime,' he boomed. 'Out goes fat Matt. In comes fit Matt.'

He walked into his office, closed the door and stripped off. Then he covered himself with a towel and walked back through the outer office to the shower.

'Don't worry,' he shouted. 'You'll get used to it.'

His secretary turned to the girl with whom she shared a desk, who was giggling.

'My God,' she said. 'I didn't know they did personality transplants.'

Standing beneath a hot shower, Matthew offered up a small though atheistic prayer of thanks to the understanding Professor Sturrock. He felt they'd really hit it off, perhaps because of the similarity of their professions. After all, wasn't a lawyer's task to understand human beings and make sense of what they said and did? His assessment of psychiatry, based on his admittedly limited knowledge, was that its goals were much the same. Professor Sturrock had quickly got to the point, and then come up with a rather clever strategy. That's what lawyers did. As for the idea of taking up cycling, it was hardly high-level psychiatric medicine, but it was a perfect fit for Matthew. He'd hit the dreaded one hundred kilograms last summer. Plus, he'd been growing a little concerned that he needed to do more on the environmental front, and cycling instead of driving to work could count as doing his bit. What's more, it seemed to have mended his marriage at miraculous speed. As he soaped the sweat from his skin, he was smiling at the contented Sunday he and Celia had spent together – a late breakfast with the papers, a walk to the Orange Tree pub where they had lunch sitting by the pond, then out for tea with their friends Trevor and Helene, all in the most harmonious manner.

So he was feeling what his old pupil master used to call 'chipper with golden knobs on' as he went back to his office to put on his suit. What he hadn't banked on, however, was a chance encounter with Angela to disturb the new post-Sturrock equilibrium. He was striding to his first case conference of the day, in Meeting Room C, when he met her in the corridor.

'Angela?' said Matthew, trying hard not to look or sound fazed. 'What are you doing here?'

'Been seeing Andrew. Got a case together.'

'Right, I see. And, er, how are you?'

'I'm fine. You?'

He didn't know what to say. Should he tell her about his new life of fidelity and fitness, or would that seem boastful, or possibly callous

– as if their relationship meant nothing to him? Perhaps it would be better to say he missed her. And when he thought about it, he did rather.

'Miss you,' he whispered, memories of their time together flooding back.

'Miss you too,' she said, and she winked as she said it, which had him remembering the mind-churning impact she'd had on him when he first saw her. The eyes. The smile. The hair. The hint of cleavage peering out from her white blouse. The body that looked so prim when clothed, as now, in her smart, sober barrister clothes but which he had seen naked and wild so often. He wondered if he could imagine feeling the same way about her again. And he could. He had no doubt about that. Even now, despite his assumption that one or two curious eyes would be staring into his back from the glass-fronted offices and conference rooms behind him, he felt himself shifting his body a little closer to hers.

'It'd be nice to see you again,' he said.

'Do you think that would be sensible?' said Angela.

'Probably not, but it'd be nice.'

'Well, you know my number,' she said, and walked off towards the exit.

He stood in the corridor and watched her go. He said to himself that if she turned round, he would call her later today to fix a date. If she didn't, he would take that as an instruction to leave her alone. It was tantalising. It reminded him of the excitement she had brought into his life. As she went off down the long corridor, her hips swaying just a little, he kept his eyes fixed on her backside and recalled the time he screwed her from behind in the shower at her flat. 'Turn round,' he muttered to himself. 'Turn round.' But she walked on oblivious, pushed open the door and disappeared.

'Probably for the best,' he said to himself and strode on to Meeting Room C. He doubted that riding a bike round country roads would give him quite the same pleasure as screwing Angela from behind in her shower. He would give it a try though. He liked the old Professor. And he owed it to Celia.

30

'You all right?'

David was stunned to see her. He hadn't expected Amanda to be at the entrance to the warehouse. He'd been hoping to get through his shift without bumping into her.

'I'm OK,' he mumbled.

'New rules,' she said, handing him a leaflet with a picture of a mobile phone on the front, and a big red cross superimposed on it. 'We've got to leave our phones in our lockers. They think we're all chatting instead of working.'

'OK,' said David, and hurried off to the locker room. When he got there he sat for a while on one of the low, hard benches. He was surprised that bumping into Amanda had not disturbed him more. He felt fine. Tired but fine.

He felt in his pocket for the folded pieces of paper which held his essay on humility. He was tempted to read it again, to give his spirits a further boost. He'd been surprised by how much he enjoyed writing it. He'd never been any good at essays in school and when Professor Sturrock first introduced regular homework, it had taken him several weeks before he felt he was expressing himself properly. But when he'd starting trying to write this, in the churchyard, the words had just poured out. He had spent all of Sunday afternoon working on it, and then much of the night revising it. He could imagine Professor Sturrock reading the essay, and being impressed, and that thought pleased him.

At 1 a.m. that morning he had saved the document one final time, under the name 'Humility', and then prepared to send it. He stared at his computer for a while. He felt he should also add an email explaining how he came to write it.

> Professor, you remember you said you wanted me to write about humility. Well, I have, and here it is. I hope it is what you had in mind. I hope it is not too long, but it is what I really think. I was in the cemetery at Mum's church yesterday, doing the headstone exercise. I can't email it because it is a drawing. I will bring it on Friday.
>
> I felt very low after our last session, but I guess you knew that. I felt I was falling even lower than before, and I was worried I was going to do something silly. Mother was really irritating me when I got home, even though she was doing nothing wrong. I know I will never harm her, like I won't harm myself, I hope. You think that too, don't you, I can tell. I hope you're right. I think you are. But I was down at the bottom of the curve, and I always get nervous then. Experience tells you the rhythm will kick in and move upwards but there can always be a first time, can't there, when you stay down? That's what was making me anxious, I think. Also, I could not for the life of me work out why you wanted me to think about my own gravestone. But I tried to keep faith in you, and do what you would have wanted me to do. And it worked. I felt better. And doing it got me thinking about humility, and it made me want to write something about it for you.
>
> You know that phrase you liked so much? Well, the storm has passed and not a blade of grass has moved. Thank you for that and see you on Friday.
> David

Afterwards he'd enjoyed a deep and seemingly dreamless sleep until the alarm went just after six to wake him for his shift at the warehouse. Now, sitting in the locker room, he felt better than he had for some time. He knew it wouldn't last, that sooner or later there would be a curve back down, but at least he had the feeling that he was much better these days at dealing with his depression. It didn't scare him like it used to. And he had seen in his mother's eyes, as he had said goodbye to her this morning, the happiness and relief she felt in sensing that he was starting the week calm and reasonably content.

31

Sturrock was on autopilot, and his patient knew it.

'Are you OK, sir? You seem really tired and distracted.'

'I am. Sorry, you're not meant to notice.'

'Training, sir.'

'Yes indeed.' He had lost count of how many times he had asked former Lance Corporal Spiers not to call him 'sir'. Spiers was a war veteran who had served in Northern Ireland and fought in both Afghanistan and Iraq. He had lost a leg in a roadside bombing near Basra, and been invalided out of the forces. He suffered chronic depression and had constant flashbacks not just to the attack that lost him a limb, but previous incidents which prior to the bombing had not really worried him. Sturrock had been seeing him for four months and they'd been making progress. But today, he was finding it impossible to concentrate.

'What's wrong, sir? If I may ask . . .' Spiers said, laughing at the way their roles were reversing.

'It's a long story,' said Sturrock. 'I was forced to play host to an unexpected overnight guest.'

In fact, he felt a failure as a host. On waking up this morning, he'd tiptoed into the study to check on his visitor. Ralph was still fast asleep, and looked quite peaceful. Sturrock sat briefly on his swivel chair, staring at his house guest. He didn't know what to do with him. Wake him? But then what? He'd have to talk to him, and what was he going to say? He decided it was a conversation he didn't want to have, and took the coward's way out, leaving a note on the kitchen table. '*Ralph, I left early for the hospital. I hope you slept well.*

Help yourself to the fridge. I'll call you later and we can talk about the kind of clinic you might be able to go to. In the meantime, stay put. Martin.' Then he'd slipped quietly away, closing the front door as gently as he could.

As he headed to the tube, he felt himself walking more slowly than usual. He stopped at the cafe in the station parade and ordered a double espresso and two Danish pastries. He hoped the coffee would lift him. It didn't. All around him he could see pictures of Ralph Hall on the front pages of newspapers, and headlines recording his patient's demise. It felt as if there was nowhere he could escape his responsibilities. But it was Aunt Jessica who was really hanging over him.

The stop for coffee had made him late, which meant he couldn't call Stella, or prepare for his morning's consultations. He'd counted on having some time in the morning to think about the patients he was seeing, particularly Hafsatu. He had imagined going down the corridor to Judith Carrington's office and asking her permission to refer Hafsatu to her. He liked Judith. Perhaps he would have sat down and had a cup of coffee with her. Perhaps she would have asked him how he was.

'Have you tried Red Bull, sir?' asked Spiers, leaning forward to get his attention.

Sturrock was jolted out of his reverie. 'No, I haven't.'

'Wait there, sir.'

Spiers levered himself up from the chair with the help of his stick, went to the door, opened it and asked Phyllis to join them.

'Would it be possible to get the Professor a couple of cans of Red Bull?' he asked, in his politest voice. 'He needs it.' He turned to Sturrock. 'You get an immediate massive caffeine hit and it will just keep the exhaustion at bay till you get to your bed later. I promise you, sir.'

Sturrock nodded at a bemused looking Phyllis, who was not used to being summoned from her desk by patients. She needed his assurance that this was appropriate behaviour.

'It's fine,' he said. 'Take it out of the lunch money and I'll have it instead of coffee.'

The Red Bull arrived between his 10.15 appointment (a young student who was a recovering drug addict) and his 11.15 (a borderline personality disorder). He had barely been able to keep his eyes open as the student went through her diary of positive and negative feelings, though he was able to note she had been in a far better frame of mind than for some time.

'On Wednesday, you have an entry for every one of the twenty-four hours,' he said. 'Did you not sleep at all?' He was hoping she would say that no, she hadn't slept. She was looking perky today and it might make him feel he too could survive the near sleepless night he had just endured.

'I had a great night,' she said. 'What I did was think about my dreams in the morning and kind of guess what my feelings might have been in them.'

'I see. Well, you seem happier than you were.'

'I enjoyed doing this. It made me think more positively than I have been. I was actively looking to feel positive things, which was a bit of a first.'

'Good. Well, let's do the same homework next week. Just keep going with it.'

Though cheered by her improvement, he used it to end the session early so that he could try the war veteran's Red Bull medicine.

It definitely worked. He had been so exhausted that the backs of his eyes were beginning to get pins and needles, but shortly after he took a large gulp, he felt a surge of energy. The effect lasted and halfway through the hour with his borderline personality disorder, he began to feel able to engage with his patient in a way he had so far rather failed to do.

Stella had called Phyllis twice in the course of the morning. He had felt so tired, and so beaten down in his own mind, that he had not been able to bring himself to return the calls. As the Red Bull kicked in, he could face it, just about. He called her as his borderline personality disorder left the room.

'Hello,' he said. 'How are you?'

'OK, considering.'

'Where are you?'

'Still at Jack's.'

'Oh.'

'Yesterday was intolerable,' she said.

'What in particular?'

'That man, in my house.'

'Stella, try to have a little compassion. He has a serious drink problem.'

'His fault.'

'He has lost his job and his wife.'

'His fault.'

'He has the press trying to hunt him down so they can add to the shame and humiliation.'

'All his fault.'

'Perhaps, but he's my patient and I have a duty to help him.'

'Well, you have lots of patients and they're yours not mine and I do not have a duty to have them in my house.'

Sturrock felt pumped up and strangely exhilarated. The Red Bull was taking him to places he did not normally go.

'Stella, I know it's not nice for you. I know you like your own ways and you don't like them to be disturbed. I know it's inconvenient. But just for once do you think you could follow the creed you seemingly believe in, and show a little fucking humanity?'

She was shocked. He hardly ever swore and when he did, it was not at her.

'I beg your pardon?'

'I think you heard. Look, I'm sorry that Ralph Hall is in our house, but he needs help. Sorry I screwed up with Jack yesterday, but I had things on my mind. I'm sorry too that we don't have a great marriage but it takes two to make it work and two to make it not work. There are so many things I can say sorry for but in the end *you* have to stop feeling sorry for yourself.'

'Martin, this is outrageous. You land me with a drunken politician and you say my being angry about it is feeling sorry for myself?'

'No, I'm saying that if it wasn't this, it would be something else

237

that you would make me feel I should be saying sorry for. Well, I'm sorry, Stella, but my "sorry" days are over. I've had enough of "sorry". It hasn't worked and when things don't work, you have to change tack.'

'I see.'

'Good.'

He had about a third of the second can of Red Bull remaining. He felt strong. He slurped down the last bit and felt stronger.

'So, are you coming home?'

'That depends,' she said defensively.

'On what?'

'On a number of things, but firstly on that man leaving my house.'

'Well, Stella, in that case we might not see each other for a day or two because my plan is to allow him to stay until I can get him checked into a clinic.'

He slammed the phone down. He could feel a thin layer of cold sweat on his forehead and his eyes were stinging. What should he do next? Call Ralph? Call his sister? He looked down at his desk and saw his diary where Phyllis had written in the rescheduled appointment with Hafsatu at two. She'd put a big red ring around it: 'REMEMBER.' How could he forget?

He called Ralph on his mobile. It went to voicemail. He called his own home number, thinking Ralph might answer if he was still there. He heard his own voice asking callers to leave a message, and hung up. He suspected Ralph was still asleep.

He had half an hour before a meeting with the trust budget team. He used the time to sketch out a eulogy to Aunt Jessica. Simon had sent over some basic facts. Dates, places, jobs, associations. It was helpful enough and would certainly provide some padding. He scribbled out a structure:

- Facts about the world of her birth and the world of her death. Google later.
- Birth and childhood. Needs funny story.
- Family. Something about Father, and her being the last sibling.

- Marriage and own children. Something about the three boys.
- Grandchildren. Something funny one of them said about her.
- What she stood for. Steadfast, rock in a changing world. Over the top but OK.
- Acts of kindness.
- Stoicism in death.
- How she would want us to remember her fondly and then move on.

He sat back, relieved he had at least got something down on paper. It wasn't much but it would do for now. If he had not a single second more to think about it before the event he would be able to get by with that. Hopefully he would find a little more time to flesh it out and make it more personal. For the moment, he silently thanked Lance Corporal Spiers and the stimulant properties of Red Bull. With fifteen minutes before the trust budget meeting, he closed his eyes and tried to sleep. The Red Bull had other ideas. He gave up trying after five minutes and asked Phyllis to get him a coffee. Then he called Jan to see if she could drive their mother to Somerset for the funeral. She couldn't.

'Oh Christ, Jan, that's a real pain.'

'Sorry, but I've got something on first thing I can't get out of. I don't suppose we can trust a cab to get her there?'

'Think how that would make her feel! Plus it would cost a fortune.'

'What about Stella?'

'Not exactly on the best of terms at the moment.'

'Oh, sorry. Jack?'

'Ditto.'

'What about Simon? If he's asked you to do the eulogy, surely he could help out.'

'He'll have lots of other things to sort out. Don't worry, I'll do it. Just the last thing I need. I'm feeling a bit under the cosh at the moment.'

'Yes, you sound it. Can't you take some time off?'

'Got a refugee who was gang-raped coming in shortly, and I have a particularly difficult patient seeing me at home.'

'Martin, there's no point pushing yourself so far that you go over the edge.'

'But I have patients, Jan. I can't not see them, not help them.'

'Mmm, maybe. But just remember, nobody ever died saying they wished they'd spent more time at the office.'

'Thanks.'

Sturrock made next to no contribution to the budget meeting and left as soon as it was over, avoiding the small talk over sandwiches sent up by the canteen. Phyllis had put a cheese roll on his desk, but he couldn't face it. He tried to sleep again, but his mind would not still. Ralph hadn't called, and was still not answering his phone. He had another look at the outline of his eulogy to Aunt Jessica but failed to think of anything else he wanted to say about her. There was just five minutes now until Hafsatu arrived. He was back to feeling cellular tiredness, as if every particle in his body was crying out for rest. But he had to keep going. He wondered about getting more Red Bull, but decided against it. He suspected the current crash would merely herald something even bigger if he tried to lift himself again. Just one more patient, keep going, he told himself. Keep going.

32

The moment Emily woke up, she felt the need to go outside. It was only just light, and the Caledonian Road was surprisingly quiet. She'd never seen Sami's shop in the morning. Surrounded by deliveries, he was frantically trying to sort newspapers and get the milk cartons into his fridge before the customers who stopped by his shop on their way to work started to arrive.

'Do you want a hand?' she asked.

Sami grinned. 'So you've finally decided to take up my job offer then?'

'I'm not sure,' said Emily, 'but I thought I'd give it a try. Where do I start?'

'Great. Well, you see this machine, do you know what it is? It's the thing that puts the prices on the produce. And it's all set to go for the cans of soup in the back. So you get going with those, and when you're done, come back and I'll show you how to change the price for the next thing.'

It took her a while to get used to pressing the button with just the right weight so the little ticket stuck on to the tin. Once she got the hang of it, she got through the first batch in five minutes.

As she went back into the store itself, her headscarf loose and her face clearly visible, a young man standing looking at the magazines caught sight of her and grimaced. Before he could stop his reaction from translating into sounds, the words 'Christ alive' came out followed by a return to the teeth-baring grimace.

'It's OK,' she said. 'You get used to it.'

'I'm sorry,' he said, 'it's just that, you know . . .'

'I know. You didn't expect to see anything like that here. I understand.'

It was a wonderful moment. If anyone had said to her, just a few days ago, that by Monday morning she would be able to be in a public place, with her whole face exposed, and react as she had just done to a young man's involuntary revulsion, she would have seen this as over-optimism on an Olympian scale. Her joy was matched by the young man's embarrassment.

As he left, a copy of *Angling Times* under his arm, she went over to Sami and told him what had happened.

'I just can't explain it,' she said. 'It's like I've discovered a new me and a new way of looking at the world.'

'Perhaps you've found God?' he said. Often, in their late-night chats, she and Sami had discussed his faith. He had told her how, when his wife died, he found the only place where he could feel any comfort was the mosque. Emily always listened politely but doubted that the Catholic Church would ever provide her with such solace. Now she was not so sure.

'I don't know whether it was some kind of spiritual awakening, but I think I know better what people mean when they say they've seen the light. I'm not sure how it's happened but I feel so happy, Sami, and a lot of that is down to you.'

'Nonsense,' he said. 'It is all down to you. It is what you are inside that has been trapped by the pain you felt. And now it is coming out. It makes you happy. It makes me happy. It makes everyone who knows you happy.'

She worked in the shop all morning and then went home to get some lunch. As soon as she got back to her flat, she sent an email to Professor Sturrock telling him what had happened and apologising for what she saw as unnecessary aggression towards him last week. She concluded by saying, 'This weekend, I have experienced something that I can only describe as "spiritual". I feel strange using that word, but I'm sure it's the right one. When I lived through the fire, I felt I lost any faith I might have had, along with any real will to live. I couldn't see how a world with a loving God in it would have allowed this to happen to me. It was a purely selfish thought, wasn't it, and that thought was trapping me. That's what you've been saying, I think. That's what your raisins were all about. And in realising it, I feel happier and more liberated than I ever have. Is that not just mind-blowing? I think so.'

33

As Ralph Hall realised where he was, he wondered how he had managed to sleep on the tiny sofa in Professor Sturrock's study. It couldn't have been more than four feet long yet somehow he had slept through till late morning. He was feeling ill, and very sorry for himself. He threw up, but more briefly than most days of late, and he was able to down the litre of orange juice and a couple of bananas that Sturrock had left for him on the kitchen table without bringing them straight up again. He took a bath, shaved, brushed his teeth, then turned on the TV in the study. He realised to his dismay that it was already lunchtime. He was still the lead story on Sky News. Seeing himself on TV made him feel even worse. He switched it off and went back to the kitchen in search of more fruit juice. But then he spotted a bottle of wine. It spoke to him in a way that nothing else in the fridge did. It said temptation. It said prospect of pleasure.

He took the bottle from the fridge, placed it in the centre of the table, next to the fruit bowl, and sat staring at it. He didn't feel an immediate need to reach out for it, which was a good sign, but he wanted to know if he could last at least half an hour, just staring at the bottle, and not opening it.

He had managed ten minutes, and was feeling a little better about himself, when he heard a key turning in the front door. He could sense that the presence it was bringing in was not a happy one. Barely a noise. Door open. Door closed. Light steps walking towards the kitchen.

It was Stella Sturrock.

'Hello,' she said.

'Oh, hello.' He saw her notice the wine on the table.

'Sorry,' he said. 'Just doing a little test.'

'Did you pass?'

'So far, yes.'

'That's good. Can I get you a cup of tea?'

'Thank you, please.'

He picked up the bottle of wine and took it back to the fridge.

'I should apologise for yesterday,' he said. 'You probably noticed, I was a bit desperate.'

'Yes, I could see that.'

'Desperate.'

'Have you spoken to your wife?'

'No. I'm afraid I'm too much of a coward.'

'You should, you know. Or go and see her.'

'I don't want to venture out, to be honest.'

'I can imagine. Hard to get away from you out there. Still, I should think she'll be worrying about you, even if she doesn't want to admit it. If you like, I could give her a call. To tell her where you are, and to say that you'll be calling later.'

'That is really kind of you, but are you sure you want to get involved in this? I've brought enough chaos into your family already.'

'No, I'd like to help,' she said, sitting down at the table. 'I think I owe you an apology too. I was not in a happy frame of mind yesterday. Far from it. Martin and I were getting on each other's nerves. You probably noticed. But I shouldn't have been so harsh with you. I should have shown a little more compassion.'

She was wearing the same clothes as yesterday, but she looked very different. He thought she was more attractive without make-up. The fierceness that had rather scared him when he arrived at the house had gone. There was a gentleness there today that reminded him of her husband.

'I really don't think anyone should apologise but me,' he said. 'I completely understand why you were angry.'

'So long as you understand I wasn't angry with you, so much as with Martin.'

He smiled, and she smiled back.

'You're not the only man and wife to go through the odd rocky patch,' she said.

'Indeed. You seem a very strong couple all the same. This feels like a strong couple's house. Does that make sense or am I talking like a politician?'

'I'm not sure you'd be saying it if you heard us yelling at each other earlier today.'

'Not about me being here, I hope.'

'Don't worry. We both had a point. They just got lost in the noise and the baggage.'

The kettle had boiled.

'Do you take milk and sugar?'

'Milk please.'

'Have you spoken to Martin?' she asked.

'No.'

'I imagine he will have been trying to call you.'

'You're right. I should have checked my mobile. I've been avoiding it.'

He was conscious of how much of an imposition his presence must be on them.

'Are you in the same game as Martin?'

'No. I trained as a medic, but just did the house and the kids really.'

'Same as Sandie, till the kids left.'

'Maybe I should do something now they're all grown up. Not sure what though.'

They found themselves flitting in and out between small talk about their families and big talk about his situation. Sometimes, her questions linked the two.

'How long have you been married?'

'Over thirty years.'

'She won't want it to end just like that.'

'Hope so. Hope she's avoiding the papers too.'

'Your family is more important than your work. You know that, don't you?'

'I do now, yes. Now I don't have one.'

She asked if he minded her putting on the radio so she could hear the weather forecast. Then came the headlines. The lead story was the Prime Minister saying the government would quickly recover from the 'temporary setback' of Mr Hall's sacking. He said it was more a personal tragedy for the former minister than a lasting problem for the government. Daniel Melchett was visiting a hospital to spell out his commitment to the NHS, and pollsters said the immediate response from the public seemed to be that they thought the Prime Minister had handled it decisively. 'Meanwhile, mystery surrounds the whereabouts of the disgraced former minister himself, who has not been seen since leaving his department last night. We now go to our reporter Suzanne Crowther outside Mr Hall's home.'

They both laughed, then she switched off the radio.

'Thank you for putting me up. I am grateful to you and your husband. He's a very good man. You're a very lucky woman.'

Mrs Sturrock looked down, and stirred the tea in the pot.

34

'Hafsatu is here,' said Phyllis, putting her head round the door.

Sturrock stared hard at his desk. Perhaps he should simply cancel, say he was ill. But Hafsatu would have travelled all the way from Chigwell to get here, probably an hour's journey. And she would have taken the time off work, unpaid time that she could ill afford. And did he really imagine that he could let her come so close, and then let her go again?

He went to the door to call her in. As always, her beauty shocked him. Every week, he hoped that as he summoned her to his consulting room, he would view her as any other patient. Every week, she seemed lovelier. She rose from her chair, and as she walked towards him, he hoped neither she nor Phyllis noticed how closely he was watching her. She was wearing her hair in braids. It made her face look even more slender, her cheekbones even higher and stronger. Her eyes seemed darker, more seductive. As she walked by him and into his room, he closed his eyes, and told himself to push such thoughts aside.

But when she sat down, he knew he couldn't do it. So often during their sessions he had lost his train of thought gazing at her strong muscular body. She always dressed smartly. Today she was wearing a white jacket, black blouse and tight white skirt. She loved clothes. He'd built on this in their sessions together, suggesting that, every time she felt a traumatic event from her past surfacing in her mind, she think of a design for an outfit, imagine a fabric she'd like to make a dress out of, try to see how colours might work together. He had no idea if it helped her or not.

'How are you today, Hafsatu?' he said, as he settled into his leather armchair.

'I'm good, Professor Sturrock, good,' she said. She grinned. She had quite the whitest teeth he had ever seen. There was a slight chip on one of her lower teeth, but it did nothing to diminish her smile. The overall effect of her today was overwhelming. Black skin, white suit, white teeth, black blouse.

I must find a way to tell her that I think she should transfer to another psychiatrist, he thought. But he couldn't see how to do it, so stalled for time, desperately trying to recall what homework he'd set her at their last session. Goals for the future, that was it.

'So how did you get on with your three goals?'

The fact that he had set her this exercise was symptomatic of the way in which he was failing her. It was too early in her treatment to ask her to set future goals. They hadn't done enough work on her past. But he shied away from hearing about it. He was fine talking about her childhood in Sierra Leone and how all the suffering and conflict around her had affected her. But when she talked about being forced to work as a prostitute, about how she felt when made to have sex with strange men so that her controllers could make themselves rich, he felt he was probing himself more than her, and he didn't like what he saw there. He felt hypocritical whenever he sat nodding in sympathy at the life she was forced to lead, knowing as he did that he regularly used prostitutes. It was not as though he did not suffer enough guilt already. What he did offended his upbringing, his religious education, his marriage vows, his self-image, and what he felt he really believed. And yet he continued to do it, and that simple fact was inescapable when he was sitting down listening to a woman who, in different circumstances, at a different time, would have been allowing him to indulge his desire for a quick sexual hit. The guilt was worsened by his inability to master thoughts about her as a prostitute, and him as a client. With every such thought that came into his mind, and every struggle to banish it, he felt a little more tired.

She had written down her three goals on a little card. *1. Build a life in Britain. 2. Own my own business. 3. Raise a family of my own.*

'How hopeful are you of achieving all this?' he asked.

'Quite hopeful.'

'What business would you like?'

'I don't know yet. Perhaps fashion.'

'Yes, you like clothes.'

Was he treating her, or chatting her up? He felt at a loss as to what to say next. He was dancing around big issues, and wasting her time and his. It was the kind of conversation she might have with a stranger she met on a train, not a conversation between a consultant psychiatrist and a deeply damaged patient.

Fortunately, she broke the silence by taking the lead.

'May I ask *you* something, Professor?'

'Yes, of course.'

'You ask me how hopeful I am about meeting my goals. How hopeful do you think I should be? What can hold me back?'

What could hold her back? So many things, himself included. He wanted to tell her this, to reveal to her the extent of his duplicity and hypocrisy. He wanted to apologise and tell her that his colleague Judith Carrington would be able to do so much more for her.

'I see nothing to hold you back, Hafsatu. Re your first goal, you have proper status. Re the second, you are intelligent and determined. Re the third, why not? You should be confident. You have your life before you.'

He felt sick. It was a cop-out, and he knew it. She wanted his proper analysis of where she was psychologically, whether he felt she was through the worst, whether a wretched past was sufficiently well addressed to let her imagine the future she had scribbled on her card, and he gave her this empty, platitudinous, over-optimistic answer. That was because he wasn't really thinking about her. He was thinking about himself, his tiredness and his wretched desires.

He wondered whether she ever sensed that he was not really going to the heart of her issues. He was able to talk to her about the rapes in the boat that brought her to Britain, because that was before she was made to work as a prostitute. And yet it was the prostitution that had left the greatest physical and psychological scars, the fears and anxieties, the lack of self-esteem, the difficulties she had in trusting or believing other people.

He dreaded to think about how many prostitutes he'd had sex with. Jack must have been about seven when one night on his way home from work, he decided to call in at a brothel he had driven by hundreds of times. It was seedy from the outside and even seedier inside but once he'd made that first visit, a second followed, a third . . . Then he found other, less seedy places. He discovered that his local paper could provide him with addresses he could visit, where there was no receptionist or risk of running into other clients, just a nice flat or a nice house with a nice enough prostitute living inside. And before long he had a network of women he could call on, and the rate at which he did so remained fairly steady. Some months just once or twice, some months several times a week. For a moment he thought of Emily and her physical deformity. She was lucky. Her disfigurement was inflicted on her from outside, and in time she would come to terms with it; whereas his deformity was inside, self-inflicted and impossible to live with.

In an effort to stop his eye from falling on the place where Hafsatu's short skirt was riding up her thigh, he tried to focus on her hands, but watching her long fingers move was just as challenging. As she stroked one hand with the other, and he imagined those hands on him, he felt deprived that he had never met her when she was a prostitute. He imagined what it would be like to make love to her, and also what it would be like to have sex with her, and he could feel the beginnings of an erection stirring. He stood up abruptly and walked to the other side of the room. What should he ask her next? About what she saw as the difference between having sex and making love? Given the difficulty she had forming relationships, and given her goal of raising a family, that would have been a perfectly legitimate line of psychological enquiry for him. But he felt inhibited from pursuing it. So he danced around, and she danced back, and he got to the end of the session, not just tired but drowning in shame. He had to get someone else to see her. But how would he explain it without admitting that the reason was that he *did* want to see her? Too much. It was all too much. He was too tired to think.

'See you next week, Professor,' she said as she left, and he wanted to pull her back and say, 'No, Hafsatu, you mustn't see me. You must see Judith and I'm going to set it up right now.' But he didn't. He just watched her go and then sank back into his chair.

Phyllis came into the room.

'You remember I'm leaving early today, Professor Sturrock? Can I get you anything before I go?'

He looked at his secretary, and felt a sudden fury at her unending efficiency, her refusal ever to display any kind of emotion, beyond annoyance at a missed appointment.

'Phyllis, can I ask you something personal?' he asked.

Before she had the chance to reply, he went on. 'Do you ever actually *feel* anything?'

'I'm not sure what you mean, Professor,' she replied, looking guarded.

'You know, *feel* sad, happy, angry, sorry . . .'

'Are you all right, Professor? You seem a little under par today, if you don't mind my saying so. Is there anything I can help with?'

He could read the concern on her face, and he felt angry with himself for having challenged her like that. He felt angry with her too though. Theirs was the workplace equivalent of the relationship with Stella at home – stuck, unsatisfying, unchanging, going nowhere. Both women have spent so many hours in so many years with me, he thought, but neither really knows anything about me.

'It's OK, Phyllis,' he sighed. 'You can go home. I'll see you Wednesday.'

'Thank you,' she said, adding as she reached the door, 'I hope the funeral is not too painful for everyone.'

Alone in his room, he logged on to his computer for the first time that day and was immediately confronted by an inbox of unopened emails. Most were from patients. Guilt threatened to overwhelm him. All these people he had failed. What had been happening in their lives? Things that he could have sorted out if he hadn't been so caught up in his own petty and despicable problems. And now it was too late. He might as well just turn the computer off. There was nothing he could do.

He was just about to shut down, when he noticed an email from David Temple at the bottom of his inbox. He couldn't ignore something from David. He clicked on it and saw the attachment: 'Humility'.

As he read it, he had in his mind an image of David sitting in the cemetery, writing slowly, stopping to think about every word.

I am as important as you are . . . You are as important as I am. We are all important to ourselves and to the people who matter to us, and the people we matter to. There are not many people I matter to, but I matter to them a lot. I matter to my people as much as all the people who matter to a king or a queen matter. The king and the queen probably don't know it though. Because they're not truly humble.

Kings *could* be humble, you know. Humility is not about military rank or where you are on a social ladder. Humility is knowing we are all as important as each other. And even the ones we think are really important, the ones we see on the TV or put on the pedestals, in the grand sweep of history, and amid the great forces of nature, they are grains of sand.

Everyone wants to control the world around them as best they can. Of course they do. Even the freest spirits in the world have to have a bit of order, don't want to be surrounded by chaos, want to make the things happen that they think will make them happy. So we try to keep that control around us. We might have some success. But there are forces bigger than all of us, and they are the things that should make us humble. History. Time. Nature.

There are some people who can shape history. Most of us can't. Nobody can stop time. Nobody can control nature. We can mow the lawn and prune the flowers, but it is other forces that make them grow.

We can only leave a small stamp on the world. Even the

kings and the queens, when they go, the world stops and talks about them for a while. Some cry. Some mourn. Many remain unaware. Many who are aware are unmoved and uninterested. The world carries on turning.

There are points in our life when we feel we matter more than others. When we feel stronger than others, when we feel we own our own universe. But at any point in our life, had I died, had you died, the world would have gone on. There is no place on earth that cannot be filled by others tomorrow.

In our workplaces, it sometimes feels like there are big people and there are little people. The big people are bosses. They have power and authority. But the big people can't function without the little people. The little people can't always do the big people's job, but often the big people can't do the little people's job. The king of one country can't get to see the king of another without drivers, pilots, security men, secretaries, typists, translators. They are all part of a team. If one part doesn't function properly, the whole doesn't function properly. We are all of equal worth. Not all the same, or capable of being the same, or wanting to be the same, but we are all human beings who owe our existence to others and who cannot function without others.

When a great bridge is built, we fete the person who designed it or we remember the place where it is built. But think too of all the little people who dug and carried and did the dirty work. When a great building goes up, the architect gets the glory. But I think of the little people too, the ones who put it up there. Because we should be humble.

Fear can humble. It makes us confront our limits and our mortality.

Anger can humble. It makes us small.

Poverty can humble because it sees people tolerate a life we cannot contemplate.

Change can humble for we can be reminded of past failings.

We can learn humility if we learn from mistakes.

The process of life is humbling. The human body is humbling. The human mind is humbling. Death is humbling.

There but for the grace of God and all that, that's humbling. We could all be the down-and-out, the tramp, the battered wife, the abused woman, child, the man with the dead-end job. We should be thankful we are not, spare a thought for those who are, do what we can to help them. We are our brother's keeper and all that.

I have no idea if this is the kind of thing you wanted me to write. I've gone on enough now, I think.

Sturrock sat back and closed his eyes. Then he opened them again, and read once more the 'grace of God' paragraph. He was none of those things, not down and out, not battered or abused, yet he felt all of those things. David was the man in the dead-end job yet what power he had to move.

As before, he struggled when confronted with David and his words to see him purely as a patient. There were times when David spoke as he spoke, articulated concepts as he might do, or even better. Sturrock noticed that there were two religious references in David's piece, and he ended both with 'and all that', as if consciously trying to dismiss them. That intrigued him. At points, he seemed to be making a structured case. At others he was in stream-of-consciousness mode, but there was a sophistication to the argument that seemed completely out of keeping with someone who had left school at sixteen with one GCSE.

He reread David's accompanying email. It was beautiful. It told him everything he needed to know about how David had been feeling. The storm had blown in, then blown out, and fundamentally, nothing had changed. What was more, David had managed to cope with the plunge himself, pull himself out of it by using techniques he had taught him. He felt so proud of him. But could he follow him?

He saw in David's plunges the mirror image of his own. He too never knew when they would start, or how they would end, but when they happened, they were all-consuming, and it was impossible to imagine life in anything other than this state. The feelings were so powerful that he felt trapped, he would never be able to break free from the grip of a mood he had never asked for, but which felt like it would last forever. So the storm blew in and it raged, and he grew angry that Stella couldn't or wouldn't help, and he didn't know anyone else he could reach out to, so he went in deeper and deeper on himself. But David had found a way out. Was he trying to send him a message with his talk of humility? Was there something here that he needed to learn? Suddenly he knew what he had to do. Talk to David. David would understand. If he could talk to David, perhaps he too could get to the other side of the storm. Wiping his eyes, he picked up his telephone and punched in David's mobile number.

35

With the extra staff, the car wash was running so well that Lirim decided he could slip away for half an hour. He went and sat in Jose's Cafe, where he ordered beans, egg and chips and a cup of coffee. While he was waiting for it to arrive, he took a postcard and pen from his pocket and laid them carefully on the table. The postcard had a view of Priština on it. It was one of the few non-essential items he had packed in his bag when they fled the city, and he'd treasured it ever since.

He'd had his Priština dream again last night. Again he'd been fishing in the Sitnica. Again, Arta brought a picnic. They started to make love in the same way. The same farmer shouted at them to get off his land. Then he'd woken up. As he blinked his eyes open, and realised he'd been dreaming, he felt the same disappointment, but deeper this time. Though the river and the farmer and the picnic had disappeared with the dream, the erection it inspired remained. It must have been about five in the morning. Arta was sleeping soundly beside him, her face turned towards him. He was close to being overwhelmed by the desire to wake her and make love to her gently.

Alban had been conceived, he was sure, on a morning when he'd woken, aroused, from a dream about Arta. It had been in a different bed and a different home in a very different country, but the moment had felt the same. Then, as now, he could feel her breath on his neck and chest, but on that distant morning he'd felt no inhibition about kissing her, little tiny kisses all over her face and shoulders. After a few seconds he'd felt her stirring alongside him, and he'd pushed back the sheets and taken his lips and his tongue over her breasts and stomach, and though she had not once opened her eyes she was suddenly awake and excited. It was over in minutes, and they were asleep again seconds afterwards, but it was wonderful, and when Lirim had finally woken again, he had been momentarily unsure where his dream had ended and making love with Arta had begun.

This morning, as he felt her breath on his chest, he'd wanted to relive that moment. Then it was easy. Now, it was not so easy. His wife was sleeping and she seemed at peace. If he were to do what his desire told him to, and kiss those slightly parted lips in the hope that she'd wake up with the desire she felt the night they made Alban, how could he know what her reaction might be? If he were to push back the sheets and kiss her body as he had done so many times before, how could he know that in her mind this would not be the act of another man taking her against her will? Yet to wake her properly, and simply tell her he felt this overwhelming desire, how bad might they both feel if she then said no?

He stroked her hair, softly at first, just skimming over it, then a little more firmly, running his thumb slowly around the rim of her ear, until he could feel her scalp too. He put his lips on her forehead and just left them there, blew tiny gusts of air, then blew a little harder so that a few hairs at the front of her head felt his breath too. He was now stroking her neck beneath her hair with one hand and caressing her hip with the other, and she was stirring a little. He blew a little harder on the forehead and then kissed her on the bottom lip.

'Arta, my darling, my beautiful darling Arta,' he whispered, 'I want to kiss you like I used to kiss you. Is that OK?'

'Mmm.'

'Is that "Mmm, I'm not really awake and don't understand what you're saying", or "Mmm, that would be nice"?'

'Nice,' she said. 'Very nice.'

They kissed, for as long as they had kissed in his dream when kneeling by the river. He kissed only her lips and her tongue. He stroked only her neck and her hip. But then she took his hand in hers, and slid it from her hip to her belly, then lifted her own hand away to circle his penis with her fingers. He felt so happy he could have cried.

As, later, he'd left for work, he'd felt as though they had made love for the first time. He couldn't tell if she felt the same. She seemed a little subdued. But he felt the weekend had taken them in the right direction, that things were going to get better. Sitting now in the cafe, he picked up his pen. '*Dear Professor Sturrock,*' he wrote on the postcard. '*We have not met, but I would like to thank you for everything you have done for Arta. Yours gratefully, Lirim Mehmeti.*' He would put it in the postbox on the way home.

36

David's mobile went straight to voicemail. Sturrock thought about leaving a message, but then he wasn't sure what he would say. Instead, he called the warehouse. A machine spoke to him, gave him options, and asked him to hold for an operator if none of the options applied. He held, and listened to lift music for a while. He was about to hang up when a voice finally answered.

'Sorry for keeping you waiting. How can I help?'

'David Temple please.'

'Do you know which department he's in?'

'Packaging, I think.'

'That's just about everyone, sir. We're a packaging company.'

'Oh, I see. I don't know.'

'Let me see, just hold for a moment.' The voice disappeared momentarily, and then returned.

'He doesn't have a line as such but I can page him. Would you like me to page him?'

'Is that a slow process?'

'Well, hopefully if he's here he'll go to the nearest phone and just check in straight away and we can connect you. Like me to do that?'

'Yes, please. I need to speak to him quite urgently.'

Back to the lift music. It was a version of Vivaldi's *Four Seasons*, but bastardised for muzak. Odd, he thought, how something so inspiring could be made to sound so ghastly. He wondered if that was what Jack's friend Charlie did, take beautiful music and make it ugly. He leaned back in his chair, rested the phone on his neck and closed his eyes. He would count to fifty. If David had not come to the phone by then, he would assume he was not there. He counted to eighty-five. No sign of David. He hung up.

He emailed him. 'Hello David, got your email. Glad you're feeling better, and well done on humility. Look forward to seeing your grave-stone exercise. It would be good to speak to you. Please call if you get the chance.'

He was as troubled by his need to speak to David as he was by his desire to make love to Hafsatu. In both cases, he was treating a patient incorrectly, drawing them into his life for his own selfish ends. He was letting David down by putting the onus on his favourite patient to help him. Just like he let down Ralph Hall by not being able to help him save his job. Just like he let down Emily Parks and Arta Mehmeti when they stormed out last week. They were like family to him, all these people, his family, his charges, and not one of them had he served well.

He felt his panic mounting. It was tiredness, he told himself. Calm down. Breathe. Breathe deeply. Do it again. Calm. Calm. He sent David a text message – *'Please call'* – and then he felt yet more guilt, because he knew that right now, this second, he needed David Temple more than David Temple needed him. He couldn't think of anyone else who would properly understand the cauldron of clashing emotions that made him feel his head was close to ripping apart. He picked up his briefcase, put on his coat and took the lift downstairs.

There were already three people in the lift. Two were talking, but too quietly for him to be able really to hear. He felt they were deliberately trying to exclude him from their conversation. They looked like visitors. They looked as if they'd had bad news. They were sad, and whispering. He wondered if he could help, but assumed they already had a doctor looking after them, or at least looking after whoever they were visiting. The lift stopped at the third floor. The third person got out, and two more people got in. One was a hospital porter carrying an envelope marked X-rays. The other was a patient who was probably heading to the canteen. The lift stopped on the first floor. The patient got out. The porter got out. The couple were still whispering. As the lift reached the ground floor, Sturrock took the woman by the arm and said, 'If there is anything I can do to help, you must let me know.' They looked confused. They left the lift. He followed them out into the street.

He stood for a few moments, breathing in the cold air and trying to still his mind. A colleague also on his way home patted him on the shoulder. 'See you, Martin.' Sturrock watched him scurry away, and tried to analyse whether that was a friendly 'See you, Martin' or a hostile one. He concluded it was indifferent.

The traffic was grinding by and the pavements were heaving with people. The thought of going on the tube made him nauseous. He wasn't sure he would be able to stand the noise and the dirt and the mess of people swirling around him. What if he met someone he knew? He felt talked out. He didn't want to speak to anyone. What if some of the fragments of thought flashing around his mind led him to speak out loud, and attract those funny looks you get when you allow private thought to spill into the public space?

He checked his pockets. He had £43 and 27p. The last time he took a taxi home it cost £35. Would it have gone up by more than £8.27? Surely not. Anyway, hopefully Stella would be home so she could come out with cash if he needed more. Or would she? He remembered Ralph. He wondered if Ralph was still there. Would he have cash?

He stood on the yellow line by the pavement and waited for a cab. Dozens went by, but none had a light on. What would he do if none came by? Was it possible that every cab would be taken, for evermore, that every time one emptied, it would immediately be occupied by someone other than him? Perhaps he should move to a different street. But then perhaps the different street would become the street that never saw a vacant cab. Was this an issue of cabs, or streets? He thought maybe if he closed his eyes for a few moments, his mind would still, and a cab would come.

He stood, eyes closed, and told himself to count to ten. Don't go beyond ten, he told himself, you might fall asleep, and if you fall asleep you might fall into the road. So count to ten. It's not sleep but it is rest and it will calm the mind. But what if the cab with a light on comes during this time and you miss it? He opened his eyes again. Red buses as far as the eye could see. Black cabs, but none with lights. Cars grinding along full of people going home, or out, or to work, or to see friends, or to see an elderly relative who had to go to a funeral tomorrow.

Oh my God, he thought. I'd forgotten about the funeral. I haven't finished the eulogy. When will I finish the eulogy? But you have an outline. It's rubbish. It's just a sketch. It has no life in it. It has no colour and texture. I don't have stories. People's lives come alive with stories and colour and texture. I just have a sketch, an outline, no colour, no texture.

And how will I get Mother there? I'll have to get up, shave and all that rubbish the normal person has to do to start the normal day, finish the eulogy, sort myself out, get to the home, get Mother, get to the funeral, meet up with Stella if she's still coming, then do the funeral, eulogy and all, small talk, small talk, cousins blah blah, get Mother back, settle her, God, I hope I don't have to undress her, I can't cope with that, I know I should but I can't and that's that, I know I'm a medical man but she's my mother and I want to remember her as young and life-affirming, not old and wrinkled and unable to hold everything in. I want good memories of her because I have only bad memories of him, and maybe that's why this eulogy is so hard, because I didn't really know his sister, certainly not after she turned, and I didn't really know him, and what I know and remember I don't like, and every time I think of him I feel the world is cold and dark and I'm not safe within it, and how can I be safe when I'm standing in the gutter and red buses are going by and black cabs are going by but there are no lights on? No lights. I can't see the light. And I want to see the light, but I can't. And maybe what I should say tomorrow is that my father drove the light out of me, and ever since then, I have been looking for it, and the closest I ever get is in seeing patients, and trying to help them from the dark, and that is the only time I feel joy, when I see them face up to their demons and confront them and deal with them and emerge blinking from the darkness and into the light. And oh how happy I feel when that happens but why can it never happen to me? Me? Why can't it happen to me?

And now the private thoughts were entering a public place. He was standing in the road, on the yellow line, and shrieking the word 'Me!' and no cabs were coming, at least they were but none with a light on and he felt close to collapse now, and people were stopping to look at him, and he knew he was outside the hospital and he didn't want to go back in, but he thought maybe he needed to, and maybe he needed a bit of help, but they would refer him to the best psychiatrist in town, and that was him, so no point doing that, so he would have to soldier on, keep going, just a few more hours and sleep would come, and then dreams that were warm and bright for once and his father wouldn't be there like a great shadow falling over his face and blocking out the light.

He was about to sit down on the pavement when, finally, a cab came by, and the light was on, and he hailed it down. He was so relieved to sit and to lean back. It would take at least half an hour to get home, maybe more with rush-hour traffic, and he thought he might get a little sleep. But his mind was back on the eulogy. He rummaged through his pockets, but he'd left his fountain pen at the hospital. He asked the driver if he had a pen. The man passed through a little blue bookmaker's pen. He took out some patient notes from his briefcase and started to scribble some thoughts on the back.

'Aunt J . . . Father . . . Different era . . . Don't blame . . . They knew not what they did. Each generation must try to improve on the last.' You can't say that at a funeral. He crossed it out and tried again. 'Aunt J. Nice old soul. Father. We must forgive. He knew not what he did. Each generation must try to improve on the last.' You can't say that. It is her funeral, not my father's. He crossed it out.

'Aunt J. Nice old soul. Her funeral. But also the end of her generation. Different age now. Each generation must improve on the last.' It was getting there. He felt he could say that. 'This is not just her funeral but the funeral of her generation. The end of that generation of her family.' No. Can't say that. Her funeral, not his. He's dead already. No point reliving. Leave it. Leave it be. It happened. It's over. You can't go back. Try to forgive. Try to forgive. Why can't you forgive? You tell others to forgive. Why can't you? Because I can't. Can't or won't? Can't. Can't or won't? Can't. Can't or won't? Can't, can't, can't.

And again a private thought was entering the public realm.

'Can't,' he shouted.

The driver was taken aback.

'Sorry, sir?'

'Oh, I'm sorry. Just thinking something and it popped out. Sorry. Nothing to worry about.'

'Oh. OK.' The driver turned up the volume on the radio and started to watch his fare more closely.

Sturrock looked out of the window, trying to slow down what was happening inside his head. A lorry pulled alongside. 'Pratt's bakery. Delivering to your home. 081 454 3298.'

Delivering to your home. A message from the lorry. I am being delivered to my home. Good. That is where I want to go. But who is the Pratt? Am I the prat? Is the lorry there to tell me I am the prat? Who is being baked? Am I being baked? What happens to me when they've finished baking me? Am I the baker? And why those numbers? What put them there, at this time? Nothing is there without reason. There always has to be a reason.

'Who is the baker?' he asked. The driver, looking into his mirror, said, 'What?'

'Who is the baker?' The driver shook his head.

The cab pulled ahead of the lorry. In front now was a red BMW Series 5. Registration LS 65 BDY. LS, that must be Lesley Sissons. Bullying victim, 1998. Tried to kill herself because those bastards at her school taunted and bullied and cut her hair and ripped up her books and put dogshit in plastic bags in her locker. And twice she tried to kill herself and each time the bastards came back for more till she had to move away. Three years he saw her for and she was so much better at the end than the start. That must be LS. But why 65? She was young, not 65. Maybe she was born in '65? No, that would put her in her forties. He only saw her a few years ago. What was her address? Maybe number 65 something. That's it. It's a street number. Lesley Sissons, 65 Something Street. BDY – short for body? Short for badly? Did he treat her badly? Or was it just that life treated her badly? BDY? Be dead yesterday. Could be. Who? Who was dead yesterday? Me? Could be. Or maybe it's about Aunt Jessica. She died before yesterday. But it's the funeral tomorrow. Be dead yesterday. I don't get that one. Another lorry pulled alongside. 'Bernard's – Removers You Can Rely On'. That must be Bernard the depressive who thought his wife deliberately made him depressed. He has his own removal firm, isn't that good?

They passed a road named Archer Way. Harry Archer. Done for murder. Reduced to manslaughter on grounds of diminished responsibility. He was a schizophrenic. OTO. Must have been nine years ago. Some OTO that was. Broadmoor. Hated going there. Nice people. Some caring staff. But sad cases. Really sad. And no escape. Prisoners. Bolts and keys and gates and barriers. And their minds a prison too. Harry Archer. Dead now. Must be dead. Did he kill himself? Hope he didn't kill himself. Lost soul, but not a bad man.

Grove Park. Grove? Malcolm Grove, three years ago. Drugs. Heroin. Crack cocaine. Delusional. Hated his parents. Both of them. Not just his father. Did cold turkey. Did fine. Wrote poetry. Still kept it somewhere. Grove Park. Who's the Park? Norma Park. Was she drugs or drink? Both maybe. Nice woman. Couldn't cope with her kids. Hurt one of them. Cry for help. But lost the kid. Social services took her away. He advised reunion after seeing her for a year but it never happened. She moved away in the end. Must be living with Malcolm Grove. Nice they named a street after them. Lovely touch. Will they ever name a street after me? Sturrock Rise – that would be nice. At the junction with Temple Way just down from Sesay Gardens. That would be nice.

The meter said £37. He wasn't sure where he was but reckoned he was just a few miles from home now. The traffic wasn't great. He decided he would get out at forty quid, wherever they were. Forty quid took them to the corner of Holt Road and Mansfield Bridge Road. Holt. Never had a Holt. Had a Halton. Margaret Halton. Anorexic. Got to the bottom of it eventually. It was her mother. Thought she was being nice, kept telling her daughter she wouldn't want to be remembered as 'the jolly fat one'. Lethal. Just got her at the right time. Mansfield. Alf Hixon. He came from Mansfield. OCD. Traced it back to a bullying brother. Bridge. Christian Bridge. Sad. Really sad. Three suicide attempts before he was referred. Saw him four times. Killed himself anyway. Never got to understand him. Really sad.

'Do you want a receipt?'

'I don't think so.'

'OK. You take care now.'

Sturrock didn't like the tone. Patronising. You take care. Not take care, which is just like hello or goodbye, totally insignificant. But 'you' take care. In other words, I, esteemed taxi driver, have decided that 'you', i.e. I, Martin Sturrock, need to take care. What does he know? Patronising bastard.

He thought he knew a little short cut that would get him home more quickly. He walked up St Leonard's Hill. Leonard, as in Len Appleton, widower, broken-hearted when his son Stuart was killed right in front of him, victim of a hit-and-run driver, an accident which he survived but the boy did not. Perhaps one of the saddest cases of his career. It was terrible to see a man suffer so from the death of a child, needed major trauma support. Or Len Temple, David's dad. No saint he. Hill, as in Rosalie Hill, post-natal depression, six or seven years ago, took to drink. Moved north in the end. Fine now. Always sent a Christmas card. No relation to the other Rosalie in his life, the first girl he had sex with.

He was walking past Mizzi's. He stopped and stared at the pink door. He told himself he mustn't go in. He had been there many times before. It wasn't clean. It wasn't nice. The woman who ran it was old and rancid. The working girls were, so far as he could recall, poor to average. Don't, Martin. Just walk on. He was staring at the blown-up photo on the pink door, of a nice smiling face surrounded by flyaway blonde hair. She was lovely, but neither the face nor the hair would be beyond the door. Many men had been enticed in by that photo, for a 'massage' or a 'sauna'. They didn't even have a sauna.

Don't join them, Martin. Go home. You upset your wife today. Go home and make it up. Do not go through that door. But in another part of his mind, another voice was speaking. You're tired. You're stressed. Just get a massage. You don't need to go further than that. But I will, the other voice said. I know I will. If I go through that door, I know I will have sex with a prostitute. Then another part of his mind, the practical part, joined in. You have no cash. And you can hardly use a credit card, can you, not when Mrs S will see the bill?

The practical part set the other two voices back at each other. 'Don't walk through the door' was saying that if you don't have the money, it is the man upstairs telling you it is not meant to be. 'Go through the door and only have a massage' was saying there is no such thing as a divine force shaping the world because if there was, there would be no need for Mizzi's in the first place, we would all meet the partner of our dreams and live in godly union happily ever after. For heaven's sake, 'go through the door and only have a massage' was saying, it is only a massage and you deserve it. Then 'the minute you walk through the door you'll have sex' was saying give yourself the option. Go and get money from the cashpoint round the corner in Sutton Road and give yourself the option.

Sturrock couldn't think of a patient called Sutton, or any connection with Sutton. The Sutton Road voice won the argument though and he went to withdraw £120. On the walk back, 'treat yourself to a massage' won the argument. He went through the pink door. He asked for a massage. The madam smiled knowingly, took his cash and said Angelica would be along soon.

As so often before, the moment he was in there, cash handed over, girl allocated, clothes taken off, massage underway, he wished he had been strong enough to withstand the urge. The expectation, so often, was better than what followed which in turn was followed by the surge of guilt and then, days later, the steady romanticisation of what had happened so that nice light and nice towels, dark sexuality and the stirring of desire could be recalled, but leaking taps, used condoms lying in bins and needle marks in the arms of sad girls were not. His mind had calmed a little on being forced to communicate with someone else, first the old woman who welcomed him and now 'Angelica'. He was in a state of heightened anxiety which led to him being more quickly aroused than was sometimes the case and once that happened, he just wanted to get it over with. He imagined that suited Angelica as well.

'A blow job will do,' he said.

'You paid the full whack, love.'

'No, it's fine. Please.' He had suddenly felt repelled by the idea of seeing any more of her body than was already on display. As she started to suck him off, he was trying to paint his mind blank. He closed his eyes, tried to push aside all thoughts as soon as they came in. Work. Patients. Kids. Parents. God. Stella. Booking holidays. Remembering to get the stamps for Stella on the way home. More patients. Kids again. Stella again. Once, he could almost see the blank, but then a thought crept in, filled out the space and as soon as he chased it away, another would float in. And down below was Angelica. Never was a name so ill-fitting. Demonica would be more apt. The mind full of angels and demons. The whorehouse full of Demonicas called Angelica. He could feel her hair stroking his stomach, her hand working up and down his penis as her mouth played around the tip. How many times had she done this? What did she think about? What did she think of the men she fucked and sucked? Did she see them as clients, or patients? Was she repelled by them, or by herself? By both, or neither? Did she have kids? Would she want her daughter to do what she does, like once he had wanted Jack to be a psychiatrist, and his father had wanted him to be an engineer? Was she any more or less worthless than he was? What he did to the mind, she did to the body, tried to take stress from it and add pleasure to it. They were both in the happiness business. Their patients/clients all came from somewhere in a land named Not Happy. He was a prostitute of the mind, she a psychiatrist of the body. Yet he needed years of training, while she needed no more than the ability to fight repulsive thoughts about repulsive men.

He tried to separate his mind from his body, see his penis as something entirely separate from him. If he let his mind influence his body, he would be here all day, thoughts about where he was and what he was doing making him shrink and wilt and long to be away. He had to let her carry out a purely physiological act. But then he found it was Hafsatu Sesay who was the thought crowding in on his space, and he didn't object. He was desperate not to think about her, even more desperate that he could not stop himself. His mind linked back to his frantic hunt of the Internet, the time he thought he found her there, and he was so happy, but then on closer examination he noticed the girl in the film had a chain tattooed around her ankle. It wasn't her. He gave up looking. But the mind could summon up images too, and as Angelica sucked away, he had only Hafsatu in mind, no matter how hard he tried to push her aside.

He was glad when it was over, even gladder when he was dressed and out of there. Gladder, but not happier. Ever since he'd left the hospital, his mind had felt as though in a vice and the two ends were closing in on each other. He had vaguely hoped the visit to Mizzi's might stop the vice from tightening, release tension, give him space to recapture his balance. But it hadn't worked. If anything, he felt worse, more tired, more stressed, less sure he could work out what was happening to him or where it was leading.

He looked at his wrist. The elastic band was still there, digging into the flesh. He'd noticed it when he'd held on to Angelica's hair in the final moments before he came. Slowly, deliberately, he took it off and dropped it into the gutter.

This isn't right, he said to himself. Come on, come on, you're an expert in this, you know what it is, it's like a psychosis, you're undergoing some kind of psychotic attack, you've seen people, hundreds of them, you've helped them through this kind of thing, well, not through but after, you've helped them recover, you've heard them describe what it's like and it's like this, you know that, but you're different to them because you're an expert, you know what's happening, you know what it's about, so come on, deal with it, get a grip of yourself, calm, calm, try to calm it and then take stock. But there's no room for calm because even saying 'calm, calm' to yourself is just like a prod, a hot prod, a prod to the other part of your wiring that is saying sod the calm, no to calm, you're not going to do calm, we're taking this all the way to the brink, my boy, you are not calm and you're not going to be calm any time soon because you don't deserve it, you useless little fucker.

He was still standing outside Mizzi's, on the pavement, his brief-case between his feet. He put his hands to his head, hard against his temples, and bent over to get his head down towards his knees.

'Shut up, shut up, leave me alone,' he shouted, and a young boy walking by thought he was talking to him. The boy looked scared, and hurried along quickly. A man came by, weighed down by two shopping bags in either hand. He looked tired and dejected. 'Why is it happening?' Sturrock said to him. 'Why is this happening? Is it because I don't do the shopping? Have you escaped because I didn't do the shopping and you did?' The man shook his head, and pulled close towards the buildings, away from the kerb. A bus passed and on the side was an advert for a new Kellogg's cereal, and as it sped by, he shouted at the man as he walked away. 'It's not you. It's not because of the shopping. It's the cereal. It's because I eat the wrong cereal. So don't worry.'

He thought about going back into Mizzi's and asking if he could have a bed to lie down on. No sex, no girls, just a bed. He would be happy to pay full price just for a place to lie down in. That's how tired he felt. He took his phone from his pocket. He scrolled down to the Ds in his address book and found David Temple. He hit the call button. Three rings, then into voicemail. Why was he not answering? Was he on a downward curve and he had thrown the phone away, knowing he was incapable of speech? Was he calling Phyllis again and trying to get through to him? Was he trying to call Amanda? Had she agreed he could go out with her? That would be good.

Out there, somewhere, unless he had killed himself, which Sturrock doubted, David Temple was doing something, standing or sitting some-where, or walking, or lying down, looking at something, thinking something, breathing in, breathing out. He might be coughing. He might be writing something. He might be sitting downstairs at home with a book on his lap wishing his mum would be quiet. He might be out by the canal, or in the park, wishing he had put his coat on, because where he was, it might be starting to rain, like it was here. And Sturrock couldn't reach him. They were blocked. No contact was possible. And there was nobody else he could turn to. Nobody who would understand the same. They were all out there, all his patients past and present, but he didn't have the same relationship. If he called Emily Parks now, and told her he felt tired and stressed and he didn't know how he was going to get home, she wouldn't understand. She would think it very odd, even though she was always nice and polite. Arta wouldn't get it. She found Britain a strange place to live, and this was beyond her range of comprehension, he thought. She didn't have David's depth of understanding.

David was the only one who would understand and be able to help. David knew this feeling. He knew the lows, but he also knew this, the racing from thought to thought, each thought worse than the last. He knew what it was like when the mind was like a giant paper-thin stained-glass window full of beautiful images in beautiful bright colours, and inside his mind he had just two little hands and he was trying to hold the glass together and carry it safely as the body moved and jangled everything in the mind, but the longer his hands inside his mind were holding on, the heavier the stained-glass window became, though paper-paper-thin, and then the arms and shoulders inside the mind started to ache and it became God's own struggle to hold on, and the images started to crumble one by one. There goes Jesus. There goes God. He's gone. He's disintegrated. The disciples are there at the edge of the glass and they're starting to go, and then he sees old friends from university, where are they now, crumbling into shards in his mind, and old teachers, they're crumbling, and then he can see past girlfriends, and there in the corner a multicoloured mountain of prostitutes lying naked on top of each other, and the mountain crumbles and there are the pictures of his patients, some are dead but they come back to life in the stained glass, some younger than when he knew them, some older, but all there, dozens, hundreds, and their families too, so there's David Temple and his mother Nora, but they're crumbling too and the glass is shattering, and then there's his own family in the corner, holding on, but now they're gone as well and all he can make out is his father, looking on stern and not a flicker of worry in his eyes even though all around him the glass is crumbling, and David knows that feeling, David alone of his people knows that feeling but he's not answering his phone, so what to do, what to do? And now the glass is in thousands of little pieces and the fragments are flying into every corner of his mind and they hurt because they're sharp and they cut and graze, and even though he can hear music now, it doesn't help because it is layer on layer of music, not just one calming symphony which might give him space, and help him breathe, but song upon song, symphony upon symphony, and how can it be that music can be so beautiful, so soothing, so calming when played in its own space, yet so terrifying when as now it is layer on layer of clashing sounds, beautiful song crashing into beautiful song, and the result is ugly, and it hurts and the songs are crashing into the glass and now it feels like the glass will cut right through his head, go out from in, and holes will appear in his head, and his brains will start to pour out on to the street, and he really didn't want his brains to pour out here, in the road outside Mizzi's, it was demeaning and it was bad, so he had to calm himself somehow, just be calm and try to buy time.

'Are you all right? Can I get you anything?' A woman tapped him on the shoulder. She was a large version of Mrs Temple, short but stout with symmetrical black hair.

'I'm trying to find David Temple,' he said. 'Once I find David, I'll be fine.'

'Is there anything I can do in the meantime?' she asked. 'You don't look at all well.'

He read genuine concern in her face and for a few seconds, he calmed. He was suddenly embarrassed to be causing a scene, sufficient to attract a little crowd of people who were standing outside the bakery.

'I'm fine,' he said. 'I'll be fine. Thank you for your concern.'

Only even as he said it, and as he walked slowly away and up the gentle incline of St Leonard's Hill, the traffic heavier and noisier now rush hour was in full swing, he knew he wasn't fine. He wondered for a moment if it was too late to go back to the hospital and ask for help. But he had no money and there were no cabs to take him and it wasn't right to call an ambulance, not when there were so many others who needed them. The fat version of Mrs Temple had soothed him for a moment, brought him up short, but it was just a lull in the storm, and by the time he had passed the bakery and then the pharmacy with the single word 'Prescriptions' lit up in red, and then the charity shop for St Giles' Hospice, which made him think of the Le Gassick wing where he worked, because Le Gassick was an anagram of 'sack Giles', and he was sure he didn't want to end his days in a hospice, and his mind was back to racing mode, and though the music had quietened, the glass shards were still cutting into the side of his head, and he was trying to put the glass back together again, and the hands inside his mind were getting cut to shreds and now the blood was running over the fragments of glass, and he just had this great mess inside his head and he didn't know how to clean it up.

He didn't want to die in a hospice, all alone but for nice caring staff just counting the days till you're gone, and he didn't want to die in a care home like Aunt Jessica, they were no different to hospices, just places where people were sent to die because their families couldn't cope so they paid peanuts to others to do it for them. How on earth was he going to collect his mother if he felt like this, and when, for God's sake, when was he going to write the eulogy? And now the crowd outside the baker's had dispersed, though one or two were keeping an eye on him, including the stouter version of Mrs Temple. He had passed the charity shop and next on the parade there was an ironmonger who did keys and shoe repairs, and he passed that and then a fruit and flower stall and then a little cafe serving Arabic coffee and one or two old men were outside smoking and after that there was a butcher's and then a bookshop, a tiny scruffy bookshop which specialised in children's books, and then there was a tanning salon, then a hairdresser's, and he wondered if they were owned by the same person because the shopfronts looked similar, then a phone and

Internet access shop full of foreigners, then a laundry, then another cafe, which was empty but for a man playing on a fruit machine, then the funeral directors and the instant he saw the word 'funeral' he felt this was where everything that had gone before had led him, and he decided he couldn't face tomorrow, he couldn't face collecting his mother, he couldn't face thinking any more what he should say about Aunt Jessica, he couldn't face the prospect of standing in front of dozens of people and speaking to them with his head full of glass shards and music that clashed with the funeral march. He looked through the window. A single candle was burning alongside a Bible opened at the Book of Job. He took out his phone and called David Temple. It went into voicemail. Staring directly into the tip of the flame from the candle, he said, 'Hello, David, it's Professor Sturrock again. Sorry to bother you. I'm not feeling too great, and I wanted to say that if anything happened to me, I would like you to say a few words at my funeral. Thanks. Take care.' Then he texted him. *'PS I have never known anyone better describe how this feels.'*

He felt he should call Stella, but what would he say? It was beyond her range of comprehension too. He scrolled down to the Ss in his address book, clicked on her name, called up her number and looked at it for a while. He couldn't face speaking to her. He decided to text instead. *'David Temple to do main eulogy, Ralph Hall to say something about need for improved psychiatric services, and Hafsatu Sesay on evils of prostitution.'* He hit the send button. Then it struck him that apart from Ralph Hall, Stella had not heard of any of these people. He sent her another text. *'Phyllis knows how to get hold of them. You can choose hymns and rest of order of service.'* He pressed the send button again. Then he sent her another text. *'PS Sorry. Not just about Ralph. About everything.'*

He knew it ought to bother him that he had no desire to speak to her, or to his children, or to his mother who he felt would be stoic whatever happened to him. Stella would be shocked, then feel liberated. The children would be shocked, but once the shock subsided and all the rituals were over and done with, it would give them something to talk about forever more. It would make them more interesting in the eyes of friends and colleagues. He was doing them a favour, he told himself.

He thought he would have a better chance of a clean hit if he crossed the road to face vehicles coming down the hill. St Leonard's Hill was a bus route and they picked up a fair bit of speed in their own lanes. He waited for the next lull in traffic and crossed the road. The noise in his mind seemed to have stopped. He felt almost serene. He knew he was doing the right thing.

Beyond the traffic lights, he could see a lorry behind a line of three cars. The lorry driver's life was going to change for ever. Sturrock felt bad about that. He might be far from home. He might be speeding home to a family who love him. He might be late making a delivery. He was going to be further delayed. The police would need to talk to him. He wouldn't be able to move his lorry for hours. There was nothing he, or Sturrock, could do about that. He was simply in the wrong place at the wrong time. It wasn't personal, Sturrock told himself as he stepped from the pavement on to the red lines in the gutter. He waited until the first car had passed and then stepped into the bus lane itself, and began to inch towards the road. As the second car passed him, he picked up his pace a little. He timed it to perfection. The third car passed as he crossed from the bus lane to the road. The lorry driver slammed hard on his brakes as soon as he realised the smartly dressed grey-haired man carrying a brown leather briefcase was not going to stop. But it was too late. The lorry hit him so hard he was dead by the time the nearside front wheels rolled over his neck, and the lorry veered onto the kerb and into the front garden of 148 St Leonard's Hill where, later that evening, Angelica would be the first to lay flowers. The exact time of death was recorded at 18.04. David Temple called at 18.06, but the call went straight into voicemail. 'This is Martin Sturrock. I am sorry not to be able to take your call. Please leave a message after the tone.'

'It's David Temple. I hope you're OK. Sorry I didn't get back to you before but I was at work. Your messages worried me. Give me a call. Bye.'

The Aftermath

Simon ended up doing the eulogy at Aunt Jessica's funeral. He had thought about postponing in the light of events, but the crematorium in Yeovil was fully booked for the next week and a half, so he had to go ahead. In the end he surprised himself by how well he managed to speak about his mother, not breaking into tears once. He put it down to the shock of Martin's death. He was able to draw on happy memories of their childhood days and so focus on his mother's warmth and energy, her delight in other people. She'd always loved Martin, and had been so sad when he stopped visiting her. He wanted to pay tribute to that.

Professor Sturrock's death was the third story on the late regional TV news on Monday night, once the police announced a name, and an unnamed source told *BBC London*'s crime reporter that it looked like suicide. When the same source told the *Evening Standard* that there was no note, but a text message to his wife instead, the press went into overdrive. 'SUICIDE TEXT – TRAGIC SHRINK'S FINAL ACT' was the front-page headline of Tuesday's first edition, above an old picture of Professor Sturrock, taken from the inside flap of his book on grief and trauma. And alongside that they mocked up a Nokia phone showing the message: '*Darling, I won't be home tonight. I'm going to kill myself.*' The national dailies followed in similar vein on Wednesday morning.

In fact, Stella Sturrock hadn't interpreted her husband's text messages as signalling his imminent suicide, more as an attempt at emotional blackmail after their bitter exchanges over Ralph Hall. She'd seen the messages after she finished a long phone conversation with Sandie Hall, whom she'd called to say that Ralph was on his way to the South London Alcohol Rehab Centre for an initial assessment. She read them several times, and then tried desperately to call her husband back. When she got no answer, she'd tried Phyllis, but the office answer machine was on. She was just putting on her coat to walk to the tube station, in the hope that he might be on his way back home, when the WPC rang the doorbell.

Even as she walked to answer the door, and saw the silhouette of a hat through the frosted glass, she knew what was coming.

She took the policewoman through to the kitchen and showed her the text messages.

'I knew he got down from time to time, but I had no idea he was so unhappy,' she said. 'I thought it was just me.' She waited until the WPC had left before sitting down at his desk, where she banged her fist on the pile of books by the computer and repeatedly asked herself, first silently, then quietly, finally loudly, almost a shriek that burst out with the full force of her lungs, 'Why?' She calmed after a minute or two, then she imagined he was there sitting on the violet sofa littered with tatty cushions, where sometimes he would sit and read, and she asked him, 'Why, Martin? Was it really so bad? And how do I tell the children their father didn't want to live a moment longer? How do you expect them to live with that thought for the rest of their lives?' There was a photo of the children on the wall above the sofa, smiling, Suzanne with her arms draped around Professor Sturrock's neck. 'They did love you,' she said. 'You just couldn't feel it.' And she finally cried, because when she asked herself if she loved him too, the answer wouldn't come.

Obviously, neither Stella nor Sheila Sturrock could attend Aunt Jessica's funeral, Stella because she was dealing with the repercussions of her husband's death, Sheila because nobody could collect her. Jan spent most of Tuesday with Stella and then drove to the nursing home in Coldicote to tell her mother what had happened. She couldn't bear to tell Sheila her son had killed himself. Instead, she said he'd been involved in a road accident, and had died instantly, without pain. Mrs

Sturrock looked bewildered, but didn't cry. Jan wondered if she even understood.

'You realise what I'm saying, don't you, Mum? Martin's dead.'

Mrs Sturrock nodded. 'I think I should go to the funeral,' she said. 'It would mean a lot to your father.'

Jan left the staff with strict instructions to try to prevent her from seeing newspapers or listening to the news. She departed with the rather desolate hope that if someone did tell her mother what had happened, she wouldn't understand.

David Temple was on his way to work when he found out. His mother called him on his mobile, almost breathless with panic.

'Have you heard, have you heard? Your Professor is on the breakfast news. It's all over the telly, David, he's dead, I can't believe what I'm hearing.'

David stopped walking. He stood, his mobile pressed to his ear, and across his mind came an image of Professor Sturrock hanging from a tree. He said nothing.

'David, David . . . Are you there?' his mum was calling.

'Did he kill himself?'

'So they're saying on the news.'

'I thought this might happen,' he said, and told his mother about the weird messages on his phone.

'Have you deleted them?' she asked. 'Because if you haven't, you should take them to the police.'

'No, I kind of had a feeling they were important.' He felt a lot calmer than he imagined he would have done. Perhaps it was because he had thought about Professor Sturrock dying before, so his mind was ready to accept it. It was his mother who seemed to feel a greater upset.

'He was such a lovely man, David. You know that even more than I do, but I know it well enough from that one time we met. I just don't know what we're going to do without him. They'll have to find someone else for you.'

'I guess,' said David. 'But there are bits and pieces he's left behind, which will be a help.'

He wondered about asking for the day off, but then asked himself what Professor Sturrock would advise. He'd advise him to work through to the end of the day, and maybe shed a tear on his way home, walking along the canal in the dark. That's what he would do. He told his mum about the Professor wanting him to speak at his funeral, which panicked her even more.

'You can't stand up in front of all those people, and talk, David.'

'I think I can, Mum. I'd give it a go anyway, maybe ask Father Nicholas for a bit of advice.' He knew she would like that, and she did. It would give her new reasons to go to the church between now and whenever the funeral was to be held.

Matthew Noble thought nothing of the *Evening Standard* billboard – 'TRAGIC SHRINK'S TEXT SUICIDE' – as he freewheeled through two lines of traffic queuing at red lights. But as he looked into the back of a car he was overtaking, a businessman being driven home was reading the paper, and Matthew recognised his psychiatrist in the photo on the front page. He braked, then looked more closely, sufficient for the back-seat passenger to give him a dirty look. The nearest garage was three minutes away. He tried to pick up speed but the combination of bad traffic, fumes that were making him cough and a mild sense of panic meant he was wheezy as he followed a red Vauxhall onto the forecourt. The paper was staring at him from alongside the cashier's till. He just couldn't take it in. He read the story over and over, several times. Then he fished out his mobile from the zip-up pocket on the back of his Mitchell's cold-weather jacket, and called Celia.

'Have you seen the news?'

'What?'

'Professor Sturrock. Dead. Killed himself. I'm reading about it now.'

'Oh my God. Are you kidding me?'

Then they told each other how they couldn't believe it, and how shocked they were and how tragic it was and all the other things people say when someone they know has died in shocking circumstances.

All around the South East, and in the wider world of psychiatry, conversations like that were happening. Arta burst into tears when she heard it on the radio news as she was cleaning the kitchen floor. She packed Besa into the buggy and raced as fast as she could to the car wash to tell Lirim, who thought of his thank-you card arriving on an empty desk and deeply regretted not having sent a letter to Professor Sturrock before. Emily's mother Lorraine let out a little scream as she heard it on the Classic FM news. She called Emily who was at Sami's. Emily had to go and sit in the back of the shop. She sat there for a long time, crying quietly. Then she went to church to pray for him. Patients, colleagues, porters, taxi drivers, nurses, newsagents, fruit sellers, prostitutes – dozens and dozens of people heard the news and reacted with varying degrees of shock that someone they knew was all over the news in such a horrible way.

As the police investigation pieced together the last days and hours of his life, it became one of those stories the twenty-four-hour media just couldn't get enough of. They loved the text angle, which sparked a huge debate about whether there were any limits to what could be considered textable information. 'What next? The text-message divorce?' Then there was the issue of psychiatrists and who supports them when they're on the edge, with Professor Sturrock's own guidelines for his hospital published as a big whooshing breaking-news exclusive by Sky News. Once the police learned that he had visited Mizzi's half an hour before dying, and had what sounded like a crack-up on the pavement outside, the newspapers had the sex angle that every long-running story needs. And Ralph Hall's Saturday-night antics, with the political sex scandal already in place, provided the cherry on top once the police leaked out that he was the last person to see Professor Sturrock at home.

For the people innocently caught up in it all, it was a nightmare. The lorry driver was a father of four from Ghent in Belgium, but couldn't get home until the police were finished with his vehicle. The owners of the garden he drove into were away on holiday, and had to rush back from Majorca. The girls at Mizzi's had to give statements. Several were found to be illegal immigrants and faced deportation.

The immediate challenge for Stella Sturrock was to organise the funeral, knowing that even though her husband's mind had been disturbed, his text saying who he wanted to speak was as close as she got to a declaration of his final wishes. She felt she had to respect those wishes. Phyllis, though shocked to the point of devastation that such an important part of her life had been taken away from her, was helpful in providing all the phone numbers. In fact, in the days that followed, Phyllis was constantly at the family's side. 'He asked me if I ever feel emotion,' she said to Stella. 'I do, and now I wish I had shown some. I kept my efficient face on because that's what I thought he wanted. But I was worried about him. So worried.'

Once Suzanne and Lucio had come home from Italy, Stella and the children sat at the kitchen table and tried to agree an order of service. The death was so hard to take in that the details that emerged subsequently, like the revelation of his visits to prostitutes, were somehow not as shocking as the fact that he had died by his own hand. Mrs Sturrock coped a lot better than friends and family expected her to. There was just one moment when her guard dropped. She had noticed Michelle draining of colour as, lost in her own thoughts, she was clearly going over what her father went through as he made the decision to take his life.

'I can't believe he's done this to us,' Mrs Sturrock said. 'His life is over. We will carry this, every day, to the end of ours.'

The girls cried the most. The flight home had been the worst journey of Suzanne's life. She came close to collapse when her mother called and told her, couldn't stop saying that she found it impossible to accept they would never see him or speak to him again. Michelle felt dreadful that she had not come to Jack's birthday lunch, and had made up an excuse about watching a friend play rugby. Jack was wishing his last meeting with his father had been friendlier. He was also hurt that his father had not asked any of the children to speak. Mrs Sturrock said his text had not excluded the possibility. 'He clearly didn't want us to,' said Jack.

'It's best done by others,' said Michelle. 'Family tend to crack up and cry and it gets embarrassing.'

Mrs Sturrock decided they should have a church funeral, partly because Martin had been baptised, but also because she felt she would need to rely on her own faith much more now. Reverend Fletcher, at her local church, was an old friend, who would see her through. It would also mean more people would be able to attend than at the crematorium. She imagined quite a lot of his hospital colleagues would want to come.

However hurt Jack might be that his father preferred his patients to speak at the funeral, from her point of view her husband's text made it much easier to shape the order of service. She simply needed to choose the music.

Phyllis made the arrangements with David Temple. Mrs Sturrock spoke to Ralph Hall and Hafsatu Sesay herself.

Hafsatu hadn't known what to think when Mrs Sturrock called her the day after her husband's suicide. She was walking from her safe house in Chigwell to the tailors where she had a part-time job. She had not heard the news. When she did, she gagged involuntarily and felt faint for a few moments. Then she listened as Mrs Sturrock explained how her husband had left a message saying he would like her to speak out against prostitution at his funeral. At first she thought it was some kind of trick. She even wondered if she was being set up, that the gang which had controlled her had found out where she had been moved to, and was closing in. She asked if Mrs Sturrock could prove she was telling the truth. Mrs Sturrock said if she wanted proof he had killed himself, she only had to pick up a newspaper. For proof that he wanted her to speak at the funeral, she would have to see the text message he had sent. They arranged to meet on Thursday, at Mrs Sturrock's house. Once Hafsatu went in, and saw it was a family home, with crying children and a widow trying to organise a funeral, she felt dreadful at having doubted Mrs Sturrock.

It was such a shock to be asked though. Why her? Why did he feel so strongly about prostitution given all the other issues he dealt with and all the other patients he had? It was when she read in the papers about his visit to Mizzi's, and then learned he regularly visited a number of brothels in the area, that she realised why he had thought of her in the last desperate minutes of his life. She was in a difficult position now. She was angry at Professor Sturrock's hypocrisy. He had sat and listened to her explain what prostitution had done to her, how it had virtually destroyed her dignity, her sanity, her self-worth, her ability to relate to other people, and yet he had used women in exactly the same abused state as she had been in. He had no idea where they came from or how they got there, but he knew the psychological damage being done by the lives they were forced to live. And he contributed to all that. The thought of speaking in front of a church full of people was bad enough. Speaking about prostitution was unimaginable.

Mrs Sturrock led her to the sitting room after asking Michelle to make them some tea.

As she looked at the pain etched in Mrs Sturrock's face, witnessed the subdued organising going on around them as the children made and took calls, each one requiring emotional energy or practical acumen, Hafsatu felt the rage inside her growing.

How dare he presume to invite her to do this, and invite along with it the fear of being tracked down, and the shame of admitting what she had done? Yet she did not want to upset Mrs Sturrock.

'How well did you know my husband?'

'I was a patient. I saw him every week.'

'And you knew him only as a patient?'

'Yes.'

Hafsatu knew the real meaning of the question. Both were embarrassed by the silence which followed.

'Your husband was helping me to recover.'

'Ironic,' said Mrs Sturrock. Hafsatu nodded.

'I am sad he has died. I am angry at what he did,' she said.

'Yes, I think we both have cause for that.'

'He seemed to understand. It was like slavery and I told him everything, the rapes, being made to work in brothels, my escape, and then
having to live in fear, and trying to start all over again. I thought he
understood.'

'I'm sure part of him did understand.'

Hafsatu looked unyielding. 'It is such a shameful thing for a
woman like me. He was helping me overcome that. Now I learn
this . . .'

'At least he was trying to help.'

'Yes. But he harmed others.'

Mrs Sturrock nodded.

'He talked a lot about demons and angels. He once said I had
been full of angels, but others had filled me with demons. Nice thing
to say. He said nice things . . .'

Michelle brought in the tea, and silence fell once more, which
gave them both time to reflect. Michelle stayed, sat on the arm of
her mother's chair, took her hand.

'Hafsatu is the patient Dad wanted to speak at the funeral,' said
Mrs Sturrock. 'She's quite worried about it. And angry about things
he did.'

She and Michelle looked intently at their guest, who seemed to
be fighting back tears.

'My father was clearly not well,' Michelle said to her. 'Perhaps for
far longer than anyone knew.'

'To take your own life – what is it the coroners say?' said her
mother. '"He killed himself while the balance of his mind was
disturbed." I don't think he meant any harm in asking you to speak
at the funeral. He was disturbed.'

Hafsatu looked crushed now. Mrs Sturrock knew what she had
to say, and was relieved to do so. She didn't particularly want the issue
of prostitution raised at the funeral.

'Hafsatu, if you don't want to speak, I'll understand. So would
Martin.'

'I really don't want to. I'd be too scared. I could say good things.
He helped many people. But I would have to say he did bad things.

He called prostitution evil in the message to you. It is. It does not mean he was an evil man. But he encouraged some who are.'

'I understand that. I hope you will come to the funeral. But you don't need to speak.' Hafsatu nodded, and promised to be there.

The Funeral

Stella Sturrock picked Ramsey & Sons, undertakers for five genera-
tions, to handle the arrangements. They had done several high-profile
funerals in the recent past, covering as they did an area full of well-
known people, and suggested setting up a 'media pool' outside the
church, but not allowing any cameras inside.

The hearse and two cars arrived at the house just after eleven on
Monday morning, a week to the day since his death. Since waking
up, Stella had been busying herself, making and taking phone calls,
checking everything was ready at the church. She had decided on a
public funeral, private burial, then family and close friends back to
the house for refreshments. The girls were following her lead, trying
to find things to do and people to speak to, as much to kill the time
as to achieve anything worthwhile. One or two neighbours had popped
in to see if there was anything they could do to help. Jack was the
one who seemed most detached.

As the funeral cortège arrived outside, all the chatter of fuss and
preparation slowed to a halt till all that could be heard was the sound
of wheels turning on gravel. Michelle had been chattering away but
gasped when she saw the coffin; Stella Sturrock put her hands to her
mouth, then shed her first tear of the day.

In the hours since Martin's death, she had felt sad at times, lonely,
confused, hurt, bitter. She had also had the occasional moment of
culpability, feeling there must have been more she could have done
to spot what was happening to him. But then as those waves of guilt
came over her, she would tell herself *he* was the psychiatrist, not her.
He was the one who understood the human mind, not her. It was at

the sight of the coffin that, for the first time, she felt sad for him, and sad too for a marriage that had given neither of them the happiness they thought it would.

The undertakers stood at the cars and waited, as they did several times a day. Michelle and Suzanne walked out with their mother, Lucio and Jack following on behind, and they all squeezed into the first car. Jan, Stella's brother and sister-in-law, and the Sturrocks' next-door neighbour, got into the second car. The second car was a bit of an extravagance. It had been ordered on the assumption that Sheila Sturrock would attend. But the senior nurse at the care home had decided she was too frail.

It was as the cortège pulled to a stop outside the entrance to the church that Stella realised she had not asked the printers for enough orders of service.

'My God,' said Suzanne, 'I've never seen so many people.'

'We've rather underestimated the turnout,' said Reverend Fletcher, coming over to the car.

'Will they all get in?' Stella asked.

'Some may have to stand, but we'll do our best.'

He gave her and the children an order of service. There was Martin on the front, smiling, wearing his favourite old sports jacket.

'Lovely photo, Mum,' said Michelle. Stella nodded.

In the emails she and Phyllis had sent out about the funeral arrangements, she had said they would like people to bring a flower to lay on the coffin at the end of the service. Dozens of the people queuing to get into the church were clutching single roses, lilies and sunflowers. Suzanne was carrying the flowers for the family.

'Florists are doing well,' she said. Stella nodded again. The under-takers were standing ready to carry in the coffin. The vicar and his team had just about squeezed everyone in. As Stella stepped from the car, she noticed for the first time the little gaggle of journalists by the fence. She turned to find the hand of one of her children. Jack gave her his.

The organ increased in volume as they stepped into the church.

'Jesus,' said Jack. It was the first time he had spoken since they left the house. 'Who are all these people?'

Every space on every pew was taken. People were standing two- and three-deep down the sides. Stella was well into the nave of the church before she saw a face she recognised, one of Martin's friends from university. Then she spotted colleagues from work, doctors and nurses, whom she had met in the days when she and Martin socialised more. Towards the front were all the cousins and the rest of the family, and she was glad to see they had brought their children too. But who everyone else was, she had no idea.

The organist played even louder as the coffin was carried in. They had thought about having medical colleagues as pall-bearers but there was too much politics involved in the choice, so she decided to let the undertakers do it. Mr Ramsey himself walked ahead of the coffin. As it passed her, she began to cry again, and so did Jack.

Reverend Fletcher didn't know Professor Sturrock well, but he knew Stella and addressed his opening remarks to her and the family. 'Well,' he said, 'if Martin ever wondered if he was loved, I think this would give him the answer, would it not?'

It was meant to help, but it made Stella feel even more distant from the event. He had killed himself, she imagined, because he didn't feel loved by the people he most wanted to love him. She sensed her children feeling the same. She leaned over Jack to take Suzanne's hand.

The chance to stand, clear throats and blow noses during the first hymn, 'Abide With Me', helped calm things a little. Then Ralph Hall came up the aisle.

Although Ralph was used to speaking in public, he had never felt more nervous. He'd been allowed out of the rehab centre for the funeral, provided he had a 'minder' to take him straight back afterwards. He had never felt more in need of a drink, yet already, just one week into his treatment, he was getting strength from the 'one day at a time' approach to abstinence. He walked slowly to the front of the church, bowed his head to the coffin, then to the image of Christ on the cross on the huge stained glass that dominated the back wall, then went to the pulpit. He had no notes. He'd left the piece of paper on which he'd prepared what to say on the worn ledge of the pew in front of his. He stared out at the sea of faces before him, and took a deep breath.

'My name is Ralph Hall. I am an alcoholic.' He bowed his head again, this time because of the effort it had taken to say it. He had been thinking about whether to admit to his alcoholism in public for days, had weighed all the arguments for, all the arguments against, but he knew it was one of those decisions he wouldn't make until the very last minute. Now, having made it, and having uttered the words, he felt as if he was going to cry. But as he stared at his feet, and breathed deeply, he heard the beginnings of applause at the back of the church. He looked up, and the applause spread through the congregation towards him. He stood up straight again.

'That's the first time I've said it, publicly. I am an alcoholic. And the man who taught me to say it is the man inside that box. When I heard he was dead, I vowed I would never drink again. I have gone seven days. I will dedicate every day without the demon that is drink to his memory. Because he took my drink problem and he made it his problem. When my world was crashing around me, he took me in. He didn't have to, but he did.

'It has taken me a long time to be able to say this to anyone, even to my wife, whom I told far too late, but I was a patient of Martin Sturrock's. And I know there are many of his other patients here today.' He paused and took a deep breath out of relief that he was going to get through it, and because he felt strong and confident in what he was saying.

'Stand up,' he said. 'Stand up if you have ever been treated by Martin Sturrock.' A murmur went round the congregation and there was a lot of rustling as dozens of people got to their feet. It took courage, he thought, to stand up and be counted, but they were prepared to do it. About a quarter of the congregation was now standing.

'Now stand up if you're a relative or friend of one of the people he treated.' Now over half the congregation was standing.

Stella craned round to look. Never in her life had she felt such conflicting emotions. She saw all these people whom her husband had cared for and felt excluded. She spotted Hafsatu standing at the back of the church, and felt shame. But amid her shame at his use of prostitutes, and any failings in her that led him down that path, not to mention the anger at what lay ahead for her and the children, she also felt so very proud of him.

'In all my years as an MP,' Ralph went on, 'I have never felt so much part of a community as I do now.' Stella turned back to the former minister as he continued, struck by how well he looked compared with the day she met him.

'And now stand up if you were a colleague of his, or a student, and you feel he taught you something that helps you to help others.' Apart from the few rows of family and friends at the front, virtually everyone in the church was on their feet. After a brief pause, he motioned to them to sit down, and waited for them to settle.

'So we all owe something to Martin Sturrock. He gave, and we took. And I don't know about you, but I never for one second thought he had problems of his own. He seemed so strong, so in command, so clever and compassionate. That's why we were all so shocked, is it not? We saw our problems, with his help, but we never saw that in taking our problems, he added to his own.

'If there is one group of people who should know that human beings are not machines, it is us. Yet do we, as patients, and in my case as a politician also, do we not expect those who look after us, and those who carry out our bidding, to be machine-like, to have all the answers, all the solutions, be there when we want them, how we want them, regardless of what they are as human beings?

'In his text message to his wife, who I also thank for her kindness, Martin said he wanted me to call for extra resources for psychiatric services. I happily do that, and will press my successor in the Health Department to fight for them too. But perhaps more important is a call for greater understanding of the pressures on those who handle pressures on our behalf.

'None of us will ever know what was going through his mind as he decided to take his own life. But if I knew him at all, he would have been thinking about every single person who stood up. I hope

I am speaking for all of you when I say to him, thank you for easing my burden, and sorry for adding to yours.'

A fresh round of applause accompanied Ralph to his seat, and as he sat down, moved by the reaction but glad it was over, he wished Sandie was there. But Sandie Hall was at home watching the news, where a reporter was being filmed talking excitedly outside the church above a 'breaking news' box declaring 'Ralph Hall funeral confession – I'm an alcoholic'. And she was thinking that, given that he was finally facing up to his problems, perhaps she should collect him from the clinic after all, once his treatment was finished. After that, they could see.

Reverend Fletcher introduced the next hymn, 'The Lord is my Shepherd'. Emily Parks hung on every single word. She felt the hymn spoke to her and her situation. She had to fight the urge to go up there herself and tell Professor Sturrock's family how much she owed him. Her mother was standing to her left, from where she could see only the burnt side of Emily's face. The headscarf was gone, and as Emily sang loudly of her soul being restored again, she had a smile that had Lorraine Parks weeping with a joy she had feared she would never feel again. She could scarcely believe the change in her daughter in the last few days. Emily had told her that she planned to go back to teaching next year, possibly after doing an RE teacher training course.

Two spaces along from Ralph Hall sat David Temple, alongside his mother and Father Nicholas who had come to give moral support, but who was dressed in normal clothes out of respect for this being an Anglican church. Unlike Mrs Sturrock and her children, David was not surprised to see the crowds. He had often wondered how many hundreds of patients Professor Sturrock must have had during four decades as a practising psychiatrist. Even though he felt he had something of a special bond with the psychiatrist, he assumed the majority of patients would warm to Professor Sturrock as an individual, as he had. Some would feel they owed him their life, others that he had helped them in large ways and small. So it was inevitable, given how big the news had been over the last week, that people who wanted to pay respects would come to the funeral.

He had written his eulogy on Friday evening, and had rewritten it many times since. But the rewriting was just an expression of nervousness. The basic structure and the basic messages were unchanged. When he had doubts about a certain word or thought, he would ask himself what Professor Sturrock might say, and take guidance that way. He also found Father Nicholas helpful with some of the tips he gave about how to stand, how to pause, where to look, what to do with his hands. But the message was his, and he felt special that, of all the people here – the doctors and managers and academics, the charity people and the politicians and the patients – he, David Temple, possessor of one GCSE, and probably the lowest paid person in the church, was the one asked to have the final word.

His mother had dipped into her savings to buy him a new suit and shoes. The shoes were pinching around his toes as he tapped his feet and waited for Reverend Fletcher to call him. He was conscious of his collar feeling tight and prickly against his neck. When the moment came, he clutched his speech firmly in his right hand and walked to the pulpit, reminding himself of some of Father Nicholas's tips. Deep breath. Pause when you get there to accustom yourself to the surroundings. Look for nice faces to talk to. Project towards the back. Speak slowly.

He was taken aback at how loud the heels of his new shoes were on the church floor, and it made him even more conscious of the fact that the focus was falling on him. When he reached the pulpit he took a deep breath, looked from one side of the church to the other, nodded towards Mrs Sturrock, then began.

'My name is David. I have been a patient of Professor Sturrock's for almost two years. I suffer from depression, and plenty more besides.' There was the beginnings of a titter at the back of the church, so he paused, as advised by Father Nicholas, to let it grow to mild but friendly laughter.

'Every week, he gave me homework.' That got a few murmurs of recognition too, so he paused again. 'He loved it when you did his homework.' A few people laughed. Arta turned to Lirim and smiled. Lorraine whispered to Emily, 'Even if you did it late.'

'One of my homework tasks was to describe the best and the worst moments of every day. On the day he died, hearing the news was the worst moment. I'm sure I wasn't alone in that. And the best was as I walked along the canal on my way home from work, and I was crying. Not sobbing, not weeping, crying. Tears just welling up in my eyes and trickling down my cheeks. And why was that the best moment of the day? Because earlier in the day I'd asked myself what he would advise me to do to get through the day, and I decided he would say I should finish work as normal, and have a good cry on the way home, in the dark, by the canal. So that is what I did. And every day since, my worst moments have been when I've thought about how he suffered, or I've thought about how nervous I'm going to be when I stand up here, or I've thought about what's going to happen if I get a new psychiatrist who doesn't understand me like he did. And all my best moments have been when I've asked him what he thinks, and somewhere in my mind, I find the answer.

'So in my mind, he says to me, "I suffered for all sorts of reasons, because I'm no different to anyone else. I have good days and bad days. I have weaknesses as well as strengths. And things just got too much for me." And when I've been nervous, he's said to me, "The key to your humanity is your humility, David. You're nervous because you're humble, but we're all of equal worth, and I trust you to get up there and say what you think, and in saying what you think, you'll do fine." And when I worry about getting a new psychiatrist, he's saying, "You were nervous about me at first, but we got along well in the end, did we not?"

'We did. We got along very well. Even if some days I couldn't face going. And I want to take this opportunity to apologise to his secretary Phyllis for the appointments I missed.' Tittering. Pause for mild laughter.

'Professor Sturrock knew more about me than anyone else alive. I wrote down here on my speech – he shared my burden. That's what Mr Hall said. He shared my burden. He shared our burden.

'My father left me and my mother when I was a kid. That was my burden. I never liked to admit it, but it was. It's been interesting these past few days to learn all these new things about Professor Sturrock. I thought he had five children, not three. I used to get jealous of these five children in my imagination, three boys and twin girls, because I thought he must be such a great father to have, when you're like me and you've never really had one. But what do I know? Did I ever think he would kill himself? No. No way. He was the man with the answers as well as the questions. So all I know is what he was to me, not what he was to himself, or his real family.

'Was he a father figure to me? Of course he was. There was nobody I respected or relied on more. But also he respected me. Before he died, he sent me a message saying nobody described better than I did "what this is like". That's when I knew. I'd had an inkling before, but then I knew. He got depressed too. Really depressed. Being depressed is not the same as being fed up or a bit hacked off with life. Being depressed is when you can't face the day. When you wake up and you feel like heavy weights are attached to your eyelids. When the knot inside you has grown and grown so you don't know where the knot ends and the rest of your body begins. Every little thing requires a big, big effort, and then you're knackered when you make it. And we used to talk about downward rhythms and curves and I sometimes had an inkling it was a fellow sufferer not a doctor speaking, but it wasn't my place to ask. I wish I had. I wish he'd told me his dreams like I told him mine. Wish he had told me what he wanted on his gravestone like I told him what I wanted on mine. Wish he had told me what his demons were. Demons and angels. He must have said that to all of us. He said we all have them. Every one of us. And some days the demons win and some days it's the angels. And on the day he died, the demons stormed the citadel and they won. But I remember the angels in him. We gave him our burdens. He gave us his angels.'

David tapped the side of his head. 'He's in here, somewhere, keeping an eye on the wiring for me, having a word every now and then. And when his gravestone is carved, it will be for his wife and children to say how it should be inscribed. But I hope it says something like this: "A humble man, he gave more than he got."'

He was on to his last page. He had just two sentences left, one saying he hoped Professor Sturrock's family would find the strength to rebuild their lives, the other saying he wanted to say thank you to Professor Sturrock on behalf of all the patients who had come to the funeral. But reading out a gravestone inscription for Professor Sturrock had hammered home the finality of what had happened, the fact that all he had left now were memories and words, and the hope of an ongoing influence. He felt his heart pumping, air swirling around inside his guts, and tears building, ready to pour. He couldn't go on. He said, 'Thank you for listening,' and hurried back to his place, for the first time in his life hearing hundreds of people applauding him.

Father Nicholas leaned over to him.

'That was the most beautiful eulogy I have ever heard,' he said.

Reverend Fletcher did the bidding, then asked the family to come and lay flowers on the coffin. Mrs Sturrock had a rose, Suzanne and Michelle sunflowers, Jack a carnation. Jack went to kiss the coffin lid, and started to sob uncontrollably. Reverend Fletcher went to comfort him, placed his hand on his shoulder as with the other hand he urged others to come and lay flowers. Lance Corporal Spiers was one of several war veterans who filed to the front. Matthew Noble and his wife went together to lay their bunch of lilies. Arta laid an iris and went to hug Mrs Sturrock.

Then there were those Professor Sturrock hadn't seen for a long time. Harry Archer wasn't dead after all. He was in his fifties, didn't have a flower to lay, but walked to the front to touch the coffin anyway. Malcolm Grove hadn't known they were meant to bring flowers, so he sneaked outside and stole a rose from the church borders, and took it forward. Margaret Halton was there too. Weighing in at a healthy nine stone three pounds. And Len Appleton, who never fully recovered after seeing his son killed right in front of him, had a camellia, and he took it to Mrs Sturrock at the front. 'Give this to his mother, will you? I know what it's like to lose a child.'

It took twenty-five minutes before people had returned to their seats. The coffin had hundreds of flowers piled up on it. Many more had fallen to the floor. The choir sang 'Thou Knowest Lord, the Secrets of our Heart', Mrs Sturrock's favourite piece of music. 'Purcell,' Mrs Parks whispered to her daughter. 'Beautiful,' said Emily. Then the coffin was carried out. Hundreds of mourners, many in tears, rose to their feet as Mrs Sturrock and her family filed out behind it: pew upon pew of flawed people come to bid farewell to a man who healed many of them, but never healed himself; who preached forgiveness, but could not forgive himself.